Whirlaway

ALSO BY ROBERT WINTNER

Snorkel Bob's Reality Guide to Hawaii

Whirlaway

A NOVEL BY
ROBERT WINTNER

 Edward R. Smallwood, Inc.
Tucson, Arizona

Edward R. Smallwood, Inc.
Tucson, Arizona
Copyright © 1994 by Robert Wintner
All rights reserved. Hardcover edition published 1994
Printed in the United States of America

00 99 98 97 96 95 94   5 4 3 2 1

Distributed by Atrium Publishers Group

Publisher's Cataloging in Publication
(Prepared by Quality Books, Inc.)

Wintner, Robert.
    Whirlaway : a novel / by Robert Wintner.
    p. cm.
    Preassigned LCCN: 93-087798.
    ISBN 1-881334-30-9

    1. Hawaii—Fiction. 2. Boating industry—Hawaii—Fiction. I. Title.

PS3573.158W45 1994   813'.54
                                      QB194-341

Fact: 97.73 percent of all adult males first arriving in the tropics—stepping onto the tarmac and feeling the balm sink in, feeling the bunk and delusion of life fall away— think, *"Yes! I was meant to be here. This is what I had in mind."*

Corollary: 100 percent of those males first experienced this conviction between the ages of seven and twelve, usually between intense desires to be firemen or Indian chiefs.

Whirlaway

# What it is

It's been awhile now. I watch the water, maybe like a moth watches flames, for the movement, for the life and death inside, for what went on there, and what might happen next.

I think guys like me, got nothing, never had much more, reach a point and think they never will. Then a taste of the good comes along—yacht, women, liquor, drugs, fast times. It's all bullshit, but it's pretty good bullshit. I'd head out to Honolulu for a week if I had the money, get all fucked up, burned out on honky-tonk and crowds, just for a chance to come home. I never felt better about a place to come back to.

As it is, here I be with what I got, which is nothing. It's clean and not so bad, if you know how to apply it.

I breathe deep, walk into the ocean, swim so far out that Jack says it makes no sense. But it's not a question of distance, I tell him, it's a feeling. He plays it close, always has—I try to tell him it's the water and the surroundings that count. He doesn't get it. I tell him he's stuck on the rational plane, tell him he can't think of it mentally, because it's not an idea, it's a feeling. Moving through the water way out there gives the void some dimensions, gives a man something to grab onto—feel it flow by. It's a relief.

I swim out, then I swim back, walk out of it a different person, lay myself on the sand, strong and warm. I breathe deep, thinking this is what happened to me. This is what I've become, what I am. This is living. This is good.

I watch dusk shimmer on the sea—like yesterday and tomorrow. Tourists pass by and drivel fills the air, forlorn talk of a world gone mad with pavement, cars, crowds, things to buy and the creative influence. Little waves toss my way, like tourists speaking drivel.

Then comes dark, stars and peace. I rise and move easy, cruising deep, for opportunity. I feel at home now, dark, peaceful, fluid and slow.

# Gomorrah

Good times was a way of life, nothing to do, plenty laughs. Hanging in was the big test, waiting to see what changed for the better because everything did, until it didn't. Hard times was the hungover funk that got old quicker than we did. Some of the boys threw in the towel, got jobs, lost the spirit. The women got hooked up when they could with the boys who'd thrown in the towel, or else they got careers and ruthless. Some prettied up pie-eyed like the nubile girls they were twenty years ago, before the late nights, liquor, drugs, fucking and good times like no tomorrow. What optimists they were, walking around with that *now I'm ready for the good* look on their faces, that innocent flirtation and lilt meant for far younger girls, as if all those pleasure bent times left them none the worse for wear.

The boys left wanted more. We clung to hope like survivors adrift grasp the flotsam, because it floats. We knew luck would save us, because it always had, and we had nothing else to know or believe in, and so we waited, drifted and waited, sustaining each other on our daily ration of joints and beer. Life was full time and anything could happen, anything, so long as you stayed alert, eyes open, ear to the ground.

I played a resource then, a woman who allowed me in, put me up when I was broke as long as I could stand her noise. I copped her garden gloves for the bitter cold, and she bought a new pair. She said she hated it when someone was all set to work in the garden, and then the gloves weren't there, and the garden could use some attention, and it wasn't all that cold. I could soak up that noise; it was only bitchy and mean. I promised a good weeding, first thaw. Meanwhile I'd hole up there on a good long binge, give things outside a chance to change. Annie had the liquor, and she said I could stay around. It wasn't the kind of arrangement a grown man feels good about, especially in hindsight, clearly seeing how whacked out she was. But poverty means death, unless you get lucky and keep your losses down to compromise, heart and soul, so you can rebound sometime soon and make it big, like you were always going to do.

Annie was lonely, so lonely she got sensitized to it, like a dog beat bad one time who won't trust another stick. So people hung around day and night, in and out of her house. Service people fixed the appliances, a carpenter worked five weeks on the garage door, a pro car waxer set up in the driveway, smoked joints with the garage door expert and lived in his van out front—maids, cabbies and all the wayward crowd knew the door was open there. Annie liked the company. She called them her friends. She was Clara Barton on the misfit front.

She had dogs too. First was a big Irish Setter who was purebred stupid. Then came a smaller and unbelievably dumber dog whose discretion with the mating act was hardly keener than Annie's—Annie would fuck nearly anyone, if they would just talk to her, or at least listen. One week shy of a puppy gusher, Annie bought another dog. She'd had a lonely flash on her way home from her AA meeting. She needed more company. A dog will listen. The cats wouldn't, didn't even care, no more than the other fringe freeloaders hanging around. Annie said she hated cats sometimes. They would have starved if not for me. God knows where they are now, without me around for chow and commiseration on too many dogs, too much noise and no affection. Outside, the garage door man and the car waxer pooled their savings for a gram of snoot. Annie got up at eleven, showered to eleven thirty, watched games and soaps in her robe until two, when I took a break for coffee. I became a student those days, full time, catching up on the school I'd missed, because nobody gets away with hooky in the big U, and besides that, any man in his prime wants to improve himself. It was my observation, by and large, that the general proportion of smart people to stupid people was relatively constant on all rungs of the socioeconomic ladder. That is, most people have little idea how many hard luck guys are smarter than they look, know more than most, nurture a wisdom blended sweet and sour with life on the street. I knew those guys. I was one of them, and we did want something more.

I studied, loved the learning process and the escape to sensibility. Guys like me didn't have the college student compulsion for finishing a book just because it was started, or assigned. I went through books like a shredder. Let a story stumble half a page and it was on the shit pile—I got that from experience. Cut your losses. School students don't learn that for years. They learn in tidy routine, with grades, spring breaks, graduations. I was real, focused, getting smarter all the time.

Annie went along and agreed to memberships in three book clubs. In fact she got a better deal than most, with a live-in reviewer letting her know what was worth her time and what wasn't. She was a busy woman, pushing piles of old bills and junk mail, some of it postmarked two years ago, into drifts along the table ledge. She wrote another list, reams of lists. She whimpered, soft and persistent, dialogue with herself, a blend of climax and constipation. She surfaced in her normal voice and asked, 1) Could she ask me a question? And given the nod, 2) Would I do something for her, a favor? Would I go to the grocery store for her? Annie had nothing to eat and was very hungry.

Annie and I knew the deal. She got a guy like me hanging around in exchange for shelter. It wasn't enough for her because it never is. She wanted dominance too, just a smidgen for the fun and excitement of it, and then too she got to see a guy like me practice subservience. I understood, so I said yes of course, anything anytime, and I carried my coffee back to my nook. I, on the other hand, favored passive control, life was so short to be wasting any more time on loonies like Annie. That day marked the beginning of another end.

Annie's first meeting at three was good. Coming home at five was bad. I'd fetched no groceries, and she was serious. So clomping through her house on spiked heels, she came to attention at my nook, where I searched for meaning in a book propped on my knees. She plucked her grocery list from thin air, as if from her foul mood, and watched it curlicue down. I scanned it too.

She needed cottage cheese and hot dogs right now, about four pounds of each. She blended them for the dogs, who howled, barked, puked, pissed about the living room, choking on anticipation; something had to give. She gave them free run as she'd been given, to figure things out for themselves.

She kept a wicker basket in the kitchen full of change, about forty pounds of nickels, dimes and quarters. Annie hated pennies. She was classy that way.

I charged her fifty cents a pop for insults, but I listened to her. Her shrink charged her eighty bucks a week for fifty minutes. I gave her a better bargain, because that's what friends were for at Annie's house.

She was up to four dollars, harping overhead when I told her, "Woof." She clomped off grumbling *fuck* and *shit*. I gave her a discount on aftermath and closed her tab at five-fifty.

She got her own goddamn groceries coming home from her last meeting about eleven, way past doggy dinner time. She clomped and bitched and joined the dogs in a late snack, cottage cheese and hot dogs. She was plenty pissed, but she couldn't deal with my disrespect, not now. Now was a time for savoring.

The alcoholic leader had chosen Annie. He wanted her unhappiness documented, for sharing. That would keep her busy, and a busy mind is not a thirsty mind. Annie loved assignments, especially when someone reviewed her work with her, and extra especially when review led to discussion on the meaning of relationship today. Sometimes she got laid.

She was up until four writing tales of social trauma. I skimmed her notes once, incidents of rudeness by others mostly, usually dinner guests—mean, aloof people who hadn't invited her back and wouldn't be asked back, never, no way. She'd taken so many into her heart, where they could share their thoughts on life and feel good about themselves. She made a list of old boyfriends too with paragraphs on their shortcomings, illustrations of their failures.

The cats and I relaxed up front in the dark. I told them Puss 'n Boots. They liked it and wanted more, so I told them The Lion and the Mouse.

They thought the lion was unreal—they bit the heads off their mice.

We cat napped that night, me, Kotcha and Bernice. Annie shrieked at her dogs when they nuzzled her in the middle of a thought—"Can't you see I'm working!" Or when Fido woke up and shuffled to Rover's bowl—"Fido you fucker! Get away from there!" She wanted sibling respect among her dogs. She joined them in a late snack, cottage cheese and hot dogs. She said it was good for a mother to taste what her children ate. It was natural. She was nuts.

Annie's wealth was third generation inherited, three generations atrophied in the fundamentals of self-care. Ragged blue jeans offset her bony ass and piano legs. A cashmere sweater too big in the arm-holes exposed her childish torso, her pubescent breasts, dark nipples and thick black hairs. Her mother told her thick black hairs on nipples were not pretty and sent Annie to the electrolysis clinic for removal, follicles and all, forever. Her nipples became a source of pride then, little girlish and in. She bought new sweaters with bigger arm holes.

Annie loved the common crowd. They listened when she announced her wealth. She attracted short run friends, but she pleaded poverty too, to keep them at bay. She was helpless, a certain public ward if not for her trust fund. Born into wealth, she could see and want, want and have, anything with a price tag. The teapot on her kitchen counter with its crackled veneer and rose gray luster looked old and rich, a thing of beauty—and her four-tier armoire, was crowded with lustrous teapots in a wall size texture, coarse acquisition.

So the single teapot on the counter was just one more, with a purpose—she dropped it. She sluffed it off. "Oh that. It's nothing." She replaced it with another from her hutch, and if the new friend properly gaped in amazement, she would make a gift of another. They ran around two bills, a pittance. She'd make it back tomorrow simply getting up before breakfast.

"Please don't," was her response to excessive thanks.

She shrieked, "Please God balance my checkbook!" She tried balancing her checkbook once and failed, right at the part where she couldn't find her goddamn calculator. She wanted to discuss checkbooks, or balances, or failures, or anything. Short of new friends, or discussions, she opened a new account so the old one could "mellow out," and she could discuss banking with someone paid to listen.

Her AA friends called her "one of us." I called her a waste of oxygen, a worthless piece of meat. I imagined a phone call—Annie got smashed by a Mack truck—just for the fun of it. I savored the prospect of calmly hanging up, checking the TV guide, thinking about dinner. Of course it was a harsh fantasy, but reality was more severe.

Insanity is contagious. It was dark again, and as I slunk back to my burrow in search of a better world, she said, "Oh wow. You know, I can't even imagine making love to you. I mean, I couldn't even imagine what it would be like."

I turned back slowly and agreed, it was a nasty vision. Her eyes cocked sideways like a dog's in playful ignorance. Below them her mouth circled an empty voice asking why.

Spinning away, she clomped off. Exits were her strong suit. She shrieked down the dark hallway: "You dogs are self-centered! You don't really care about me! After all I do for you!" I knew she included me in the pack. I hated her and wished her gone.

It worked. She went directly to a late meeting, her fourth of the day. Her normal dose was three meetings, and she wasn't an alcoholic, didn't drink much at all, hated the taste of sipping whiskey—but they took her in. They talked to her. They listened.

I dozed, dreaming that Annie's book of lists and crayon doodles was discovered, sold heavily by A Major New York Publisher, called Brilliant!, Blockbuster!, A Riveting Read!, Not Since Jackie Collins! I dreamed Annie made it big, soon to be...AN...N...B...C...MINI...SERIES...

I woke at dawn in trembling cold but relieved, only a dream. Literature in America was not much worse than it was last night. A dog had lost to diarrhea, however, and that was overwhelming, especially when I pulled the window shut, warmed a bit in the thick shit smell and wondered how a man could find the sensible world. I wanted distance from the cold, the shit, the crazy. I wanted away, someplace better, just as a third world peasant dreams of America.

It was a still life, man in a funk, in cold and stink, tired and tired of it in the early morning. A pissed on, dried out, chewed up paper from another morning lay between me and the shit, open to the comic strip. Scientific Facts asked: Reduced to the same proportionate size, the skin of the earth would most resemble that of what object? A ping-pong ball is the answer. I felt that from the same proportionate distance, life looked equally smooth. It was up close that the cold and hunger and stink of it spanned deserts, enraged seas, made mountain ranges. The cold outside and in was like yesterday, and so many seasons had passed like days of the week. Pushing forty the circle turns quicker than it did at twenty. Little Black Sambo watched the tiger chase its tail, and turn into butter. So the days mercilessly passed for me too, another year gone, melted into mush. My horoscope said today is lucky for love. Today is also good for travel, but bad for business. With Mercury in retrograde, disintegration will prevail.

I went for a walk just like I used to go for a walk when the acid was coming on, and physical movement helped ease the transition, kept you grounded when you knew the earth could slip away. A field first seen two years ago, when it was rye grass rolling in waves in the breeze, now was weeds and wind. Side street names known by heart in every direction led to contemptible familiarities. On the way back

I passed a college crowd dressed for the New Age, mostly in pueblo peasant rags, baggy satins, breeches and boots.

Young idiots with rich parents and angelic smiles, they mulled on the sidewalk, experiencing intellect together.

I told them they were ugly, maybe out of frustration. Looking at them pissed me off, but I had nothing on them. One said, So? Another said, Thank you. I went them one better, told them they looked dumb as dog shit. Another one laughed with a knee slap.

The new load of dogs was born that night. I wondered how strong the anti-abortion lobby would be if dogs were born one at a time, and people came in litters of nine, and the unwanted were gassed humanely.

I didn't sleep. Annie shrieked to everyone (all the dogs) to keep the fuck away from her puppies, just keep the fuck away. I prayed for her quick death.

The next day would have been good for leaving if life was neat as a book. I was broke instead, no place to go. I walked around by the ocean, because that's where guys go when they have no money, no direction.

Three men stood by the fence on the bluff. A young one stared in longing at the seductive horizon. An old one watched the pounding surf, remembering the energy once his. I was nowhere, adrift, out of sight of the world around me, looking from side to side and out to the middle distance, wondering what would survive me.

I walked away from the ocean, as guys who have no money, no direction do, unless they jump in. Insight came hours later, in the shower, when another empty voice sputtered in the hot cascade. "I'm sick of everything," it said.

I laughed as the curtain was pulled aside, and Annie said, "Is my soap in there? You're probably using it to jack off. I know you guys jack off all the time in the shower. Do you jack off in the shower?"

My last thought before soothing hot turned tediously tepid was that all heroes need the same thing: heroic odds. The older you get, the harder glory is to come by. I toweled off allowing Annie to watch, carefully stretching out my dick to dry the bottom side of it while I told her I'd fuck her for two grand, because compromising your soul won't last so long if you can make some money and change things, I thought. She shrieked that I was disgusting—sick! and disgusting. I asked if it was time for me to leave. "Sick!" she said, and she left.

Sometimes a sensitive fellow knows when a girl is coming on.

I heard Annie's shower running like an invitation to her confessional, where she would tell her love of showers and passion, show her gear with abandon. The garish fantasy ended with a shriek, No motherfucking hot water!

I locked myself in Annie's "study" and got down to basics, in outline form, because a good escape plan begins with assessment. Mine went two words: Cold. Nuts. I could go nuts anywhere—I trembled. But I knew a guy in Hawaii, Jack Witte. I rang him up, that simple.

In Hawaii it was hardly noon, and Jack watched the world from his condo deck, outside, warm and dry. He drank a beer, smoked a joint, hanging in. No, he was not employed, or busy, nor were prospects imminent. No, he had no ideas. Yes, he might be up for something, another beer and another joint didn't sound too bad. Yes, come over. What the hell. "You can be poor here," he said. "Or you can stay in America and be poor and cold." Jack understood the situation right off, was at home with no resources, little hope. He sounded smart that way, and comfortable. "Hey. It's my birthday next week. We'll party." He sounded like old times, good friends, family, as it were. That's how it was with what was left of our crowd, the old boys, getting older all the time.

I had an hour to closing time so I left quick and headed uptown. Outside the car waxer offered a hit of a joint and said, "You oughta fuck Annie man. She's alright."

"Hey alright," I said, appeasing Annie's entourage, taking a hit of the joint, telling them again, "Alright."

The car waxer's head pumped, "Right on, Man," as if meaning beyond the grunt was understood.

I stopped and turned. "Is it the whole scumbag world or just me?" But I didn't wait for an answer. I spun again and marched double time. Hope was folded in two and tucked in my wallet, like life, a blank check on a closed account. The check could swap easy for a ticket out, to someplace else; God bless America, where clean and white, or at least looking that way, can get you anywhere you want to go. The car waxer wasn't a bad guy, but I had a plane to catch.

Telling the travel agent, "Yes, it's time for warmer weather," I wrote the check. I sat back with the ease and confidence of a busy executive looking forward to some time away. The travel agent was soft and sensitive, the kind of fellow for whom sharing the joyous anticipation of others was gratification in itself. The soft man stared at me and then smiled. I smiled too, wondering if this was preliminary to an invitation, prelude to a kiss.

The soft man paused, that cagey, wary moment that says: you're dead meat boy, bad check and all—and he leaned forward, reaching under his desk for his secret alarm button. But I held him eye to eye, tooth for tooth, maybe with a little flirtation thrown in, after all. "I'll need a minute," was all the soft man said, most likely leaning forward to rub his knob. He fetched the ticket with a coy wiggle, as if he wasn't such an easy pickup, or I was supposed to call him later, or something.

The walk back to Annie's house was different, because I was already gone, and the same old same old looked more like used to was than here I am. Gone too was this day of uncertainty, these days of waste; sundown headed clearly into a night of meaning, a world of sense, where life in its prime waited to be lived. It was change. It was growth. It was sentimental.

So too was Annie, waiting, sentimental and sweetly curious. She'd been "seeing" a radical American Indian she met at AA. His name was Red Salamander. I called him Sal, but radical American Indians don't take good to nicknames. He wanted to be called Red Salamander, but was too proud to ask. So he glared—one pissed brave take um scalp from white man just you wait and see. Nnnnnnuuuuuhhhh! He was nuts, like Annie. He said he knew why he got drunk: to drown his rage. No more. Now he was radical.

Annie couldn't get enough of hanging out with an authentic member of the minority oppressed. She complained, however, that all Sal wanted, ever, was blow jobs. Night and day Sal wanted blow jobs. She said a woman has her needs too, and she finally put her foot down. He'd left her high and dry. Sal stood up straight, spread his legs, folded his arms and said the white man owes it to the Indian. Annie went along with that too, for awhile, until she had no choice but to cut him off, which was two days ago.

He'd called while I was out, while Annie was in her bathroom waiting for her hot water heater to catch up with her need. He'd left a message on the phone machine, a rendition of the Stevie Wonder hit, I Just Called to Say I Love You. He squealed at the end: "And I mean it! From the bot-tum of my heart."

Annie was near tears, and perplexed. Was this it? Was this what she'd been waiting for? She wanted my opinion as she overhauled her face, sprayed her pits and crotch.

But the scene was removed, in the past and apart from reason. I was a man witnessing my own escape, slow motion. "Holy screaming Jesus I hope so," I told her. She threw her arms around me and said she knew she could count on me. I was a true friend. It was her most touching moment. She cracked a Dom, then another, and another still even though she and I were drunk. And though she felt she did love Red Salamander the way a woman dreams of loving a man someday, she couldn't possibly call him in this condition. She got depressed and swilled the third bottle, down the hatch, until the bubbles popped out her ears and nose, foamed from her mouth and dribbled down her chest. She felt better when she burped, and better still when she lay down and best yet when she snored.

I answered the phone at ten and listened to a grunt. "Ugh," I said, and left the continent near sunrise.

 # Erratic Behavior

Jack Witte knew if he let it, the world would get him. It always had, from the first hand it dealt him. His mother was a showgirl in the olden days, but she nurtured the dream—marriage and family. So she danced till forty, married an ogler from the third row, a regular, Max Witte, had a family named Jack and spent her last thirty years looking for the goddamn gin. Jack hid it, she drank so hard. They adapted to straight vermouth, but grudgingly.

Jack Witte said he wasn't Jewish, not really. His father was Jewish. "In Israel I wouldn't be Jewish. They wouldn't count my mother. I got shit in school for being a Jew. Cocksuckers. I'm that Jewish; I got the shit for it."

Jack had a photo of his own olden days, with long hair, when victory and independence, from the suburbs or something, was declared nightly, rolling a wake up reefer before turning in.

He grinned in the shot with a joint clenched in his teeth, kneeling on the deck of a boat half built in his back yard, gripping a big staple gun in one hand—the other hand on deck trickled blood, stapled there. That was fifteen years ago. He finished the boat and sailed it west with a wife and a book: How to Navigate.

That little token of youth and glory and blood in black and white hung in the kitchen, over the sink near the dim yellow stove light. From the living room floor it was only a hot spot on the grease flecked wall, one more frayed reminder of what victory and independence came to. The fold out sofa was lumpy. The foam mattress on the floor was better, but sleep was off kilter—the lumps, the past, the musty, muggy air, jet lag. I drifted in and out of it, sorting white noises outside: the fan, the breeze, the surf, a passing car, the void.

Jack's condo was cheap rent—hallway mostly, between a ten-by-ten sleeper and matching parlor. The kitchen was a slot.

A light went on in back and Louise whined again, "What are you doing?" Louise, the girlfriend, looked like a dry season, trickled in like a long, skinny drink of water, lanky with bony elbows, knobby knees and mouse brown hair dyed black because "Jack likes it not to match, you know." She came on warm, dropped back for mystique, or maybe it was only a mood, meditation on another hunger.

Jack liked that act too, maybe in pleasant relief from what his life boiled down to: money and pussy, and in good times drugs.

Louise looked away and said she didn't care. She looked back and said now she was Nada and her friends should call her Nada too, unless Louise "felt better." She said she was "into numbers." Louise was a five, Nada an eight. "What I'm really kind of excited about is when as many people call me Nada as the ones who call me Louise. It should make me a six and a half, I think. I feel like John Glenn or something. It's sort of an experiment."

I felt her excitement. She was like a yard child, dirt poor, Appalachia or Ethiopia, happy with the simplest toys, like a coat hanger or a chicken foot, or a piece of paper and a crayon stub. I asked Jack how he found this one. Jack never hung out with the cosmic crowd. Jack said Louise had a thirty minute plan that made the psycho babble okay. "Fine," I said. "But how did you meet her?"

"I asked for it," Jack said. "You don't get more than you ask for. You ought to know that."

Louise shrugged and said she and Jack would grow together.

"You just walked up and asked for a little piece of pussy?"

Jack lit a smoke, looked troubled but then sat back and grinned. "That's all there was to it, Harry."

"It was so cute," Louise said. She looked worried and said she thought they would be good, eventually—her chart anticipated him. She thought she might be psychic. Jack said there was no goddamn money in fortune telling. Louise said, "Psychic. Not fortune-telling." Then she spent an hour in the kitchen cutting celery, fluffing sprouts.

Dinner was quiet, sprouts, soup and more hunger. Bedtime was early, because people in a bind with life know that sleep stops the gnaw for a few hours anyway, sometimes. I couldn't see how anyone could sleep in that heat, but I didn't care, Annie was no more, falling away, back and gone.

It was deep night when Jack boomed down the hallway, through the parlor and across the complex: "That's why I can't live with you anymore! Because I have to answer stupid questions all the goddamn time! I'm taking a shower! I'll take a shower at three in the goddamn morning if I want to! I got three hundred fifty dollars in bad checks out there!"

The running shower became another noise to sort. Another light went on and the bathroom door opened. "What are you doing up?" he bellowed. She cried and ran back to the bedroom. Several doors slammed for drama. And after a couple hours quiet, dawn broke like a taunt. Then came sleep for an hour or two, ending with the smell of coffee and cigarettes, the sight of Jack pacing the lanai, figuring birthdays and life. He came inside and said, "Another year Harry." He lit another smoke. "I guess we might as well get drunk."

It made sense. We called it a transition, because calling it something helped it make sense. We drank a case of beer that day and set a limit. It was hot and we had a birthday, but more than a case a day was for hopheads. We stayed stoned but didn't count joints because we couldn't count, because Hawaiian legumba turns your brain to syrup and made Louise's number game look like nuclear physics. We couldn't count, but we got good at staring and giggling.

We got up halfway through the second week, once we'd taken the edge off the gnaw, got our little revenge on the bad deal that kept coming our way, once we'd taken the life out of the living. It had

grown bad, turned sour, but it was eased off now. Sure it could come
back harsh again, but like Jack said, we were warm, sometimes even
breaking a sweat, and we stayed ready with another doobie, another
brew.

It was one morning before first buzz that I suggested fresh air. Jack
said yes, a couple guys should head down to the yacht harbor, watch
the boats and see Jack's friend, Masao. On the way he asked how
much money I brought. I brought every cent I had, and a few cents
from Annie's change basket, maybe hoping I'd see her again so she
could insult me some more. I had about a hundred fifty in cash, but
I lied. "About a hundred bucks, Jack. Seeds and stems." Jack grinned
and said a hundred was plenty, and since it was Thursday, we ought
to go ahead and get a gram of cocaine. I said that a gram of cocaine
would take half the hundred. Jack lit a joint and said, "So?" Jack made
rough sense like that.

Stoned again on the seawall, drinking some strong coffee because
it was morning, we shared the doper's view of life as a cartoon, when
a sleek yacht came in from its morning sail, loaded with tourists. "It's
a money machine," Jack said. "Every body on board is a fifty dollar
bill." Jack's friend, Masao, at the helm, coughed into his fist, *blow job.*
This cracked Jack up. Masao backed the yacht into its slip, and we
went aboard. We drank beer in the cabin while Masao exchanged
farewells, stowing lines.

I said I knew a guy in San Francisco, Lyles Warren, who worked a
boat just like this one. Jack said it couldn't be the same boat—this one
was special, special engineering, special resins for special rules, for
twenty tourists, not just six. It was set up special, to make much more
money. "We had one of these, we could make a ton of dough."

"I know where we can get one," I said. Jack's stupefied stoned stare
was a blend of belief and doper fun. I said this guy, Lyles, drove a
boat that was the exact same as this boat, and it was for sale, would
have been in foreclosure, except that the guy selling it had married
the woman who tried to buy it, so it was back in the family instead
of in foreclosure. So now the boat wouldn't cost more than a quarter

million—*Whirlaway* was the boat. Jack worked his smoke, took it down to the filter. He lit another on the burnt plastic. I said, "I can get us a boat, if you can find a slip to park it in."

Jack grinned, stoned enough to realize the break he'd been waiting for. "Well," he said. "Well, we could cut a deal with somebody who has a slip in the harbor." He smoked and thought. "Oh hell, we don't need a slip. We could put the bitch on a mooring off the beach with a couple three anchors and some chain and a ball, no problem, it'd make a goddamn fortune, I swear it would." We sat there stoned the way stoned people do, waiting to see what the cartoon would do next. I lit a smoke—Jack giggled—I was now a thinker. I giggled too over luck in America. We couldn't think of a single reason not to buy a yacht, but why should we? That would have reflected bad attitude, something we'd both been avoiding for years.

Jack gave it half a rest thrusting his head out the companionway, ferret from the lair, to scan for dockside action, maybe easy prey, maybe a basket full of cash and a few blank checks and a couple three teenage nymphomaniacs to go with our new yacht. What he saw amounted to the same thing, another delusion—"Oh Jesus, there's Booth Linda!" Booth Linda, short and stout, tip her over—she had the waterfront concession on cocaine, and came around regular as the Good Humor Woman with ice cold refreshment for the boat crews and the women who hawked boat ride tickets from wooden hot boxes called booths.

Back down in a blink and a twitch with his hand out, Jack urged, "Come on come on come on. It'd be a shame to blow it now for a lousy hundred bucks." He meant we should escape the reefer daze and save the empire. "Linda!" he yelled. Drugs came next, and then the world.

A couple in their mid-forties waited on the dock while Masao spoke low with their daughter. He would meet her that evening. The parents looked nervous, smiling, small talking, avoiding the truth. The daughter at seventeen was nobody's little girl. Masao at forty looked like a character from a tropical smut comic with his lopsided leer and undersized Speedos with what looked like a wash cloth rolled up inside. Jack lit a smoke and giggled. "You'll love this guy." Jack meant I would love him because he was so sleazy and such a relentless pussy hound, and didn't that spell victory over the deal or what? And oh, Masao was a good guy too.

Masao said, "Aloha." The parents liked that. The daughter stared at his stalk. Then the father said aloha too, and the anxious threesome strolled up the dock. Masao came down grinning. "You got to set it up in the daytime. They don't trust you after dark." He set his cabin in order, at right-angles, told who to sit where, took the navigator's seat for himself, called for a beer and pulled a mirror and a blade from the nav cabinet.

And soon the world was ours, with that sweet invincibility only a hundred bucks can buy. Masao said yes, a fortune could be made, and so could more pussy than you could shake a stick at. Jack giggled, nearly blew away a set of fat lines. He recomposed, grunted one up and asked if Masao thought he would score with the lovely daughter. Masao took the mirror and the straw and said no thinking required; he scored last night, after having dinner with the whole family. He grinned. Mom and Dad came down to the boat for Sis right in the middle of a hump. The daughter yelped, "Oh Mama," but not for her mother. Masao looked proud, as if relating unsolicited tribute to himself. I wondered if Masao was pathological or simply demented. Jack stared in awe at prospects for the charter trade.

Sincerely, Masao said he provided a service, for the parents too, first as a baby-sitter, second in showing the young girls the art of love—Masao was a likeable swine. He said shit, if it wasn't for him they'd be out fucking riffraff, or something. There were older girls too, some over thirty. He stared seriously up the companionway as Jack laid out more lines, and no one laughed, like nothing was funny.

Masao spoke low and in simple terms of the simple beauty of the charter business. Then he asked where the money would come from. Jack leaned into a line with a grunt and said the money was all taken care of.

I nodded and said I could possibly put it together, maybe. Maybe I knew a few people with money who might be interested. Just for fun, Jack got paper and pen from the nav table and made three lists: income, expenses and capitalization. The pleasant delusion evolved.

But an hour, a half-gram and a six-pack later Masao said he had to prep for the afternoon sail. He said Jack and I should come along. I asked what needed prepping.

Masao grinned. "I take one dump." Among the afternoon passengers were two sisters, fourteen and eleven. Masao showed his stuff. I wasn't comfortable with it, but Masao said, "Seventy-five pounds. What the fuck? ..." Then he spoke low, briefly to each. Each giggled and mumbled back. Masao reported that the girls were ready. "But Daddy one mean billy goat. He know. He want kill skipper now." Daddy sat in the cockpit squeezing his hands, cracking his knucks and looking tense. Masao got busy with a sail and said, "I must be one nuts guy, hump children, but I crave young taint."

Jack giggled: taint is the stretch part, between the shit and the sashimi. It was a nowhere scene rife with perversion on a beautiful backdrop, the first of many such scenes. And maybe staring at the clear, blue sky, telling no one in particular, "This is what happened to me," I should have had at least a clue that something, leading to everything, was coming undone. Several people stared at the man visibly lost and confused, talking to himself, maybe on drugs. Masao gave Jack the helm and tugged my sleeve to help him shag a round of soda, beer, bag wine.

"Cannot do that," he whispered to me. I gave him a whacked out look back, one I'd learned from Annie that I'd never dreamed would be useful. This guy was telling me what was acceptable and what was not. Maybe that's why the deal had been so bad, because guys like me couldn't get our values right, couldn't get the hang of the do's and don'ts. Shitfuck, I didn't have to look normal for anyone, especially a sex criminal who looked certain for hard time or violent death.

The afternoon sail ended peaceful. Jack and I hung out at a bar during the sunset sail, enough of sailing for one day. We talked numbers and wealth and went back to the boat for more answers and numbers for the pro forma. Masao served beer and the mirror. Another two hours of numbers shrunk the gram and made a profit of two hundred twenty grand a year. Nobody factored equity because it wasn't spendable. I said, "That's conservative," feeling more businesslike all the time.

"But not realistic," Jack said. "Besides, we're going for broke."

Masao said, "For broke. Imua." He scratched out two twenty and inked in two fifty.

Jack said, "Yeah. Now. Let's get some more toot, you know, just to hold the deal together."

Masao said he was too tired to go out, so maybe he'd just wait for his date to show up. He said he did that sometimes. He laid back in a berth and reviewed income and expense projections. He approved. He was the guy who made them up. He looked up and asked again, "Where the money is coming from?"

I said I knew this rich, whacko bitch named Annie, and I told the boys about dogs and Indians and blow jobs. I thought she'd go for a boat deal, but if she agreed to put the money up, somebody would have to listen to her, and most likely pork her regular. Masao said no problem, especially for money.

I told Masao he was a babe in the woods when it came to earning money. No, Annie would be more maintenance than a yacht, even for a hard-core bilge rat like Masao. And as I cringed saying her name, I knew it was wrong. A clean break is forever. No, not Annie.

But I remembered another bubba, an old homeboy from way south, another deviate who took the deal and made it his own, for better or worse, a guy who'd broken free of poverty mode and stayed in my pocket for just such an opportunity as this. I told my colleagues, "I know this guy, south of San Francisco, Nuel."

~~~~~~~~

 Nuel

The man was a killer, fairy godfather with a laser wand.

Nuel, the bubba who sent the boys to the ball, was whacked and dangerous. His license from the American Medical Association let him slice heads for a living, human brains. He was further sanctioned by the Federal Reserve to own anything, based on belief in his ability to find another scalp to part. .

I met him at a party, a gathering of renegade sophisticates, small-time hustlers mostly who'd done well enough to flash their cash, who hadn't got caught, hadn't lost their spirit and fancied some savoir faire—drug dealers, insurance hustlers, a torch or two, a stickup man, some lawyers and doctors. I fit in, working baggage claim and credit cards at the time. The question: What do you do? was not asked here, faux pas. What you did was measured in dollars, your success determined by the glint in your eye, the purity of your bullshit, your presence, free, on the street.

Nuel loved the question, especially from females. He worked the pigeonhole offense, scooping cocaine recklessly from an eight-ball bag. He could pack a nose and offer a ride in his dream car quicker than the second sniffle, and if she still hadn't asked by the time the console was adrift in Peruvian flake, he'd call the other coast or talk about tomorrow's flight or show her his quaaludes baggie—anything until she asked how he got so many wonderful things. Then he'd go loose, lizard-eyed cool and say, "I'm a brain surgeon."

Nuel said he was from Virginia. Pressed for where about, he'd allow West Virginia. He'd been a yard child in Appalachia, played with coat hangers and chicken feet and maybe a few chicken heads. Adult life for Nuel was compensation—revenge was so indelicate. First he compensated for his past, then his present, thrusting headlong like no tomorrow.

A boy from the hills can join the Navy and get out with a scalpel and a strop and then get rich. It was that easy, learning medicine and manners, and though most people heard speech impediment in his molasses drawl, Nuel heard charm flowing from his lips, sweet as honeydew. The hillbilly mushmouth flooded the gates when he got pissed, but then they wadn't nothin' nobody could do about that. "De monkey's on yo back now Bubba. I'm gone be on yo ass nat'n day. Nat'n day Bubba, jist lack I'z on Bascum's 'n you said I wadn't." Bascum was a thief. Nuel was learning how. "Bill Bascum is a very complex individual," Nuel said. "You boys just don't unnerstan the man."

Nuel understood complexity. "I don't know. I jist always wanted a be a brain surgeon. You should see how girls react when I tellum." Many nurses knelt down, mostly ignorant of the danger lurking in front of the initials M.D. Nuel was a doctor in search of vast wealth and genital contact. He'd had four wives but no close friends.

I knew the last two wives. In the third divorce settlement Clarisse won fifty grand now and fifty grand a year. Nuel didn't care. "Shit boy, fifty grand. Shit." He took up with a sleepy young thing and soon decided to marry again. "Oh, I know I've had a lot of wives," he reflected. "I suppose I'll have some more." He saw himself in VistaVision. His oldest son was older than his fourth wife.

At home with fate, Nuel knew true love had found him again on a date, by chance. He remembered with sentiment: "Oh we'z jist out driving around you know. We stopped up there by Sea Cliff 'n it was so clear 'n all it was beauty-ful. You could see all the stars 'n we jist stood up there 'n you could look out over the whole bay 'n everthing and you know what she did I mean just standing right there? She gave me a blow job. It was beauty-ful." Nuel was a romantic after all. He married the fourth wife a month later.

But that was many months later. When I met him he was only halfway through the third wife, and drunk. He'd pigeonholed a female with a big knife. She wanted out, so he dropped quick to the God act. She'd complained of a pain between her breast and her arm pit. Nuel said best have a looksee and was on her with the knife quicker than she could say self-examination. He topped their goblets. That calmed her down, and Nuel loved a good Bordeaux before surgery—"Eze sonzabitches'll run you five thousand dollars fo they done. Tie yup five days in a surgey ward—shit—little old bah-opsy."

She laughed it off. He moved in. She hit rape defense mode. Nuel got bedside, "Darlin', why this procedure's fundamental, first year shit—teensy tiny little slice, shit, wouldn't feel like hardly much more'n a skeeter bite and I bet my DeLorean to your Jag whoever's throwing this dance has a needle and thread around here somewhere." The female looked sad, then frustrated, then desperate. Nuel read her and stopped, set the knife down and told her be still for a minute. Then he slipped his hand down her blouse, copped a little feel and moved into the suspect area. He nodded slow, step 1, The God Act. Then he breathed deep and got down to the Big C. "Darlin' it ain't mah place to be sayin' sixty days or less and such like that at a party like this, but Ah swear it if it is, well, it won't be because you been denied the skilled hand of a medical fuckin' expert." He turned around slo mo, got the knife, wiped the blade with a towel, heated the edge with his sterling Zippo and advanced...

She screamed: "You crazy fucker! Get away from me!" All the civil outlaws hushed, agape at Nuel and the knife. She pulled her blouse back on to her shoulder, adjusted her bra, huffed and puffed and walked away. Nuel shrugged, dew-eyed dumb as a sleepy hound. He set the knife down and shuffled on over to the crowd nearby, where talk centered on the new career, criminal law and local wine.

Nuel sipped his. I said I couldn't tell the difference between fa fa Chablis and a decent couch white. Nuel said: "You jist drank

Chardonnays fo few years, till you git you taste buds wuhked out."

He made an impression. Nobody knew how far he tipped either way, daft or dangerous. Talk turned to tax and cash laundering. Nuel grabbed the lead with a deal, simple as brain surgery. "I bought me some empty office buildings in Utah from a fellow never drank nor smoked nor nothing. He's about sharp as they come, old J.D. I tell my 'countant now, you don't do a goddamn thang without you talk to J.D. now. We gone fuck old Sam I mean black'n blue."

Nuel was strange but colorful, whacko with a quotable flamboyance. I saw a resource, because guys like me who don't spot them and remember will never break out. Old J.D. saw the resource first, but it looked like plenty more to go around.

Back to America, back to Annie's on a thought process that was itself dreamlike, I could see the world changing. I understood credit cards and how to make them work, understood the rich vein of cards to be gleaned in bars and bistros, restaurants and spas, especially in tourist places. But a flight on a stolen card is only good if you got nothing to lose, so when they walk down the aisle looking everyone in the eye, you flat don't give a shit. A business executive on the fast track can't do that sort of thing, and besides, that stuff can follow you for a long time. So I borrowed three bills from Masao for the ticket back and settled with the airlines on fifteen hundred for my two lost bags. Lost bags are clean, and I had a deal to keep moving forward, no time for penny ante hustles. And within the week I plunked down a grand for a ninety day option on the sailing yacht, *Whirlaway*. I wrote it up myself, because I'd studied the law, way back when I had time on my hands.

I'd had a few drinks with Nuel in the months after we met. I never got to know him well, but we understood each other, friends. We hadn't seen each other in a year or so when I called. Nuel said, "Hey Bubba, what you fittin-a-do?" I said I had a deal, looked right up his alley, a yacht deal, warm weather, the tropics, you know.

Nuel said, "Thank you Bubba I do preshate ju callin' me on a deal but my er uh working capital is all tied up rat now." Nuel said he had deals coming at him he just couldn't move on, what with J.D. and Utah and such. But he was cordial too, so he said, "Sho, come on. We have dinnuh."

Jane, the designated fourth wife, was learning to cook. Her Julia Childs cookbook was swamped in dribblings—tomato sauce, clam nectar, ripe Brie, flour, spices, cocaine and fine wine. Nuel cut more cocaine from his rock on the dining room table when I arrived. It was ritual procedure, not entirely unrelated to surgical procedure: cutter, chopper, gold tooter, goblet of fine wine. Nuel called for each instrument. He was served by Madelaine, intensive care nurse, whose patient that night was me. She put a little hug on me, gave me a peck on the cheek and a warm smile with my goblet of fine wine. I sniffed the delicate bouquet, sipped the flavor of success, felt warmed all over by my arrival. A businessman who thinks success will find it.

Nuel said come on. He wanted to show his new answering machine, the de Luxe model. It was a few thousand dollars—Fuck I don't care about the money—voice activated so he could say Hey from a stupor in the night. The lost soul on the other end, in the emergency room, could get The God Act from right there in Nuel's bed. Nuel could tide a patient over with drugs just like he tided himself. "I seeum soon'nuff, first thang after muh rounds, first thang after brunch."

He led back to the dining room where a dozen wines waited on the sideboard, price tags ranging forty bucks to three twenty. After another line and a light Chardonnay, I said, "I been drinking these a couple years now."

But Nuel missed the joke. He said, "Good, you should." The phone rang on cue, Emergency Room on a car wreck. Nuel listened, snooted a line, drank some wine, prescribed phenothis and barbothat and said don't worry. He rang off and recalled fondly a few he "saved" that day. He said he felt a whole bunch better with his new answer box on line.

He snooted again, sniffed and snorted and said, "You see Bubba, I know the perceja so well I can tellum what to do in my sleep. Then they fuck it up and say I toldum the wrong thang. Now my machine'll record ever goddamn word spoke on my phone. I'll git them little fuckers in that 'mergency room. Ha ha ha." Nuel was a benign God after all. He remembered his favorite car wreck, ever. "Iss Negro walked in de 'mergency room with a goddamn rearview mirror poked in his head." He said the chance of surviving a rearview mirror poked into your head is one in a zillion, the chance of surviving its removal is less. "Iss boy's shuckin'n jivin'—I saved him. Hell."

He gave Jane and Madelaine a little nosebag all their own so they could retreat, powder down and girl talk while Nuel and Bubba took a look at this boat deal. Jane said dinner was almost ready. Nuel said, "I don't give a care we order out Chinese ha ha ha."

Nuel caught me watching Madelaine's ass as she walked out. He said the poor girl had a bad disk, needed a papaya enzyme shot in her spinal cord, since that was about the only procedure anyone had come up with so far, and it was only a fifty-fifty chance. "Hell, she run sixty forty with me on a spike. Hell some folks jist die! right on de table!" The spinal shot cost five grand regular, but "Fuck it I'd do up Madelaine for free. She's a real nice piece 'o pussy you gone see." Nuel said he'd tell me one thing—"Ahteya wunthang"—she wouldn't want nobody fucking around with her spinal cord but him, not around there.

I smiled in appreciation and stood up a little straighter. I presented two pages of pro forma numbers but Nuel got stuck on the first two lines. He cranked up his computer for a detailed analysis. "Hell, I can feed isshit right in de machine." But the machine stalled. He found his computer instruction manual and said he was afraid his computer wasn't working right. He popped another cork, mid-range at $89.95, and laid out another pair of lines. It was fun. And in a little while I would get to fuck Madelaine. Life gets better when you move in the right circles, and I felt better already.

An hour later Nuel was on page 30 of his computer instructions. Coked up and drunk was a consensus. Nuel dispatched two more emergencies on the phone, another crash and a stabbing, and told the ER nurse to call him back if the most-dead one got any worse.

I said, "Look Nuel, don't get hung up on a few numbers. You got your cash flow right here—these figures are conservative, based on a boat just like ours. We doubled maintenance money and that's it, except for insurance, advertising, printing and incidentals." At last Nuel scanned the numbers. "Down here you got your depreciation and tax credit. We'll split the tax benefits among the investors." It was a hot button—tax benefits—a surge in pulse was a lead to follow. "Nuel. Look at this." I unrolled an architect's drawing of the boat. Nuel either studied it or zoned off, his head dropping slightly in scrutiny or unconsciousness. "Nuel. Look at this." I shuffled shots of Masao and boat loads of women near naked, then laid out two more lines, browsed the wines left up and picked a nice white near the high end—two forty—for closing.

Nuel studied the boat loads. "Shit, Bubba," he said.

The wine was given a chance to breathe. Nuel and I weren't. We snorted and rambled—adventure at sea and big profits. I said I wasn't sure how far I'd have to go to piece this thing together, but if Nuel would go fifty grand I knew it would come together. Start up was only two fifty, boat and all.

Nuel, in the business rendition of The God Act, dumped his baggy on the top photo, the waxy flake sparkling over the bronzed skin beauties. "You don't need no pieces. I want it."

I sat back slow and easy, poured the wine and repeated the proposition: "Nuel, you want to finance the whole project. That's two hundred fifty grand."

Nuel said, "I guess so," mumbling for the girls, staggering to his computer. "I know iss'll work."

The phone rang. Jane was quick, said Nuel was out and hung up. Nuel mumbled that he'd just bought a yacht. "Fuck you. My dinner's ruined." She found the straw and lunged for the pile.

"Be good fo breakfast," Nuel mumbled, scratching his head, seeking focus on the numbers. Then the wine was ready, and it was bedtime. It was beauty-ful.

Amazingly next morning, Nuel was still inspired, the deal was still on. I found him early in the kitchen, saving a goblet of wine in the microwave. "You put it in de fridge 'n'en give it jist 'bout twelve seconds 'o radar, it'll be fine." He said what the hell, if he could get into a deal like this one without too much cash he didn't care, and he'd get his depreciation and his tax credit—"I git mah taix craidit." And of course he would be a yachtsman.

A crash victim had died in the night. Nuel said it was expected. "I knew he would. Hell he was dead soon's I heard his brain pressure." He dabbled at his lasagne. I had an eye-opener, kissed my date and told Nuel we'd talk in a day or two. Nuel said, "You be careful now Bubba."

It was dawn in Hawaii when I called Jack and asked for status. Jack said he was broke and back to whacking it. Louise moved out, good riddance. He shit and brushed his teeth nearly every day, so he wasn't doing too bad.

I listened. Jack rolled over and lit a smoke, inhaled deep and recalled an uncle who died of asshole cancer because he sat in meetings for hours, for years, holding it in. Another uncle died of prostate cancer, never whacked off. Jack feared that kind of death. But Louise was one more bitch, gone and forgotten. He said he didn't need her—he had some sox.

I said the boat money was done, a quarter million bucks.

Jack smoked. "All of it?"

"It wasn't easy."

"Nuel?"

"Yes."

"Your friend Nuel wants to put up all the money?"

"Yes."

"What did he say."

"He said he guessed he would."

"He just said, 'I guess I will?'"

"Not exactly. He said, 'I giss so.'"

"I'll be goddamn," Jack said. He said he'd love to talk some more, but he had to catch some guys at the harbor before their morning charters. It was a new day, sunshine, blue sky, the smell of success.

Louise moved back to Jack's place the following week—he called his place Mexico, or, The Little Brown Hut, or Adobe World, or Mondo Condo; he said his life so far was a third world state of mind. She didn't ask if she could. She showed up, "home," which was her whole speech coming through the door with a bag of groceries. Jack had yelled at her for the short shrift life gave him—he couldn't even buy a lousy goddamn chicken, he was so broke. So she came home from a week gone with his measure of happiness, a chicken, some celery, carrots, potatoes and, creme de la creme, a cold six-pack. It turned his heart to mush.

She'd seen a psychic. Jack asked how much it cost. It was a hundred fifty bucks, but by the time she told him, the chicken was baked, the beer drank and a shitload of good news imparted unto him. Emerald Sea, the who-do, could feel the vibes from a phone call or letter for fifteen bucks and give a fair account of what was and what would be. The hundred fifty dollar special, however, got Emerald looking deep and far ahead. She saw many years together for Jack and Louise, decent health and prosperity—but it wouldn't be easy. It could happen though, with work. Louise was willing. She trembled and shed a tear—the who-do saw a boy for Jack, a girl for Louise. "A hundred fifty bucks?" Jack said. "That's a honk and a half."

A strange woman would come into their lives, and Jack would strike it rich in packaged fish. Jack guzzled his last beer and said "Ho boy," feeling good.

The next day on the phone, fed, fucked and rested, he said, "The bitches all want back in when things are going your way."

I asked, "Status?" Jack said, "Yeah yeah, I'm headed down right now."

Annie's place was bad, but not as bad. She'd reconciled with Red Salamander and spent most of her time at his tepee, no shit, in a park in town. The white man owed it to the Indian. Red got coverage. Annie, main squaw, was all beads and fringe and ecstatic over social justice. It was the debut she never had.

Nuel

It was good times for Nuel too. With unemployment and the wholesale price index down, more people could afford the knife.

I fed the dogs and cats, lucked onto a series of good books, and every few days drove over the hill, to Nuel's place, where wine, cocaine, Madelaine and talk of sea adventure led to a modern male bond. Nuel and I were friends, joked with each other. I asked how many melons today. Nuel laughed. The melon count was good, our fortunes intertwined.

Nuel said he averaged four grand a head, "unless it's a insurnce job. Then I can push close to five, and if Medicare, Medical, Medicaid or Medifuckall's in on it, shit, I'll tweak her on out to sixty-five hunnerd. Motherfuckers take a year to pay."

It was a time of comfort, with a nurse who knew how, plenty drugs and wine and the money secure. Jack complained, no luck, but that was Jack's nature. I felt good. It was quiet days, easy nights.

Nuel called one day with an invitation—dinner with a special friend I should meet. I anticipated another nurse with a remarkable figure, lip gloss perhaps, most likely with good manners. And by week three of the yachting trade, another evening of fine wine, the best in drugs and sexual relations with a beautiful, intelligent and talented woman seemed a matter of course, a pattern anticipated, naturally. I felt foolish with roses. The friend was another doctor. Ralph and Nuel had swilled about six bills in fine wine by the time I arrived. Ralph was quiet. Nuel rambled. Nuel was proud. Ralph reflected.

Dinner was rack of lamb and endless chatter—status quo at Nuel's. It was a long evening with no nurses, no snoot. Jane cooked and left so the men could drink, eat and talk. Nuel was a sloppy drunk, slurring and muttering, not sentences but phrases. He praised Ralph as the greatest—"I'm talkin' greatest Bubba they ain't a muhfucker greater'n he...you..." Ralph was the orthopedic surgeon Nuel brought in last week on a tough case. A boy of twelve had a tumor on his spinal cord and a terminal prognosis—one to three months left. His parents bought Nuel's advice: go in with the laser beam, Nuel at the joy stick, deep fry that sucker and maybe, with the help of Nuel and God, some miracle might put the cancer into remission.

So Nuel sliced the boy open—wielding a cleaver in the retelling—and Ralph disassembled the spinal column. Nuel worked the laser through the scope with the precision and power of a genius. Then came the procedure unheard of, unimagined, undreamt by mortal doctors, now destined for the front cover of *The Journal of the American Medical Association.* Nuel directed, Ralph bent rebar—"You goddamn right Bubba—con-crete rene focemunt. Iss muhfuckah right here made a reeee bar samidge wi'de code in de midduh..." Nuel rose off his seat, floating, then settled back down, tears forming, the Light of God upon him.

"You shoulda seen iss fucker! Bubba, we had blood 'n shit all over at muhfuckin' place! 'N iss fucker right here he don'give a shit he jist bendin' em rebars 'n I'm shoving em fuckers into this boy's back...Man! It was the bloodiest shit I ever seen. God." They sewed the boy back up, the two bars sticking out just under the neck. "Aw hell, they only stuck out a few inches."

The story ended. After silent tribute, Nuel popped another (three bills—near the top) and toasted Ralph and himself, who by God gave that boy his only chance. If the boy only lived another twelve days, well it was twelve days knowing the best goddamn talent money could buy had tried—tried like hell to save him.

Then, shit ass drunk, spilling wine on his chest, Nuel made it clear why I was there: to hear that Ralph would come along on the great adventure, sailing *Whirlaway* across the ocean. It was news to Ralph too, who begged off. Blood and shit were one thing, seasick was something else. He mumbled that he enjoyed meeting me and left. Nuel said, "Well. I guess so." Then he faded clean away, fell plumb asleep right there in the his chair, lay his sleepy little noggin right down beside his din, right there on the crumbs and flakes and spills, snoring serenely near his rack of lamb. I took it for a cue and also took my leave.

Driving home I figured it out; near the higher echelons, idiosyncrasy is just part of doing business.

 The Bank

I checked in next day and Nuel was again alert and cheerful. I said thanks for a great dinner. Nuel said, "At's okay, Bubba," and he said he had to run—business was holding up better than ever—several melons waiting. Nuel said his record was six melons in one day, and today the record could fall. He was up slicing at sunrise and had two sliced and done back up, one more sliced and waiting—he only stopped back home for a little breather, and then it was back to the shop. He had enough melons on hand for the record, if he could hold up. "Oh bidness good, Bubba."

Nuel averaged twelve melons a week then, and a strong economy gave him freedom from lobotomies, his non-elective standby, his bread and butter cut in hard times.

And the forecast was strong. So I felt good when Nuel said his lawyer was preparing the documents. The feeling lessened with the forty page, single-spaced diatribe on fuselages, grease fitting maintenance and a full array of judgments for crimes against Nuel. Under two lines at the bottom were printed my name and Jack. Nuel asked on the phone, "What's at other boy's last name?"

We met next day at the lawyer's office—gray walls, carpet and furniture, filtered air and windows stuck shut, a gray piece of meat to match behind a desk. The lawyer looked like Nuel and spoke in the same soft monotone and sat slumped and shapeless in a very expensive suit. He looked like a motherfucker too, or a childfucker or any kind of fucker; convenience and revenue looked like the order of his day, you know, like the kind of lawyer people think about when they think fucking lawyers. Everyone shook hands. The lawyer read. He spoke legal speak, and it came out eulogy; the deal was dead, could not survive the hundreds of remedies for disrespect to Nuel or Nuel's pocket. But then again a guy like me, down but not out, but goddamn it down and down and down some more, knew when a dead deal had to be brought back among the living. I said I didn't give a shit how the lawyer spent his last two days, and who paid for it didn't make any difference to me either. Nuel laughed his nervous laugh, the one he saved for embarrassing times like this one, with a potential partner in shirt-sleeves, who said shit in a business conference. Nuel was keen on form. I suggested that Nuel and I review the document in private, maybe over cocktails at his place, where we could work things out.

Nuel and his lawyer looked at each other, and then Nuel gave the nod. He'd take care of everything.

Outside, Nuel had a new show'n tell, and with a 'lemme show you sumpm Bubba,' he pulled a cardboard case from the back floor of his dream car. He set it on the hood, opened it and pulled out a nine millimeter automatic Uzi. He attached the grip, the butt and the silencer. He slid a clip into place and said he just wanted me to see it. He sent in for it from his mercenary soldier magazine. He said he loved it— made his M-16 seem like a child's toy. He said if he ever killed himself, he thought it would be fun to head down to faggot town and take out about forty, fifty faggots first.

"Nuel," I said. "I didn't know you hated homos."

"Oh hell. I don't," he said. "Hell, I might jist go on down a corner here and take me out a mess 'o lawyers." I laughed and said go ahead one time, squeeze off a few rounds. Nuel laughed too and said he'd joined a combat club. That weekend was his first scrimmage—they used blood pellets that hit with a sting and a splatter when they took you out. He was graduating "orientation to combat," and he said, "Fugzample, don't ever peak around de corner on a building like they

do in a movies. Bullet'll rickashay flat straight on a surface in from
where it hits." He stroked the muzzle. "I kill you in a minute."

"Why would you want to kill me, Nuel?"

Nuel laughed low and put his new toy away; goodbye, no hand-
shake and no invite to come drink wine, snort cocaine, have a nurse.

On the way home I figured I'd duck out, get a job selling insurance.
I came to my senses over dinner—rice, tuna and beer. After all, life
and the good are sometimes as much of a compromise as the downside can get to be. Annie and now Nuel—it was a world o'whackos.

Nuel called a week later. I said the forty page document was on its
way to Jack, and it won't be long now. "Well," Nuel said, he'd gone
ahead on his end too, with his personal banker, Weems, who understood brain surgeon financial power. The money was ready to go.

I leaned on Jack that night. What was taking so long? Could he
find a parking place or not? Jack said some people have to work to get
by, and his end of it was tougher than snorting cocaine and fucking
nurses with Nuel. I cried foul. I was the one in the snake pit, and han-
dling creatures who could turn on you at any minute wasn't easy.
I hadn't felt so good, and the nurse had her bitchy side too, got tem-
peramental and wanted to talk about life and love.

That calmed Jack down enough to spew his troubles more calmly.
He worked on a tourist barge for seven dollars an hour, which shrunk
to four fifty "after the cocksuckers fuck you in the ass on taxes and pay
backs on your company T-shirts." He was starving to death, full time.
In his spare time at night he went to captain's school, prepping for the
Coast Guard exam. His license would qualify him to captain
Whirlaway for hire. In his spare daytime he was looking for the perfect place to park a yacht, but it was tight—too many boats, too many
desperados cutting each other's throat for a better chance at the good
life, or a new life, or just any life. "You got sixty slips in the smallest
harbor in the Pacific and only thirty commercial permits and about
two thousand assholes trying to get them. I got holes in my pants and
dirty socks, Harry. Who the fuck am I supposed to be? A rich guy?
A guy with a fancy racing yacht?"

I let him light another smoke and calm down again. Jack said he had two possibilities, but one guy was so dull he looked terminal. "The other one is a macho meatball. It doesn't even matter. Neither one believes me. I told them my partner'll be here soon with a quarter million dollar yacht, but I'm still a boat nigger with a big mouth. Get the picture? I got credibility gap. But I'm working on it." He wasn't sure what I would owe him for getting so much more snoot and gash than he had on this deal, but he'd figure it out.

I offered to sign a forty-page document from Nuel's lawyer, giving Jack snoot and gash parity. "Yeah, right," Jack said and hung up.

With forty days left on the option, Jack had nought—one cocksucker or another wouldn't listen to reason. But he knew the score. He'd make it work. Don't you worry.

Nuel lost interest under pressure from J.D. in Utah. I ran a spread sheet on investment performance, ran the photos again. Nuel would be the first doctor in history with a boat and a profit. Nuel came back into the fold with renewed interest after telling his buddies, "I got me a couple boys workin' on it for me. Couple boys over there workin' my front end." Nuel clearly saw envy in the faces of his doctor buddies, most of whom had taken it foursquare up the asshole on can't-lose propositions, especially with boats. Nuel was a genius again.

Nuel told his lawyer how foolproof and free of work the *Whirlaway* deal shaped up. Nuel's lawyer called me to say he would draft that intent into Addendum One. He sent a bill for thirty-five hundred bucks two days later.

Not to worry, that wasn't even a whole melon. But Nuel called after midnight demanding two-thirds of the lawyer bill right now. "Rat now! I mean rat now, Bubba! At's a deal we made—one thud, one thud, one thud!" He slurred like a drunk, yelled like a fascist.

I heard cocaine and liquor and said me'n Jack'd pay in the morning, first thing. Nuel said he had to pay his lawyers "rat now! At's what I payum for's to keep my ass out trouble!" Now how are they supposed to do that: "Nahadaypostadodat..." If I don't pay them: "fadompayum... Rat now."

I said I hadn't realized the gravity of the situation, and I was writing a check and pulling my pants on too for a walk down to the mailbox rat now. I asked if that would do until tomorrow's detailed interface. Nuel said, "Well. I guess so."

Jack made a deal with the dullard with thirty-five days to go. The deal fell apart with twenty-five days to go. It was sleepless nights until eighteen days to go, when Jack cut a deal with the macho meatball, who wanted the world if he was to enter a deal. I wanted a profile. Jack said the guy's fishing boat nearly sank this week when the head jammed open on Kotex. So the guy said no goddamn kotex could sink him, and he put a Chrysler starter motor on his toilet. Then he flushed his hat at 200 amps, 800 rpm. Now he wanted 80 percent of the gross. I said I'd take over.

I called the meatball and said, "Yeah, okay, forty percent of the net."

The meatball said, "Well, I got to roll the numbers around in my head." I waited, practically expecting to hear an echo on the line, reverberations of numbers bouncing off the walls of his small but uncluttered brain cavity. In a minute the meatball said, "Okay."

"I can't wait for you to meet Dr. Nuel," I said.

"Yeah, I oughta," said the meatball, whose name was Bill Bascum.

The hat flush story had everyone dockside har-harring; oh boy that old Bill Bascum. But nobody said nothing nor got into range of Bill Bascum without one eye over a shoulder, for self-defense, for the Sunday punch. Cute story, but the guy was scum, a clinger, like the ring in the bowl. Jack said, "Hey. He's the only guy left. What do you want to know? He smokes a ton of dope and crosses his arms all the time. He's got a big mole on his neck with greasy hair on it. Is he okay? You want me to have him call Nuel's lawyer? Fuck."

Jack lit another smoke and said, "Hey, I got my ticket." He was a captain, licensed by the U.S. Coast Guard. I wondered if they were more stringent than the A.M.A. or the A.B.A. It all shaped up like Howdy Doody time, and a man with the first snit of smarts could easily have known that this cast of clowns could not, ever, on any day in the history of the world, generate the kind of results described in all the documentation and professed intent.

Nuel's lawyer cranked up the paper mill for another inch of it, and with four days left, everything was set. The lawyer grinned—he just happened to be heading over to Hawaii with his family. He'd be happy to meet the meatball for a signature.

He checked his family into the Hyatt Regency and charged another three grand for the last stack and another twelve hundred for personal delivery. Nuel said don't worry about it, they had that Bascum fellow bound and gagged with legal parameters, and he needed to take care of his lawyers now, "'cause they the boys keep me outa trouble." Jack and I decided not to worry, not with all the money we'd make as yachtsmen.

Jack came over with Masao and Herbert, his cousin, six-five and shadow dark, who said Howzit Brudda, we like cross ocean with haole boys please also yes on da kine new boat. They spoke pidgin, which isn't dialect but is slang, imprecise, insecure and demeaning.

Whirlaway was hauled out, surveyed, repaired as necessary, bottom painted and buffed out stem to stern. Jack worked the wax and dirt out of the boat and into himself until he was nothing but dirt and grit and the boat shined, until he looked like he sounded but *Whirlaway* was bright as the future. His imminent command gave him what he'd been without: purpose, and a little respect wouldn't hurt.

Closing day was two days before the option expired. Rumors flew that the boys didn't have it together, but the boys knew better. But at two hours before it would be official, Nuel came to the boat yard in his dream car. *Whirlaway* was showroom clean, rerigged and ready to sail south across an ocean. Jack was a smudge, wax, sweat and blood. I watched from the pay phone where I called for survey, insurance, yard bills, life-support, materials, parts, gear, groceries. Jane got out first and sat on the hood smoking a cigarette, a menthol 100. Nuel shuffled some papers, made a phone call and got out. He thrust his hands in his pants, behind his belt and said, "Boys. We got a problem." The boys waited. "Prefuuuuuhed ship's mortgage." The boys still waited. "You can't git one."

Remorse hung over Nuel like a cloud. The great one was weak. Jack said, "Bullshit, Nuel. All a preferred ship's mortgage is, is what the bank calls a mortgage on a documented vessel." Nuel said his lawyer couldn't get one. "Give him a few more grand. He'll figure it out."

I had seen money guys disappear, get cold feet and run away, sometimes because the money isn't there, and the so-called money guys were only jacking you off for the tribute they couldn't get anywhere else. But mostly it was plain and simple buyer's remorse, figuring at the last minute all the other stuff all that dough could buy. That wasn't the case with Nuel. He had the credit line. The last minute factor in the equation for him was disrespect, a hard fact to accept for a Doctor God from the surgery ward, and then came the fear; what if his boys got worse? I yelled from the phone booth. "You want this boat Nuel? We're talking ten, twelve melons cash. That's three days downside. I don't get it. You want it to work or don't you?" Nuel said sho, 'course he wanted it to work, he was only relating what his lawyer told him, that...

"Hey Nuel." Jack buffed again. "Fuck your cocksucking lawyer. I'll get the preferred ship's mortgage."

Nuel laughed, pulled his tie loose and opened his collar. "Well. I guess so." He ducked back into the dream car and made another call. Jack and I leaned on the keel in the shade, in trouble, no way to play it but straight. I strolled over to the dream car and knocked on the window. It was as goofy as the rest of the car, as goofy as the guy driving it—it only opened six inches, and with cold air pouring out into my face I asked Nuel where the money is, for closing. Nuel said he had a call in, to Weems, at the bank.

"A call in? We're closing today." Nuel said not to worry, cranked up the dream car and left. An hour later he was nowhere. An hour after that he called and said closing would be set back a few hours, not to worry. *Whirlaway* went back into the water. We went to Annie's. The seller had called—no extension on the option, a Texan waited with cash plus fifty grand.

"Alright," Jack said. "Instant equity. I nearly got a degree in accounting you know."

Annie was on the outs again with Red Salamander for a debt she refused to pay for the white man. She got happy, flitting about her kennel/living room, with three new men, Masao, Herbert and Jack. In her vulva jeans and sweater that was mostly armholes, she plied every angle. Masao said, "Carrot legs. Funny looking tits."

Herbert laughed and said "But she one nice lady yeah, take care so many dogs?"

Masao and Herbert, on their second case of beer, smoked a joint with a few dogs on the sofa, figuring odds on getting home. Nuel showed up with false confidence to report that Weems would call this number soon. "Soon? Nuel, is it ready or not?"

Nuel reacted then. He called me pushy, said it was my worst trait, acting like a Jew like that, and he wouldn't be pushed, and he wouldn't deal with his bank on that level—"on at levuh." He prescribed patience and drank a beer. He demonstrated calmness in the clutch, on the sofa. Jack and I paced a half hour. Masao asked Herbert, "You think he pushy?"

Annie said she had to go, all the men were so grumpy. She liked happy, "up" people, like herself—people who could talk and share. She left for AA with two dogs.

I told Nuel to call Weems, now. With all eyes on him, Nuel called the bank and asked, meekly, for Mr. Weems. He waited a minute and said, "Yes... Yes... No... Yes... No... I see." He hung up and asked Jack and me to join him please in a bedroom.

He paced. Then he began. "Boys. I'm gone tellya 'bout bidness. Bidness is like life." He said a bidness deal sometimes gets sick. It needs surgery just like people do. So you put the deal on the operating table and damn it all to hell you do your best to save it. But sometimes it'll die on you. And death is one of those things strong people learn to accept.

The bank would not make the loan.

Jack asked me where I found this fruitcake, then he moaned: months of life wasted, poverty coming on, broken promises. I ducked out to the living room and called the bank. I wanted Weems, life or death. Why wasn't the loan ready? Weems said he wasn't at liberty to discuss a client's loan status further than it had been discussed that morning. The loan was denied. If "the doctor" wanted to come in and discuss it, they would be happy to discuss it. I said the option was up in twenty hours. Weems said he certainly couldn't help that, and he hung up.

The next hour was silent and depressed, like death row right before sunrise. Jack smoked half a pack, yelled fuck and broke a few tea pots.

Nuel said he was sorry boys, but that was the way it was.

I smoked a joint, for perspective and nausea, drank three beers quick and walked down to the beach, to think, to fight surrender, because the best points get scored with no hope, no time.

In the next two years I would face fifty-knot head winds and big black seas with Jack Witte. None of it looked so grim as that nasty sea of tomorrow.

Jack came down with another six-pack, and we remembered guys from high school who made it. Jack said he should call his brother who worked in L.A. for ninety grand a year—he'd know what to do. Near dark we went back up and took turns calling long distance, to guys from high school who made it and Jack's brother, fifteen hours to go on the option. All we needed was two hundred grand overnight. Our old friends from high school all sang the same chorus of bullshit bullshit bullshit; neato, a sailing yacht, God, that sounds so much better than the humdrum life I got. Then it was a minute or two for remember when and gee, it's a shame you guys didn't call sooner. It would have been great to get in on something like this. Right.

In deep night, surrounded by dogs, dirt, hair, stink, sleeping drunks and Annie working on a list of grade school teachers and their wrong deeds, I gave up. It wasn't the first time I ever gave up, and it didn't represent the most work lost, but it was the worst beating. The future was gone again. Slouched in a chair, I delivered my summary report: "Fuck it all."

"Yeah." Jack poured the last of his beer onto the floor. A dog shuffled over and sniffed it, then shuffled back. Silence sounded grim then. Annie sounded worse, mumbling motherfuckers at the whole lot of them. We sat still again, knowing that dark and still and surrounded by stink is what everything changes to.

And it was a change for the better, but sometimes people confuse tangible loss for spiritual loss, and in their confusion they strive to regain what was lost, when in fact the loss was a blessing all along. People sometimes deny the natural order of things, insisting instead on the perverse, the unnatural, the rich reward in dollars they have been taught is necessary to lead a good life. And so it was in deepest night that a visitation, suddenly, from nowhere, broke the stillness, moved my tired carcass from all heaped up on the sofa to standing to moving to Annie's table, where the arms of it took a sheet of paper and fed it into the typewriter and the fingers hit the keys causing words to appear on the paper. It was a letter to Weems, saying that a contract was signed with the meatball, that I, Nuel, was on the line for three to five million dollars in lost revenue, I, Nuel, would seek restitution directly, forthwith and forevermore, from the bank. I would sue, big. It was a page, signed, Nuel. Jack snored. I sat still again, and two hours later woke up to another day, another drive to Nuel's. I went in alone. Nuel sat at his table in his jammies and his robe with a glass of wine, a cup of coffee, the morning paper. "I made a few calls last night, found us a hunnad thousand dollars," he said. "A hunnad thousand, Bubba. It was beauty-ful. How'd you'n Jackie do?" He was up early for his rounds.

I knew what escape looked like. I sat down beside him, put the letter in front of him. "Sign it."

Nuel read it and said, "Well..."

I was run down, run over, pulled off the road and stood back up, beat and sleepless, and when Nuel didn't sign it, I clarified the situation for him: "Sign it Nuel. Sign it. Sign it, or I'll break your hands." Even I was impressed with the overall dramatic effect of a face full of sleeplessness and some shakes and wearies.

Nuel signed it and looked hurt. A man once praised takes poorly to rough treatment. He said he'd need a few minutes to get dressed, he was coming along. I said stay put, by the phone, and left him looking hurt.

Back in the car I gave Jack the letter. Jack laughed and said last night Masao and Herbert went drunk to a pub at the harbor. The waitress bitched when Masao flung macaroni salad at a group of girls, but when she threatened to have him booted, he went spastic and garbled, "My slip forked!"

Jack started on the prize pussy they almost scored—I said shut up. Jack looked hurt. "Focus," I said. "Focus. Focus. Focus."

Jack looked a little bit confused at the concept, but he shut up anyway. Downtown a hooker walked home. Her stretch mini, pushem up and spike pumps looked like low budget props in the morning light. Jack leaned out and yelled, "Hey bitch!" He grinned at me.

We made the bank at eight oh one and wanted Weems. "Do you have an appointment?"

Jack said, "Look bitch..." He wore his shorts, his orange and green aloha shirt and his baseball hat.

I held him back in slacks and a white shirt. "It's an emergency." She called a loan officer.

I told the loan officer: It's an emergency. He said he made car loans and home improvement loans. I showed him Nuel's threat letter and said he better lead the way to the man who made real fast boat loans, because—watch check—in eight hours the shit hits the fan. Nobody knew exactly how much shit would hit, but Lord it would be some shit and I, for one, frankly didn't see how anyone would come out alive, much less clean. The loan officer read the letter, wrinkled his forehead and said, "Follow me."

Jack said, "Good man here, Baldidge."

"That's Baldridge."

Baldridge lead the way to Weems. Weems' office had glass walls. He looked snug inside it, well fed and secure, all needs tended to. And he looked young, hardly thirty. Jack whispered, "He's younger than us."

I said, "Yeah," stopped at the door, turned to Jack and smiled. "Pretty fucked up, isn't it?"

Jack giggled, and he relaxed. I'd made a joke, meaning the good old days were still on, because we were still a couple of fuck ups still fucking up, trying to rob a bank this time. Baldridge said, "Gentlemen," and held the door.

Jack said, "Thank you, Baldridge."

Weems listened to the liabilities at hand, the threats and desperation. Jack carried stacks of Coast Guard regulations as evidence of authenticity. The bankers perused the Coast Guard papers. They set Nuel's letter aside. Jack rambled over Coast Guard regulations and the penalties for violation. After two hours of interrogation, the bankers spoke.

Nuel called a couple months ago for a boat loan around two hundred thousand. Weems said yes, the bank would make the loan, come on in, we'll talk.

Weems paused.

I said go on. Jack said yeah, go ahead on.

But Weems shrugged; that was the end of the story, the end of Nuel's financing. Jack said fuck. Weems said this was a regular problem with doctors, God bless them.

Jack said fuck.

The bankers reflected, stepped outside, mumbled some more and stepped back in. "Follow us." They led up, third floor, pure theory, and The President.

Jack and I breathed deep and ran it again, Baldridge and Weems filling in. I checked my watch—three hours and counting.

The President asked one question: How could the bank lend money on a boat that would be three thousand miles away? Jack was quick: "I'll be there!" The President stared off, into the oblique plane of pure theory, and he nodded.

The bankers conferred and said they wanted to see "the doctor." I said I would call, that Nuel was standing by at the lawyer's office, had cancelled three melons today to deal with this. The bankers said fine, right after lunch, around two, or three. I smiled across The President's table and said, "If I were you bubbas, I'd order out."

Nuel wasn't home. Jane said he was making rounds. I called his answering service and said, "Find him. We have a major hemorrhage in a bicipital lobe. This is Dr. Hurt." Nuel called back in five minutes. I said be at the pasta parlor down the street in ten minutes for a briefing.

Nuel showed up in his three piece, thousand dollar suit, carrying his newborn calf briefcase.

Jack had ordered a cauldron of spaghetti and said the great thing about his aloha shirt was that it didn't show spaghetti sauce.

I briefed Nuel: no matter what the bankers said or how hard they leaned, he was not to go into a room alone with them, but should insist on his partners' presence.

Nuel said he didn't like my tone of voice.

I said, "If a tone of voice is all you have to worry about you'll have a good day," and I smiled again at the change between us. Nuel hadn't flexed the dominance muscle any more than Annie had, hadn't shown more kinky curiosity at seeing a grown capable male like me in the subservient position than she had either. But Nuel had fucked with the future, so he'd earned himself more than despicable disrespect. He was made to understand that for some people life was real, downside and terrible loss a significant possibility, and he had become one of those people. I was more myself now too, more like an animal trapped, and the crackpot, drunken quack who was pretty good to drink wine with was someone else, a long time ago.

I left swiftly, leaving Nuel twitching resentments, leaving Jack slurping. Nuel left next, leaving Jack with the check. Jack signed Nuel's name and phone number.

In a first floor gathering at the bank, Weems said in his pleasant voice that he would speak with the doctor alone. No one moved.

Nuel said his partners should stay. Weems said it was personal bank business. It was a banking move, all the bankers standing up in a banking posture that said they had as much pulse as the rest of the furniture, they didn't care what happened, as long as they had their little conference. It was a moment of weakness for me and my partner Jack, and with no parry we stepped outside. From outside the glass, we watched the bankers drill. Nuel nodded.

Weems came out alone and walked right past us, headed out toward the parking garage, wagging a finger for us to follow. Outside, he said the bank would make the loan—Jack grinned—as long as Jack and I would share the risk, with personal guarantees.

Jack said, "Give us the dough Weems. I'll guarantee you a goddamn blow job."

Weems said, "No no no. We need signatures. But they can't be made under duress."

I asked, "Duress? What is duress?" Weems paused, as if in rational thought, then led the way back in.

With ninety minutes remaining Jack and Nuel and I signed here, and here, and here, and here. And here, and here, and here. I yelled to Baldridge to get his ass on the phone, call the seller and tell him the funds are in escrow. Baldridge liked the excitement. It was fun, like teamwork, the kind of banking in the spirit of community development that he'd imagined.

Outside in the flush of victory, wadding up the credit applications from Weems, I breathed deep. Jack lit a smoke and chomped it in his grinning teeth. But glory was brief. Nuel lagged two steps back, head hanging. "Boys. We got a problem." He said the bank loaned a hundred seventy, thirty grand short—Nuel got bent, in there alone. "I figured I might as well get what I could." I got the shakes, couldn't talk. Jack kicked a Mercedes, kicked it again. Nuel said, "Well, I could put the thirty on my credit card, but I really don't want to."

I spoke around the lump in my throat, said Jack and I were off to the boat yard to get signed off in the next...fifty two minutes. Nuel would be along with the rest of the money—didn't matter what it took, because anything less would cost so much more. Breathing was rough, pain evident, and with a struggle I threw in sincere anticipation of better times just ahead, blue skies, sunshine, full sails, yachting, plenty greased up women, just like in the pictures, just like we knew was now close at hand.

Nuel looked sincere too and wanted to know, "Are you with me? Are you boys with me?" Jack laughed, flicked his cigarette away, put his arm around Nuel and said, "We're with you Nuel."

 # Das Boat

The Whirlaway Syndication closed with five minutes to spare. The Texan was already comfortable on deck, at the end of a boot scuff trail. Jack jumped aboard with his first command. "Get off my boat." The Texan obeyed.

Nuel felt redeemed. He called Jack Jackie and asked what he should do. Jack flicked a butt overboard and told him go make rounds or whatever he wanted to do, just stay out of the goddamn way. Nuel laughed, undaunted.

Two days of adrenaline, hot dogs and cottage cheese and a major bank heist led directly into overdrive preparations for a sail across the biggest ocean in the world tomorrow at sunrise. And now we had the grand back from the option, according to the forward thinking terms of the deal cut by the fast track yachting executive, me.

Jack and Masao took four bills to the grocery. Herbert and I took four to the liquor store. Everyone got back near dusk with enough groceries and beer for a sail across an ocean, and enough brandy and cocaine to forget the same span in cares and woe. Jack got himself a jumbo beefburger drooling with funky lettuce and tomatoes. He looked like a python engorging a monkey, mustard and mayo gobbing down his palm treed chest. He grinned, garbled that he didn't give a fuck, inhaled several beers and capped off with a lethal pull on the brandy bottle. Looking as insane as a man still free on the streets can look, he said, "This is living."

Masao came aboard with two junior barflies, naked under their baggy blouses. "Let me see that cocaine," he said, and the party was underway. One young floozy slid in beside me, interrupting my feeble attempt at reality adjustment. I tried again with a man-size swig on the cognac bottle and foolish snoot straight from the bag. That was a boost and brought me closer to the spirit at hand, and in a fire engine flush I turned to the strange female beside me and said, sincerely, "I'm a yachtsman," and I believed it, because it was true. It was what had become of me. What a difference a day makes, people sometimes think.

Jack announced that five grand a month, mortgage and insurance, put the cost of the evening over a hundred seventy dollars.

I cried, "You're right. Party's over. Everyone out!" And so we laughed till we choked, till tears ran with more laughter at the funniest thing in the world, which was Jack Osborne Witte and Martin Zane Lusk, yachtsmen.

Then we drank and snooted some more.

Some people plan two years for an ocean crossing—we set departure for seven tomorrow. Nuel said he had to go home for a few things, but he'd be back as close to seven as he could. Jack said he could come back at eight, if he wanted to.

Three hours got us down to three fingers, brandy, a half-gram of toot. Masao dumped it out, lined it up, and final blasts boosted the crew up and out, to town for more women. Masao's girls went along, as bait. I was wired, tired, nauseated, drunk and spastic, and with another attempt at realization I sat still, and in a minute I was alone at a milestone in life.

No noise or bodies crowded in. It was down to the dim glow of the cabin light, the crisp night air of Northern California, and with a last little line and a modest shot, all fell still and quiet on a gentle rise and fall dockside, rich and tingling aboard the ocean racing yacht, *Whirlaway*.

Fifty-two feet long with a fifty-seven foot stick, a thoroughbred, she felt calm and ready. With a strong body and good lines she promised a good race—to the future, and wealth. I disappeared then, blended with the bulkhead, the chart table. Stiff as a board is what I was, and glowing too, warm as well-oiled mahogany. My soul floated in misty cabin light with no doubt that happiness was real, drugs were only fun.

Goodness was no longer an idea but had become a feeling; the vast ocean and its bully waves were just another ride, downtown.

I carried a cushion topside and lay down in the cockpit under the stars. Two fell into my head, blinking and twinkling diamond light and prospects for the following day.

I woke briefly two hours later to the pitter-patter of fat feet, a squeal and a whine from below to "Eat me! Oh eat me! Eeeeeat Meeee! Eat me all the way to Maui!" From somewhere in the haze that passed for consciousness, Jack grinned with a smoke. A fat girl beside him grinned too, a mouth breather, big and slack jawed as an open hatch, with a nose bright as polished brass in moonlight.

Jack said, "You want some you know what?" But the girl's birth control skin blotch moved like paisley on acid when she said she couldn't orgasm if she wasn't sucking on it, and my brain could not figure what I could possibly want. Jack giggled, and she said don't laugh, you didn't laugh five minutes ago.

I rolled over, back to the dream. It was short, leading to a megabeacon right in my eyes. It was tomorrow. The future had begun.

Jack, fresh as a daisy, stood at the helm ordering dock lines off. I had a waking vision then that Jack Witte would die young. But he'd die quick too, and that made him the better man. Masao and Herbert freed lines and climbed aboard. Nuel arrived as *Whirlaway* passed the last dock. Jack pointed to the fuel dock at the harbor entrance and passed it close.

Nuel jumped aboard with his luggage—two grips, a black bag with enough drugs for a discotheque, his Uzi, in case of pirates, and a baker's dozen Krispy Kreme jelly donuts. He said, "You boys lucky to have a survaval expert like me on bode. I be able a tell you exactly what to do, if I have to."

I moved and learned a new pain. A steep southerly swell, residual from the Mexican hurricanes, rolled under cold, gray skies and directly into the backwash off the coast. I remembered the dream, the promise, rolled over and puked overboard, then dragged myself below, to the head, for further wringing out. Herbert said, "Drunk sailor, squeeze tight in middle, give back debauchery from both ends."

I trembled back on deck. Herbert served up the last of the brandy and said, "Hair of dog what bit."

Jack at the helm had molted as well, looked more insane than last night, but different, removed from lubberly corruption, at home on chaotic swells. "Nothing beats the life at sea, Harry," he said. "If you don't count the cold, the wet, the constipation, no women and big fucking waves breaking behind you and over the port bow too—" He dropped his torso with both hands on the kingpin, weaving out of the spot where two swells crashed.

I remembered the dream, the promise, and felt earthly want fall away, considered death in terms of pro and con. Cold and wet felt bad. *Whirlaway*, big and racy at the dock, was down to proper size on the watery void. Hardly different than the flotsam flung by the hulking rollers, she loped down the backsides, languored in the troughs, alongside a Big Mac styrofoam box. Death was as close as the rail. I would have jumped, but it seemed even colder and wetter.

First nights at sea are difficult—winds gusting to thirty-five and swells crashing on the cabin top, swamping the deck. The boys on watch came up spitting. Jack yelled back at the blustery seas, "Fuck me in the ass! Whore!" Another wave broke overhead, and he asked meekly, "Why me?"

It was cold salami and mustard on white bread for two days, since sea legs and appetites take a while, and because the helm needs a close watch in the fluky breeze and stray breakers the first few hundred miles.

Masao navigated a rum line—two-forty south-southwest, a straight shot, Gomorrah to Babylon. He brought a sextant, sweat clothes and a raincoat. He'd crossed ten or twelve times, give or take.

Nuel came on deck before dark the second day wearing two grand in foul weather gear and safety harnesses, looking like Robby the

Robot, looking for a place to hook his tethers. Jack wore sweats too. He flicked his smoke to the wind and told Nuel to shag a beer.

Nuel paused, processing strange input, then nodded from the shoulders and struggled back down the companionway. He shagged beer.

Jack said "Thanks. Stay below. Save yourself for later."

Nuel paused again, shrugged and muttered, "Well." Jack yelled after him to tighten his chin strap before he farted, and we all had one more laugh.

Nuel mastered Loran electronic navigation the third day out. "I got it all figured out boys!" He got a fix in minutes, made Masao's sextant obsolete, until that night, when Masao cut the Loran from the master panel.

The cold gray clouds cleaved early the fourth day, and patches of blue sky boosted moral. Herbert at the helm looked overboard at a dull spot on the dawn shimmering sea as *Whirlaway* passed near it. It rolled over, casting a sad eye up. "Oh you little baby," Herbert whispered, and the big whale sank.

More blue above eased the steel gray below, and though two thousand miles remained, spirits rose with sunshine. Six spinner dolphin leaped from a water wall, ten more followed, and a hundred fifty more jumped quick off the bow, tailwalked abeam, smiling like hosts.

The sky shed doubt by noon, swells off the port bow ceased, and a steady following breeze of eighteen knots hinted tradewinds, downhill run to the tropics. For the first time in nearly a week all hands relaxed on deck in the movement the open ocean provides, in which men can know themselves. Masao read smut comics aloud, allowing panel discussion on blow jobs, asshole reaming, stand up fucking. Herbert found a pair of brown striped panties in a lazaret puka. Jack looked proud. Masao stared sadly west and popped another beer. Nuel went below for his Thai sticks.

Firing up, he said, "Bubbas, you ain't smoke shit till you smoke isshit." So we got stupid on Thai sticks, watched the azure sky, rode the one-way sea and shed clutch anxiety like bubbles in a wake. Nuel said he had morphine too, enough to numb everybody, just in case.

Reverie settled in like tropical balm, and in awhile Jack spoke low. "It won't work like this, hating Nuel. He's leaving anyway. We ought to put the shit behind us. We need to pull together and let it work." Nuel smiled.

I shrugged, shook Jack's hand on it and we both shook with Nuel. Masao turned a page. Herbert went below for the rum, for a toast, friends more better.

So the day rolled along, as if time was movement between sky and sea. A Godlike warmth eased the wayward souls from wet and cold, until Nuel stood up, scanned north, then south, shielding his eyes, fore and aft. Legs spread like an ancient mariner, he folded his arms and said, "I give any man here fit-ty thousand dollars a kill my ex-wife."

I laughed. Jack flicked his butt overboard. Masao turned a page. In a minute Nuel said, "I fucked a girl one time in a ass. Shit. I pulled mah dick out'n it had a piece 'o corn! Jiss hanging off a end of it." Then he gazed west, like he was a salty dog, and these were the glory days.

Herbert at the helm said, "He thinking. That man always thinking."

Nuel turned and planted his feet, facing Masao. Masao studied his fuck comic, turning soggy pages gently. Nuel said, "You know Bubba, you got a tumor in your brain." Masao looked up and smiled—his smile was crooked, one side curled up, the other stayed flat. "I was gonna tell you if you wanna check into my hospital before we left, why, I'd a took a look at it fo you. 'Eze muhfuckers, ha ha, they had us all in a rush. You want me to, Bubba, I take a look at her once we get there. Probly cut it out pretty easy if they got the laser gear." Masao looked at Nuel, then at Jack, then at me, and then he laughed and looked at his fuck comic.

Then came crimson dusk; red sky at night. A mahi mahi hit the hand line. Landed, killed, filleted and skinned, the fish hit the pan for a saute, white wine and oyster sauce. After dinner was topside again under benevolent twinkling skies. The waxing moon rolled in a phosphorescent wake. Masao and Jack stood watch midnight to four,

Herbert and I from four to eight. At ten Nuel said, "You boys go on get some rest. I drive iss bitch for awhile." And in the spirit of new trust and camaraderie, Nuel was given the helm. Jack slept for the first time in two days, an hour and a half. He was back on deck at eleven thirty asking what the fuck—the wind had swung around to the north, up five knots to twenty-three.

Too much sail for the course had pushed Nuel sixty degrees south, because running downwind is faster with fewer bumps than reaching across it. He stood at the helm with his legs spread. "We haulin' ass now, Jackie! We rollin'!" We were headed for Tahiti.

"I'll take it now, Nuel," Jack said.

Nuel went below and yelled, "God at's fun!" I went up and steered while Masao and Jack changed the foresail.

Jack took the helm muttering. "Sixty degrees off course. First cocksucker in the history of the world to miss the Hawaiian Islands."

Eighteen knots of wind made for twelve knots of boat speed all night. The breeze went light by sunrise, and another mahi mahi came aboard. The morning warmed, and the tropics seethed as we shed shirts and pants like soldiers in a truce. The sun seeped in like balm.

Herbert trailed a rope, dove off the bow and swam fast for it, then hand over handed back to the boat. So we shared a Thai stick and another day at the swimming hole was officially underway. Jack luffed the sails because Nuel couldn't reach the rope in time. He grinned at me and said, "One a these days, Alice. One a these days."

But it was swim stop that took Nuel from his two grand in foul weather gear and his thousand dollar cashmere suit, took him a long way from his four foot TV, his thousand dollar answer box, the dream car, the nurses, the drug and wine cellar. No God Act here, swim stop took Nuel down to naked. Pale and flabby and hung like a jellyfish, Nuel was only a fat man in middle age. Herbert stood beside him and laughed, maybe in kindness, maybe understanding what a half million a year can make up for.

Next to Herbert, tall, tan, muscular man of the tropics with a leaping tiger on one arm, a butterfly on the other, Nuel looked harmless.

"An amorphous blob," I said.

"A ball of snot," Jack concluded. Nuel was, there naked in the open ocean, a megalomaniac forgiven. He squeezed his nose, held onto his cock and jumped in.

We swam fore and aft. Masao dove thirty feet. Herbert told of sharks following, patient for the morning swim.

The wind died so we motored till noon, cleaned and checked the rig, the engine, the bilge. Herbert slipped and cut his toe on the rail, and Nuel was quick with injections, antiseptic and anesthetic, then stitches and a bandage. Herbert turned pale and said, "Doctor Fun. One brain surgeon." Nuel basked, saviour once again.

The wind came up quick to twenty-five, and trimmed to it *Whirlaway* made good time three days running.

Then the wind swung north and rose to thirty-five, gusts to forty. Nuel said bear south. He said a boat should change course to play the wind. "Ah wanna see this bitch run!" he talked gusto. Masao said in his opinion... Jack chucked his smoke over and said opinions are like assholes...

"I have asshole," Herbert said. He said boat no like too much sail, and he went forward, changed the headsail, shortened the main. Jack agreed and stayed the course.

Night fell quick as the wind came up, and *Whirlaway's* fastest time yet, fourteen knots over the bottom, was wet again but not so cold. Enough ocean had flowed under, enough breeze blown by for easy sea legs on deck, as if the world always heeled, yawed and pitched, reaching across the wind. Black clouds covered a three- quarter moon, or else split over a lit horizon. Squall lines came up quick then ran away, or else they swooped down to dump a deluge on deck.

I drove midnight to two, weaving through the rollers. Herbert lay in the cockpit. At two, Herbert sat back on the life raft, steered with his feet on the low spokes of the wheel. With the wind steady at thirty *Whirlaway* surfed down a steep backside at twelve, fourteen, seventeen, down to the hollow on his toes, to nineteen knots and a certain beeline to the bottom, but the bow came up, came closer to the wind halfway to the crest and punched through to surf it again, fourteen, seventeen, nineteen knots. Herbert whooped and cater-wauled like a banshee on a sleigh ride.

Masao and Jack came up at four. Herbert took Masao's berth, sighed once and snored. I hung out between the head and galley, wet and tired, amazed at the hard work of a dream and a promise. Horizontal, hanging out between sleep and a daze, between rising wind and hissing sea, between Masao's voice—"Kind of spooky out here," and sudden blackness, I bolted, rolled out and up. A goblin cloud swallowed the moon. Jack froze, profile in fear. Masao laughed loud in self-defense.

Dawn nine days out was clear and warm with twenty knots from the southeast for an easy reach home with a reefed main and small genny. Home—a hustler knows he's growing old when sentimental concepts sneak in—I tripped on thinking it. After a week and a half at sea Jack Witte looked like a reasonable man. Unshaven, salt oil in electric hair, sunburned and burned-out, he looked like struggle, snoot, liquor and no sleep. He cursed the two ten from L.A., over-head at dusk—it carried people who had regular jobs and got paid on Fridays.

The ham came up near dinner, gone off, its stench lunging from the icebox before it and after it and lingering like remnant stink of a former life. More corpses followed—rancid burger, butter, turkey, more pig and worst of all, slimy wrappers. Herbert chucked it over in handfuls. Nuel took pictures. Jack pissed in the wake.

Herbert brought tequila on deck for happy hour and said drink quick, so it no go off. Then as night fell, and little twinkling stars peeked down from their cosmic loft, we took turns shooting them from the sky with Nuel's Uzi. Herbert shellacked a vibrant red one overhead and it streaked across the sky to oblivion. All the drunks cheered and laughed. But Herbert whimpered, said he shoot one star from sky—he aimed askew, because everyone knows the atmosphere diffracts, and now he killed it. Nobody laughed, because Herbert looked down, said he was sorry and went below quiet with the gun.

Masao told then of Herbert's hard season. Two close friends were killed, one drowned, one shot.

Chili beans for dinner went down like bowling balls, and the next day passed slowly, farting out loud and cabin fever, looking west, no jokes.

I drove the last night at sea, four to six, and doused the compass light for fun, or spite, picking a star to steer by. I wondered who else it guided, if it still existed, or if it shone only as illusion of its former self, dead and gone, its light a half aeon out front of the truth of it. It drifted off course, one more lost mark on the gray thin line. Compass light on, I focused on the short run.

I sat by at sunrise, Herbert at the helm, when a pair of mahi mahi jumped a perfect arc ten feet high, fifty feet back, making for the lure like dawn after night. One fish hit. I grabbed the line and pulled the fish to four feet back and hung on to it, watching the hooked fish slice the water more easily than *Whirlaway*, as if quick sleek movement was a simple meditation. The bull was hooked. You can tell by the shape of the head, square on the bull, round on the cow—she swam with him in perfect tandem about a foot behind, staying with him, unaware that her soulmate would be plucked clean from reality in a heartbeat, and her life would never be the same. Herbert watched and encouraged a quick landing, which would lead to quick cooking. But I let the line go slack. The fish spit the hook, and he and his mate experienced the heartbeat together, poof and gone. "You let him go," Herbert said.

"They mate for life," I said. "I admire that."

"I admire breakfast," Herbert said.

"Give a fish a break."

Herbert laughed. "You jump in water. You see who give you one break." Then he yelped like a stuck pig. Horizons broke, jagged line rising like civilization's teeth.

Near the point at Kaanapali on Maui's west side, three miles before the windline and the true entrance to Pailolo Channel, cane fields dazzled radiant green from the sky blue sea. Rounding the point with three six-packs to go, we drank quick, so we would arrive with only three beers left, and it would look like perfect planning.

Jack made radio contact with Louise, Whiskey Alpha Romeo six one two do you read me baby?

Arrival to champagne, leis, adrenaline and fame was good to noon, when the lunch charters begin. Then we wobbled up the dock among the tourists who wondered aloud how deep is the water. We wondered how fleeting fame would be and where, already, is the womens?

Louise swept Jack away to a place with four walls and a door for a thirty minute drill. Herbert stayed aboard with a Thai stick. Masao wafted down the dock like a cool breeze to a female he one time fucked. He grinned his charming grin and said come with me. She threatened him softly, and he too left, for the pay phone above the harbor, his office, where he worked his little deck of cards, each one a name and address and a word or two on kink. He called them his Tarot cards, since they outlined his entire fortune. He set them in a neat stack beside his pile of quarters, and he dialed.

Nuel stood by *Whirlaway*, hands in pants, waiting to make his move. He moved on a young woman in a pink designer golf shirt and a villager skirt. He let her admire the source of the excitement that morning, before he stepped up behind her and said, "I own at boat."

I wanted away. So I slid up to a booth where a dock girl sold boat rides, a hefty lass with fine big tits who looked familiar with the other side of midnight. I wondered what men say when they come in from the sea, and wonderment was the best possible line. She said I looked good, really good—I looked over my shoulder and then seeing nobody looked back with a dumb as dogshit, just in and just paid grin. She'd seen it before. "Do you have any cocaine?" she asked. I said I felt good, really good, and yes, maybe I could get some.

Jack materialized from a nine minute drill to agree that yes, maybe we could. Jack said I was something, scoring a sniffette quicker than Masao. I said, "She's no sniffette—too big. She's a sniffalo." And we giggled along into a brave new world.

So the next five bills were spent in air-conditioned comfort, debauchery with a view, as if cash flow was just around the corner. Jack had opened a business account, had wanted one for years. He wrote checks. It was fun. Jack said a guy needs a payday, after all, don't worry, food stamps came last week.

We surfaced three days later refreshed, relaxed, changed. Strolling dockside like yachtsmen, we got good news: Nuel shacked up two nights with the preppy girl, bought dinner and cocaine for her and many drinks for his new friend, Bill Bascum, over a talk that went long into the night. Then he'd flown out, yesterday, for a surge in the melon market. Jack lit a smoke. "That cocksucker'll be twenty grand richer by the weekend." We laughed—even Nuel's unbelievable share of the good couldn't dim spirits then.

A Lifestyle

It was simple. It would be simpler when the money rolled in. Jack would keep the books and run a few charters, more charters when the whales and tourists arrived. He would visit booking desks with charm and goodwill for more business. I would continue my education. Everyone agreed: I was otherwise out of it, happily home in the apartment I would rent, pursuing personal development.

But Bill Bascum only passed the joint. He was boss, on paper, so he stood by *Whirlaway* with his legs spread, arms folded, like a statue whose butthole needed space, smelling like a jar of old roaches. He smoked it—pakalolo, lolo, da kine, el ropa; same rose by any name— pre-dawn, for his fishing charter, again at noon for lunch, then every little while for life. It left him a man of few words. He told Jack and I that first morning, "Nnnuuhh..."

Jack said, "What?" Bascum walked away, gone fishing. Jack said, "You know I worry about that boy." But Bascum opened up the first week, when a large, black tourist shucked and jived stem to stern, talkin' bout dat man on *Sea Hunt*, swim like a damn fish. He jumped in cocksure and drowning. It was Jack's first day, so Jack jumped in too, for a kick in the head and a death grip on his larynx. He dove, and the big black let go. Jack got clear, called for a life jacket and saved the man with it.

Bascum lit up, "Nigger can't swim. Don't you know that? You put a nigger in water, shoo, he sinks." His eye sockets drooped down his face, eyeballs hanging in by mere suction. Advice driveled out the mouth: "I'll tell you what. Don't take no niggers on a trip. Just don't do it. They can't swim or else they say they can but they can't. You take niggers out there and they'll be sucking on them snorkels, and the people see that and think, 'Well I wonder if a nigger ever sucked on this snorkel.'"

"Fucking-a," Jack said.

I said, "Niggers." So ended the first conference with Bill Bascum. He squinted through his stupor, rethinking what he said. He nodded slow, walking away. Jack yelled, "Hey, thanks Bill." Bascum's head ticked back once for you're welcome.

Vague got bad when Captain Bascum went mum again. Jack drove one day a week. Bascum's right hand man and alter ego, one Duane Crawly, known thereabout as D.C., a short, puffy fellow with bleach blond hair, drove the other six days. D.C. looked like a little big time wrestler, coming on strong, huffing and puffing, beating his chest and insisting, "I'm D.C.!" He told me, "You can't just come in here from the mainland and boss people around." This on day one, first meeting. But I'd been around the block enough times to know new-boy shuffle, and to recognize bad cocaine and too much of it. D.C. had gone and mushed up what little bit o' brains God gave him.

I said, "I understand. Don't do anything I say." Oh, Christ, a wise ass. D.C. jerked himself this way and that as if in self-containment, as if not breaking a peckerhead in two wouldn't be easy.

Beefy forearms usually mean a knockout punch, but D.C.'s tiny hands didn't match. Jack said, "Little hands mean a little dick." Jesus Kee-ryste, that made D.C. mad.

I said, "So far we don't have to worry about that." D.C. huffed and puffed, kicked a booth with a booth girl inside, then chain-smoked and buffaloed up and down the dock, claiming territory, looking back quick. He heard dogs barking, common quirk in the neighborhood, caused by too much speed rush and acetone jolt mixed into too much snoot.

D.C. was skipper of *Whirlaway*. He called it my boat, unless Bill Bascum was around. Then it was Bill's boat, unless Bascum wasn't paying attention because he was too stoned and campaigning a snif-falo. Then it was me and Bill's boat.

Bascum beefed, second week, that I wasn't out hustling more business. I told him I was not a hustler. Bascum said if business didn't pick up, no money for me.

I tried a threatening death stare, but I could have just as easily pointed a gun. Bascum walked away, stoned stupid, and by week two, hostility evolved.

Jack, Nuel and I had a partnership. Nuel owned *Whirlaway*, and the partnership leased the boat from him with an option to buy it for a price equal to the mortgage balance. I structured the deal. Nuel's lawyer wrote it up on sixty pages for another four grand. But business was slow, and Bascum took all the dough for his pocket. It was obvious and visible theft, but the only complaint came from Jack and me, getting broker all the time. And who would listen?

My own apartment shrunk from good idea, to concept, to tiny speck on distant horizon. Mexico got hot—the dirt yard, dumpster row and the spilled rubbish described the boundaries of life, where chickens scratched out a prosperity equal to ours. I sang: Oh, Mexico, I never really been, so I don't really know... Heat ripples veiled the gray monolith. Rain made steam. Running for a six-pack in the mud, Jack leaned over and dug his hands into it and came up flinging glop onto the building. He said they forgot the mud; anyone knows adobe needs mud. The fridge took the beer down five degrees from ambient Mexico, its endless compressor humming in the hot, dank shadow. The fridge stayed hot to the touch and would have worked better in the arctic.

Relaxing with a six-pack, we drifted, dreamed of better times. We laid odds on the future and in our innate, soulful way, we took a hard earned rest from trying to get ahead. The heat stifled the noise—bad bearings in the fan, the stuck compressor, the TV fugue—all of it carried idle minds away and eased the pain of days wasted.

Hard times got loud. I couldn't nap anymore, so I walked down the road, let the place cool off, or I sat, watching Jack pace and mumble cocksuckers. Louise asked every afternoon if anything was better. She asked every night when it would get better. She left five dollars every morning for a six-pack, and she left for work.

Monthly accounting and first payout approached. Business was slow but was good for grocery money at least. When Bascum ignored my calls, Jack took the bookkeeper's spread sheet down to the *Whirlaway* booth. He wrote checks for our fair share, or at least our share on record, from the *Whirlaway* checkbook while the booth girls and deckhands watched, aghast. Then he waited for Bascum's signature. Bascum unfolded his arms long enough to sign, his scowl unthawed. We got thirty-four bucks each and began month two.

It passed by the hour.

When Jack went again for month two, he found payouts for Bascum's personal bills on *Whirlaway* check stubs. The bookkeeper called it "a discrepancy, inadvertent, I'm sure."

Jack took the cancelled checks written on the *Whirlaway* account to cover Bascum's personal stuff and said nothing. Business was better, month two. With nearly fifty bucks each, we reckoned a new year, an end to poverty.

Business boomed three days before Christmas. Hostility boomed too—Bascum said anybody messing with his business wouldn't stay healthy. So we hung out on the wall by the walkway in front of the booth, late afternoons when Bascum strolled by stoned, past *Whirlaway* for the hand off from his booth girl, several grand in vouchers and cash.

By then D.C. told a story about his single-handed delivery of *Whirlaway* from California. He told it daily on board, and again loud one night at a bar, when a small man stood up and yelled D.C. down, yelled Spam thief liar! The small man had sailed with D.C. and knew another story from a crossing low on provisions, down to rations. D.C. hid Spam in his berth, ate Spam at night, in the dark, with two hands. Stealing Spam was a lingering indictment, a rallying point for the unhappy crew on that hungry voyage, a cause for commiseration and social justice. The small man at the bar was still plenty pissed and wouldn't hold still for any lies D.C. wanted to tell, even the little harmless kind.

Of course the bar crowd wanted a fight. D.C. grumbled. The little man yelled, "Spambo!" The bar crowd guffawed, and D.C. walked away. His humiliation felt good. But our pockets stayed empty. Frustration grew. We called Nuel.

Nuel oozed hello bubbas, sounded faintly satisfied, talking long distance with two paupers. Hearing the dilemma, he sounded uplifted, risen again to rightful stature. He said, "Well, you boys went 'n fucked it all up didn't you?"

Jack said, "Yes, we fucked it all up, Nuel."

"You boys cain't go through life thinking you can push anyone around you want to. Why, I didn't appreciate yo rudeness one bit. It was unnecessary. You boys ever git lucky, why, you might learn you some manners before it's too late."

"Yes, Nuel."

Nuel said, "Well... You know old Bill, he's a very complex individual. I had a drink with him, while you boys went off with your bitches. I told him keep a eye on you boys. Don't let you tell him what to do."

"You mean you fucked us Nuel?"

"I ain't fuckin' nobody. And iss ain't personal. It's bidness, at's all." Nuel said Bascum owed four grand a month, according to the lease, to cover the loan payment on the boat. He said he hoped Bascum would come across with some profit money. "But hell, even if he don't I still get my 'nvestment tax credit 'n my depreciation. At ain't so bad."

Jack banged the phone on the table. Nuel said, "I told you iss wadn't personal. It's bidness." Then he spewed his fake laugh. He said, "Well. Alright. I have a little talk with Bill, see if I can't getum to be nice to you boys."

Jack hung up. "Squeeze play," he said. "Nuel told Bascum he could keep all the money. Just pay the four grand. Fuck us." He smashed a beer bottle into a wall, then another.

I went for a walk.

Christmas in poverty would have been worse cold, or if youth and health were more gone. The future slipped by fast, and Christmas eve was good for stealing soda cans. Cashing in next day was good for a twelve-pack and a chicken. Christmas was merely bleak. *Whirlaway* grossed two grand a day. Jack called his brother, who called Nuel, who said he'd "had a call in" to Bascum for a week and didn't know why Bascum hadn't called back. Jack's brother called us back and yelled at Jack that he must be some kind of fool to get tied up with a maniac like Nuel. Jack said, "I didn't find Nuel. You want to talk to my partner?" Jack's brother said he'd send over a thousand dollars for a lawyer.

I found a lawyer on the third day of the new year. He was forty minutes late, then came out in a shirt that looked slept in. He chewed sunflower seeds and dribbled shells down his chest. He didn't sit in his chair, he lay back in it and said, "I quit smoking."

Jack said, "I didn't," and lit up. I presented the case. The lawyer knew about Bill Bascum, said he'd help get *Whirlaway* back with a retainer, twelve hundred. Jack said, "We got eight."

"Eight'll get me going. Get the rest."

Jack counted eight hundred while the lawyer took a call. Jack mumbled cocksucker and laughing, said, "He's younger'n us too, Harry. What'd we do wrong?"

Down at the harbor another thousand dollars rode out on the afternoon charter.

Two weeks later the lawyer wrote a letter to Captain Bill Bascum, saying the lease was in default, please give the boat back. Two weeks later I called the lawyer, who said he didn't think it was working. I asked what came next. He said litigation, for another fifteen hundred, and he was fairly certain he could make a case of it and get *Whirlaway* back in six months, maybe eight.

I hung up. Jack lit up and threw a lamp against a wall. I asked him what we'd do with *Whirlaway* if we got it back anyway. Jack yelled, "We're on the note! I'd like to sink the bitch!"

I headed out for another walk down the road, past the heat-rippling mailbox telling myself that rich guys everywhere would trade places with me for my health, and relative youth. I walked two miles to the highway and another mile to a gas station. I asked about a job, asked if maybe they had something or other for a guy to pick up a few bucks at. They said no, no jobs. That was a relief. I walked home. Jack got back soon after with a grin and a cold six-pack. We drank. Jack said Masao wanted none of it, but Herbert was all for it, said he knew some crazy Tongans, don't worry.

I called the lawyer and told him the plan, take the boat back by force. The lawyer said state law favors the tenant. I asked if he knew that before the eight hundred, or if the eight hundred paid for research. The lawyer said it was piracy, and worse, Bascum could get it back easy, legal.

I told Jack, who lit a smoke, threw his beer at the fridge and said, "After a while this shit tastes like soap."

February passed on food stamps, soda cans and what was now a resource, the spirit of vengeance. That Bascum, Crawly and Nuel had pulled a squeeze play was not so hard to take as the consequences were. Destitution seemed unacceptable.

March began with a major airline strike. Business slammed shut. Louise got laid off. *Whirlaway* sat idle. Jack wished for a hurricane to go with the airline strike. I called Nuel to see if Bascum sent a check yet and to see what could be done.

Nuel said, "You can't deal wif bidness like at. You can't go jumpin'up'm down like you boys do ever time someone don't pay a measly chickenshit few thousand dollars. Shit. You boys don't know much about bidness."

"Jack and I make a majority, Bubba. We held a meeting and voted to call Bascum in default. Now, you want to undermine the majority, deprive us of our livelihoods? You know that could get expensive, Bubba."

Nuel said, "Bubba, you can't sue me. You'n Jackie ain't got no money. I got money to keep a battalion 'o lawyers on you boys. N'at's how it works, Bubba."

I said, "You know Nuel, you outsmarted me again. Let me ask you something. How long you and Bascum be asshole buddies if the strike goes on a few months, Bascum can't pay?"

Nuel said, "Well. What difference would it make to me whether Bascum can't pay or you can't pay? I told you boys, iss ain't personal. It's bidness. Hell, I wish you boys had some money, but I can't hep it if God made some people be born wif d'bility to be rich'n some people, like you'n Jackie havin'a be poor. It ain't my fault you boys ain't got shit, why, I had it all set up for you'n Jackie to make twenty thousand dollars a year. At's good for somebody like you'n him."

"I hadn't thought of it like that. Hey how's the melons?"

Nuel reflected, said, "Bidness good, but I'm tired of California, the traffic 'n crowds 'n all the trendy buhshit. I usually git inspired every few years, move along, conquer new worlds. I still make plenty dough, nobody knows how much, but Bubba it's plenty. Two thousand brain surgeons in the whole damn world and Bubba I one of um. Old J.D. come up with a couple more empty office buildings in Utah I hate to pass up so I suspect I buyum, but I just got that bug, you know, just want to get out my flight jacket and hit the road."

"Well. How about a few hundred bucks, for your bubbas in need?"

"Well. Things a little tight right now, Bubba."

I chuckled, "Well, Nuel, don't you disappear until this boat business gets cleared up. I feel like something got to give soon, and if you pull a vanishing act, I'll find you. Then you'll see how tight it can get."

"You'n Jackie can sink at piece o' shit." He laughed. "That'll suit me jiss fine."

Watching *Leave it to Beaver* reruns and sleeping long hours for three weeks led to baseball season. Jack said he could have been a pitcher in the majors if his goddam brother hadn't made him throw his arm out. He answered an ad for a job at a furniture store, but when he got there the guy said he realized nobody wanted any fucking furniture. On the way home Jack stopped for two bucks regular and picked up an application for a gasoline credit card and said the day was worthwhile. He felt good with small projects like that. The credit card application took him an hour to finish, an hour free of spilled beer and broken lamps. He wrote ninety grand by salary and Whirlaway, Inc. for employer. He said extra plastic on land is like extra provisions at sea.

I took up jogging because walking was too slow. And with Louise home, asking when, when and when and not leaving five bucks, Mexico suffered overpopulation.

I called Nuel in April to remind him that Bascum missed the March payment, and would stiff April too. Nuel said, "I only bought that boat 'cause you boys said it'd make money. You never said a goddamn thing about a airline strike. You boys said it'd make money."

"New plan," I said. "We move it to the south end, by the other hotels, fuck that shit hole harbor. We'll run charters with a motor launch off the beach."

Nuel said, "Well. I'll have my lowyer draw up some papers. I want personal notes from you'n Jackie, whatever you got."

"Draw'mup."

"Now. When we gone go in and steal her back?" He babbled what he'd learned at combat school. He knew about weapons, ricochet and trajectory, blood and bayonets and shit. He outlined his pathologies again, his boyhood needs. He said, "Don't tell nobody I'm comin' Bubba. I be travelin' incognito you know." He would bring his Uzi, his assault rifle and a couple three .357s for me'n Jackie.

I said we'd make radio contact when it got firmed up. Nuel said, "Shit. Iss'll be fun!"

I planned the assault. Between innings I read aloud from documents written by Nuel's new lawyer. With the new stack was a note: Sign these and return promptly to my office. He'd sent demand notes for a hundred fifty grand each, payable anywhere, anytime, at his discretion. They made good entertainment, especially with a joint. Another stack came the next week—the new partnership agreement. It was like the first one with a change: The Doctor would be King.

He called Saturday, late, coked up and drunk. It was a small world after all, because we were too, had stolen eight mop buckets with built in wringers from a hotel and made enough for a tank of gas, a gram of snoot and a cold pack. I answered the phone like a bumpkin uptown, like Nuel: "Helloo?"

Nuel said, "You a liar. You a cheat. You a fuckin'... crook! You a no good...rotten...goddamn...piece o' shit!"

"Well. Sometimes you got to overlook the small stuff, Bubba. Whatsmatter Nuel? Melons running low?"

"Well... I guess so." He got tough again wanting to know why hadn't he got no demand notes yet? I told Jack it was the C.E.O. Jack took the phone and said he saw some hot fresh turds smelled better than those notes. Nuel said he needed a check for eight hundred bucks rat now to pay the lawyer for drawing up those notes. Jack choked on his beer and handed back the phone.

I said, "'Em notes worfless, Bubba. Why any pork butt knows two times a hundred fifty grand equals three hundred grand, and the bitch didn't cost but two hundred."

"Well. At's okay. You git your own notes, but git em'n'en gitum back to me rat away. You boys ast me to get those notes drawd up'n I did. You ast me'n you know you did, so don't lie about it, 'cause I did. Now you got to pay for um."

"I writing a check rat now, Bubba, pulling on my pants too for a walk down to the post office, it's only a mile, the check is in the mail."

"Well. Sign at new agreement too, because the old one wadn't no good, because my new lowyer said you boys put a fucking on me, a good one. About the only thing you did right so far was call it straight on the first lowyer—at worfless piece o' shit. Iss new lowyer now, he's sharp. He said you boys got to put something up! It's called consideration. He said it's the law! It's required by law for you to put up some consideration."

"Hey fuckin-a right, Bubba, we sign'm all in octuplicate and getum off tonight with a check too for several thousand dollars."

Nuel said he'd sent off for a new marksman rifle that shot hollow core bullets and he'd put one of um perfect, right between the eyes if we kept on messing up, wouldn't have no other choice—"ratbuh tweeny az, Bubba. You know I can do it. You know I can."

"You bad, Nuel. You the baddest."

And on the cocaine talked until I asked why he leaned on his bubbas so hard for a few bucks? Something wrong at the melon stand?

Nuel said it was the principle of the thing—de principoo. Then he got serious: "I can sew up thirty stitches to the centimeter if I want to.

I coulda been anything I wanted a be, if I wanted to. Two thousand of us in a whole damn world...and I'm one of um..."

"Good night, Nuel."

"Good night, Bubba."

The airline strike ended at the end of peak season. Another month passed with another lawyer for Jack and me with another grand from my mother—her social security check, because she believed I wanted to be a good boy, if only I could get the chance. The new lawyer discovered the lease was not on file with the Harbors Division. The copy on file showed no profit sharing, only the flat rent. The new lawyer was proud—repo was easy, no suit, and only another five hundred.

On a hunch that night I looked under I—Intensive Care, called Madelaine for the straight skinny on Nuel. Why was he calling around, coked up and drunk, leaning hard on a measly few grand? She said Nuel had a bad surgery, put steel rods along a boy's spine and gave him ten days to live. Infection set in at the rod ends, so the parents called another doctor because Nuel the brain surgeon was on answering machine mode. Amazed, the new doctor advised immediate action. The boy was moved to another hospital the same day and the rods came out next day, when newer doctors found the tumor on the spine. Nuel missed; a piece of good spinal cord was gone. They got the tumor and sewed the boy back up. He was discharged a month later and back at soccer practice with a limp the month after that. Nuel got sued for seven million. The insurance company required a hundred grand deductible, cash up front and then settled out of court. Nuel was no longer insurable in California. Nuel be gone.

Redemption

Summer hit hard. Heat rolled like lava down the mountain, breathless, in waves. Sanity was a far away place. A good day was break even or not much loss—the phone company must have been bluffing, the line stayed on.

Jack called State Harbors Division, Commissioner of Harbors. He asked the big man, how long would it take to get a slip in the harbor? Commish figured a hundred years, maybe, if you sign the waiting list today. Jack said what the fuck, them bastards bring in a fancy yacht, *Whirlaway*, just like that, no list, no wait, no nothing, just walk on by the poor working stiffs because they got big money—he heard they had a brain surgeon from the mainland behind the operation.

The Commissioner said he didn't know about that, but a man with a slip can lease another man's boat and charter it from that slip. Jack asked how that's fair if the boat owner gets a profit? Why wait, if you're rich? Commish agreed: if the *Whirlaway* deal made a profit for the owner, it was worse than unfair, it was illegal.

Jack sat up, lit a smoke and said, "Good. I'm one of them bastards and I got profits from Whirlaway Charters."

Commish said, "I don't get it."

Jack said, "I got the motive which is money and the proof which is a cancelled check, signed by Bill Bascum. I'm turning myself in, Commissioner. I can't live with it anymore." Commish said he'd look into it. Jack asked when.

Commish said, "Well, this afternoon."

Two days later Bill Bascum took *Whirlaway* from his slip and dropped anchor in the roadstead, the main traffic channel outside the harbor. He'd been told, give up or lose. And a couple down and out-ers came up again off the canvas, on a well-placed phone call.

Victory was a cold dousing. Mexico was hot with numbing sounds—the fridge, the fan, seventh inning organ. The first wave blown off in the first gust was wake up call in the face after senseless months. The blustery channel looked the same as any day, but today was different—we jumped in, swam out. I choked on seawater yelling that it must look nuts, swimming in the roadstead, up the yellow line through the thickest boat traffic in the mid-Pacific. Jack yelled back, "You got to work hard and fuck hard Harry! It's time you learned that!" I sputtered thank you, and the down and outers clambered along the smooth, slick chine cursing Bill Bascum, *Whirlaway* and life itself while normal people with regular lives wondered why two men struggled to climb aboard when anyone could see they would never make it. We couldn't possibly pull ourselves up. We could make no purchase, achieve no grip, gain no traction, gather our wits, calm our breathing.

Until Jack sacrificed feeling in his fingers gripping the backstay chainplate, loving the stern like it was Louise, the way Louise was finally learning to love, and he squeezed, pulled, cut, bled and grunted his way over the rail. He threw the swim ladder over so I could come up easy, like a tourist.

Jack took the helm. I took the foredeck. And like figures in a dream, we laughed again at reality, two wetbacks suddenly yachtsmen.

I cleared the anchor while Jack cranked the engine. Clear of the roadstead I raised the main, then the headsail—*Whirlaway* heeled and loped like a thoroughbred to the stick.

The down and outers were up and in—owed the bank four grand a month, had no place to park, no office, no phone, no stationery. Under sail in a steady breeze on a balmy day it didn't matter. We'd pulled the biggest bank heist in the neighborhood, and now we'd commandeered a racing yacht. Sailing past Lanai and the Navy ships it didn't matter either who we were or what we weren't or the price we'd be made to pay. Nor past the verdant mountains and valley at Olowalu, around the horn, McGreggor Point, where the balmy breeze blew stink—forty-five knots on the nose, tradewinds jamming the mountain gap, did it mean a good goddamn. Beating into it, into the surging shallows of Maalaea Harbor for a mud anchorage near dark and another swim to the sea wall, nothing mattered still.

Resting there watching the mosquitoes feed, we talked need and capitalization strategy. Bascum cancelled the insurance. That was a laugh. We wanted to call Nuel collect but he was on the lam. New insurance would run two grand down. A mooring off the beach just down the bay would run three hundred feet of three-eighths inch chain, three thirty-five pound anchors, a concrete sentinel block, thirty feet of half inch chain, thimbles, shackles, swivels and a mooring ball. Brochures, minimum order, snorkel gear times twenty, an inflatable boat and outboard motor—drydock in Honolulu, the compulsory annual for Coast Guard inspection. "My God, it's been a year," I said.

"We can do it easy for fifteen grand," Jack answered. He called Louise. She showed up in time and said unless someone had a couple bucks for gas, we'd be on the shoe leather express to Mexico. Jack said fuck it, just drive.

The next morning on the phone I assured Weems that Nuel was out of it but we were in it, back in the saddle in sixty days, new management, new location. Weems said sixty days would be fine, because foreclosure doesn't start for ninety.

"Yeah right," I said, setting the phone down and settling in to a strange comfort—ninety days, a half-assed idea, Nuel's boat, Jack's need and tradewinds to knock you down. It didn't look right, wasn't the set up set out for. It was hopeless, and that felt good, finalizing defeat. "Now we can calm down and fuck the dog in peace," I said. "And to think we came this far with no money down."

Jack paced and smoked. "You're just upset." He tossed a beer back and said the smart move now was to visit the six big booking desks at the south end for a market survey on *Whirlaway*.

"What for? To make sure this is a good idea?"

"Fuck it, I'll go alone." But I humored him and went along and listened to the bookers say yes, good idea. Jack said, "See?" But I said it was only the smart answer to a couple stiffs on the ropes offering twenty percent off the top on a quarter million dollars in inventory with no risk. Jack smoked hard and stared out the window. "And what about the jack, Jack?"

I always figured action to follow thought, but I realized then that the converse was true in Jack Witte, who by nature jumped now and then wondered how and why, who cursed the world for constantly sending him a bad spin of the wheel.

Jack got a clue on the jack when we passed the weather-beat shingle of Acme Finance. He swung me one of his Cheshire shit-eating grins, as if to say our luck was changing and would keep on getting better if I could keep my bad attitude out of the way. And he swung the truck hard right and sped through the crummy little shopping mall to the five-by-five of future dreams today. "You'll like this place," he said. "The guy in here says the bank doesn't think my credit's worth a shit, and he thinks it is." At the door he said, "Just keep your mouth shut."

"No parla Inglesa," I said.

Jack barreled in. "Yeah, my friend here just came over from the mainland and I want to show him a good time. I been thinking about it anyway and I guess I might go ahead and pick up a little inflatable for myself with an outboard, nothing too elaborate maybe six seats, twenty horse, I don't know maybe five grand. I guess I'll look for a used one, but maybe..."

The Portagee behind the counter raised both hands, as if the stick up would be on him. He'd heard enough, slid the loan ap over. "No loan for used equipment. Must be new."

Jack said fine, he'd get a new one. He filled in the blanks, listing all the furniture in Mexico and the frost free fridge under assets, along with his truck, a gone beater, mostly rust, bad muffler, weak linkage, poor brakes, iffy skins, one headlight and a couple bucks regular. It sat around the corner—value: five grand. The Portagee punched Jack

Witte on the computer. Jack lit a smoke and flashed a grin just before the Portagee turned and matched it. "I looking for red flags." The computer beeped a little tune.

The Portagee said, "Oh, too bad. Look here like you got bad debt. You owe department store four hundred dollar."

"That's bullshit. My ex-wife ran up that charge. That cunt. Dressed like a fucking hippie for ten years—wouldn't shave her goddamn armpits, fuckin' legs—I couldn't even get her to shave her goddamn pubic hair where it sticks out of their swimming suits right here you know—" He showed me and the Portagee, rubbing himself high on the inner thighs. "Fucking cunt—she goes out and runs up four bills just to fuck with me—that's bullshit!"

The Portagee liked Jack's spirit, said he'd call for confirmation, since a bad debt after divorce shouldn't hurt the non-debtor spouse. "Ex-spouse!" Jack said.

Pacing, smoking, waiting while another Portagee far away researched Jack's ex-wife, Jack called Dinghy City, priced, haggled and settled on a six seat inflatable with a twenty horse outboard for forty-nine ninety-nine ninety-five. The other Portagee called back, "Da Witte guy okay."

Jack said fucking-a right he's okay and walked out ten minutes later with a check for five grand, thirty-six months to pay, twenty-two percent annual interest. Who cared? I followed, three steps back, impressed. At the corner Jack said fuck, which verbalized his simple longing for a six-pack. He drove to the bank, opened a new business account with a small cash out for the beer, and in minutes we cruised again, drinking a cold one, feeling good.

I pointed out we were still ten grand short of capitalization.

"Easy," Jack said. "That's why God invented checks. You know sometimes I wonder how you ever got this far."

"You go to jail for that," I said. "And I'm amazed myself."

Jack said, "Well, they get real pissed alright, and they say they'll put you in jail, and sometimes they do, but not if they think you can pay."

"Write checks," I said.

"Checks," Jack confirmed. "Shit, we get twenty-one days in the Federal Reserve outbasket right off the top—for free! This is America goddamn it. Why you think they set it up that way?" Jack made feeble sense, which fit neatly into marginal reality.

And any kind of sense and volition was springtime for two guys down, counted out. Two six-packs were small celebration on a grand down on the boat and motor, because the guy at Dinghy City had in-house financing. Jack said that was a real break, because they won't let you out of drydock without a bank check.

"You mean they know about us?" I asked, but Jack wouldn't even respond; I was losing the attitude struggle yet again.

Near midnight Nuel called, coked out and drunk. He wanted the plan. I told him: restart the charter business off the beach at the south end. Nuel took charge. "Looka here! A monkey's on yo back now, Bubba. It used to be on Bascum, but now it's on you. I'm on be on yo ass nat'n day. Nat'n day, Bubba, jist like I'z on Bascum's 'n you said I wadn't."

"What did you want us to do Nuel? Nothing? Or leave town and hole up somewhere and relax, like you?"

"I'm here in a hot seat where you'n Jackie put me, now that you put a fuckin' on Bascum jist like you put it on me. He gone sue. He gone sue'n I'm gonna be on yo ass nat'n day. Nat'n day, Bubba. You boys fuck wif me'n I gitcha. So hep me. Ratbuh tweeny az Bubba. Ratbuh tweeny az."

"Nuel. Where do we send your share of the profits?" Poor Nuel, slipped easy on profits, rattled off his new address in Florida. His new phone was just as easy. Weems wouldn't be able to find us after tonight, but Nuel was now found. I asked if Florida looked good, could support another melon cutter.

Nuel said, "Oh, I guess so."

We traded goodbye Bubbas and rang off.

Months of lethargy led to days and nights of work, sweat by necessity. The hundred mile sail to Honolulu was set for midnight— Honolulu for annual haul out, repairs and Coast Guard inspection, only a month late; Honolulu, where a boat like *Whirlaway* could get a lift out of the water. I packed sardines, crackers and beer. Jack lit a smoke and jerked the phone out of the wall as if wrenching the head off an enemy. I asked him if Louise would drive us down to the boat. "Truck's empty," Jack said. In the bedroom he woke Louise and said it was time, Honolulu and dry dock, and he'd be going it alone afterward, don't worry, he'd pay her back for the beer. She cried big, but he was back out front. "Come on," he said. "Let's get out of here."

I followed. "What now, Sir. How do we get a ride at midnight, no traffic?"

"You ought to do something about your pessimism."

"It's been chronic, even in school. But I do want to be a criminal, I really do." Jack marched in a huff. Louise's whimper faded in the gravel crunch underfoot.

Mexico didn't look so bad in the dark, under the stars. Marching across the dirt, past the dumpsters, down the access road to the highway, where maybe luck and a late drinker would come along, Jack stopped. "Wait a minute," he said, laying his paper bag on the ground. He ran back up the hill, back inside. In a minute he ran back out. "I told her keep the fucking TV. Christ, it's worth a hundred bucks."

I took the lead then under the warm night sky, in the fresh air. I asked Jack how it felt to be pushing middle age with everything he owned in a paper sack, heading down to a highway at midnight to catch a ride. Jack thought it over and said, "I don't know, Harry. How does it feel to you?"

I vaulted the ditch leading with my thumb. A truck stopped. We ran for it. "Piece of motherfucking cake," I said. Jack gasped, on the run. "You ought to do something about your health, Bubba."

It was two rides twenty miles to the harbor at the far end and a walk all the way around it looking for a dinghy to borrow, since no one wants to leave on a hundred mile sail in the dark, wet. A funky, half flat rubber boat looked like it might float the fifty yards to *Whirlaway* and had a paddle, which was good, turning around from up the creek.

Loaded up, the funky skiff only sank six inches when I stepped in. It sank another six with Jack's weight and soaked the paper bags. Jack called it a whore, but it didn't sink deeper, and fifty yards was only five minutes and dry above the calves. Aboard I chucked our bags and lay down on a berth. Jack drank a beer, had a smoke and then another, checking the gauges and pumps and oil. Jack liked the action.

While I half dozed, Jack called the National Weather Service on the VHF—steady trades in all channels, fifteen to twenty knots, seas four to eight feet. I dreamed when Jack called the Coast Guard, Whiskey Alpha Romeo six one two, that he and I were yachtsmen. I woke up to Jack's nudge. "Come on. Let's get out of here."

Then back out of the harbor into Maalaea Bay toward McGreggor Point and past it and past Olowalu, past the mountains and Lanai, motoring on a compass bearing four hours until night thinned, the gray veil rose, and sails went up to a clean run in following seas before the trades, past Kaanapali to the Pailolo Channel.

Whirlaway loped easily at twelve knots, to the windless flats behind Molokai. Jack said one day we would round Molokai on the front side, where mountain met sea in the most dramatic plunge of sheer cliff and waterfall, where a yacht could pull into any one of three coves he knew, around to good shelter from the wind and good anchorage. "But not today. First thing you know the cocksucker blows forty and you're in a world of hurt. Lee shore. Fuck that." So we motored all morning around Molokai and met the trades again near noon.

Five miles into the Molokai Channel Jack said, "Goddamn it this feels good." Down to trunks and caps, we trimmed her good and surfed down the backsides, flew up the fronts, ultralight. Jack said he needed rest and went below for a nap. The next seventy miles was another dream for me, a good one.

Honolulu teemed, a vibrant city on the tropical horizon on a hot afternoon, but the scene closed in on Tuna Packers Boatyard at sunset. The scent of it got real, like a surprise intimacy. Day shift changed to swing at the packing plant next door. The boatyard was closed. With one fender, flat, and no pump to fill it, we tied up by the rubber tires on the fishing dock, and Jack cursed every surge that made black marks on the hull. Then he cursed the tuna smell and Tagalog chatter from the Filipino plant workers. He cursed the tuna boats coming in, making *Whirlaway* move five times in the night.

He cursed the burger stand up the street for heavy grease and high prices, and he cursed the mosquitoes every time he slapped his face. The heat quit at dawn for thirty minutes of sound sleep, until graveyard changed to day, and a thousand Filipinos came and went all talking at once. Jack cursed them too, "Fucking Madangdangs."

I got two coffees for a buck at a Madangdang breakfast cart. Jack paid another buck for greasy donuts, considering the long day ahead, and we ate dockside, dried out from wet, half rested from bone tired, windblown, unshaved, bleary eyed and waking up to another reality. A Madangdang walked up looking like the old man on the mountain in his billygoat beard, surveying the fancy yacht, assessing us. He asked, "Is your boat?"

Jack said, "Yeah. It's my boat."

The old man asked, "How did you get it?" Jack smiled, making the Madangdang a man to remember.

The boatyard opened at seven and *Whirlaway* was first on the railway—yachts need lifts, but the other boatyard was full, so Jack said fuck it, we'll use the railway. *Whirlaway* looked way overdressed among the fishing boats. She rolled up the rails in the canvas sling mounted on a frame with steel wheels on railroad tracks. High and dry in the sling, she rolled along the rails to her place where we would scrape, sand, repair and paint her bottom. The four Samoans on the rail team steadied her in place with posts, wedges and big mallets.

They moved quick, spoke quicker—"Hoy!"

"Ooba!"

"Oo!"

"Oobie! Hoy! Oo!"

"Ah! Oo!"

"Ooba!"

"Oobie! Oo!"

Jack broke in, "Hoy! Ooba! What does it look like, a goddamn motherfucking tuna boat? It's a fucking yacht for chrissakes!"

He shut up when the four Samoans regarded him like a ripe coconut, and he agreed, "Ooba." More calmly, he said, "Paper-thin hull. Please. Very careful." He took a mallet and gently tapped a wedge into place.

The biggest Samoan pulled Aqua Velva from his hip pocket, dabbed it on his moustache, over the fuel and shit smell of the harbor water he'd just swam through to get the sling around the hull, and he turned and walked away. The others followed, leaving the posts and wedges. Jack called, "Mahalo," Hawaiian for thank you.

The big one turned back. "Mepwa!"

The others laughed. I called, "How you say: 'Mepwa?'"

The big one said, "Mahoney." All the Samoans laughed and left.

Jack lit a smoke. "Fucking Mexicans." And he smiled again, making it twice in one day. "Well, Harry," he said. "How does it feel to be looking down the barrel of the worst fucking week you'll ever experience in your life?"

"I don't know, Jack. How does it feel to you?"

"We're fucked if the bottom dries," was his answer. "This shit turns to rock," and the next four hours were wet and copper blue—awash in oxidized bottom paint, hot, dizzy and nauseous, scraping and wet sanding till noon.

The local tap water was half shit, but it fit well in the budget and comprised most of the diet for the next three days of scraping, grinding, sanding. Jack lost some of his gut. My ribs showed.

Knocking off two hours early the fourth day, when the old poison was off, and it was only a quick roll on with the new poison, the budget opened up on a twelve-pack, a turkey loaf and new bread. I found some old mustard in the galley. I cooked. Jack smoked and drank in the cockpit and yelled at the Madangdang tuna packers to get to work.

Living on the boat in the boatyard, with the deck fifteen feet off the ground, compounded the dream of those days. The heat and mosquitoes allowed two hours sleep a night. The copper paint and tap water sustained the daze and the runs, and the layers of grunge seeping skin-deep looked like poor men's tattoos. I was light by the third day, dazed and confused by the fourth. Stock-still I wondered, Who am I, where and what? It happened in the galley, in sandwiches. Holding bread in one hand, knife in the other, it all quit—even the essence of bread and knives and mustard... went away. I waited easily for something to move, and a horsefly chomped my shoulder. Don't ever think it can't get worse. I moved, from the eyes mostly, squinting in pain, squeezing the sting, watching mustard roll down the knife, form a globule and plop to the counter. Tears rolled down my face—not from sadness, and I didn't know from what, except I didn't think they had anything at all to do with mustard, or bread, or anything. Then I forgot what it was. I was lost.

It got catatonic, still life in drydock, broke down, shut down, me staring at a fly swarming mess. Jack came down to the galley and eased me aside, made his own sandwich and on his way out asked, "Ready to hang yourself yet?" I meditated hanging another minute, but it was like all the ideas that held up long enough to make sense then. I had no rope. I dropped the bread and mustard, chucked the knife in the sink and went up for my six, quick.

That took the edge off, until mosquito wake-up after dark. In the swelter below, the roaches convened for bread and turkey loaf, yet through the buzz and sting and roaches I had a vision: jumping overboard was the thing to do, as if the ocean was overboard, but perversion seemed complete when I realized jumping overboard would land me head first on a parking lot. An ember glowed in the dark. Jack in the corner echoed death in the sweet, acrid smell far from rage or revenge, low and hollow, "The mosquitoes want your blood. Roaches want food. Flies, shit." He passed half a joint, the first in a week started long long ago. "You need this." I smoked it, got smoked. "Mosquitoes not bad with a fag lit," Jack said. I eased into a berth and waited with my business associate and a smoke for sunrise.

Trading scrapers and sandpaper for resin, hardener and acetone the next three days we rebuilt the keel where big Duane Crawly had backed onto a coral head. Jack laid up the fiberglass matt and fiberglass roving, varying weaves and coarseness for extra strength in nasty weather, cursing nasty weather then cursing the work at hand until his mantra, matt, roving, matt, roving, took the hateful sting out of the work. I cut the cloth, rolled on the juice. We called Nuel from a pay phone one night, five a.m. in Florida, collect from Matt Roving. He answered and wanted to accept, but his answering machine wouldn't shut up. Jack yelled, "We're all gonna die!" and hung up. He giggled and felt good.

Fiberglass dust from grinding mixed with sweat and settled in, itching. It and hair came off with duct tape, or else it mostly wore off in a few days. I smashed a finger replacing the cutlass bearing on the strut. Jack wound the grinder out to five thousand rpm, but the pad was rated for three. It disintegrated at five and made his face look like an old dart board, but it missed his eyes.

The United States Coast Guard came out on request the sixth day, after new through-hull fittings on the head and the knot meter. The inspector heard about Bill Bascum and the idiot D.C. who buggered up the keel, and so on stem to stern. The inspector inspected. Jack rambled endless ill will. The inspector checked squares on his clipboard and signed off *Whirlaway*.

New bottom paint would finish it. Seventy percent copper and fresh, it made a strong man weak, puked out and dizzy. But day seven ended the work, and sundown was back in the water, motoring down to Ala Wai Marina for gas on Jack's credit card.

Timing was good, tying up by a waterfront bar for maybe eight hours sleep before heading home, so dawn would be halfway across the channel, calmer then, easy breeze. Two dollars was enough for coffee, and happy hour would have been chicken parts, ribs, carrot and celery sticks.

But looking like bums dyed blue and feeling worse, the down and outers were down again, couldn't eat. The long week, no sleep, the heat and dust and fumes, the long night and task ahead: beating south across the Molokai Channel, eighty miles upwind, uphill, trades building, twenty-five to thirty knots, seas to twelve feet.

I ordered Bloody Marys. Jack said they wouldn't take a gas credit card. I asked Jack what he would lose if they didn't. Jack watched me sideways, like I was catching on to the attitude game a little too good, or maybe going lighter still. I took it for respect from a guy like Jack. He drank big and ordered two more, mahalo, mahalo, yes, that's our yacht and yes, we should probably take a six-pack or two for the road. Jack didn't smile but followed back in a shuffle, half lit and hoping beyond hope that life was a dream.

I lay down. Jack lit a smoke, took a puff and tossed it over. He walked forward checking rigging, fittings, fasteners, cotter keys. I didn't move, and twenty minutes later the engine started. Eight o'clock, seven hours ahead of schedule, Jack worked quick and nervous with a seventh wind way past sanity and human endurance. "Let's get this whore out there," he said. "I can't sleep." I obeyed.

Cold and wet were around the corner—out the Ala Wai and bearing south for Diamond Head, a two star twinkle through the last cleft in the cloud cover beckoned. Then it was gone. Night thickened, folded over, a dark, windless world, waiting. Down to adrenaline, time for shoes, socks, sweaters, raincoats and caps. Flying a triple reefed main and a storm sail, Jack and I stood side by side at the helm like two guys at their own wake, in silence save the single word Jack announced as Diamond Head disappeared to port behind the hunched back of an eight foot swell on its way to the distant rumble: "Reality."

A cloud break drifted under the moon and mercifully passed after lighting up the no-man's-land ahead; natty white manes and disfigured faces howled the pleas of all the lost souls of the sea crowded that night in tumultuous endeavor. They stood on their heads, turned cartwheels, fell rigidly down on deck like dead men dropped on pavement—or else they vanished, leaving the blessed moment of weightlessness, of hope that somehow hell had passed. The sickening fall came next. The crunch of all the tons of *Whirlaway* in the boil boomed in our hearts and in our heads beyond doubt: disintegration, destruction, annihilation with no trace.

An hour into it, numbed down to amazement that life went on, Jack yelled to go below, rest.

I lay in a berth listening to the war outside, knowing the rig would come through the deck and kill me quick—the nauseating noise of wood and fiberglass fracturing pounded in my ears. I drove my fingers into them and said, God. An hour later I went up. "It's building!" I yelled in the black and horizontal spray.

Jack yelled, "No! You forget!" And he stepped aside as I braced at the helm. Jack watched me dodge two and take a third on the chin, then yelled instructions for steering through the breaking seas. His words were lost on the wind, drowned in the spray, and he went for his hour of hell below, away from the pummeling on deck, below to questions of fate, free will and circumstance.

We weathered it, as if by choice. Sunrise lit the faces of two prisoners, liberated, who could not stop shaking from the cold of the night before and the fatigue of the sleepless week. Jack came up with a six-pack, and the first two went down quick. The next round was slower, and approaching the North Shore, Molokai, Jack stood up straight on the transom and yelled back to the hurly-burly channel he knew had tried to kill us: "Fuck you, whore!"

We were drunk again for brunch, home by two and speechless till way past dark.

~~~~~~~~~~~~

 Cash Flow

Jack built a plywood box, swiped some rebar and cut it with a twelve dollar hacksaw he was glad he hadn't paid for, it broke so many blades. He backed the truck to the same site next day and told the foreman he'd swap charters for concrete, two yards.

I hitched west and wrote bad checks for anchors, chain, shackles, swivels, thimbles, a mooring ball and groceries, two bags. I hitched back south and wrote a check for rent and deposit on a beach condo fronting the mooring. I ordered ten thousand brochures C.O.D. while Jack shackled, chained and swiveled. Herbert got cousin Darryl's outboard and two air tanks to set the mooring. I told Herbert we'd swap charters with Darryl. Herbert said, "Darryl got money."

Jack pushed the concrete block overboard when Herbert called, "Here! This side reef, that side deep." Herbert dove and set the block, rebar loop up. Jack lowered anchors northeast and south, against trades and konas, and Herbert dove again to set them in. He dove again with shackle hardware and it was done. *Whirlaway* rode on her mooring at dusk.

Next day early Jack went for the dinghy and motor. I called booking desks to announce Whirlaway Charters, new management, new location, send passengers. A hotel desk said hold please, then came back urgent—six people leaving tomorrow needed a sunset sail. "If you guys have room, gosh, you'll be heroes," the woman said.

I thought about need and heroism—and six geeks on vacation. "We'd be delighted," I said.

I meditated wealth; net that night to Whirlaway Charters would be a hundred seventy bucks. That day's nut was three thirty-five. Jack got back swearing vengeance on Dinghy City—no motor until next week. But he'd lucked out at The Liquor Hut, Red Goose Sparkling Champagne, closed out at a buck fifty.

I said, "We'll show them a thing or two about need," but Jack was down the beach in long strides to the surf shop, where the surf shop boys said yes, use their outboard—a four hundred pound, fifty horse monster that fought back on the long lug down to the water. Bolted on, it sunk the dinghy stern.

Jack said, "Fuck it. I'll keep a little way on." Heavy trades easing up were followed by a south swell rolling up the beach in four foot breakers. Boarding would be in the lull between sets. But first the dinghy needed enough depth to keep the prop off the bottom, test run. I swam out front, backwards, pulling down on the bow, keeping it into the waves. Jack climbed in and laughed, "Don't let go, Bubba, or you'll get your dick caught in the pickle slicer. He didn't laugh, mumbling cocksucker on the first three pulls. After three more he yelled, "You cocksucking cunt whore shit!" The rope broke on the next pull throwing him into the bow.

The surf shop boys called support—"Fucking shit!" They laughed. I swallowed big water when a wave broke blindside, filling the dinghy. Choking, cursing and bleeding we fought it back in, fought the outboard off, drained the dinghy, fought the outboard on and the dinghy back out, out past the breakers. I pushed, swam fast to the bow and jerked it seaward, kicking clear of the prop as Jack pulled and pulled and pulled and cocksuckered himself speechless until he sat down chomping his smoke, fighting for breath. I ground sand in my teeth, watched Jack seize in the chest, waited for the big one but Jack held steady with a hiss and a wheeze, and another hiss, "I wish Nuel was here."

The motor started on the next pull, sputtered black smoke but ran smooth enough for taking six normals to *Whirlaway*. It wouldn't run in two hours, late dusk, but the future was too far away for thought, except for the cash—late dusk, a hundred seventy, real money, secure. The normals were twenty minutes late. Jack was sanguine. "It's their goddamn nickel."

Two were women, eighty-something. Two more were third time newlyweds, fiftyish. He wore a dinner jacket, white ducks and patent leather shoes. She wore a formal muumuu with a slit to show off her sequined panty hose and stretched calves over four inch pumps. The last two were beta normal profilers who looked unready for anything, noses high, voices low, telling the second couple, "It's no secret. Real estate has been very good to us."

Jack was brief. "Aloha. Chop chop, let's go, we're late." But it took ten minutes more to explain the wetness of water, the physics of boats, the bummer when keels meet bottoms and the consequent need for wet feet, up to the knees, and a dinghy ride. The old women were game. They viewed death like down and outers: incidental. They hiked up their shrouds and hobbled to the water. The newly-wed couple, still in the blush, were flexible. He shucked his shoes and rolled up his pants with a hardy laugh and a big why not? The new wife shared the game spirit, peeled off her panty hose, yes sir, stashed them and her spike heels in a bush by the surf shop. The couple blessed by real estate went along but pooh-poohed. Then they all climbed into the dinghy where it sat, high and dry on the sand. They climbed out when Jack explained in his voice for stupid children, that boats out of water can't float. Then everyone lugged it ankle deep, me'n Jackie grunting with the beast on the back end. A new set of four foot breakers did not require explanation. With all eyes on him, Jack mumbled, "the joy of yachting."

He called it twenty seconds later, go, right now, chop chop. He saw in the next moment a late breaker, saw the normals dumbfounded at the oncoming wall. All scrambled, except for the eighty year old women, who couldn't move much faster than hundred year old women. Jack chanted, "Out out out out out out out..." But too late— it was old ladies face down like dough globs under a rolling pin, sprawled, soaked, sputtering, spitting sand.

Helping them up, brushing them off as though water was dust, fearing the law, Jack said, "That's it. Party's over."

But one old woman sputtered, "Oh dear."

The other shook her head and hobbled again to the dinghy. "Not yet," she said, and the dinghy of fools rub-a-dub-dubbed out to the beautiful yacht.

Once on board the maiden crowd got the royal treatment— Sparkling Red Goose, pretzels and chips—and they took to *Whirlaway* like the happy take to life. Sails unfurled, she heeled gently and ran before a balmy evening breeze. Jack drove. I poured. All bemoaned the weather back in Cleveburg and had a lovely yachting time.

Luck stayed good two hours: the outboard started and beach drill was mostly dry. The real estate people said it was the time of their lives. The newlyweds said it was the second best part of their trip, and the old ladies said they'd be back next year. A market was born. The hundred seventy in vouchers payable in thirty days was good as gold if the system worked, so I wrote a check for it at the surf shop, and the night was made for celebration with a twelve-pack and a gram of snoot.

Jack said sometimes a guy has to let go. He got sentimental late, recalling Louise, spunky gal, soft head sometimes, maybe, but a free spirit. She could get down and have some fun. He called with good news and an invitation, say, fifteen minutes. He was two weeks without, in love again. Louise showed up in ten minutes looking taller and skinnier, milky white in a white chintz see-through, ghostly, hairless except for the odd fuzz on her throat, like the fuzz some women grow below the navel. Jack said that fuzz grew there because of him.

But perversion was her idea, he insisted, and frankly he could live without it, unless she insisted. Louise wore black silk stockings and no shoes. Jack lumbered, just behind his fat gut, under his furry shoulders. Louise floated down the long hallway and lit like a mayfly on the wall. She loved the contrast, and she loved her beau, especially when he insisted. She pegged it—"You're in a mood."

I took my cue and headed out for a walk, maybe a few beers. I said hello on the way out. She whispered, "Comet dust."

"Yes," I said. "Welcome home." Louise stayed on with new fervor, howling now in response to Jack's pneumatic affections.

I considered reaching old age without.

The next week changed that, and then I considered reaching old age without post-orgasmic calmness. A housewife on a separate vacation swore she loved her husband. Short and plump with a yak like a new motor, she stayed on board, peeled off her bikini top, massaged her breasts and asked if I would take over. She asked if I liked her breasts. Her husband thought they were great. I said yes, your breasts are great. In the sack she went directly down and asked if I liked that. Her husband liked it best of all and often said she was terrific at it.

I said yes, terrific, till way after dark, when fatigue and a headache called for quiet and solitude. "I can't believe I'm a grandmother," she said. "Can you?"

"No. I can't believe you're a grandmother." She talked about her children, her grandchildren, her husband again, and then she got peeved—no tampons aboard. I said I'd go ashore for some, hoping she'd stuff a few in her mouth. She called me a dear for offering, ate me again and said no, she really must be going. Goodbye never felt so sweet.

Jack and Louise snored on the sofa, pleasure spent, TV on. She woke up and asked how it was. I shrugged. She said, "It's tough getting loved in spurts like that."

"Yes. Too few spurts. Good night."

Too much sun and wind, hard work, no money, little sleep, few women, save the odd stew or housewife, the stray sniffette, and a debt that no sooner shrunk by month's end than it swelled afresh on the first. Whirlaway Charters grossed thirty grand in two months, but spent thirty one three in the same period. All the checks stayed afloat. With thirteen hundred late on the mortgage, Weems threatened, but softly. I felt good enough about Weems to ease him out another five hundred for groceries, beer and morale booster, since without the boost, Weems was lost. With morale intact, high season approached, easy money. One night's snoot equaled one week's groceries, but everything is expensive in yachting. And besides, who could pass up the bargain Herbert gave?

Herbert deal da blow. His network of uncles and cousins at all levels of law enforcement, patrol cops to undercover, was old family, immune. "I set up good, syndicated." He'd been hungry, down to saimin—thin broth, thin noodles. Now he shared good fortune—snoot at cost plus ten percent, with a credit line when the wind blew so hard all we got was beat. Herbert gave up on boats then, he was so busy flying one island to the next, driving one end to the other, picking up, delivering, staying on call. In two months he was two bills up and said, "It good."

I stopped warning him on the drug trade one night after a sit-down drunk at a bar up the mountain. The road back was narrow and winding, so we doubled the dose on liquor antidote, for safety. Heading back down Herbert eased his new syndicate truck to sixty in a thirty-five, because it was best to drive conservative even though the antidote let you take it easily at twice the posted speed limit. Then he eased it to a stop when the flashing red came up behind with an air raid warning. Two snoot wrappers sat on the dash, a couple straws and razor blades lay on the console, empty beer cans strewn across the floor. Jack and I shoved stuff under seats. Herbert whispered, "Be cool."

He rolled his window down and grinned when the officer said, "Herbert! Howzit Brah!"

Herbert slurred, "Howziiiit, Thomas." He turned back in. "Thomas. He my good cousin."

Thomas said, "Ey, Herbert." Herbert got out, spoke low, and a minute later the truck sped along again at sixty. Herbert said, "Thomas my good cousin."

And who was I to counsel Herbert anyway? I lived in a fog, example of unsuccess. Fun was rare, money more rare, energy bought in plastic pacquettes. In two months I'd beaten foreclosure, saved Nuel and averaged two bags of groceries a week. The boat was paid down three grand more, for Nuel, who was still bound by the purchase option, but he could vanish anytime, and who wanted the boat anyway?

Worse than poverty was fear that minds would follow bodies in the charter trade, burned, beaten, worn haggard, no prospect for change. Jack said I worried too much, that a business could not be judged in two months, much less before high season, when we looked most likely to gross forty grand a month on fifteen overhead. So I agreed, set worry aside and got in the groove, up at six, on the beach at six thirty, iced and stocked by seven, boarded by seven fifteen and off the mooring by seven thirty, answering every day the normal questions: How deep is the water? How much was the boat? And you get to do this every day?

And off again to a shallow crater eight miles out for clear water, plenty fish, easy anchorage because the bay is flat all morning. Then the long beat home, trades on the nose, forty, fifty knots some days, enough to get a load of beta normals shrieking their endearing mix of fear and fun. At least the trades first crossed the wide isthmus between the mountains, so gale winds made only small waves, no fetch, no rogues.

In the thick of it, with skin dark as Herbert's, faces lined and leathery in permanent squint, hair frizzed and fried white, we hardly noticed twenty knots or thirty. I noticed thirty-five. Jack called forty a whore, and the whore went to forty-five. Fifty was rare, and sixty-two was the record headwind coming home—a hurricane on the Beaufort Scale.

Then all the normals who feared going below because they'd heard going below makes you puke, went below. Jack stayed at the helm in mask and snorkel, sputtering cock fucking sucker at green water rolling over the bow.

But a down-and-outer finds relief in anarchy; let chaos reign, so the beta normals could have a taste of it too. Still I worried that disaster would be incomplete, would leave a five grand deductible to pay. And how long could disaster wait, back and forth and forth and back so many times to the snorkel grounds? Poverty was already an in-law. With major damage, his whole family would show up. Jack said fuck it and drank a few beers. I drank one and fell asleep.

The normals came in all styles. Jack hated them, mostly because they had the money to pay for a boat ride. Business was less than it would have been, if me'n Jackie were nicer guys. We knew it, and we discussed it. I said we'd have even less without the truth, without righteousness in our hearts. Be realistic.

Jack went along with the truth and moral righteousness, and the next day when the headwinds howled fifty, he told the folks: Every day. Every goddamn day.

One normal from Chicago named Chuck looked and nattered like a chipmunk—short, red hair, freckles, puffy cheeks and a motor-mouth. He came out with his wife, whose stayed tutu revealed once-splendid breasts. Chuck made friends quick, talking about life, what it's really all about, God and wonder—pissant Republican middle management suburban with sincerity. Jack stretched his neck for a deeper shot down the vortex—Chuck's wife leaned forward on cue and hunched her shoulders.

It was routine, Chuck's wife letting Jack see her tits while Chuck talked shit. Chuck hovered nearby, watching Jack look down his wife's swimsuit, jabbering sailor lingo like, "She's a beauty alright!" and "Aye aye Captain!" and "Steady as she goes!" Chuck was adventuring, out at sea.

I said, "Arrr Billy!" and stepped up by Jack for a look.

Chuck's wife was as good a show as tits and squirm can get. Jack sat down. I hardened the main. Chuck chattered his way down to the cabin where he ranted nautical, rifling the nav station, taking up floor-boards, perusing the bilge, searching gear, muttering love, for boats. "God she's nice."

Ascending he asked, "Is every day this great?

"Sometimes greater," I said.

Chuck said, "God, I'd sure like to be aboard her in a heavy storm sometime." He looked hopeful.

I laughed, "Fuck you Chuck."

Jack giggled, lost his beer down his shirt.

Chuck sat down, grinned stupidly, shrugged and said, "No, really," and shut up.

That afternoon *Whirlaway* got shit-listed at a booking desk— Chuck's. "Fuck them too," was my market analysis. "We got twenty-eight more."

Soon after was a sunset sail with two school marms far from home on a boat ride, waiting for a difference in their lives. They huddled forward by the mast, sipping Red Goose. The other couple aboard stayed aft, by the action. Stacy, the wife, focused on sailors' crotches. Joe, the man, ran the Harley Davidson shop in Big Toe, Texas and had the tattoos to prove it. He twitched near the helm, asking if it was okay to, you know, I mean, snort, grunt, gobble, snort, I mean you know is it okay on the boat and all?

Jack said, "Do you have cocaine?" Joe grinned. Jack called a school marm to take the wheel and followed Harley Joe below. Joe used a teaspoon, dumped a dollop on a plate, and the down and outers dove in, honked way too much, until we too twitched, nattered nonsense and felt inexplicably, unreasonably excellent, just like Joe.

Joe's wife came out of the head wearing a macrame bikini with one inch mesh, covering nothing. She had a great figure, a tattooed past. Harley Joe asked, "Hey, one of you guys want to fuck my wife?"

Jack asked, "What do you do? Watch?"

"Yeah, well?" Joe said.

"How about if she just tells you about it?" Joe liked that, that was a good one. He plopped out more snoot on the ridiculous pile, powdery monument to anarchy. I'd had enough, knew enough, headed topside for school marm banter over depth, cost, daily habit, awe and wonder.

Back up, shrugging, grinning, Jack blurted, "Fuck that guy. Wants to watch." The school teacher went purple. Putting an arm around

her, I swelled in the shorts over the pure innocence of the creature—
it was sailor talk, that's all. I am sorry. I comforted her. The wind came
up, *Whirlaway* heeled, Harley Joe lost some powder, Stacy got goose
bumps all over. The school marms whimpered. I said, "This is what
happened to us." And the wind blew away all thoughts of language,
toot, tits, tattoos, school or differences.

I had a recurring dream those first months of chartering, with more
wind and sun in a day than most people get in a year, and four more
beers quick before bed was basic relaxation. I dreamed of perfect
peace, that it was divisible by three. The three parts, profound in
dream slag, were: speed, impact, settling. I feared the dream, because
I thought it was a death wish, and though I believed I wasn't afraid
to die, and it would be a relief, I felt bad about dying before I had a
taste of the good. Then I welcomed the dream, for comfort, slept in
motion, like a rock, sinking. The difference was that easy, arbitrary,
irrational.

I sank to dawn, to a thud on a clump-clustered bottom thick with
questions. I breathed slowly, carefully, between the water.

The dream blew away in the wind, vanished in sunlight. A shrink
would say weeks later that the dream was a defense mechanism
whereby mental process removed itself—occurred elsewhere, apart
from the difficulty at hand rather than shutdown completely. The
shrink called it a form of repression, healthy in the short run, leading to psychosis over long periods. The shrink said the dream had no
fear, no pain. That was good. That was life, sustaining itself.

The sun and wind and work built strength, to a point, then worked
the other way, until tired felt like old and tired. The surf shop boys
were only thirty and had a clear advantage. I blamed the liquor and
snoot. Jack said, "What are you going to do?"

The days were clear and sunny, tropical. The normals laughed and
drank like hazard was one more station on the dial, until they
clammed up, white knuckled at thirty knots on the nose, deathly pale
at forty. Then Jack worried about sail trim, the reef, complaints at the
booking desks. But we only skimmed the reef and had nearly twenty

desks left. The days were simple, wrestling the shore boat, pulling lines until muscles hung like rags on rungs, no more left to squeeze.

Then the surf shop boys yelled wussies, and sometimes ran down to help if a teenage daughter was on board. Jack said the surf shop boys knew nothing but shore break, that their futures didn't exist. I said no, not like ours. The surf shop boys looked humble, evenings at the bar, where humility passed for manners, shirts and pants for adulthood, and they had only to sit still, speak softly, drink slowly and get by. Jack said thirty years old and not a pinch of shit to show for it. I didn't press the issue.

Afternoons, the surf shop boys on their skim boards shot down the slick to the hollowing break then launched up the faces to perfect flips. They competed for height and form and cheered for glory, or for eating it bad. Farther down in tamer, lapping waves, too weak to lift the dinghy, beat and limp with no teenage daughters, we waited for help.

Or else we hung around for a sunset sail, watching the surf shop boys lug rental catamarans to the water and back. At five the surf shop boys headed out on small cats and sailboards for solitude at high speed. I envied their waking dream.

With no sunset sail quitting time was two. Windows shut, curtains drawn, air-conditioned to sweater weather—Jack fell on the sofa, I took the floor, by the tube. The washing machine droned with the day's dirty towels, lunch ruins dripped half rancid in the sink and *Andy of Mayberry* or *The Beverly Hillbillies* or *Hawaii Five-O* played the dirge, endless and monotonous into sleep.

Weather reports were automatic—trades up blew the door open and forty-five down the hall, through the living room blowing pictures off the wall. Lamps crashed, down and outers cursed and one got up to close the goddamn door. Kona winds came from the south, could run *Whirlaway* off the mooring onto the reef or the beach. Kona winds rattled the big sliding door, and we lay still and awake.

I woke one day to a Public Broadcasting documentary on harvesting the sea, wondering how PBS got on when *Petticoat Junction* and

Gomer Pyle were running special back to back that week just down the dial. The big slider rumbled in its slot—waves flung spume and sea snot onto the glass. Pulling the curtain showed stage-one kona storm, weather rampage from the south. It could change steady combers to monsters breaking a hundred yards out, rolling in fifteen feet high— boat death weather. The trick was getting aboard quick, running north to lee anchorage. Lead time was minimal, but strength was too, so I let Jack sleep, since a couple hours lead would do, and sleep would be rare if we ran from the storm.

I left the curtain open and lay down again with anxiety and a laugh—if we ran from the storm—when a Japanese fisherman in rubber boots and dungarees, layered shirts, gloves and a tattered vest came on the tube, standing in a work boat, feet apart. The scene was Nokomani Pond, where Japanese aquaculturists set nets, four feet wide with wide mesh. As the fisherman heaved the net, empty except for the slime, a voice said sheer energy, photosynthesis, was harnessed to make algae, a primary source of nutrition and a favorite food in Japan. The algae is dried, pressed into thin sheets, nori, then cut and rolled for sushi.

The empty nets weren't empty, and that was what harvesting the sea and action had come to, no danger, no life, no death. The fucking Japs are taking over, I thought, drifting off, dreaming of a white rice blanket and nori wrapper.

I woke after dark to balmy breezes, northeast—tradewinds—and easy surf. Under full moon all was well, no run tonight. And no run tomorrow, with the balmy breeze climbing to forty-five by sunrise. That left time to rest—and think, as if thinking over events, chance and free will would lead somewhere, a point, maybe, instead of hopelessly onward, close-hauled with a lee shore. Of course it didn't. It doesn't.

Louise got a job selling helicopter rides but was quickly on probation, said she couldn't in good faith sell rides for Thursday, because after all, it was November 22. "Rhubarb, rhubarb, mumbo jumbo," Jack said. He called it cosmic shit, her greatest perversion, but he got nothing. Louise read the numbers, and the numbers don't lie.

I asked, "How come then one and one are three?"

"You're so fucked," she said in her quivering hostility.

"Oh."

"It's the eleventh month. Don't you see?" Louise tolerated ignorance. "Everyone has a number. It's real. It counts the letters in your name and the day your were born, and the way you do it is you add the digits, like fifteen is really six."

"And Nada is six and a half." I remembered.

Louise liked that. "Yes," she said. "Of all the numbers, only eleven and twenty-two don't add up. They won't reduce, ever. They're that heavy."

"It sounds heavy."

"It is. Eleven/twenty-two is like Christmas and Yom Kipper rolled into one. John Kennedy died that day. That was heavy. It's kind of like Friday the 13th. It can be good or bad—but it's heavy, whatever it is."

"Heavy."

"I'm sick of that shit," Jack said.

"That's plain to see," Louise said in her spookiest lilt. Two days later, 11/22, business was off. I sat on the seawall. An African tulip in tiny whirlwind fluttered madly, like a coquette gone insane. New breezes skimmed the bay like hot breath on a cold glass, like ghosts.

Watching the world speak in undeniable omen, I knew it was nothing. Nature is balanced, if not benign. Truth resides in science. I listened, watched for momentum or submission in the fickle breeze. It faded. It was nothing, and I felt weak, approaching zero, turning to froth and foam like the scuz blown off the wave tops.

The trades stayed down a week, and nothing chased the heat away.

Business was up again with cold weather in America and holiday normals avoiding depression, seeking sunshine and blue skies as a backdrop to the realization that nobody really loves them. *Whirlaway* anchored at the far ledge of the crater in a lumpy surge, but the tourist crowd was smaller there, because bigger fish hover just beyond, waiting for helpless prey sucked over to the deep. Grouper big enough to slurp a fat normal whole can sink quick four hundred feet and digest in comfort. Implosion is only a belch. I lived the dream then, serviced normals, sold the act of adventure as some women sell the love act, wondering where those who sell it find it for themselves, wondering if something packaged and sold is lost, wondering if that was blood on the anchor cleat, knuckle flesh on the thimble.

A Thanksgiving sun rose on down and outers welding a shaft strut removed yesterday at sundown, reinstalling it soon after sunrise in a grunt and choke, taking turns with the wrench underwater, then telling the normals yes, every day, then reducing sail, ignoring happy faces asking how deep, how much, as the bay went steep and frothy white with screaming trades, horizontal spray.

Louise made a tofu-turkey loaf. Jack threw it over the seawall. "You're supposed to eat a goddamn turkey on Thanksgiving." And our waterlogged, weatherbeat, mystified little troupe went out to dine.

A partner as contrary as Jack Witte made life easier for me, like a depressing book used to pull me from a funk; as in: you think you got it bad... Between us nothing was sacred, nor could honor exist as long as life held our noses to the wind, put sand in our teeth, reminded us that every tick of the clock cost money in the voice of Weems. Ours was a dim light then, glowing with liquor and drugs. But I was different from Jack—I was a dreamer. I had control of the dream, except the part where I tried waking up and could not. Sometimes up on the mountainsides crawdad eggs lie dormant in the hardtack for years, until a decent monsoon floods the ditch, and life begins again. Scientific facts like this were a comfort. Comfort was somewhere else, and we longed to be there.

I dreamed. Jack bore on. One balmy sunset in the doldrums—two weeks before Christmas, when the charter boat crowd starves, food stamps gone with two weeks till paydirt, when Weems called daily to say this is it, we must foreclose, when the four-normal minimum was down to any stiff with a few bucks for the magical interlude made famous by *Whirlaway*, Red Goose included—Jack bore on.

Three normals on a champagne sunset was a windfall—found money—groceries, two bags, with a twelve-pack and a chicken and rice through Christmas if bad came to worse. The reservation came one morning after five days of no normals. Happiness was talk of food on the table, swabbing her down, icing her up, a six-pack and the lull before sunset—and fuck it, a bottle of Red Goose wasn't so bad, with holiday cheer.

Due at four, the normals called at three thirty to cancel. I took the call and listened. Papa Normal said Normal Daughter cut her foot bad, might need an ambulance. He hated cancelling very very much and thank you, in these extraordinary circumstances, for a full refund. "Hold please," I said, and I told Jack, "Says his daughter cut her foot and needs an ambulance and he wants a refund." I knew Jack well enough to hold the phone towards him.

"He's a goddamn liar!" Jack said.

"Should I tell him?"

"You can tell him fuck his daughter and fuck her foot and fuck the hospital too. He doesn't get one dime back!"

I told the man, "Sorry. Your five hundred dollar charter was already discounted to a hundred five. You can check your voucher for the 24 hour cancellation policy. No refunds tonight, Sir."

Papa Normal breathed deep, then he said, "Okay look... We'll be there in thirty minutes."

The normals showed up on time. He looked like Sigmund Freud. Mama Normal was slim and pretty, but too pale for good health, and bony. Normal daughter wore braces on her teeth and a band-aid by her ankle. He said hello. She gazed at the horizon. Normal daughter looked down, apparently repressed, which repression I would soon learn was healthy in the short-term. He was a shrink from New York and said he didn't mind being called a shrink, not like some of them. Jack said that was fortunate. The shrink said he came to the tropics for a seminar on creativity and madness.

Jack grinned and said "Wonderful. Get in the little rubber boat." And it was rub-a-dub-dub, out for a lovely evening of yachting.

The shrink looked into his Red Goose after sipping it and said he really didn't mind cheap champagne, not like some of them. Jack said that was fortunate. The shrink studied it. The wife chose bag wine and studied the horizon. The shrink looked up at last and said, "Well."

I offered the daughter a slug of brandy. She giggled and took a soda. I asked if her parents ever got down and c...c...cu...cu...cut her loose. She giggled again. "No."

It was one of those eerily calm and sensible evenings, warmer than usual, populated by two who knew they were nuts, two who wondered why and their daughter who had little time left for innocence. I sat between the shrink and the wife, watching her watch the horizon. "You're too skinny," I said.

She said, "Yes. I know that."

I turned to the shrink. "You don't have to drink this shit. Want some brandy?" The shrink hung his head and nodded. I liked these people, profiling normal, but so obviously as unhinged as a couple down and outers. They too questioned life, even though they were rich.

Jack grinned, steering across the light, fluttering breeze. I took a snort and passed the bottle. The shrink liked that, living at last. He glugged, choked, wiped his chin and looked proud.

I lay down on the opposite seat and said, "Tell me doctor. Why?" The shrink leaned forward, elbows on knees, chin in hand. Then he took another snort. I watched, and asked, "How long have you felt this way?" The shrink smiled down, nodding slowly. I went below for some funk on the stereo, then came back to point out the perfect breeze, the perfect coral tint of the waning perfect day, the purple golden shimmer on the surface of the sea.

Whirlaway heeled gently, sliced easy at five knots with no effort. I said, "Hey Doc, come here a minute." The shrink obeyed, followed to the stern, held on while I tied loops on either end of a line, hooked one end to a stern cleat and threw the other end over. "Hang on, take a ride."

The shrink studied the wake then turned to the wife, who gazed at the horizon. "Honey."

I said, "Come on. You won't believe it."

The shrink asked, "Are there sharks?"

I said, "Doc. Don't ask me. Ask yourself. Are there sharks? You know the answer for chrissakes. People pay you what, three, four hundred grand a year to tell them about the sharks." The shrink studied the wake. He nodded slowly. "Fuck the sharks," I said. The shrink nodded. "Am I right, Doc? Am I right?"

"I'm an excellent swimmer," the shrink said.

Jack turned around from the helm. "What the fuck good's excellent swimming do you high and dry?"

"Come on Daddy," the daughter chimed in. The shrink sought eye contact, first Jack and then me, like a condemned man mustering spirit, as men removed from spirit must.

He took the line and flexed, then stopped, stuck on hesitation, like a word breathed for but unuttered. "I'll be wet," he said.

"Using your degree now," Jack said.

I touched his shoulder. "Yes, Doc. You'll be wet. Then you will be dry. Doc. What is wet?"

The shrink jumped in. His trunks slid to his ankles. He held the rope with one hand and pulled his trunks up with the other, but the trunks slid down again when he gripped the rope with both hands again. Jack laughed and said to get him back aboard so we could talk about investing in the yachting business. Instead I yelled, "Spread your legs!" The shrink sputtered, confusing speaking with breathing and got his trunks up again. "Spread your legs!"

The shrink spread his legs and his trunks only slid to his knees. Then he weakened, legs closed, ankles fluttering like streamers, trunks gone. Jack called don't worry, he'd come about for the trunks. I yelled don't let go. The shrink blubbered through the water rushing up his chest, pummeling his chin. Finally, giving in, he took to the tow, spinning to go under, spinning again to come up, weaving dolphin-like in the wake. When his arms went weak and stretched straight back from his grip, I pulled him in, helped him up. The shrink grinned and breathed, said it was the best thing he'd ever done. Jack came about for the trunks.

I said, "Ever?"

The shrink nodded. "And ever."

I turned to the wife. "Come along dear."

"Fuck the sharks," she said.

Jack asked the shrink, "Was she always a cunt?"

"No," the shrink said, and therapy was underway.

Nothing came of the evening but vast potential—the daughter drank six sodas and puked—both the shrink and the wife called it good, a purge, transcendence and growth by way of total immersion. Meanwhile the wife lit into Jack, telling him she knew from the first that he was far past misanthropy, that he hated society and probably himself, that he needed help quick, whatever form it took. She told him he suffered the worst maladies of modern man, including breast fixation, severe chauvinism, tremendous guilt and worst of all seething instability, most likely carried over from a nasty childhood burdened by a careless aunt or who knows, maybe a visiting stranger who'd used him, yes, used him to her own ends.

I took a snort from the bottle and told the shrink, "You know she's very good."

Jack took a snort and said, "So?" She went below.

This while the daughter guzzled pop and turned green and the shrink kissed my ass for seeing his need, loosening the reins. As his daughter's belly sounded reverse, he asked, "What is a man anyway? A beast of burden? A beast to pull the load that is the future? What about now? Ha! That's what we just figured out."

He freely gave of his two bills an hour time, confessing numbness and paltry insight from the confines of the city—"Oh! If I had a yacht and a piece of rope like you do!" he said. Jack went below.

I described my dream then, my sinking peace of mind, my yen for the drop. "Am I nuts, Doc?"

The shrink said, "Yes. But it's short term. Don't worry yet." He spoke of death as a good thing, in the figurative sense, necessary for change. Below in the cabin the pretty, bony wife had peeled her swim suit down. Standing before Jack she ordered him to "stare upon my nakedness." Jack stared easy enough, and she wrapped his hand around her breast, told him to "feel of my breasts."

Jack squeezed each and said, "The right one's a little bigger, huh?"

"Do you think this is sexual?" she said.

I listened to the shrink less, strained downward more. Jack got sincere, said he felt almost free, could he try a blow job, please? Have a snort if it'll help.

I was relieved when she pulled her top back up, then climbed up, announcing that nothing ailed Captain Jack that twenty-four thousand volts wouldn't cure.

Attention undivided, I asked the shrink how long was short term, how would it end. The shrink said, "The short-term is relative."

"Come on, Doc, cut the shit."

The shrink nodded and said three or four months most likely. "It's simple, really, irrational beha ior, loss of distinction between what is real and what is not."

Jack stuck his head out and said, "It's been six months." He handed up the brandy.

I drank. "The lie, Doc, what do you do about the lie?" The shrink smiled. "What do you do about knowing you don't mean it every time you talk civil? What do you do about people every day, getting up in the morning. What do you do?"

The shrink grasped my arm. "Stability. Cling to what won't move." He let go and sat back profoundly.

"Genius," Jack said. "Sheer fucking genius." The daughter wretched, and it was time to turn for home.

At the mooring Jack said don't worry about the mess; two niggers show up first thing in the morning for that. So it was rub-a-dub-dub back to the beach in the dark, where everyone shook hands, hugged and agreed that the evening had been wonderful, and don't forget the meaning. The shrink said, "We need to cut the bonds more often, working our way to always, all of us."

Then the wife said, "We love you." And she walked up the beach with the shrink, daughter between them, headed back to their rented condo to plan tomorrow's fun. Jack said nuts, but he liked them. He headed up for a couple three margaritas. I looked north and south, up and down, and wondered what to walk toward that wouldn't move.

 An Older Woman

Life droned on. Rising heat and howling wind signaled springtime in the tropics—it blossomed coeds. Whirlaways offered its first discount, they were students after all, so young, so fresh. Herbert wanted work, please, to help in time of need, and he worked easy on deck, with mystique—tall, dark, local boy with leaping tiger tattoo, pull this line, slack that, hoist, strike, reef, flake, ease, come up, rig and heave to, moving like a cat on a fence. People asked, How much? How deep? Every day? Herbert said, "Hoi! Ooba."

Jack stared at one coed or another, muttered intense desire to suck air through her asshole. Herbert whispered yes, her shit must taste like marshmallows, it must. Jack wondered aloud if she swallowed or spit it out, and Herbert said she hocked it on the wall, she must. Then they'd laugh. It was routine.

I watched the water move.

Herbert charmed the coeds, especially the loud, coarse girls whose tropical agendas called for tall, dark and local. The perfect coeds didn't move or talk at all, like they couldn't, stuck in perfect beauty.

On a day like all the rest, hot, sunburned, half drunk since dawn, tired and tired of it and hardly amused that Herbert gave a private snorkel lesson in the head with a loud, short, fat coed, after the hard beat home, forty knots on the nose and five foot bumps, after dinghying ashore in four trips, losing one load under a pooping wave that turned rub a dub broadside to the next wave that turned it turtle, left it flopping, splashing, gurgling bloody murder and refund six feet deep, after gathering the bodies and gear with a good laugh for that adventure, after cleaning and securing *Whirlaway*, wondering if the outboard was ruined, ignoring shredded knuckles and festering sun welts, eating three aspirin and lugging the two ton, sand laden whore-dog high and dry and dragging our sorry asses up, away from the heat, we sat and breathed in cool, dark, calm, no normals, just four walls. Silence.

"It don't make sense," Jack said.

Herbert said his blow job was only so-so. Jack went for the mail. I listened to the shade, sought stillness, watched my skin burn.

Jack had fallen out with the resident manager, a retired marine called Colonel Klink, who said, "Nobody runs a business from my condos!"

Jack explained: "Why don't you kiss my fucking ass." Klink understood, and the issue went away. But it left Jack bitter, with the world still at him. "The cocksucker's got nothing else but to get on some stiff trying to turn a buck." Jack hated management.

He got back with the mail bad-mouthing the "over the hill, semi-fox they got down there as secretary now." He tossed three letters at me—one envelope said I'd already won ten million dollars. Another was an old dentist bill, forwarded four times, and the feds still wanted their student loan money. Jack settled in like a disciple before a sage as Herbert got down to detail on the fat, baby coed, down to tongue action, lip compression, congeniality and talent.

I took a break. Herbert would bullshit to sundown, and Jack would listen, as if to the secret of life.

Two women in the front office wore muumuus, a Friday tradition begun by the missionaries, maybe because Friday was the day for fish and no pussy, because muumuus make every woman look the same, like a sack of spuds. One spoke fast, smoked hard, paced, looked anxious, looking a man over. The other, younger, had to be the semi-fox. The old one finally shut her yak, stared at me, set me up for my how do you do, but I froze at the plate.

The pretty one wove her fingers under her chin and said, "Your roommate was just here. Doesn't he give you your mail?" And she smiled—she understood.

"Yes." And I stood there stupid, until the twitch got me, and I turned to browse the paperbacks. I read Sidney Sheldon, Sidney Sheldon, Sidney Sheldon on to Jackie Collins, Jackie Collins. Nothing had changed.

The old one rattled—her teeth hurt, gums bled, sinuses were plugged, her hair was fucked up, her tubes were off. She left to call her friend, her doctor, for some test results.

I pulled up a chair like a tourist checking in, plopped down and sighed. "Tough day?" she said.

"The charter business is shit."

"You look like proof." I leaned over her desk, drawn in maybe by a woman who could call me shit and still show an interest. She asked which boat, what kind, how long, how much for a ride. She'd always loved boats. She talked boats, animate with good hands, feminine with a middle age wrinkle slanting from her neck. She was to the fat, baby coed like cool shade next to high noon at sea. Her voice, manners, poise and patience were elixir to a tired man. "Why do you look so beat?"

"Too much sun, too much wind, too many normals talking shit, stuffing their faces. And I'm old." She thought it over, sat prim and pretty like the cross your heart bra woman, or the Brylcream secretary, or my sixth grade teacher, a normal, suburban, wholesome woman who most likely kept an active passion tucked under the sheets. "And no money," I shrugged. "Maybe a guy might want to take a girl to dinner. What do I do about that? Use food stamps?" Her fingers wove under her chin again. The old ones were so much easier, so much nicer, so much more caring.

"It doesn't cost much to take a girl to dinner."

"Then you'll go?"

She sighed. "You're broke."

"I'll borrow."

"No. It would only be one more bill to pay."

"I'm comfortable with debt."

"I'll go but only Dutch."

"We can go Jewish if you want to, you pop for all of it."

"I'd like that, and to send you roses too, but I'm not making much here either."

"You look too smart, too good to sit behind that desk, hid away and broke."

"Yeah, you too." She sighed big, sweet and innocent. Yeah me too, I thought, mum again, since I couldn't just ask her to stand up, muumuu beef check, so I could see if our date was still on. But she got onto boats again, wanted a ride, loved sailing and the sea, and I feared warmth and friendliness with chunky thighs and a fat ass...

"You're not even listening." She looked out the window, lit a smoke and stretched her neck. "I'm forty-four."

I nodded slow—way older than my sixth grade teacher, but then the urge was still in me when she moved like a woman moves when she wants to look like a woman, just like my sixth grade teacher used to do right in front of all the wet dreaming boys. I smiled that far away smile that would one day let people know I'd gone past the edge of reason, smiled because it was already twenty-five years since the sixth grade, and I still wanted to put my pee pee in her tee tee. The phone rang. She answered official then dropped into phone voice, the intimate one echoing desire or experience or both, with giggled agreements of fun and yes, again soon.

I ducked out, shuffled back and lay down for a rest, until six a.m., yachting time again. Seven hours of sun, wind and spray later was mail call.

But she didn't work Saturdays. Two steps back, Jack said he sometimes liked watching other people catch fish as much as he liked catching them himself. He said let's sniff around the pool. I followed like a dog to chow, and there she was, passing the bikini test with honors, a knit in black with beige piping. She lay on the chaise lounge, knees up and spread. Jack whispered, "Excellent bush."

She swung her legs over, sat up with a warmth undeserved by some and said, "Hello stranger."

"Hey."

"Good trip today?"

"Wonderful." She got up for two chairs looking good, turned around in best profile. "You don't look forty-four."

She showed a confidence that said it isn't so old, considering what's left, what is known of giving. She pulled a chair to her chaise. "Now sit." I sat. She offered her hand. "My name is Renette."

"Unusual."

"My mama couldn't decide on Renee or Lynette..." Oh God, country western goes tropical. She had a little grunt for a laugh. "My baby sister is Lynee." She did it again—her baby sister was only forty-two. Dewy-eyed as a country lyric, and just as sincere, she spoke in simple terms, believed in simple shit. I wanted her right now, wanted to muss her up and fuck fuck fuck her, and it seemed so easy. I would soon learn another lesson, how want can turn on a man, can up and chase him down the road.

Sure I was horny—maybe extremely horny—horny and beat—too beat and too broke for cocktails and dinner. So I stared, wanted and said fuck it. She said, "What's a matter, Baby?" God, it came out like butter.

I knew the numbers going in, that she was old-fashioned cornball and no matter how good the friction, the profile was possessive, insane jealous, hornier than me when I was seventeen. I knew going in that it wasn't all that much time between high school and thirty, and thirty was only yesterday, and in that same brief span she'd be around the bend toward sixty, which isn't all that old as people go, but it's a long way from high school.

"I'm Martin."

"Mmm. Martin." She loved this pool more than the pool at her condo, and well, she knew I needed some good news when I checked the mail, so here she was. She was married twenty-five years—I'd only begun nocturnal emission at the time of the wedding—but she knew from year two it wouldn't work. She took another twenty-three to get

smart enough to head out on her own, and to let her kids grow up—
they were eighteen and nineteen.

I was only just nineteen. She regretted the coming week, in which
she would neither join me for dinner nor yachting because her recent
husband arrived last night from Northern Idaho. Not to worry, the
husband was a bonehead. He was violent too and jealous, but she
didn't know why because she hadn't slept with him in nearly six
months and even then it hadn't been too good, and she didn't plan to
sleep with him now—oh she might sleep with him but she wouldn't
do it with him.

I understood, watched her enjoy my fall into hormonal submission
as she lay back in perfect glisten, subtle writhe.

I felt different, as if here at last was a break in the tedium. Eyes
closed, she said she was sorry I hated my situation, that she, like most
people, would give anything to go sailing every day and make a living at it. I said I would too. She asked again if I would take her yachting. I said sure, an overnighter, if she wanted to. She said you don't
even know me. I said fine, week after next. That would allow time to
know each other, time to cancel if sexual attraction seemed too little to go on. I enjoyed my own bullshit, knew it didn't matter if
nobody else caught on.

She oozed in and sighed. Good looking women enjoy the same
confidence, maybe more, because flesh is tangible. She must have
known it all the way from Booneville. Good looking women attract
the niceties of life, until the looks fade, or the confidence fades. She
looked mid-thirties with years of experience—one dimensional, and
just the right dimension. Meditation stopped on a whiskey voice from
yonder, "Oh, Netty!"

"Oh, Netty?"

She rolled over slow and said, "It's here. Go now." And the slow roll
showed yet another angle of the figure a man never tires of.

"He sounds fat."

"He is fat—fat in the head." She curled up on the chaise lounge,
pulled herself in fetal. Then she sat up, as if in some bumpkin ritual

over love gone sour—sat up and moved a strap from behind her back to around her neck in a poolside gyration middle-aged women with good tits know will plop a bronze and perfect one from its halter. She re-set it slo-mo so we could see—husband arrived—just how good her tits still looked, and no tan line.

Shifting quick to phone voice again she said, "Walter meet Martin." Walter and I shook on it, and she said, "He owns a great, big, huge, fifty foot racing yacht." She twisted it, so I told Walter that Renette had looked forward to his visit, and maybe they could come out on *Whirlaway* while he was here. Walter said thanks just the same but he didn't do too good on boats.

"I know just how you feel." I left, looking back from the gate at Renette soaking it up, Walter squirming, undead in a trap, sharing a sad mortality, youth gone, magic remembered.

Back in the condo Jack snored background to *The Munsters*. I lay on the floor and dreamed of fair winds through *Petticoat Junction*. I woke after dark, from a dream of youth, when Saturday night was a time for fun. I sat up blinking, wondering what she was doing now. And I smelled a roast.

The trades were down, so tomorrow would only burn, no slap in the face. I asked where Jack learned to cook.

"My mother."

The dream lingered, blended with the scent, gave rise to another question, why? I told him, "My mother used to pack my lunch in a bag in summer so I could head out all day alone. I'd hang out all alone even then. Strange, huh?"

"Compared to what?"

"You think we'll get out of this? I mean, clean? I see people on TV with tons of money and no sunburn. I got more brains than some of them. How do they do it?—Get into the chips, and all we get is beat to shit and broke."

Jack slid two plates down the coffee table—pot roast, spuds and carrots—no wind, no clouds, clear night. "This is living, Harry." He set a six-pack on the table. "You better stop worrying about that shit, loosen up and enjoy yourself. You'll be dead a long time. This is it."

"I know you're right." I didn't ask Jack what he thought an aging sniffette might be doing. I knew what Jack thought. So I shut up and agreed to a mutual fund—eighteen bucks—to go cruise the bars. Louise was out until late, at a who-do talk.

Jack knew about life but not about women. He wondered aloud on each one's perversions. Drinking through the eighteen bucks the down and outers headed back down the beach agreeing that a man's best friend is liquor, since a man knows he can get drunk. Louise came home inspired. Jack got laid.

The next day and the next day and the next day were like all before, all to come. Routine made the work easier, gave us the second sense, so each would know what the other would do when the dinghy got pooped or a normal got drunk on the foredeck in the face of a likely header or the wind blew fifty knots. We took turns with the shitty end of the stick, cleaning the head, swabbing the bulkhead where normals lunged from cockpit to cabin, puking halfway. Cleaning up tourist puke was degrading.

Herbert swabbed puke one time and said he could cure the problem. The next time a normal turned green, Herbert stood behind and softly said, "You puke down there, I kill you." The normal puked overboard, amazed.

Nights were routine too. After sleeping off the beer, which didn't seem like much at one an hour, or maybe two when the sun got serious, but added up to six or twelve beers a day, we woke fresh enough to speak, after a couple aspirin and a beer. Sometimes we drank wine at night, since variety is the spice of life. We were usually drunk.

Jack's birthday came again. I was up late the night before, insomniac from too much alcohol, but late nights were a relief, in the secret hours when the world shuts down, no wind, no sun, no questions. It was easier then to put your mind somewhere else, to imagine the going, the exit, the vanishing act, and why not skip town and leave the bitch to Nuel's bank? What could they do? So fuck it. Fuck them. I wanted my life back, what was left of my youth, or something.

Jack came out after midnight. He popped a beer, walked to the sliding glass door framing the dark night and lit a smoke. Sitting on the couch with Jack at the window in that still, oppressive silence was no different than waiting on the foredeck with Jack at the helm in a nasty sea; a word, a movement, a gesture comprised the efficient language of survival in the storm that was. Jack lit another smoke off the butt of his first and said, "It's my birthday."

I got his address book from the end table, flipped through it and dialed direct, gave Jack the phone and sang, "Happy birthday, birthday Bubba... It's five a.m. in Florida."

Nuel picked up with a groggy helloo. Jack laughed and handed back the phone. I grunted, squealed and hung up. Jack said thanks, he really liked his first birthday gift. He said it felt good.

"Your birthday's as good a time as any to deal with the situation. We got to figure something out."

"What's to figure out?"

"You want to fuck the dog the rest of your life?"

"No."

"That's what's to figure out."

"You figure it out," he said. "I got a charter to run in the morning."

"I think I got it figured out."

"Yeah? What?"

"You'll figure it out." Maybe it was a mistake, getting Jack down on his birthday. "I might split."

"Fuck it. Split." Jack went to bed.

Eight normals next day meant a gross of four eighty, which was about three eighty after commissions, three fifteen after lunch and beer, two eighty-five after insurance, one forty after the mortgages, fifty after short term debt on the dinghy and all the charter gear.

Fifty bucks was something, until the welder who fixed the strut last month was waiting on the beach at sunrise for his seventy. The truck was out of gas and had a flat.

The welder got forty and a promise of the other thirty next week, which wasn't good enough until I said it's Jack's birthday, for chrissake. The eight normals were from Washington, D.C., six men and two women. The women made sixty-five grand annual, each. The men ranged ninety to one twenty. All were early thirties.

Salary histories got traded on the way out to the snorkel adventure as one young man walked dreamily fore and aft, gazing up in wonder at the mast and sails. "God," he said. "You guys got it made."

"Fuck me in the asshole," Jack said.

The young man reflected and said, "Mmm. Not so good, huh?"

Jack said, "Ah, it's not bad. It's really pretty good." He flicked his smoke overboard on his way below for two quick beers that would make it pretty good. He came back up smiling and told me, "We'll never sell the whore if we say she's a bad fuck."

That afternoon I bought a barbecue grill for four dollars, guaranteed good for two barbecues.

Louise gave Jack the future—she'd done his chart and was scheduled for an interpretation that night in the crater, eleven thousand feet up. She knew his attitude toward the stars, but she knew her own faith in them too, and what they could foretell. Excited and purposeful, she said she'd be home by midnight.

I presented his birthday gift, the grill, and he spotted another ten for steaks and beer. He'd invited the two women from the day's charter over.

I cooked, poked coals and asked Jack what a married man would do in a bind. Jack said, "What comes naturally." The women brought a half gallon of wine in two bottles. Jack said he didn't know if he could still drink wine that didn't come in a bag. One woman said she was so bored with men making tons of money, who were still restless, unhappy and uncertain with life.

I said I knew about life, "It's wonderful, getting better all the time. I have no money, but I'm happy, like a pig, in shit."

The other woman opened both bottles. Then both giggled, the way girls who plan to stay do, and they asked, please, for some adventure stories. Ignorant of life in the no check on Friday lane, the dirt road lane, the sundown and payout lane, they listened in disbelief to tales of checks, credit cards and other sleight of hand. They heard the saga of Nuel, they loved the leverage with Weems. Herbert showed up near ten with some birthday snoot and more wine. The women stared, the tropics come to visit, as he told stories of his cousins who had run him that evening to the Big Island and over to Oahu and back, to see the biggest cousin of all. At ten thirty Herbert split quick, off on another appointment. The women from Washington, D.C. were ready to continue their adventure.

They didn't have much to say—one was a GS-14, the other a computer rep. Still it was good, their matched whimpers proclaiming equal rights for women in Washington, D.C. Jack walked through the kitchen for more wine, stopped by my room and asked, "How's it going?"

"Not too bad. You?"

"I can't tell. She makes these noises like it hurts."

The GS-14 riding me said, "Just pace yourself."

Jack flipped on the light. "Oh, I get it, slow and easy, like old people."

Louise came home at ten to twelve. I felt bad, that such a sound sleep coming on would be so shattered. When the storm didn't hit, I strolled out, ready to see Jack, peacefully dead on the sofa. Instead I saw the computer rep on the sofa nattering with Herbert. Jack chopped a little snoot for Louise. Without looking up, Jack said, "Look at my partner. He always looks like he can't believe it. I think he might be going nuts on me." Louise looked and laughed.

Herbert said, "Jack cocky on birthday." And the party went on and on, everyone happy about how the day was turning out.

Next day was no-show on the beach, which kills business in the charter trade, not to mention eight fares and the additional loss of another day of life, in which eight fares earned a man the right to eat, sleep and breathe.

I skipped mail check five days and called it strength, but on Thursday the older woman knocked during afternoon stupor. She delivered the mail, junk mostly, and said she was headed over to the shopping center on the other side because someone borrowed one of her Nancy Sinatra albums and broke it.

"Mmm." I rubbed my eyes. "Tough break."

"She only made the two albums and then she practically disappeared, and you can't find *These Boots* anywhere. You know, *These Boots are Made for Walking?* Mine wore out, and then somebody broke it. I think she's the greatest singer ever was. And *These Boots* might be the best record ever too. I heard they got it at Shopper's Fair."

"How's the visit going?"

"Terrible. I wish he'd leave. He leaves in three days."

"Sunday?"

"Yes."

"Dinner Sunday?"

"No. Give me a few days. I lived with the man twenty-five years."

"Sure." She asked how things went. "Status quo." She leaned in, kissed my cheek. She could emanate electricity at will.

"Come down talk to me sometime."

"Next week."

"Monday?"

"You need a few more days, after so many years."

"Fine. You wait."

"See you Monday."

She walked away looking good, with a waist small enough to wrap my hands around and the smallest ass I'd seen on a grown woman— and with a look back that said from the eyes that this would be something more than one more fuck. Her face was pretty and well formed, with high cheeks and a straight nose, succulent lips and a good chin when she held it up.

Good time through the weekend was a couple fourteen-packs, a couple twelves and a surprising sixteen on Monday. I went for mail on Monday, for warmth and intimation. She wanted the last four days in detail. I told her nothing changed. I was a hundred bucks up, maybe a hundred ten, on my great big, huge, fifty foot boat.

"What's for dinner?" She leaned over her desk, with feeling, with an intent I hadn't felt from a woman in way too long.

"What do you want?"

"I want it simple. At your place."

"I'll make rice."

"Yes. I'm off at five. I'll just come over."

I drifted home, amazed, she was so easy, so pleasant, so balmy after the scorch and slap of a long day's sail.

Jack was right there with counseling, focused on extra kinky, what women need after forty, you know, like coffee in the morning, especially her, he could tell. She needed the time last week because she just fucked her ex-husband black and blue, got down on ream outs, blow jobs, hum jobs, plate jobs, you name it—swallowing, hocking on the wall, who cared? I had wondered if such could be, and I practiced further repression.

Yet Monday I knew Jack was wrong; she may have slept with the recent husband but she hadn't done him up. It didn't matter anyway, but I felt better, more developed as a human being, less jealous, and relieved. She showed up at five and suggested making love now, then relaxing over dinner.

I fantasized saying no, like guys in the movies sometimes do. I said, "Sure. Might as well. It's a shame to hurry a good meal."

We walked to the bedroom, undressed and looked at each other's bodies. She lay down on the bed and spread her legs. I kissed her once between the breasts, and she pulled me aboard. In...out, in, out, in, out, in, out, in—hold there, then inoutinoutinoutinout. Whiz whiz whiz, whimper whimper, fini.

"That was nice," she said.

"Not much of it," I said.

"What did you think?" she said.

"I thought, 'God, I love pussy,'" I said.

She sat up, got up. "Let's have dinner now." She looked pissed off. But what could she expect? It was five ten in the afternoon, hardly happy hour, and she wanted romance, drinks, dinner, dancing, moonlight and all, in three minutes.

"Hey, relax. We'll try again after dinner."

"We'll see." She postured, hooking up her stayed dacron bra. I pulled her back down but she got back up, hungry now.

She'd brought a six-pack from the office, Acme Cola, and had a quick one on the rocks with spirulina. She held her nose and still cringed with the parrot shit look and smell of the stuff and said she was learning all about good health since being out on her own.

I made Dagwoods from leftover charter lunch and served it on the lanai, where she could watch the bay and hear the surf. She said, "God. I love the water." I sat with my back to it.

After dinner was a quiet, reflective, hormonal time, time for another fuck, with a few intimacies this time and many more in, outs. She came with a flutter, ghostly as gossamer in a breeze, and afterward she counted climaxes. Two was average, three common, six the record.

She'd had sex with five men in her life not counting the husband. Four were in the last six months, since independence. She fucked one guy in high school, before marriage. She got pissed all over again when I asked if she maybe should ought to count fingerfucking too, maybe three for one fuck, or something.

"Why do you have to talk like that?"

"I'm sick and insensitive. Forgive me." She reached down slowly and clamped her cool fingers around my limp dick. "It'll be a few minutes, dear." And we waited. She was gone by ten, after what seemed like a very long date. Jack and Louise came home soon after and asked how it was.

"Good."

"Did she swallow or spit it out?" Louise waited too, curious.

"It wasn't like that."

"Like what? You didn't even get a blow job?"

"Hey. This is my new girlfriend we're talking about."

"So? I give Jack blow jobs," Louise said.

"Yeah," Jack said. "You want us to think you're getting hooked up with a bitch who won't give you a blow job?" "Take a break. Don't think for a few days."

"What was good about it?" Jack asked.

"The smell."

"Yeah? What'd it smell like?"

"I didn't say it smelled good. It doesn't stink. But I meant her smell. She smells right." I turned to Louise. "Good fit too. You know, some feel better. Pretty horny but pleasant too. I like her. If she was still here I'd want to fuck her again. How about that."

"So where is she?"

"I'm tired. We got twelve again tomorrow."

Jack turned on the late movie, peeled off two beers, plopped on the couch and said, "So the bitch smelled good. I never even thought of that."

"I think one man here could fall in love," Louise said, walking into her room and closing the door.

"She was a great fuck and I'm ready for that, a good fuck and some good company. But she was old, too old."

"Too old for what?" But the movie came on. Jack dozed off quick. Fred McMurray tried to fuck Doris Day for an hour and got nothing but farther away from it, and I woke up to test patterns, heavy trades and Jack's snoring on the couch. He went to bed with a good hour and a half before yachting time again.

At mail call next day my new date was pleasant but distant. I asked what was up for dinner. She said she didn't feel well, cramps. So six beers, nine hours of TV and sleep and five hours of questions, answers, sun and wind later I checked again. She was beat.

"Why so tired?"

She forced a small laugh. "Too much to drink."

"You drank your dinner?"

The small laugh strained. "I guess you could say that."

"I though it was you and Acme Cola."

The laugh petered out. "Hardly any sleep."

I stared at the letter from Nuel's bank, reading the return address over and over, waiting.

"Jesus," she said. "What do you want? A blow-by-blow description? I had a date."

I understood. After all, it wasn't like we were tight. But it was shit. "Did you get anywhere near the record?"

She breathed deep. Outside, a short, stubby fellow in tight trunks and a polack T-shirt rode up on a motor scooter. His thighs chafed, thick. His shoulders and back were bushy.

"Some women like that."

"You're on the wrong track, Mister," she said. The squat fellow was inside in three steps, and the introduction made his identity clear—

she introduced him and me and looked down. Squat also knew the score: me on Monday, Squat Tuesday.

Blow-by-blow would surface later, on request; Renette and Squat went at the record all night, but squat's fetish was squirting his hot snot on her chest. What's a girl to do? She sat on the edge of the bed, he stood. She "aroused" him until the last moment, when he, you know... I knew, pressed on, because nature is sometimes perverse, causing males of the human species to strain for more detail in the sexual exploits of their mates with other males. So I didn't believe the part about the last moment—she said it was the truth, honest to God, and then he smeared it around with his dick—"You want more?" She cured me, and the record was still, she felt, within my grasp. "But later. Please?"

I slammed a beer, sipped a tumbler of wine. Jack rolled over on the sofa, half awake. "That bitch fucking around?" Jack could have been psychic; I thought him tedious—tedious and cynical; she was a bitch, therefore she fucked around; cynical and right.

I drank deep, for relief, for removal to somewhere else, express. I belched like a low rent slob and felt old. "No," I said. "She wasn't fucking around. No more than usual."

She came around at five fifteen. "Where's Martin?" she asked at the door.

I listened. Jack said, "Not here."

"Where is he?"

"How the fuck do I know?"

She called at ten to say she didn't like Jack's attitude, "Can I come over?"

"No. Me either. He's a rude sonofabitch. Yes."

 Kona

Fortunes change like the weather in the charter trade. Hard knocks on the high seas with none of the good changed quick as winter into spring. The older woman took to penance like a slut marrying rich.

Martin forgive me, for I have sinned. Squat was a teacher, that was all, and no more, a liberator, slashing her inhibitions. Squat had loved her. She loved hair on a man. Absolution was physical, because "it was you," she said, "who made me feel like never before."

I beat the beast, jealousy. Through acceptance came insight. What was simple friction after all? She was married twenty-five years. What about Walter? Tall, dark and handsome—roughly four thousand fucks. And sucks? It must have been what? Maybe two zillion in, outs. I gave it up, sooner than the flesh gives up itself. Events are history as they occur, dust; she was mine. Jack said that besides all that history and future stuff, it's very difficult to wear a pussy out. He was primitive and practical. And so too was Renette, bumpkin charmer, who now called herself my property.

She ditched Squat and showed her love the way a country girl does, clinging in public, stroking my hair, staring goo-goo as a country lyric. It seemed to me an odd match, yet I craved the two syllables of my new love: in, out. And the attention I wallowed in now was all new too. I had something to feel good about, something to look forward to, to look back with and compare. I called my ex-wife, who always thought of me as a charming failure—it was that good.

Her new boyfriend, Brandt, answered with bilious joviality. Brandt made money, in the city. He said, "Hey! Hey guy! How's your Tuesday? Super, I hope. Gee it's good to hear from you—what kind of craziness you got going on now? Here. Here's Frannie."

"Martin."

"Francis." I only called to say hello, nothing new, really, business is good, yes, warm and sunny, yachting every day, and my new date was something, lovely with nary a wrinkle, stretch nor dimple, and she blew me away with attention. Everything paled in comparison—kind of like life with a messy roommate compared to a love affair.

Fran said she was happy for me, at last.

I said, "We're watching TV and she's rubbing my shoulders." Fran never would. "She whispers, 'You only hang around with me because I rub your shoulders.' I said, 'Oh yeah? And what keeps you hanging around?' She says, 'Because you let me.' It's like that. I like it."

"You would. It's sick."

"Probably. But she got flowers, dinner and drugs that night, and I ate her until she came twice." I could tell Fran was impressed—she was rarely speechless. And what harm a white lie—Renette got a flower picked outside, a joint and a two minute cunnilingus. But she was so appreciative, far more than Fran ever was.

Fran said thanks for the call, maybe next time I'd have something to say. "Ciao."

"Aloha." I watched the bay, glad I was in the tropics, wondering if tastes would change in ten years, wondering why I wondered, and if the reason was love.

Sex with Renette was simple chemistry and brought me back stronger than I'd ever been back. She drew me in, whirled my cares away, spoiled me. She lay beside me, after, rubbing my temples. "I know women are attracted to you," she said.

"You worry. I never had it all that good."

"I can understand a man like you unmarried. But I can't believe you don't have a girlfriend." I watched the ceiling, feeling the ambient smell change, smelling pressure. "Do you have another girlfriend?"

"No Renette. I don't have another girlfriend."

"How many women have you had?"

"Who's counting?"

"How many?"

"It's a stupid question."

"Why? I told you how many men I've been with."

"It's stupid because I got laid the first time over twenty years ago. So you figure maybe one new lay a month, which isn't all that many for someone as available as me—I don't mean I was that available, not like Jack, I mean... what do you get? Two fifty?"

"Two hundred fifty women?"

"Nah! I bet it wasn't half that."

"A hundred twenty-five women!"

"Yeah. That sounds about right."

She sat up. "Jesus Christ."

"Yeah, so what was big Walt? Gunga Din? You fucked that guy black-and-blue, probably chapped his noodle. That doesn't count? What? Probably about four thousand fucks there. You fucked more than me, lady."

"A hundred twenty-five women?"

"Why do you press me on this?" She lay back, waited one minute— mood change—reached over and got me up for another go. She apologized with feeling, gave me new insight to simple pleasure, let me know I'd never had it so good.

Good fortune came to Jack too. Despite his trash talk, the odd stew or wayward wife, boat pickings were scant. And he asked the women on board if they wanted to you know what, because he never got more than he asked for, but his partners in the love act were fat, loud or whacky. Jack used beer and low light to dull the edge. Hard times was two six-packs, pitch-dark.

First week in January, seven normals sought adventure. Six were three couples from Canada who asked if lunch cost extra and could they get a rebate if they didn't eat? "You know, eh, rebate?" They complained. They could have brought their own sodas and saved a few bucks, eh?

I bet it's expensive, eh? I bet it's deep, eh? You get to do this every day, eh? The seventh passenger aboard, abnormally twenty-two, five nine, dark hair, big eyes, svelte physique, smooth skin, poignant breasts, small ass, no wrinkles, no dimples, was perfect. Sent from above, travelling alone, having a fair time except for some loneliness, she honestly just hoped to sit down with somebody nice over a bottle of wine. She laughed openly and said she was horny too, she couldn't help it, and a little cocaine wouldn't be too bad.

Jack twitched. He slammed back two and breathed deep, uncertain where to start. Animus sexualis, object of premature ejaculation, she swept him away, drove him quick to fidgets.

The charter adventure wound up forty-five minutes early that day. The Canucks complained. They were told... "Get in the goddamn dinghy." Jack was pissed and hurried. They obeyed.

He pleaded, please, find Herbert for some snoot and fetch a couple three bottles of wine too. I obeyed. Jack went back out to *Whirlaway*, and an hour later hit the beach again for his party pack, his grin stuck on his face like a death mask. He jumped out, swung the dinghy back out, grabbed the party pack without stopping or timing the set and pushed back out, into the top of it, yelling over the surf. "Tell Louise I got a leaky stuffing box out here! I might be all night! Call the..." His voice drowned under the breakers and screaming little outboard as he turned around, man with emission.

I told Louise that Jack might not be home tonight because he might stay on board. Louise asked why with a tremor. "He says he has a leaky stuffing box." Louise put away her groceries and then fixed dinner. She rarely cooked because she didn't know how. So sashimi platter with seafood chowder was a fete. She cooked quietly, poured the special champagne she and Jack had saved, set the table with linen and crystal and served, and we ate in silence. I realized deep fondness for Louise, in silence. And maybe it was only honor among thieves, but I drew the line at lying for Jack.

She looked up slowly, reflectively, harking back on her sexual past. Her first boyfriend liked eating her until the cows came home, and once they came home, he liked burying his face and staying down there. Once he cried down there. She gave her opinion on penile shapes and her amazement at so many crooks to the left. She assessed Jack, sexually, and said she knew you couldn't get everything you needed. And she shared her sometime fantasy of what she would try with me, if the occasion came up. She said it would most likely be conventional, you know, just for fun. I watched my bubbly play out, sharing her struggle with acceptance and control.

She went to her room, left the door open. I downed the flat champagne. It tasted like I imagined sex with Louise would be, tart and tingling but incomplete, like drinking for the hell of it, or to get drunk. I imagined Louise in the down and dirty and thought no, she was right, on her back, legs spread would be best for her and me, because it was Jack Witte we most wanted to fuck. For truth tampering, for leading the way over the edge of the waterfall to nowhere. Louise and I shared a bad dream of a place where falling didn't end no matter how fast the bottom came at us, and maybe we shared the intimate understanding too, that we were where we were because we'd both followed Jack Witte. I wanted to fuck Louise, but then again I really didn't want to, but then again I did, and I knew instantly where that round robin would lead to given half a minute.

So I left for Renette's, where a man could smoke a joint and forget his care and woe over some prime time TV, vigorous fucking with his girlfriend and sound sleep. Ten hours later, just after dawn, Jack rode the dinghy in slow, over water reflecting his placid calm. Eight normals were due in an hour. He beached it.

"Is she aboard?"

"Unbelievable. Beautiful. Hard body. Flawless... Snatch... Tits..." Jack Witte shaped invisible beauty, snatch and tits, in the air with his hands, went dumb while his tongue floated to the memory, hovered in the ether of pure contact, hardly soul to soul but at the highest plane he had reached in this go-round. Reflecting as if on a talk with God, lighting a smoke like it was life itself, his stubby face and haggard eyes softened on the exhale, in the cloud, under the halo.

The sun stuck its first ember through the horizon. He watched it, breathing deep.

"Where is she?"

"Swallowed it. Said it was too hard to come by to waste it. She was wild."

"Where is she?"

Jack watched the horizon. "You remember when you first started getting pussy how sometimes you'd wake up and open your eyes and wish she'd split two hours ago?"

"Yeah."

"That happened to her." He grinned again. "I'm the oldest guy she ever had."

"Where is she?"

"She swam in. I think a couple hours ago. God. It was unbelievable."

So it was, that Jack found truth, saw the light, left the prairie for the mountaintop. That night at dinner he announced his love for Louise, his intention to marry her, whatever it fucking took. Louise cried, a restrained, choking sob. She went to her room again and shut the door. "What's wrong with the bitch now?" But she came back, angelic, for a hug. The woman was a paragon of understanding, or at least of tolerance.

However difficult, her chart had come to pass.

And in a run of three, good fortune came again next day on the phone—a big time tour director wanted *Whirlaway* for a five-day private charter. Jack repeated: "Five-day private, starting Monday?"

I punched the numbers: eight hours a day, two hundred per, five days. I whispered, "Ten grand."

Jack said, "Hold the line please I'll check the manifests." Phone at his belly, he said, "Off the beach. Wailea."

"Travel time. An hour each way."

"Too much."

"Okay. An hour round trip."

Jack raised the phone. "That's ten thousand and travel time, five days, another...twenty-five hundred, oh hell, call it twelve fifty... Yes... Very good." He snapped his fingers for paper and pen, wrote the credit number, said aloha and it was done, eleven grand in five days, new moods in five seconds. Gone was resignation and despair. Hot coals became the cool green grass of home. Joined in the spirit, in strength, resolve and perseverance, we felt wealth approach. Jack called Herbert, and in an hour we felt nothing but numbed faces, running our motor mouths.

Herbert knew the bottoms, breaks and outcropping at Wailea, so he came along. Day one passed at anchor just off the beach in twenty feet of water, fronting the deluxe villas where the execs enclaved, and where the Chairman of the Board and Mrs. Chairman held court. Himself's personal man and herself's personal woman kept radio contact via walkie-talkie. Each movement, itch, urge was on the air. First came arrival and unpacking. No one cared to yacht, but it was good to know a yacht was out front.

Day two held too few hours for orientation and executive interfacing, but it was good to look out and see a yacht waiting.

Day three Herbert brought a gram. Himself's man said, "He's coming out of the bathroom now. He mentioned brunch in the restaurant, but he wants a newspaper too, and he said he wanted to get it himself. He's expecting her to meet him in twenty minutes at the main ballroom, over."

Herself's woman said, "She went down to the ballroom early to check the flower arrangement. I think she plans to meet him there in twenty minutes, but not if he goes for brunch first—oh oh—she's walking across the lawn toward the spa, over.

Herbert said, "Ccchhh... We got one lost bloody Mary at pool, no can find drinker, over."

The fourth morning herself's woman called and said herself would be yachting at two, or two thirty. Jack dinghied in and picked herself up, along with himself's son and the son's girlfriend, who had a perfect wax job and didn't look too bright but knew enough arithmetic to hang on to the heir apparent and feign independence. The snorkel adventure ground was empty that hour and looked good, like before a daily fleet made it look like the Safeway parking lot. The threesome snorkeled, then came back aboard ready to yacht home.

The next morning herself's woman buzzed up and said herself had recommended yachting to the other wives, so all forty of them would be yachting that day. After four days on the hook, six cases of beer and three grams of snoot, the down and outers were down deep, splayed out. Still it was only two trips. The wives were depressing, every one plump, pale, pasty, with a few grand in diamonds and gold, shrieking bloody murder for every wave because it became the thing to do. But they responded to discipline.

After pasting their faces, packing their swimsuits, coiffing their coifs and arranging their tits, they came late. The one o'clock group finally got off at two. The three o'clock group got off at four fifteen and barely made the beach before twilight, between dark and rising breakers.

The wives got tipsy, screamed, giggled and flirted with the sailors. The sailors told them they were something else. The wives got serious to say good service, good yacht, good fellows. And with no complaints, it was eleven, two fifty in the bag—two month's closer to current status on mortgage and rent, and tomorrow was the first.

Renette and Louise waited on the beach then for the party cruise home, five miles across the bay. So it was up anchor and homeward, chop-chop into the breakers and nightfall.

But *Whirlaway* rode easy over two big swells and quit, lost way and drifted in. Jack yelled for the anchor. Herbert stumbled and kicked it over again. Once hooked, she rocked powerless, dragging slowly in the surge on too little scope. Jack was beat from dinghy drill all day and drunk. Herbert was more drunk. I went quick, the way I sometimes hoped I would go, into the darkening chop for a look see, into dinner hour for reef sharks, early evening in shallow water.

A five gallon bucket of concrete tethered to a float had moored a little boat, but now the float was gone, and the tether waited straight up for *Whirlaway's* prop to grab, wrapping itself tight around the shaft.

After a minute, looking and feeling, I came up for the knife, choking. Cocaine, beer, reefer, sun and no exercise gained new meaning, there in the clutch, growing old. I breathed deep twice and dove again.

The prop wraps cut easy, and the four foot rope was only eight inches by the second dive, wedged tight between the prop and bearing. I breathed deep again, over the saltwater rasp in my lungs. The knife was too big, so I dove with the razor blade. One hand gripped the shaft, steady in the surge, the other cut. Down to thirty seconds per dive, then twenty, I stopped, bearing still jammed.

Incoherent, Herbert stripped down, took the blade, staggered and fell in. At three minutes I dove to save him but got sent back up. Herbert came up thirty seconds later. "We go."

A breaker rolled over the bow. Jack cranked the engine and leaned on the throttle to three thousand rpm. *Whirlaway* needed eight feet to float. With ten feet beneath us, the shaft squealed. Jack leaned on the throttle to thirty-five hundred rpm, eased up, and leaned again. *Whirlaway* made way as engine heat soared, threatening overheating, but every yard gained allowed a foot more scope, and better grab for the anchor, and seized pistons are better than a beached boat. She swam out. In a minute, in twenty feet again with two anchors ready, the shaft ate the few strands inside the bearing and spun easy. Jack eased the throttle. Another minute of running, waiting, listening, and Herbert opened more wine, cranked the tunes. Jack yelled down for more snoot. I shivered madly, then followed my colleague's directive on more wine, more snoot.

Renette, still new to the rule of the sea, wrapped a blanket around me. "You're a fool, Martin," she said.

"Yes. But I'm rich."

A common key to greater profit in the cocaine trade is dilution. By adding white powder that costs twenty dollars a pound and has neutral taste, smell and effect, to white powder that costs twenty thousand a pound and feels like Hannibal crossing the Alps, a dealer can double his yield. But he must take care against greed.

Herbert used a blend popular for its subtlety—unlike speed, it caused no twitch, unlike acetone, it didn't burn. He used manitol, baby laxative that makes adults fart and shit too, but they don't care, crossing the Alps on elephants.

So the unshakable shakes that night were joined by the unstoppable shits. I ran a hundred-five by nine, and I ran back and forth from Renette's bathroom to her blankets, all piled above her heating pad.

When the fever melted in sweat, she rubbed me with alcohol. Too soon, it rose again by morning. With innards wrung tight, I lay in delirium.

She hovered nearby, a visage surrounded by delirium, describing her famous pot roast. She spoke condolence, that I would soon miss as well her famous hamburger soup. The vision changed, balled up like tripe. Grotesque in laughter it said, "I guess a hot dog omelette would be out of the question."

A day of sweat and fever eased at last to dull pain, no sound but the wind. Sitting up as if in a dream, I saw a woman and a baby out the window, just across the road. A man beside them looked up with them in admiration of the clouds. The man looked like a beta normal, good for forty grand a year if he kept at it, worked up to it. He could vacation two weeks a year, watch the clouds on late afternoons. The woman looked pleased with prospects.

I lay back down gently, wondering where to run to, falling deep asleep.

Jack came by near dusk to say it didn't look bad, only fifteen knots. A surf shop boy was set to work my deck slot on tomorrow's charter. I sat up, lay back and slept again till midnight, woke up sudden. Renette wiped my face. Eight pounds down in two days, I still fevered at one oh one, couldn't walk, but shuffled and leaned to the bathroom for another pound of purge. I'd felt worse—once on bad acid, once in the Molokai Channel. I slept again with a weak and bitter laugh when Renette said, "You've bottomed out."

Another sixteen hours sleep ended when Jack telephoned again to say it still didn't look too bad, but it was up to twenty, gusting twenty-five.

"What's so bad about twenty-five?"

"Look outside Harry." Through the groggy funk I saw palm trees leaning the wrong way, wind from the south.

Forty-knot trades didn't hurt because tradewinds hit the isthmus first, no fetch. Kona blows southerly, starts way below the equator in tropical depression, launched north like an uppercut to the chin. Seven thousand miles of wind builds waves of consequence, walls of ocean thundering down. Moored boats must run, because inch thick lines with 54,000 pound test won't hold.

"Where are you?"

"Watching it."

"How she rides?"

"Easy as pie. Swells about six feet at the mooring but not breaking. Weather service says no sweat, it won't get any bigger. It's veering off already."

"I'm not worth much."

"Less than usual?"

"Get Herbert and Masao."

"I can't find them. We'd never get the dinghy out anyway—six foot break at the beach. We'd have to swim out with flippers."

"What do you think?"

"What do you think, Martin?"

"I think the bitch'll kill us one of these days."

"I think I'm getting what you had. Did you start with a fever?"

"I think I'm glad we got insurance on Nuel's boat."

"I think that's what I think. I got a hundred two fever. Did you get the shits?"

"Not too bad. Why?"

"I'm going to hang out down here. It's picking up."

"So what the hell can you do if it picks up?"

"I don't know."

"I'm coming down."

"Good."

Renette looked troubled but didn't call me a fool. Jack waited in the bar overlooking the beach and *Whirlaway*. He looked stuck again grinning, this time like Wiley Coyote in the moment of truth, just before the anvil falls on his head, or the Mack truck creams him in the face, or he falls off the cliff with a whistle fading to a poof far below—he looked ready for it too.

He laughed, "Up to forty. You can see the rudder at the tops of the swells."

Outside *Whirlaway* rode gracefully in the building sea, her light weight rising easy up the faces, gliding down the backsides. She loped over the top of the set, sliced through the rest. The down and outers drank margaritas and broke an easy sweat.

In an hour, storm dusk thickened, gray and muddy brown. The wind blew forty-five, gusting fifty with a sickening howl. A black on gray silhouette in a buck and a gallop soon lost delineation. The imaginable was nauseating. We went separate ways home after trading assurance that boats are no less an illusion than life itself, even at a quarter-mil; that a few buckets of resin, a few spools of wire could be cold molded and strung up again tomorrow sure as day follows night.

I got home beat. Fatigue heightened when Renette sounded hurt, when I whimpered at her famous Portagee sausage pie. She'd made it just for me. It was special—her grandfather's very favorite dish in the whole wide world. Grandaddy lived to ninety-six, so it must be kind of like health food. I went to bed, ready to check out sixty years early, fuck the pie. She followed with more tales of Grandaddy. It was actually a close call on what exactly was his very most favorite—he was nuts for cheddar cheese melted over bacon—yes, and God, he really went wild for soft-boiled eggs over baby-back ribs. Her body relaxed on pleasant memory, and she breathed softly into a dainty snore.

I played the wind, rode hard at the mooring, cringing when gusts rattled the little house.

Kona winds hit sixty at first light, and in a forty minute fury the wind swung slowly west, the death direction. It climbed steadily to seventy with a turbine scream that left no doubt. Jack's call at six was anticlimactic. He said, "It's all over."

"On the beach?"

"In front of the surf shop."

"You at home?"

"Yeah."

"I'll meet you down there."

"Okay."

"Jack?"

"Yeah."

"You had coffee yet?"

"No."

"I'll pick some up."

"Great. I'll get the fucking donuts."

"I'm leaving now."

Downed power lines, trees, fronds, trash and wreckage lined the road. Ugly grays overhead swirled red in the bloodlet sky. *Whirlaway* lay high and dry, seven tons of thoroughbred, down.

Fifteen foot waves broke at the mooring.

Two hundred deathwatch normals lined the beach. *Whirlaway* had missed the near reef by a few feet, and she'd missed a half dozen rocks now uncovered on either side of her as well. She rose three feet when the waves washed under her, as though trying in vain to stand. Then she lay gently back down in the sand.

She lay there lame, the end of all we had to give—leaning into seventy knots, Jack yelled, "What do you think?"

"I think we should shoot her in the head."

"Me too. I can't tell without going aboard, but I think she's undamaged. No shit. If we can get aboard, we can sink her easy."

"Pull out the knotmeter plug?"

He nodded. "That'll do it. She'll fill up in an hour."

Another head butted in—Herbert. "I save *Whirlaway*," he yelled.

"We want sink *Whirlaway*."

He shrugged. "Okay. I sink *Whirlaway*."

I vetoed. "Night time maybe. We got two hundred witnesses here."

Whirlaway wallowed, her big stick banging between two palms, her keel digging in like the hind legs of a poorly shot beast. She writhed, down but undead.

I said, "I call insurance man." We broke, Jack and Herbert striding to the maelstrom to mount the beast, careful, since she rose gently, fell down quick as a seven ton cleaver.

I called the adjuster, who would be down immediately after brunch. It sounded like a total loss, which sounded sweetly, faintly, good. The wind too said everything must go. The surf pounded agreement.

Jack rummaged the lazarets for spare line. Herbert danced down the high rail, balancing on the surge and lift. Sliding down the foredeck to the roller reefed headsail he cut lines from it and tied them quick—lines of half-inch nylon, three strand braid at a dollar ten a foot we drove fifteen miles to pay cash for and fifteen miles back and then spent another two hours on, fitting them just right. *Whirlaway* rose and fell, bucking in her death throes.

Herbert hurled a line from the bow but the bow swung out—the line was too short for a wrap on a palm tree. He danced back, cut the main sheet, no doubt on how much or when again. Or maybe he saw another day, another drive down the road for one new mainsheet for two haole bruddah in charter business. Jack watched, stuck on prospects for another hundred bucks for new sheets. Herbert hurled it, secured a stern line and hurled it too.

The wind hit *Whirlaway* on a surge like a shotgun, recoil at seventy-five—slammed her to the sand with a sickening crunch. Jack and Herbert hit the deck hard—Jack grabbed the compass binnacle and cracked his head on a base bolt. Herbert grabbed his leg and yelled, "Hoi!" A dozen deathwatching normals ran down to the shallow bluff cut yesterday by the surf, where they folded their arms and leaned forward for a closer look.

I yelled, pulled on the stern line, took a wrap around a palm tree, and three watchers lent a hand, leaning into it, gaining three feet. Another four watchers joined in and gained six feet. Gaining three feet on the stern, she eased out of the surge, gently rolled, ready to moan.

Herbert went below. Jack stepped off the low rail to the sand and staggered up, sat down against a wall. I yelled that he looked like Cowboy Bob Ellis after losing to Dick the Bruiser—Jack's head seeped like a soft tomato. "He always bled bad when he lost too!" Jack closed his eyes and passed out.

Heart thumping double-time, I stood up wondering what comes next if you don't die. The thousand-eyed minion watched and waited. I turned around to Duane Crawly, fake laughing in the wind, "Ha!... Stupid fuck... All the way... Good!... Stupid fuck!... Ha! Ha! Ha!"

The crowd thinned quick, fell away in layers down to two, adrenaline and me. I didn't want to hurt Duane Crawly, only to cancel his existence. Duane Crawly was thicker, and a thick man wonders when a thin man who looks half dead from drastic weight loss through his asshole sprints in with an elbow to the sternum, a flat-handed nose smash, a knee in the nuts, another in the head. I stepped back for room, for the extra point, dropkick to the gut, no blitz, but Jack stepped up. "Come on. We got another dog to fuck."

Duane Crawly rolled over, got up, left without laughing.

Jack said, "Hey. You just beat up Duane Crawly."

"I don't feel so good."

And from under the blood caked on his face, Jack said, "I got the donuts."

"Jelly kind?"

The insurance adjuster arrived in time for donuts and coffee on the beach. He walked fore to aft and back, checked the bow line and stern line and the swing of the mast between the trees. He said, "Excellent work, men, securing a vessel. The company likes to see that before paying a claim." He wore a red jump suit and carried a clipboard and from the neck up, with his white hair and waxed moustache looked like the Chance man in Monopoly. He dealt cards all around: Sam Snole, Marine Survey, bonded, Adjuster and Claims Rep. He wanted to know: Who went below deck? Was she damaged in any way? Taking water?

Herbert looked at me, then at Jack, then at Sam Snole. "She tight like young you know what. I close hatches."

Sam Snole looked west and south. "We can pull her off."

Soggy donuts tasted like the future. The kona eased to fifty, in another hour to forty. The tow boat couldn't start until the storm stopped and six more boats got pulled off—they called first. Jack babysat the day. A thousand normals watched.

The kona dropped to twenty-five after dark, and the normals went home. Near ten I came for the night, and Herbert showed up drunk with a fresh wine jug near ten fifteen. So we drank wine and watched the tide come in. The mast beat harder against the palms when *Whirlaway* surged harder on the bigger breaking swells. By eleven the beating destroyed the forestay. Jack figured a new one at about a grand. He figured twenty for a new mast when it pounded hard enough to shake the tree. Herbert shuffled off in the dark. He came back with the chain saw he kept in his truck just in case. "I fix mast."

He cut the tree—it smashed one spreader coming down but missed the hull by two feet, easy. The mast beat no more. It swung easy on the surge, until a man holding his chest ran up, yelling for help—a ski dock fragment, eighty square feet of 2 x 4s, decking and nails cart-wheeled this way down the beach. Herbert hove to.

Bluffside again in baggy boxers and shaggy robes, the normals talked. The fragment would smash *Whirlaway* on the bow—no bet. The new line was on Herbert. He held the flotsam toe to toe, knee-deep, but lost way, steadily, then quickly. He yelled for rope and lost more tying the line and more still jumping up for a wrap on a tree.

Jack yelled, "Pull, cocksuckers!" Gripping life at last, the normals heave-hoed. The flotsam stopped. More normals came down, complaining they couldn't sleep, too much racket. Jack yelled, "Pull the fucking rope!" They pulled, also happy, and the flotsam went high and dry.

A normal popped a brandy, party underway. Jack said, "Yeah. Some fun." Herbert drank big. One normal said a boat like *Whirlaway* was only fiberglass and steel cable and fully insured and not worth risking a life. Herbert asked, "What risk is? What *Whirlaway* is? Anyhow, I no sleep tonight." He passed out in the surf shop ten minutes later, pau hana, all done.

I stayed up with it, one to dawn, dozing off, wakened twice by looters headed aboard for marine hardware. The first was drunk and staggered off, carefree as he'd arrived. The second was big and trouble. He swung a chain. I used a Hobie boom. The second left too, leaving me feeling big, until I turned to see Herbert, bigger still in back up, in shadows.

The morning was clear, sunny, breezeless. Three thousand normals lined the beach. The work boat rounded McGreggor Point. The glassy bay rolled flawless clean to a five foot break at the beach whomping thunder—too big for safe salvage. But the man for the job had twelve more boats to pull off, and the adjuster feared another front.

Whirlaway was dry inside and looked sound outside and on the bottom. She got turned in the sand, inch by inch, a pull on the bow, a pull on the stern. The surf stayed high. Advice surged from the normals. An hour before dark she was ready for the big pull.

Normals squeezed together shoulder to shoulder with their backs against her bottom—the work boat roared, the insurance man yelled "Push!" and *Whirlaway* budged another inch, seaward. Again, inch by inch, she struggled back toward the water—only the bravest normals stayed, backs to it, three feet deep.

She stood too soon on a three foot swell—it rolled under and down she went with a crunch. Time had come today. The Little Boat That Could billowed smoke, burned rings, leaned hard and the wounded bitch stood up—fell down, stood up, fell again, finally leaping onto a swell then crashing onto her keel as the wave receded. She fell down hard on her side with a crunch of hull and broken ribs. Again she rose, again she fell. And again, until the work boat yanked her one more stretch, and she came down liquid, swimming again.

Herbert yelled for the pumps but got drowned out in the roar of normal thousands. *Whirlaway* swam low, then lower, shipping water through a fractured hull, her pump plugged with sand. Below, floorboards underwater, Herbert pulled the boards up, yanked free the pump hose from the sandy bilge and cleared it. Then he found the manual handle and went like a piston.

Near dark the beach emptied. *Whirlaway* sat tied to a dock in the harbor across the bay looking dead and buried and disinterred, fresh from the grave. The down and outers sat in the cold, wet cabin in dim light and shadows scooping sand into little pails.

Chaos screamed in the silence.

All the winches were filled with sand. All the electronics were dead and gone, all the wiring ruined, all the rigging crimped, all the cabin covered with sand and sludge, and the port hull showed bones in a compound fracture.

Sam Snole shined a flashlight in our eyes then came below to say he was tired, it was late. So why not meet in the morning at ten for damage tally and logistics on a tow to Honolulu for haul out and repairs that were fully insured, less the five thousand dollar deductible of course.

"Stop!" I rambled low monotones over the saga of Nuel and Nuel's bank and how mortgage payments came from charter revenues. I recounted poverty, Sam, no energy, sorrow and confusion. I said it was plain to see how long a boatyard would take to repair a hull like this one, and *Whirlaway* will be in foreclosure in a month, much less eighteen months... "And me and my partner, Jackie here...we reached a happy point tonight, which is the bottom. We accept defeat. Death. But we believe, too. We believe life can get better. Most of it is still left to live too. Liberation, Sam. That's what we believe...all the best to Nuel, the bank, insurance company...Sam... We quit. It's like that."

Sam Snole had heard it before; boats. "Like I said," he said. "It's late. We're tired. Tomorrow morning. Ten."

# Dry Dock

Jack Witte and I lost our boat. Then losing our boat became another dream, and we lost it too, to another reality insisting over and over and over again: *This is no dream.*

We lost our minds, slowly at first. Then losing our minds became another dream, a soft and liquid dream that cushioned the bumps and left us feeling better than we looked, until we wished it wouldn't end, uncertain what it was.

Nervous breakdown was the phrase I heard my parents use in hushed tones, describing some poor fuck who couldn't hack it anymore. That was way back, in the time of Negroes and queers, a time of primitive essence, a time like now. So it was, to me, still a catchy phrase. Ner.vus-bray.k.down—a molting process, focused on nerve endings. The nerve endings swell up, fill big with emotion, until they crack open, spill out their juice or else make new, bigger shells; you die, or you grow.

It starts with pain, call it growing pain. So when the shell finally cracks, the soul itself seeps out. Then you win, in failure, the grand prize, which is no feeling at all. You win the gift of numbness.

All of a sudden you find yourself in drydock. Drydock—it doesn't matter what you call it, call it prison, call it a bad dream, call it worse—call it karma, call it destiny, call it what became of me, call it real and now, and horrific with no escape, no free will, no mind over matter because the matter is liquid, trickles through fingers, slams like bad surf, sucks like undertow. Pervasive as bad air, it fouls dreams too, so you get it here and now and then some.

Weems got two choices—come get Nuel's boat, down in value a bit, scratches in the paint.

"How much value has it lost?"

"You could fire-sale her for thirty grand, maybe."

"You showed appraisals at two ten."

"That was before. She got parked on the beach."

"Hold please." He palmed the talk end, leaving a clear signal—two stuffed shirts planning life for some down and outers. Weems came back jovial. "Hey, you fellows have really been through it. We know what you're up against. We're impressed by your ability to make payments. You get that boat fixed, and make more payments. How much time do you need?"

I figured eighteen months for the yard to fix it, two for Jack and me on a rush. "Five months. And we need a letter."

"Why a letter?"

"Because drydock eats shit. We work it, we need assurance, you know, something legal. That's your second choice. I guess you got other choices. You could work it. Or you might ask Nuel if he'll work it."

"I see... Alright, five months and a letter."

I hung up and shrugged, following Jack to the truck, feeling like the gravel underfoot, crunching like souls under pressure. The storm weather of two days ago was now down to breathless heat. We rode fifteen miles west in silence, me hanging out the window, for air, or life, or something. At the greasy luncheonette Sam Snole called convenient, we shuffled in, took a table with a view, sat and watched the water. Mabel brought coffee. I said, "We can get three months free, if we can fix it in two."

Jack sipped his coffee.

"I'd just as soon walk away, anywhere," I said. We let prospects of a run, anywhere, mix with fatigue and depression. "So? What do you want to do?"

"Does 'I don't give a fuck,' mean anything to you?" It was a brand new day with the same old question from Jack Witte.

"Let me think that over."

Sam ordered the special coming through the door, backed up and asked, "You guys want the special?"

"Yeah, I'll have a special," I said. Jack lit a smoke. "He doesn't give a fuck."

Sam nodded. Jack said, "Give me a goddamn special." Sam confirmed it, three specials. He sat down saying no insurance money for a boat in foreclosure.

"No sweat Sam. It's covered," I said. "The bank and us. Asshole buddies. We got a letter on the way."

"I see."

"What can you do on the five grand deductible?"

"What do you mean what can I do?"

"We don't have it. What can you do?"

"You got receivables? What about charter money coming in?"

Jack came to life. "We got payables. Big ones. We're insolvent."

"Don't worry about that now. Get your boat fixed."

"That's just what the bank said," I said. "But it's not our boat."

"Oh, it's your boat alright." And Sam gave his speech on marine liability with a reminder that guarantors of a mortgage note were on the hook, with further advice Whirlaway would best be fixed, if the true meaning of broke would be avoided.

"Can you front us some jack, Sam?" Jack asked. Sam slowed down, up close to the truth.

"We're down to credit cards and checks," I said.

"Maxed out, Sam," Jack said.

"Use credit cards and checks. I'll get you cash when I can." I didn't ask how in the hell because I liked Sam, who insisted on helping, if not trusting. Sam knew about boats and boat wrecks and once-wild-eyed boys now beat-to-shit stiffs in the charter trade.

Brunch was a gut bomb. Sam cleaned his plate in three minutes and said the tow was set for tomorrow. Easing up from business nose to nose, he recommended "an inexpensive little hotel" in Waikiki and sprung for the grunts. Jack doused a butt in his yolks over easy, and that was farewell. Sam left.

The fifteen silent miles back was followed by a silent day, scooping sand with hands, filling the fracture with underwater epoxy, patching and wondering why.

Last fucks were clinical, sleep comatose, sunrise a roller coaster— Pailolo and Molokai Channels at the end of a towline. Arrival twelve hours later, dark, was with a wish that Almighty Screaming Jesus had put her on the reef or the rocks, or thrown Herbert off before he cleared the pump—anything. Short of that, death seemed peaceful, serene. Sleep was deep again, waking involuntary.

Sam's inexpensive little hotel was The Tiki Driftsong, or some bullshit fa fa name. Jack called it Cellblock 9, because it was only nine dollars a night, no charge for dark green paint on cinderblock walls, fake shoji blinds over safety grates and once-a-month maid service. The maid was come and gone that month. On the bright side, Cellblock 9 had no rafters, only a low, blown ceiling. And the management knew Sam, so down and outers with a boat could stay indefinitely, no problem.

Dismantling began. With her backstay, forestay, babystay, upper and lower shrouds unfastened at the deck and hanging limp, Whirlaway looked like a hag in the morning. Sixty feet of mast lolled in the breeze until the crane plucked it free. We laid it on six oil drums, straight, kind of. Beheaded, Whirlaway got stripped to bare bones, buckets of cable, clevis and cotter pins.

A plan evolved, full of *Who cares?* and *Fuck its.* I called America for the exotic resins and glues and wood, ultralight. I found lay up men, painters, a mechanic, an electrician, a finish cabinet man. I got on the phone with the parts lists and drudged through it until my ear swelled up.

The good thing about Kewalo Basin Shipyard is the smell, no old tuna fermentation. The bad thing is the other fermentation, resin fumes, resin dust, paint fumes and paint dust. The blacktop amplifies the tropical sun and heats all the fumes and dusts to the perfect temperature for skin cling. The hot breeze mixes it all just right for breathing. And the gentle rustling palms are vague, burned shapes on the perimeter, swamped in the sandblasters' screaming staccato, upwind. Hot black cinders settled like endless dew on a day forever beginning.

Three days in the hulk yielded thirty-six hours times four hands scooping sand. Sam visited late, day three, to assess progress. I said it was high season now; at this rate Whirlaway would be back in service in time for the doldrums, Labor Day to Christmas, no normals, no charters, no money, foreclosure after all. "We need help, Sam. Two guys can't do it. Without help we lose two months of high season and three months of summer. We're in foreclosure without help, Sam."

Sam nodded and walked off, turned around and said, "Hey. Don't fuck up."

"No Sir, we won't. And don't you fuck up either."

Jack liked the lip. He sniggered. Sam took it walking away. Jack sat down. "Who does that cocksucker think he is?"

A tall man stooped under a cancerous hull next door. He stooped out and still stooped, out from under. With one arm crooked like a bulkhead he pointed a gnarly knuckle at Sam in the distance. "Don't push The Squire. He's good. He'll take care of you. Don't push him."

Jack said, "The Squire? I quit." He lit a smoke in the shade. I crawled back inside, back to the heat and shit that was life.

The day went slow as dull pain and by dark was forgotten. Jack held firm. He quit. I said good, I felt relieved, it was over at last. At the corner I traded my watch for a quart of tequila, and we drank it—a trial celebration.

But poisoned bodies and tired souls awash in tequila became different bodies and souls dead drunk. We became different people, slept the dreamless sleep and were awakened again by a relentless dawning. Then fatigue and poison and a brand-new day made rational thought seem like a faraway place. So we went without thinking, on instinct, like beaten dogs who still come home. The down and outers shuffled across the yard like troubled spirits, undead.

And it was another new day, the morning of Carry Lowe, all five-nine, hundred-ten pounds of him ambling bowlegged in knee sox and baggy shorts across the yard the other way. "Reporting for work, Sir. Sam sent me."

Jack groaned, "Get in there...scoop sand." Carry hopped to.

"I thought we quit."

"Fuck it." And it was no longer over.

Fuck that—I sat in the shade with a yard Danish and my mantra, "I quit. I quit. I quit..."

Jack said I couldn't quit, because I never worked in the first place, never learned about an honest day's work for an honest day's pay. "I'm not sure how I got hooked up with such a low-skilled individual in the first place, but one thing for certain is sooner or later you'll have to come to grips with work. Or you'll starve to death."

I engorged my yard Danish before it was too late, then lay in the shade with a hangover, a bellyache, Jack Witte's greed and lies.

Carry Lowe dug to the elbows in bilge scum, becoming the new and lowest form of life on the planet. Jack rose over Carry Lowe, barked orders, warning that it better be done right.

"Hey, Jack. Drop dead," I called from the shade.

Jack lit a smoke and stared, and two down and outers would have fought, to see who was more down, more out, whose fault it really was, who was right, who was wrong, but Jack clutched his chest instead, dropped his smoke with a grimace, a grin and a plea. The guy could make you laugh, any time, anywhere—that's what got us by, no fun, just plenty laughs. But Jack didn't laugh—he laid himself down. I called, "Is it the big one, Jack? Is it? Is it? Sonofabitch." I snoozed. Jack lay still.

We worked quiet that week, fourteen hours a day. Ten more hours of the day were killed in Cellblock 9, eating take-home yard sandwiches and Socco Soda on credit. Jack vented pressure on the rental car, heaving the emergency brake at thirty, then at forty when he got the hang of the skids, got used to the screech. I rode silent in back.

Carry wanted weekend work too, for the money, and Saturday night he wanted a ride to The Tiki Driftsong. He'd catch a bus home from there. Jack looked at him like he was nuts, nodded at the rental car and said, "Get in." I said the backseat was taken. Carry didn't flinch at the first light, when Jack lunged on the emergency brake. He laughed instead, and when the next light went yellow, he beat Jack, slamming the shifter into park at thirty-five.

The little rental car screeched, beat its park ratchet useless, spitting teeth in the skids, hocking the shifter back to neutral. The little car coasted to a stop, shuddering, breathing hard. Carry looked up grinning—nobody had nothing on him. At the next light, Jack one-upped the skinny galoot with a slam into reverse at forty and fish-tailed crazy in the center lane, out of control, stopping sideways. Traffic went around, and Jack and Carry were bonded. I asked Carry for a joint.

"You bet." He had a half-inch roach in his hip pocket and bonded with me too—I took it and got out. Carry giggled. Jack sped away, screeching and smoking down the road.

A man who looked fifty with graying hair walked by in torn pants, a ratty T-shirt and flip-flops. He looked me over and laughed. I lit the roach, breathed deep and savored the six miles back to Cellblock 9.

I got back at 9:30. Jack was asleep. I lay down, closed my eyes and eight hours later rose for the ride back to the yard. A new day began, just like the old one left off.

Carry was a talker from the beginning. The sludge and sand were gone. Jack cut out trashed cabinets. I wrenched water tanks and hoses. Carry worked the engine, removing the alternator, batteries and saltwater cooling system. He'd been a mechanic. "I got here four months ago from Texas. I had my own motorcycle shop and a hundred seven custom Harley Davidsons but my ex-wife got them on grounds of desertion. I got nothing, so where in the hell was I supposed to desert to?"

He'd been a male whore, managed by his girlfriend, a female whore. "She was fine, man, I mean fine. She'd go off for a week with these rich guys and come home with two, three grand and buy me all this neat shit, silk shirts and fancy pants. She bought me a new car.

She was real expensive man, and fine. She took care of me fine." She knew the ins and outs of whoring good enough to spot a niche, the sixty and older women market, right there in Lizard, Texas. Carry did fine, good money too.

Jack wanted to know how he could fuck some old bag in the first place, and how did he keep it up? "Oh, you can man. It don't have nothing to do with what you want. It's your job. But I'll tell you what, your best head in the world is old lady head. It's fine, man. You have a few drinks and need the money. You could do it." Carry could do it, but he was lost when he fell out with his girlfriend. He didn't know why they fell out, never thought about it. Carry was strong that way—all surface, everything on the table where you could see it. The guy got down, but never out. Or at least he didn't know it.

Carry worked bait slot for awhile after that for a rough bunch of friends, among whom he was thinnest and fairest and most attractive to homosexuals. "I lured these faggots home, you see, but my friends would be there and they'd roll the faggots. Faggots are rich, man. I believe you got to be rich to be a faggot. Used to be Jews, no offense. Now it's faggots." Carry reflected. "I mellowed out since then. I don't mind queers at all since then. I wondered if I was one when me and my friend fucked his old lady at the same time. I don't think I am though. I'd much rather have some pussy. I'm open-minded though. I think it's important to stay open-minded. I like to swap. I got a fine girlfriend now, if either of you do." Carry had six children, two by the same woman. Five lived in Texas. His second daughter lived with him and his girlfriend. He was only twenty-seven, so he didn't mind a little setback, losing everything, then losing his prospects too. He didn't mind his boatyard job, for awhile. But he was in the front office to quit the morning he got sent down to Whirlaway, so he decided to work it, because he liked the way it looked. "And you guys are okay."

"How did you know we were okay?" Jack challenged him.

"Shit, man. Anybody could look at you two and tell you were okay." Jack looked puzzled—faint praise. Carry fessed up, "Besides,

I want to go sailing with you guys once we get her all fixed." I said no sweat, Carry could break into yachting with a lovely cruise south, upwind in spring trades across the Molokai Channel. Happy as a bumpkin headed to town, Carry set aside his engine parts and cleaned the block, swabbing big grease spots with a rag, poking crannies with Q-tips. "Yard work wouldn't be bad with good boats to work on. They're mostly shit. Seven-fifty an hour's pretty rough too, especially when you guys get charged thirty-five..."

"Thirty-five!"

Carry stopped. "Yeah. You guys pay the yard thirty-five bucks an hour for me."

Jack computed quick—"That's... two hundred, fourteen hundred a week on a boat nigger!" He threw down his chisel. "Go call The Squire."

"What should I tell him, Jack?"

Jack sat down. "Tell him I quit."

"Right." I shuffled up to the phone, dialed The Squire and asked why thirty-five an hour for a seven-fifty man, when nobody knew how to pay the five grand deductible.

Sam said, "That's how. Call it an expense." The yard would get the five grand, through Carry. Sam set it up, loose. Don't press it.

I was embarrassed—I used to be hip to a hustle, before I went numb. "Thanks, Sam."

"Like I said, don't fuck up." Sam rang off.

Back at the hulk, Carry polished the block, prepped floorboards for stripping and oiling. "Well?" Jack asked.

"Slow down, Carry. This isn't a job. It's a position." I hit the shade. Jack lit a smoke, mumbled and chiseled. Carry slowed down and talked.

He was a welder, a sandblaster, a painter and a carpenter in the last four months, and once he panhandled a hundred twenty bucks in a day just to see if he could do it. He was tempted to continue, but panhandling had a limited future, and a father had an image to consider, a big picture to paint.

His was a color comic, where people spoke in talk bubbles and moved in quick thrusts, one frame to the next.

He paused, pulled a knee sock down and scratched his leg—wrapped in dragons, demons and filigree. He said one day they'd cover him, once he had the money his brother used to have, before the insurance company fucked him out of it.

Jack tore the vanity from the hull, pounding his chisel with his mallet and his mouth. Carry scrubbed and stripped teak, chattering away. I got up, wondering if the tequila was last night or the night before, knowing Jack was right—I was a no-skill man. I stooped and dipped steel parts in a bucket of muriatic acid to get the crud off, easy enough, until my lungs burned, but not that bad, until they closed up and I had to step back a minute. And stepping back was back into proper perspective, on buckets of acid, Carry's chatter, life itself, the long and the short of it, fucked, right before my eyes. The acid stung, let me shed easy tears, like some people do at sad movies, so past places, hustles and loves looked disjointed, blurred one frame to the next like Carry Lowe's, all lost on schemes and quick travel. Memorial to a hustler was all it was. Love was a distant land, never been.

I gripped a shackle, dug deep with the wire brush, ferreting rust and corrosion from deep in the threads. I remembered a woman—friend of a friend was how it went. I was twenty-three, immortal in New York; she was thirty-nine. Cocksure meets post prime, hormones arcing—Sure, she said, there's room on the couch. I never actually felt my New York lovers coming, she said that night, not like I can feel you. And later that night in a funky but chic cafe she said last night she swallowed it. She didn't like it. She choked. Her gay friend coached her, said open your throat. She wanted to try again. *Avec toi,* she said, like a playful romantic.

I stopped scrubbing. I wondered where she could possibly be now, and what would she want to try, pushing sixty, and how old a human being has to be before the dirt and shit and dicks in pussies make room for the caring for another soul. Was this me? Oh boy, big trouble on heavy simmer.

Carry scraped and chattered—his mother was a bad alky who brought strange men home. He'd fought his father, tooth and nail. Carry could read his comic aloud and deal with it.

I thought it nauseating, all of life, Carry's, mine, anyone's, just endless frames, disjointed, storyless, soiled, smudged, sickening and gone. Then I remembered the cardinal rule in the moment it was too late: Never look in a mirror on acid.

I reeled, puked, choked, gagged and fainted.

The view up from the mud and cinders was gray sky, smoke and dust. Jaundiced eyes looked down, yellowed by fumes, liquor, days on end. A voice bellowed, "Give him milk!"

Another said, "No! No milk! Water!"

Another insisted, "Fuck you! Water'll kill him. Give him air!"

And so on round the circle, until Jack said, "Give him some pussy."

And the circle broke up—"Haw! Haw! Haw!"—because I opened my eyes, back among the living.

I sat up, wiped my chin, breathed and croaked, "Man, this is the life." Jack smoked a cigarette and waited. I waited too, for coherence to maul me again.

Jack said, "Why don't you knock off, hit the Cellblock. Relax."

I agreed, with perspective. "We won't make it." Jack smoked. "It's got to change."

"What's to change?"

"I need rest. A couple hours. A joint." I sat there. I breathed. "We need a hotel. Air-conditioning. We need TV." Jack nodded. "Some guys make ninety grand a year, don't know what we know."

"Fucking-A."

"Guys used to die at thirty-five, forty, before AC and TV."

"I'm ready."

I struggled up, wobbled, decrepit. "This is shit."

"I've had it too."

"Want to quit?" Jack looked up at the hulk. "Fly out tonight?" Jack shrugged. I think maybe deep down inside, he liked it, or maybe still nurtured the fantasy that one day he would grow up and be a commodore, really. "Fuck it," I said. "Where would we go, without resources, without hope?" Jack turned, started back up the scaffold. "I'll take the car. How late you want to work?"

"Dark. We finish the whore or we'll never get out of here."

Toward the parking lot on rubber legs I remembered—no room phone at Cellblock 9, and the payphone in the hall was tied up with scum bags hunched low, looking both ways, like big deals going down. Glue sniffers, bums, whores, baggers and mentals—Cellblock 9, the Resort.

So I stopped in the yard store for a Socco Soda on credit and a free call. A new girl, big and local, Bastalani, worked the register. She looked nineteen and puffed up, inflated in the belly, the breasts, the arms, legs and ass—in the face and fingers too, full of many scoops sticky white rice and pig meat three times a day. She was shy, her sweet, sad eyes reflecting the futility of words.

She fit there in the yard. She needed work. She had tattoos, common on women in the tropics. But unlike the chic butterflies or arabesques the haole woman want for new identity, Bastalani's tattoos showed resignation, indifference and chaos, like the weather. Odd blotches and strokes down one forearm looked like a telephone doodle pad, fragments, swirls and dashes, initials and numbers idly scrawled elbow to wrist. The other forearm was clean, like she was saving it.

Bastalani hesitated on a smile. Not looking too good, dirty as dog shit, mud and cinders caked on the puke, sweated through and dried out, I shuffled to the cooler, shagged a Socco, stuck my head inside and crawled in. She laughed, knew that I knew. I came out—"When I was a kid I got a bath in the sink."

She looked down. "You like cold beer, call him Socco Soda?" A small whimper escaped from me, from deep inside, in twitching fluorescent light—she knew too, more than I ever would. Did I ever. She looked up like a fairy godmother: Here is the gift of life, cold beer on credit.

I shagged two six-packs and signed the chit for Socco Soda, touched her rough arm. "Thank you." She met me eye to eye and followed my smile with her own. "We need one good hotel, cheap."

"Ming Chu. Ala Moana," she said, dialing her cousin there for a room.

I ambled out with the gift of life, shuffled back to the hulk and called up, then tossed up a six-pack, and for the first time since going to hell, Jack smiled. He asked how, where, who? I said, "Sh..."

Driving to Cellblock 9 with a cold beer and then another, I marveled at simple pleasure, drank another on the edge of the bed, showered, drank two more and felt good heading out.

The Ming Chu sat short among the skyscrapers of Waikiki, clean as a tea ceremony, run by little guys who looked like Japanese Mafia—white suits, yellow ties. I checked in with the gas credit card and moved gear.

A different silence, that of reprieve, like the soft spot in a storm, settled in that night. With the AC on full bore, the big window open, TV on and a six-pack between us, the little room became an oasis on a vast and blistering desert.

I rummaged the sludge bag, found a *Whirlaway* T-shirt, XXL, hosed it down, rubbed the stains with deck cleaner, hung it up to dry and folded it neat. Jack said I might as well knock off another day. I said, "Love is a game of give and take, Jack," then took my offering to the fairy godmother, came back with two more six-packs. Jack learned the meaning of love.

Three weeks into it, the hulk was clean—down to bare bones, soaped and sponged, free of deck fittings, cabin gutted, port bulkhead and vanity gone. I called for funding. Sam came late and looked grim, first at the trash can full of empties, then at Bastalani busting out of her Whirlaway Charters T-shirt, its little spinnaker stretched across her melons.

Sam carried a clipboard, checked items off. Then he got dead serious over exact procedure for cutting the hull. Jack put an arm around him and said, "Sammy. It's ultralight. It's different. You set your Skilsaw kerf at seven-eighths—that's five-eighths for the balsa, two-eighths for the matt and roving inside. You peel that away inside and lay down some mold release. Then you lay up your new core, soak it down good with resin and lay up your new matt and roving. Then you wait a day, set your kerf at a quarter, come on outside and cut away your skin. The mold release lets it drop right off, and you lay up your matt, roving, matt, roving, ten-ounce skin for faring. You cut a hole in this whore, you'd never find her curve again."

"How do you know this?"

"Martin told me."

I drank another beer.

Sam nodded slow. "Just don't fuck up." Then he presented a check for a hundred dollars. Jack said, "What's this? A tip?" Sam looked pissed.

"A hundred bucks?" I said. "Sam, we got bad checks out there— they find us, they'll arrest us. We got new balsa due tomorrow from California, secret glue, mahogany—what do you want us to do? Write another bad check?"

Sam spoke through his teeth. "I'm doing the best I can. I expect money in three weeks."

"Three weeks?"

"In the meantime, make it work." He turned and left.

The stooped man beside us said, "Say thank you. That's his money."

Jack said, "Ah, fuck him. Everybody's doing us a big favor."

Sam came back. "This yard man you got helping."

"Yeah."

"Watch his hours. I don't want him over five grand."

Jack kicked a bucket over and sat on it. He popped a beer and said, "Want a beer Sam? We got plenty." Sam walked away.

Ten minutes later, speeding down Nimitz Highway with a cold pack, not using the emergency brake but trying to make Sam's bank before closing, Jack hunched over the wheel. I said, "You're ignorant."

Jack said, "So? You got no skills—plain fucking worthless. That's what makes our partnership so dynamic."

I cranked the tunes. Jack hit seventy, screeching into the parking lot with a lock on the brakes and five minutes to spare. He went in in a huff but came out grinning, gripping four twenties and two tens by the necks. Driving more reasonably to the Ming Chu in balmy twilight he said, "I don't know. Should we get some pussy or some snoot?"

"I'm not getting snoot."

Jack agreed. "Yeah yeah. No snoot. We'll get some pussy."

"Fine. We'll get some pussy."

In the hot shower I laughed—an evening out, drinks, drinks and more drinks, and maybe some women, after all, maybe. The mirror said no, no women, so I combed my hair elsewhere.

Jack read the yellow pages carefully, like it was the engine manual. "You looking under P?"

"No. It's not under P. It's under M—massage. What would be great is outcall. No shit, it's about twice as much but they send over these young ones. It's the ultimate room service."

"Then we're stuck here."

He stabbed one with his finger. "Ooh. I like this. Tahitian Treats. 'We specialize in young women of the South Pacific, anywhere, anytime, any service.' Ooh." He dialed, waited, spoke like a young executive, until he got to the price. He said he smelled a cunt in the woodpile. The phone went dead. "Fuck that." He hung up and laughed. "Forty bucks for the visit, forty bucks for the rub, and then you get to talk. Shit. That's a hundred sixty bucks just to ask for some pussy."

"Let's go out."

"Yeah. Shit. We'd never find outcall for a hundred bucks unless they had leprosy or something." Jack hit the shower.

Out front I said, "I don't want pussy."

"Why not?"

"I want to get drunk. I want to get away from here."

"I want pussy."

"Want to race?"

"Okay okay. Check here in an hour. I might not get pussy. I just want to sniff around." And I was down the street, out on my own. All

the trouble with life considered, we got along as well as any two soldiers in the trenches.

Maybe that's why I breathed deep, stretched my legs in long strides
and stretched my neck down the razzle-dazzle strip, feeling the
hooking hordes who knew that stride was powered by a pocket full
of cash. I felt strong, marching past tons of T-shirts, beach bags, big
combs and plenty hot pussy without a quiver or a blink, and I turned
quick into a nameless bar, for Campari and Soda with a twist, for the
taste, feeling like a rich man. One was enough, and again for the taste
I tried a Bailey's—good, close to right but too sweet. Crown Royal
neat was closer still, and brandy seemed certain—a good brandy, but
it was too early for brandy, maybe later, with coffee, and possibly a
Cointreau.

Another fifty yards up, stride shrinking, confidence holding, was
the best bar of all. No ferns, low music, peaceful and empty, except
for two women. Cuervo neat came next, with a beer chaser. That was
refreshing, right on target and warranting another round. A small
buzz floated down warm and soft, enveloped the troubled head,
turned it toward the young couples on the promenade, visitors from
reasonable suburbs to this, tropics aglitter, souvenirs, flesh for sale.

Content in the chaos, assured by return tickets home, they looked
happy and dull, like security was a state of mind, fucked, fed, free of
fear. I was none of the above and a long way from anything feeling
like home, time for another round.

The Cuervo neat with beer was good, but too rowdy. Maybe a
Stoly would at least allow the illusion of civility. The closest of the
women two seats down said, "Looks like a man with a mission." I
bowed my head, because an alcoholic getting caught getting drunk
is like a teenage boy getting caught jacking off. Everyone knows it's
a real regular event, but still it's so tasteless in public. "You visiting?"

"Yes. I have a boat. It's under repair here."

"Ooh. A boat. How big?"

"Small. Small boat."

"Oh."

I sipped, sipped again, looked up and rejoined society. "You visit-ing? I mean, you know, from...America?"

She held her breath, like she didn't want to blow her answer. "Well...," she sighed. "Yes and no. I mean..."

"Why don't you just tell him," her friend said.

The first woman offered her hand. "I'm Elly."

"Martin here." We shook on it.

"This is Corrine."

"You might as well just tell him, Eleanor," Corrine said.

Ellie hemmed and hawed, started and stopped, giggled and blushed. I said, "Tell him, Eleanor."

Ellie could not. Corrine leaned in front of her and said, "She's horny. She wants to get laid."

I nodded slowly, coloring quickly as life itself, there on the raz-zle-dazzle strip. The hard part was good posture—I wobbled on my stool. "Wrong guy," Corrine said. "He's too drunk."

"It's like this," Ellie said.

"Like this," I said, feebly grasping coherence.

"I'm a yuppie. You know, young urban professional?"

My head wobbled. "I'm a...a yrffie. Young rural failure."

Corrine laughed. "Right guy, Eleanor."

Ellie said, "Seriously. Nobody admits being a yuppie, but I am and I don't care. Except that we...I'm supposed to have this handful of emotions and increasing income. It's not enough—look, I'm smart. I'm really smart. I think I'm too smart to be happy with what I have to be happy with."

"You'd be amazed how happy you are...looking back...from a boat yard."

"Bullshit. I'm not happy and no Barnacle Bill the Sailor can tell me I am."

"No... Pardon me... You don't sound happy."

"I've been married five years, and my sex life wasn't all that great the first four."

"And now...the bars of Waikiki."

"He hasn't touched me in a year, and it's like... I need to get fucked."
I nodded freely now, wondering if I could stop. Palms up, she was
puzzled. "I can't walk into a bar and pick up some guy, some complete
stranger."

I looked over my shoulder—nobody, and I smiled stupid, realizing
I was being picked up.

Corrine asked, "So what are you doing? Chopping liver?"

"Are you healthy?" Ellie asked.

I pondered health. "Physical seven, mental two."

"I mean it! Really healthy! I'm married, don't forget. I'm going
home in three days."

"How can you give your husband a disease if he won't fuck you?"

"He will fuck me! I know he will. Some day." Happiness waited just
beyond the rainbow, in a gold kettle with some shiny coins and a nice
fuck from her husband. She came back quick to criteria, wagging a
finger. "I'll tell you something else, Buster..."

"Martin."

"I'll tell you something else, Martin. I have no intention of jeop-
ardizing my marriage. I want out of this, no love, no meaning, no
nothing out of this. This would strictly be a one-night stand. I need
some sex, to be touched and that's all."

"Yes. I could use some sex and that's all too, I think." I scanned
down, breasts, ass, thighs, looked close at her teeth.

Suddenly coy, she blinked, "I think you're cute."

"You mean like a small dog?"

"Do you have a romantic commitment?"

Corrine's head rested on the bar by this time, like an unread vol-
ume, elbows out, hands propped like bookends. She looked disgusted, left out.

"Not a commitment like you have," I said. "More of a romantic
interest."

"Are you healthy? Really healthy?" I went bottoms up and she said,
"Okay. You talked me into it..."

"Eleanor!" Corrine was up. "You're not going with this guy! I mean, come on!"

"That's the trouble with you, Corrine. Fantasize. You're very good at it. I'm tired of it. I want some memories." Ellie posed, femme fatale, cocked head to a raised shoulder, subtle tongue thrust and playful bite on her lower lip. Eyes aflutter on mine, she said, "Some nasty, kinky, please-me memories." She went limp, normal again, like herself. "I want to be ravished."

Corrine yelled to the bartender for another round of drinks, then to Ellie, "You're not going with him."

Ellie asked, "Where are you staying?"

"Ming Chu. Up the road about five minutes, but..."

Corrine leaned close, "But what?"

"I might look like an easy lay, but I have standards too."

"What are they?"

"Yeah, what are they?"

"How long you in town?" I asked.

"No no no no no," Ellie was harsh. "No phone numbers. No last names. No second dates."

"I don't know. It's rough. I think maybe it sounds rougher than I am."

She grasped my arm, slow but firm. "Fine. I don't want to be ravished. Just take it easy."

"What if you love it."

"Look, Charlie. Don't do me any favors."

"Who's doing who?"

"If you don't want to, just say so. I might fuck some weirdo stranger, but I won't beg him."

"Weirdo stranger?"

She hooked back her new drink. "I'm cooling off," she said.

I drank slow, looked out the door, then at my ice cubes. They looked animate, cold and dying with no favors for me except maybe by default, chilling my vodka. I knew how they felt, victims of convenience. "Ellie wants a door knob..."

Corrine grunted—"Too stubby!"

"So don't tell me I'm cute."

Ellie was on me. "Martin, Martin, Martin. I promise to treat you nice. I promise in the morning I'll respect you." She saw the time. "What am I saying? I'll respect you by midnight."

"No no no," moaned Corrine.

"One thing more," I said, looking forlorn as a lost pup.

She waved me on two handed—"Come on, come on, come on!"

"I can't handle a fat ass."

Corrine sprayed her drink across the bar.

"Christ!" Ellie spouted

"Stand up."

"Don't you dare!"

Corrine drooled. "He's a pig!" Ellie looked both ways.

"Say oink, Ellie," I said.

Ellie sprang to a slow pirouette, pulled her dress tight across her ass—"Oink oink." It wasn't too fat.

"One six-pack, low light," I said.

"What?"

"For the dimples," I said.

Corrine shrieked. Ellie blushed. I liked the action—and she looked good in a blush. "Fuck it. I'm drunk. Your ass'll do."

Ellie liked standards, stepped up quick—"Look at these tits." She lifted them up.

"May I feel them?"

"Go ahead, hot shot."

"No!" Corrine slapped the bar. My hands hovered at Ellie's breasts. Corrine blushed, hid her face, peeked through her fingers.

I squeezed, gently, then firm—they were too hard. "Implants?"

"Do you like them?"

I put my ear to one and shook it. Corrine shrieked. I suspected implants, just after the honeymoon, when combined incomes allowed spiritual focus, call it human potential. Corrine looked horny too, horny and embarrassed, blushing and gasping—and wouldn't Jack envy a two-bagger. But the shrieking and giggling and vying for control made me shiver. I said, "Enough. Time for therapy. Let's go."

"No!"

Ellie shucked her doubt, made for the door. "Eleanor!" Corrine pleaded. But Eleanor waved goodbye.

I lingered, leaning toward Corrine—"Sometimes in solitude we discover ourselves." Then I spun and followed Ellie.

In long strides back down the strip, she looked like a hooker. I looked like a sailor, drunk and lost in the streets and buildings that had moved in the last hour. Jaywalking in horns Ellie said, "Sometimes I like it tender." Stepping up to the curb she said, "Sometimes I like it fast."

Lights thinned. I stopped, lost, but I looked up, just up to the left, at the Ming Chu marquee. I made a new posture and grasped again at coherence. "First slow. Then fast. I got it."

"No numbers. No names. Remember." She covered her eyes. Up in the room I said, "Shit. We forgot wine."

She waved it off. "Wine is for romance. That's not why we're here, Charlie."

"Martin."

"Please. Charlie."

"My partner sometimes calls me Harry."

"Why? And what's the difference?"

"I don't know. And I don't know. Maybe he's like you, and doesn't want to really get to know me." I dropped my pants. She bit a knuckle on a second thought, watching my dick, then she ducked into the bathroom. In a minute she called, "Lights out please." She came out in the dark, lost. "Here," I called. She felt her way over in the dark. I turned the light on.

Skinny arms with freckles and no fuzz led to narrow shoulders, undeveloped since age twelve. She wasn't fat, she was shapeless, carrot legs and sure enough dimples on her ass. She put my hands on her breasts—they felt real, untrussed—and she doused the light again. She knelt down for kink, for the memory, but it was all teeth.

I grunted. She gasped. "Fuck me!" she said. We fucked. And I told her on the same rhythm as the fuck—"It's the same as the tides. In and out." A set of waves came and went. "I honestly believe love is trying to find me," I told her. "But don't worry. You...ain't...it." I rolled off. We lay there quiet, morose, and she left with a soft thank you, slow and uncertain. Emptiness took new form.

I lay still in the dark willing myself to merge with stillness and darkness—with a poof, and gone. I woke at two when Jack came in loud. "God, that was something."

Five hours later on a slow drive down Nimitz Boulevard, dirty mist and gray sky matched the mood, and the metronome wipers were interrupted only once for an opinion. "You drive like old people fuck," Jack said.

"I drive like I fuck." I pulled into Zippy's, We Never Close. "I like it slow. And I still got fifteen bucks." Jack spent his on tequila and a six-pack. He said nipping the pint was easy, but ducking into alleys for the beer chaser was unsettling. He drank and shopped, until it got too late, girls going home. He'd picked a couple honeys too. At one a.m. he hit Tahitian Treat, only six blocks down, and spent the rest of his dough.

The Zippy jingle tinkled in the traffic drone. Coffee wafted thin through drifting exhaust. A hundred dollars had numbed senses. Five hundred would have killed us—it was like that. Down the road, the inferno.

"Boy," Jack said. "Life seems pretty cheap when you go to a hooker and she drops and sucks you off and you pay her for it."

"You mean cheaper than yesterday?"

He lit a smoke. "She made me wear a rubber."

"How could you come with a rubber on?"

"It wasn't easy."

"She had to work awhile?"

"About ten minutes."

"How much more to suck you off without the rubber?"

"She wouldn't do it. I asked her if she made her boyfriend wear one when she sucked him off. She said no."

"How old was she?"

"Nineteen. She's a legal secretary. I asked her if she liked her work. She said she liked her legal secretary job, but she didn't like sucking cock too much. She was pretty, too."

"I never heard you use that word before."

"Fuck you."

"That's more like it."

The little speaker crackled, "Eleven thirteen." Zippy's sold cups, not coffee, so down and outers could beat the rule. After two weeks the cups leaked. Today, new cups, fifty cents a whack, and the daily gruel.

Gray skies and mist beyond the patio became light rain over fried eggs, weak coffee. It washed clean the fronds and foliage, but runny ocher breakfast on a runny gray day led to thin resolve, and it was two gray souls easing up, and onward.

The next ten freeway miles were thick with soot and smog from progress come to the tropics, lined with pockmarked trees that glistened in the bright, morning rain. It looked fraudulent, as if it was dead, and some prankster with a sick sense of humor had come along and painted it living. "It's a hoax," I said. Jack hocked out the window.

Whirlaway waited to soak up another twelve hours. Jack looked up the scaffold ladder—he'd unhooked the wiring at the panel for labeling, since Sam said the wiring must be salvaged. The Company must repair, not replace, if possible. He grabbed a bucket, emptied parts on a rag, walked down the dock and filled it with saltwater. He climbed the scaffold, unscrewed the instrument panel and pried it free. He poured saltwater on the instruments, to trash them. "I think the instruments got covered with saltwater. I think we need new ones." He looked down at me, for approval.

"Ay ay." I scanned the gray, dark sky, for reason. The light rain got thick, then came the deluge. Jack yelled, electric gauges should be protected from the rain, and he hurried the cover back onto the caulk.

I walked away, drifted across the tarmac like a prophet come home, arms spread like ashen fronds, hoping the rain could let me shine too.

Disintegration

Rebuild unraveled like a loose thread on a dirty shirt. Resin dust pumped from the grinder. Sandblasted rust stuck to sweaty skins, toxins clutched lungs and stretched eyeballs across brains until purple clouds drifted in a green sky. Life became science fiction. Three weeks equalled twenty-one days times fourteen hours times two. Carry Lowe was saved for bottom paint—hundred proof poison. He said thanks, he needed the work. I said, "Don't worry—we came to Honolulu to create jobs for the people."

Three weeks was halfway—breakdown to hull and deck. Reassembly looked like a mirror image, but the mirror cracked. Simple tasks grew big, grotesque and disfigured. The compass binnacle needed bronze clevis pins for shift and throttle linkage that were available in Hong Kong, and they turned inside teflon grommets from Eastern Ontario.

The new instrument panel was too big. The electrician swore he knew shit from shinola, but he smoked a pipe and thought and thought and smoked and smoked. I told him go home. He said he lived in Fiji, actually. I said it didn't matter, actually, just go away. Jack told him go to hell.

The new electrician didn't smoke a pipe—he was a headscratcher. Jack told him to get the fuck out, then he cut the hole bigger with a Sawzall, and the new panel fit. He spliced in some ignition wire and boosted the jolt with a solenoid he got from the parking lot. Sweating like a pig and bleeding from his knuckles, he said, "I swear to God, Harry, I should've been a 'lectrician."

"Or a car thief," I said.

"Yeah," he said, hunkering bolts. "Or anything."

Luck held on deliveries—balsa core, special inboard resins, exotic mahogany—all but the new spreader came the same week, so the first check didn't bounce until the goods were safely hidden.

Luck failed when the mechanic, who was fat and dirty enough to make down and outers look like Cary Grant and Fred Astaire, removed the fuel injectors, covered the ports with dirty, grungy cellophane, then lost the injectors. He got fired too, same day as the grinders and lay-up crew. I ordered new injectors from L.A. Jack charged a grinder and a gross of pads and a box of respirators, and with a vengeance swore he was the best fiberglass man in the Pacific anyway. The cocksuckers.

One night on a bad check for ten bucks we got movie tickets and popcorn. Two guys were trying to escape the Khmer Rouge in Cambodia. It was too close to home. I wrote another bad check next day for five dollars and tried again alone, a movie about a muscular comic book character. That seemed safe, until the character came on the screen, and a local in back yelled, "Fucking haole monkey!" The city closed in.

Carry stayed on at the sandblasting station. He came over with a roach when he could scrounge one up. I replumbed the head, rebuilt the toilet with new gaskets, diaphragms, clamps and hoses. Jack ground on the keel, prepping it for lay-up. Carry nursed a soda on the shady side, recalling his mother and father back in Lizard, Texas. They married, divorced and remarried each other five times, and if that wasn't love. They would have divorced again, but his mother had herself sent away. His father had no front teeth. Carry had permanently trashed three knuckles on his right hand, no small chance, right there in the old man's face. He had fourteen brothers and sisters counting holdover halves from his ma 'n pa's other marriages.

Jack ground on the keel, covered in resin dust except for circles around his eyes and over his nose and mouth. Carry said his mother brought home winos off the street who would fuck her right there on the living room floor, or if they couldn't fuck they would fingerfuck, sometimes right there in the presence of other, maybe last night's, winos, who moaned and rolled in their own puke.

Carry got confused in the retelling, and he didn't recall his past lightly. He liked a sympathetic ear, but he didn't need one, once he got rolling, it was coming out, or up, just like cheap wine he couldn't hold down no longer, there in the shade of a wrecked boat. He stammered over his primary goal then, to kill his brother, a successful Corvette dealer until last year, when he suffered an aneurysm while fucking. Now Carry's brother was a vegetable at home. Carry wanted to end it for him soon, with honor.

Carry stopped. It got quiet there in the shade and light breeze. He mumbled apology and hung his head. Life had won another round.

Among the wrecks in the yard was a sixty-five foot Swan that dragged anchor in a kona blow a year ago and bounced its keel on a reef. The hull cracked and would have sunk, but the wind quit, and the Swan took a tow.

Every day a jump-suited, respirated gang of experts shuffled from a tin shed out back and stood shoulder to shoulder on a poor man's scaffold—a 2 x 10 on buckets. One brushed resin near the keel. Another laid up a little patch of fiberglass cloth. Five more watched, then rolled the cloth with tiny metal rollers and surgical precision. It was a million dollar yacht, an insurance job.

After two hours and a smoke break back in the tin shed, they shuffled out for another cloth, another two hours.

Every third cloth stayed on the hull, the rest got ditched, imperfect. Hull surgery ran fifty dollars an hour per man. The men stayed anonymous in their space suits. But their leader was big and thick, his melon-sized head swelled bigger by a thick red mane and moth-eaten beard. He was Fatty Renken. Watching him lead his little troupe back for another shift, another six men times two hours times fifty dollars, down and outers felt good, like Fatty was a winner, had it beat, down and dirty—he walked tall and proud, made no bones, took no shit. He was a wealthy man.

The yacht owner had made millions, according to the rules of the AMA. But nature pays no homage to symbols, so his yacht got fucked, after he got fucked by the insurance company, who charged him a mint on malpractice and hull insurance. It was up to men like Fatty Renken to complete the fucking circle, get the money back down to street level. "Sometimes I love the system," I said. "When it works, all the fuckers get to be fuckees, sooner or later."

Carry said, "You guys got a car. Let's go see some strip shows." Jack stood up, stoop shouldered, head down. He shuffled off. I asked Carry if he could score a joint. "Ask Fatty," Carry said. "They stop at four and hang out a couple hours, shake off the resin before they go home. Way back in the back shed. Take a six-pack."

"I don't know those guys."

"Sure you do. It's like jail here. Take a six-pack. Hey, you want to see some strip shows?" I shrugged. Carry split. I found a bucket of rags, dried out and caked together hard, but not a bad pillow without the bucket. I laid some clean cardboard over some dirty cardboard and lay down in the shade, looking up at hull fragments. I had passed acceptance, running headlong to amazement, and it was worse by all alone. With other people, it held together, took a form—words, gestures, shoes, pants, shirts, skin, blood and so on. By myself it fell apart. I'd seen people on TV who looked at the camera and said yes, I'm not sane. I'm insane. They smiled then and usually looked nuts and far away.

A word drifting by made sense then—it held together, gave meaning to its environment, as if meaning was the tangible difference between life and death. It was disintegration. The past seemed as far away as the future once did. Roads taken seemed no different than roads not taken; meaning became independent of action. I left then, leaving the corpse under the hulk. That moment was the last. I split with the breeze, became the shade.

First lost in that logic, then shedding logic as an appendage of the flesh, I reached the waking dream. Jack showed up with two six-packs and spoke. He'd called Louise and asked if she wanted to get married. She'd said yes. They would marry in two weeks.

I sat up, happily troubled. Was that it? Was that what it came to, eating shit in a trench until you gagged, and then burying your head under a pillow and giving thanks because you had a place to stick your horndog dick?

Jack said what the fuck—he had to go home anyway to pick up his food stamps.

I stood up, took a six-pack and walked away. Jack called, "You're best man."

It echoed. Cinders passed under far below, down at the surface of that vast and empty planet. Across the dusty, noxious hostility, thoughts tumbled in the zero gravity of the schizoid break. I homed on a chasm in the canyon wall, a chink in the glacier, toward which, into which, through which I went, as if volition was a signal from Houston.

The big steel buildings formed two walls of Fatty's oasis. The lesser tin shed was the third side. The fourth side was trash in a ditch, to infinity. I arrived and stopped, blinked and gathered the scene—dirt floor, wavy tin walls, sawhorse seating and a blue sky going red for the hour at hand. Fatty's crew decompressed with spliffs so strong a wayward spaceman could lose coordinates sighing, and the moment came when a visitor drew attention to himself, stock-still as a catatonic in the Arctic.

The largest beer cooler known to man, a hundred gallon box scavenged off the transom of a dead fisherman, sat in the center. I stood by it. One of Fatty's crew gently relieved me of my six-pack and dropped it in, shoved it under the ice, popping other cans up, frosty cold. I watched and watched. "You did the right thing," Fatty said. "Welcome."

The great cooler overflowed. The same man popped a cold one for me, and another man gave me a spliff and made room on a sawhorse.

The rest watched. I got led to it, grateful they didn't laugh. I got seated and smoked. Then they laughed, passing spliffs—they'd seen it before. They'd lived it, some of them retiring from the reef to the boat yard. They knew: I'd be okay, as soon as I got good and fucked up. I did, and I laughed too, feeling good, maybe great, for the first time loving my dirty, threadbare clothes, the grime and stench to match. In another minute I loved the rusted shed, then I loved the dirt itself. A man asked, "Reef job?"

I looked up, nodding like a plastic dog in a rear window. The man smiled and nodded back. And I knew that Fatty's oasis was the place I'd longed for, that I'd stumbled on to understanding.

The beer in the great cooler turned to empties in the infinite ditch. More spliffs orbited that ring of souls, and soon, I was lost in space, comfortably, just me, sundown and the motley crew. Tattooed and scarred on sunbrown skin, they were warm as renegades can be.

Talk turned to killing flies, especially the juicy bombers buzzing the fish bucket. One man stretched a big rubber band for a tail shot on a quarter pounder. He let go—splat to the ditch—with a perfect hit. Talk turned to killing men. Voices thinned. One man said he could kill if he had to, no problem. Another said you never know. Fatty said it was easier than swatting a fly, and that surprised him, how easy a man goes dead. He remembered that man more than any fly he ever killed. He enjoyed it more—more than one of them fat, hairy sonsabitches bumping his head when he's trying to think. Much more; it felt good, like a two-tone tattoo once the sting and blood get done with. 'Course now the motherfucker had it coming. The oasis got quiet then with no questions.

One man lit a fire, another skinned the fish—it was a triggerfish, like the one I had in my aquarium years ago, before I let it go when it got three inches long. I wondered if my fish grew up and crossed the ocean and wound up in Fatty's oasis, like me. I hoped it wasn't my fish, but I couldn't begrudge the boys my former pet, good as they'd made me feel.

Another spliff came around in the cordial spirit, and the tin corrugations on Fatty's cocktail parlor rolled like little waves around the world. The sky went red to deep red to brilliant red. I watched the drama, day to dusk, dusk to twilight. Red came back, up to orange, giving way to yellow and the gray veil, nightfall. Silence fell too on Fatty's small circle of friends, in reverie and tribute to the beauty they'd come south for, a beauty no past could take from them.

A half black, half Tongan named Peter asked lowly, "Alright now. What do you call that color?" He stared at the swatch between the gritty skyline and jagged cloud line, breaking the reverie, bringing the boys back, engaging their brains at low rpm.

One said quickly, "It's yellow. Gray yellow, maybe, but yellow. That's all it is."

Peter leaned forward. "But what about the pink streak down the middle?"

"Fuck pink," the quick one said.

"I know what it is, Peter," a Mexican with a bandito moustache said. Peter waited like a patient teacher. "It's faggot yellow. Right?" The others agreed, laughing yes, it wasn't just plain yellow, it was faggot yellow.

Fatty Renken said, "You assholes." He cocked his head up. "Looks like a mahi mahi to me, you know, after you get your foot on top of um and club shit outa they fuckin' heads a few times. Dead mahi. That's your color, Peter. You could make some lipstick outta that color and be a millionaire."

"No!" The Mexican said. "You full of shit, Fatty."

Peter stood up. "Milky amber. That's your color."

The circle of friends moaned.

The Mexican said, "Milky amber. Faggot yellow. Same color, man. I guessed it first." He grumbled and left. Others grumbled too over old ladies at home, and happy hour ended. Peter stoked the fire and watched it. Fatty went into his shed to roll more spliffs. Milky amber, faggot yellow, dead mahi—all went gray to dark.

A single ember honed in—it was Jack in the night, finding his partner oozed across a sawhorse, melted onto Fatty's shed, holding a dead spliff in one hand, an empty in the other. "You look great," he said.

"I feel good too," I said, handing up the dead spliff. "Brain wash?"

He lit it from his cigarette. "Why not?" He smoked it. "Come on, we're leaving. Carry's waiting out front. Strip joints."

I rose like a time-lapse weed in a nature film, amazed again. Sidestepping through Fatty's dark door, into a cloud of smoke and low voices, I spoke up. "Thank you, Fatty."

Fatty growled, "You're welcome back. Anytime."

I drifted out. The oasis was empty now except for the black Tongan's silhouette. I followed Jack's ember toward the gap. "Good night, Peter. Milky amber. I agree."

Peter mumbled yes and poked the coals.

Then Fatty's oasis became another frame for Life Comix, pleasantly read from the natal darkness, the weightless comfort of the unborn.

Carry Lowe was a thought, then a form in the dark, following along in step, taking the spliff, narrating a wonderful evening of dance and song, beginning at The Q-P DO Cocktail Lounge.

"What? You got a charge account at the Q-P DO?"

"Sam brought another check," Jack said. "Five bills." He grinned, "And we get seven-fifty an hour, just like Carry."

"No shit?"

"No shit. Carry's got cash. We'll pay him back tomorrow."

I stopped, suddenly human again. "I'm dirty, sweaty."

"You'll fit right in."

"I want a shower."

"Fuck the shower. This ain't an interview. What do you want to do? Make a good impression?"

"I want a shower. I want comfort."

Carry said, "That's cool. The Q-P DO is only three blocks from your place." We walked. Carry picked up the step. "Oh boy, strip shows."

The Q-P DO was a dive, limp sign on rusty bracket. Inside was worse—low light, conduit, water pipe and vent duct surrounding a bar and some booths facing a small, raised stage backed by mirrors, flashlight on a lazy Susan for disco lighting.

Casing from the door, Carry said, "Keep moving," and led to the bar, ordered three beers and turned to the empty stage. Below it the busty B-girls and strippers prepped for the first show. Three B-girls came on like hookers, rubbing shoulders, whimpering over the lumps they found, rubbing chests, then lower backs, whimpering over wallets. They worked it, leaning close with the acrid scent of dog meat—Filipino—whispering, "What's up, sojer?"

I leaned away. "I'm up. You've made my dick very big." She giggled, wanted more, was there for rent and groceries.

"You buy me one drink." She rubbed my thigh, slid up once to squeeze my pecker.

"Maybe later. Not now. Show time now."

She walked away. A dancer mounted the stage. Five four, one-thirty with electric hair and softball breasts and a leopard skin handkerchief up her crack. The dancer turned around and bent over to tie her shoes, six-inch spikes, no strings. An old needle on an old record crackled old disco, set her ass in motion, set her hands to hinting that maybe, just maybe, she'd untie her spotted hanky, peel it from her crack. She teased, knowing how badly we wanted a look at the hair and brown part. She sought eyes in the mirror, flirted, spread her cheeks for a preview.

A wharf rat climbed a pipe by the stage, six-, seven-pounder, ran across a duct overhead and up through a hole in the drop ceiling. She eased the hanky out, gyrating her intimate self, verging on climax, pouting in pleasure.

A telephone rang, the needle scratched and a voice called, "Madang dang dang mac a dang mac a dang dang dang mac a dang!" Jack coughed, lost control and sprayed beer across the bar as the stripper called back, "Dang a dang dang dang dang madang dang macadang dang dang!" Carry sat up straight, looking fore and aft, up and down for blackjacks and certain death. The stripper climbed down to take her call.

Jack coughed more and louder, fumbling through a soft pack so crumpled it looked empty since yesterday. Lighting a crushed fag he said, "Let's go. I want white chicks fingering themselves."

Carry nodded, out the door in a shake, down a block to Club QT. The QT was empty, the B-girls ready, reaching for dingdongs on the sitdown with conviction. I said, "Would you care for a drink?"

Carry said, "No! They won't even dance for another two hours in here. Her drink'll run twelve bucks."

I shrugged. My girl said, "Oh, I get it. He da boss. He tell you what to do. He tell you what you can do and what you cannot do. He da boss. You da bum. Right?"

"Yes. He's the boss. I'm nothing. I'm nobody."

"Fuck you, sojer."

Carry led next to The Esquire, "It's the best place of all. I saved it for last. I really dig this music." Heavy metal—I said it wasn't music but the sound dog shit would make if it could talk.

"What?"

A dancer found her rhythm, pulled down her top and called, "Hi, guys!"

Three other men, sixtyish, ravaged by wine, rounded out the crowd. Jack yelled, "That's us in thirty years, Harry."

I yelled, "That's us now, Jack." She bumped and ground all the more for undivided attention, slithered from her tutu, waved it in the air, turned for the bend and spread, and left. The next girl was early twenties, blonde and slight, with innocence, a low mileage look, no silicone, no stretch and a delicacy that was rare, onstage. She found me in the mirror as she waited for her song. She sank deep, eye to eye—turned to me, graceful and direct, leaned over the stage lights, bent close, bottom lit, like an angel, and whispered, "What are you doing later?"

I only had to say time and place—but Carry Lowe broke in, "C'mon! Let's see some pussy!"

"Ooh," she tittered. "He wants to see some pussy!"

So the romance ended. I knew in my heart that I would look backstage after the show, even after she ditched her tutu—a gold sequined suit—showing four scars from major surgeries, car wrecks or knife wounds. Her tits stuck out, cold molded. Still she was so sweet. And I was so ready. Maybe it was only a mood.

She hid three eggs in her vagina and didn't drop a beat when Carry yelled, "Hard boiled, I bet!"

A chunky woman next hid a coke bottle but was forgotten five dancers later when we left drunk, agreeing that The Esquire was best. Carry felt good, host about town. He found the nub of Fatty's spliff and lit up. Jack waved it off then took it, what the fuck. I finished it. Good and fucked, Carry said he'd saved the very best for very last. The Pelican Chuck Wagon, We Never Close, $6.95, ALL YOU CAN EAT!—prime rib and fried chicken too. "It's fine, man."

A weary counterman in a white apron and chef's hat cut roast at the end of the line. Before that was a steel bowl of greasy fried chicken and a matching steel bowl of mashed potatoes. Steel trays, two rows, completed the buffet with canned vegetables—beets, carrots, string-beans and corn, corn bread, hard rolls and butter at the end. Carry dove in. "See. I told you it was fine." It looked like Thanksgiving buffet at a Federal penitentiary.

Jack flagged a busgirl and ordered a jar of wine, quick, chop-chop. Carry hit the buffet, sat down in a hurry, put away all he could eat with two hands. "I ate this good in jail too." And in jail he learned about the prison system, where he hoped to work some day. "Man, you know what they pay?"

"You know some places call it all you care to eat," I said. Carry shoveled beets, backed with carrots. Jack couldn't watch. "They could call this deal eat till you puke. I think I'm there." Jack spewed wine. I scraped beets, carrots, beans and mashed potatoes onto Jack's plate. Jack dumped the swill on Carry's plate.

"Fuckheads!" Carry went for another plate, another pass, more beets. At a new table, Jack ordered another jar of wine.

Carry drove back to the Ming Chu belching, dropped us off and promised pick up tomorrow. Jack puked. "God, man," Carry said. "What a pussy."

I took a walk, said don't wait up over my shoulder. I walked, waiting for the jumbled day to settle down, find a rhythm, a logic, a pace. I walked faster, looking and longing for a star way above the razzle-dazzle glitter. At a pay phone I took a chance and called an old date.

It had been a day among days, all you could eat. I sighed when she answered. I knew life itself was devious and a liar, and though she was home, Squat lay beside her, sperm crust on her tits where he whizzed and then rubbed it in.

"It's me."

"I miss you."

"Can you come over?"

"I guess."

"Tomorrow?"

"What's wrong?"

"I miss you too."

"Yes. Pick me up at the airport?"

"Sure." I gave her the number at the yard and hung on to the phone without speaking until my three quarters clanged lights-out. I shuffled back to the Ming Chu dizzy, nauseous, depressed, disgusted, drunk, aching, anxious and hopeful.

Carry redeemed himself just at sunrise with two hot coffees. No words could recall last night's fun. It was a quiet ride to Cambodia, a new day, seven-fifty an hour. I felt connected again, bought a newspaper, my first in weeks, but it was still bad news, around the world, across the nation. Locally, eight locals beat a white man for driving on the beach. Ten locals beat a white man for shushing them in a movie.

In Items For Sale I chose a Chevrolet. No money down and easy payments meant a thirty-day lead on the two-grand rebate, if I went with the top of the line. I stored that one away, because you never can tell. And I hove to on new engine vents just as the space behind the engine reached a hundred degrees in the morning sun.

Renette called soon after five in the afternoon. I drove to the airport, wishing the distance between me and the world would shrink. Two doves scratching at slim pickings in the grassy strip between the freeway and the retaining wall looked like Jack and me.

# Dissolution

Jack allowed me two days rest and relaxation—he'd take the same for his honeymoon, fuck it. I got the room. Jack would camp at Carry's and check out Carry's girlfriend and maybe fuck her on credit for an I.O.U. on Louise, either before or after the wedding, whenever she came over.

I told Renette I was falling, over the edge, couldn't stop, needed her around. She liked that. We hung out, got stoned, watched daytime movies, had sex and clocked seven-fifty an hour—it was good, but it soured. I didn't know why—we had the chemistry, but I was nuts, and she was so simple, she couldn't even see it. I stared out the window. "Dead is dead."

"Maybe for you," she said.

"Oh yeah? Miss smarty-pants. What'll happen when you die?"

"You go to heaven."

I laughed. "You mean wings and harps and shit?" She ignored me. "You believe that?"

"Yes. And I really won't like you if you make me not believe it."

I was gone again, out the window like a light beam. "What's it like, up there?"

"It's nice. I'll see my Grama and my dog Freckles." She blushed. I wanted to fuck again.

Her country corn made me horny, but she one-upped me the next day, double dared me to satisfy her. She mixed pitchers of wine/Gatorade coolers and talked trashy like the boys behind the high school up there in Booneville, where she got fingerfucked, grew tits then fucked some yokel because he had a fast car, and then she served her time with Walter for the next twenty-five years, but couldn't remember why, except that it was long ago and something never happened.

She said down and dirty was every girl's dream, no different than every boy. She dared me to fuck her, really fuck her. I tried, and she double dared another. So I tried that too and managed, in daring spirit, but got a D double dare for another—she didn't crack a smile. She complained: she "honestly and truly" felt I wasn't fucking her hard enough or fast enough, or just enough. "Why?"

"Because I'm a sorry sonofabitch?"

She said, "Yes, but how am I? How do you feel? Do you dislike me? Do you hate me? Am I convenient? You're so cold."

I rolled over. "The morning sun, when it's in your face really shows your age. But that don't bother me none, in my eyes you're every-thing." She shut up. I took a nap.

Turning two days stale as a long marriage and chafing my noodle, she bore down day three at breakfast, before the airport. It was her turn to stare out the window now. I couldn't believe it; Cambodia seemed like relief.

"You're distant from me."

"Yeah. Don't take it personal. I'm distant from me too."

Fishing her maple syrup for the diced French toast she'd drowned there she said, "Single is more fun than married. But it's lonely too." I felt her specialty coming, a love thrust—she wanted to mate, clench like fists. Don't lose the grip or you die.

"I will be home soon. You'll feel better then."

"Sure, right." She stabbed a goo ball, let it drip. "People get satis-fied, no matter how many partners it takes. I read in *Cosmo* that lots of people make love with more than one person in one day."

"Will you?"

"I don't know. No."

"Did you?"

"When?"

"Recently."

"He gave me a ride to the airport." She laughed. "Boy, and I used to be jealous."

"Why do you need so much fucking?"

"I need love."

"You need love?"

She shrugged. "What else is there? You're so...cold, what do you know about love? What am I supposed to do? Sit home?" The bitter smile of truth etched my face. She'd horsefucked Squat again. "You fucked him so I would love you more. You have no faith, as in unfaithful, as in void. Spiritual communion is what I know about love, opposed to bang and whimper, which is what you know about love."

She stirred the bowl with her fork. "That kind of love doesn't exist."

"How convenient." We drove to the airport with country music. She looked tearful. I feared her absence, breathed deep when she was gone, drove slow to Cambodia. And knowing nothing, I leaned into a grinder, pushed and pulled long and hard, turning rough and bumpy to fair and smooth. Nose and lungs clogged with dust and a peacefulness settled in, which was that of departure from the worries of the world. Gone away from all that stuff, I laughed at the pasty blue snuk flipped in the air, one nostril, and the other, then at the big blue louie gobbed up and hung on the rudder.

A man free and clear can lay down in the cinders and sleep sound as a baby into night, and cry in the dark when wakened.

Jack held a six-pack and paced at the end of his ember. I trembled, whimpered, bad dream to worse waking. Jack said awkwardly that he broke too, on his own, that no one else knew, and that somehow we would make it. "It doesn't matter how bad it gets." He took a deep drag. "It's like bad weather." He paced. "You ride it out. Or let it take you."

I breathed deep.

Jack stooped. "Thirty-five days. Not so bad. I estimate another forty." He tapped his clipboard, proof. "Come on." He pulled me up, out from under, as if to show the stars still shining at night.

We worked quick for a week, little beer, no joints and the momentum of *Whirlaway* reborn. The new mechanic installed the new injectors, new muffler, alternator, starter and ignition harness. A new control panel was epoxied in, wired up. We worked hours and hours and days on end removing the fractured balsa inside, until the sweat and fibers made us look like the dirtiest guys in the world. But the paper-thin skin left on the seventy square feet, port side, was clean and smooth. Jack applied mold release, going chalk white from the fumes. I laid up the new balsa wood next to the skin, pampered it to contour, no swells or bumps. Then came resin soak, hatches shut to keep out the wind and dust. Jack swooned, slurred his cocksuckers and soaked the poison through the balsa, stroking the drips up, up, up. Three more days of sweat, blood, grinding, sanding, matt, roving, more matt, more roving led to the next three days of grinding, sanding, cleaning, more resin, grinding, sanding and cleaning.

The new bulkhead and cabinets were done, assembled, screwed and glued into place. The keel was ground, laid up, ground and laid up again and again, until it was properly thick again. I ground it fair.

Driving to the airport in silence, numb in the hands, arms and shoulders, hurt in the head and lungs, choking on resin dust and life, Jack bolted the shifter hard, crunched the rental into reverse, grinned at its death clatter, jammed into park. The little transmission shook like a can of nuts, coasted in park, and Jack took another shot at the world—the emergency brake. Lunging back, teeth clenching a fag, fishtailing to a stop—"Little fucker's got guts," was his farewell opinion. The little fucker trembled. Jack smiled down on it and his partner. "Flipside, Harry," he said, and he flew home to shag food stamps, get married.

I worked two more days, driving slow, nursing the shot car; details, late orders, reorders, firing the new painters, hiring newer painters, listening to Sam talk trouble with money. The first twenty grand came and went in a blink. Sam held up a C note. I turned away. Sam stuffed it into my shirt, promised more Monday. "Where's Jack?"

"He's gone."

Sam nodded. "You're doing a good job. This could be the fastest rebuild I've seen."

"We're losing our shirts." Sam walked away. "We're losing our shit." I charged a six-pack and headed back to Fatty's, brain cells to weather, raising sail in funky seas. Life gets good in a storm sometimes, fucked up drunk, at peace under the winter dark sky. Evening rain blown horizontal by gusting trades got cursed—Fatty's crew moved to the big steel boat shed. I congealed on a sawhorse, buzzed triumphant in the deluge, victory in my eyes.

I flew away home two nights later and watched my arms enwrap a woman, watched my body surrender as she searched it for love, watched a day open far away from Cambodia. I was told to rise, dress in slacks, a shirt and a tie from a former life.

Jack showed up early to have his tie tied. Then it was off to the little mansion on the beach whose owner had agreed with Herbert, trade one wedding day for private charter. Herbert had two grams of snoot and two coolers iced down, loaded up, beer and Champagne—"I no care my money go. I no go nowhere."

Herbert said he'd done well—cousins and the right set-up—syndicated—made for success. He carried a cash bundle in a fag bag, paid for flowers, liquor and music, gave Jack and me a bill each, wedding presents.

Tuberose and plumeria made life smell good even if it hurt, and a honk or two in the front yard with a six-pack chaser put the hurt on hold. We got buzzed under a shade tree while watching the guests arrive—everyone Louise had ever known. Louise sat in a back room where the gaggle plied its craft, enhancing the lie, puttying up, making magic.

Herbert's new squeeze didn't putty, pencil or rouge. She was fifteen, overly developed and dim. She bom ba ba bommed across the yard in a T-shirt while Herbert enjoyed the envy of his friends. "When the girl is so young, you can train her."

"When the girl is so young, you can go to jail."

"No no no. I have paper. Father sign. I no going jail."

The girl squealed at twenty paces, "Herbert!" She knelt beside him. He had the toot. "Want!" she whined.

Herbert was mean. "No got. All gone."

"Not!" she whined.

"Go. Get Louise look good."

"Not!"

Herbert wagged his finger. "You bad girl. Look. You go make pretty."

"Waaaaaant!"

Herbert looked cross. "Okay. I give. Then you go?"

"Yes! Want! Please!" The girl would graduate grammar school in three months.

Herbert chuckled, finding his snoot stuff, dipping a small blast. "Almost all gone."

She laughed, "Not!"

"You bad girl."

She snuffed it up. "Ah!" She laughed and squealed, "Herbert! Want more!"

"What feeling. What verve. I can't believe it—Herbert and the girl, off the cuff like that, like Virginia Woolf or something..."

"What he said?" the girl demanded.

"You go. You bad girl. Make pretty." She cocked her head, rearranged her T-shirt so it clung more loosely to her unharnessed breasts, stood up and left. Herbert sighed. "The girl." He lay back chewing straw grass.

I said, "God, the dialogue—you, the girl."

Herbert smiled, closed his eyes. "Yes. We talk."

Jack say no chew grass by tree. Herbert smiled. I lit a joint. No one spoke, and in a minute or two it was home again—soft grass, blue sky, cool shade, good buzz, strong bond.

I sat up. "I'd like to pour epoxy on it." My friends turned slowly to me, smiled benignly, with tolerance, then turned away.

Jack perked. "Ooba oobie oo." A woman arrived in a flower skirt over a leotard. The down and outers stared, breathed through their mouths. Herbert called, "Marylin!" She strolled over. "Meet my good friends, *Whirlaway*, folks."

"Oh God, you got *Whirlaway*? I'm dying to go on that boat." Jack laughed—"Yeah we're dying for it too. Shit, we'll take you. Where you live?"

"No. You no take nobody nowhere. You take Louise. Go now. Be a man. Marylin like talk Harry." Marylin blushed, got more beautiful, made a heart thump, a throat lump and pants too. I looked tentative and dumb, stuck on beauty.

"I come back," Herbert said. She giggled. Herbert administered more antidote. "Champagne," he said and left, leading Jack away too. She leaned against the tree, watching me. I stared back. Want was a spark between us, no talk of who is, what was. I said, "You look young."

She shrugged. "Nineteen." I nodded. She touched me. "Don't do that," she said. Heat spread from the touch.

"Don't do what?"

"I like older men." She looked away. "I don't know. They're not so goofy."

"Older. Not goofy."

She looked back. "And they have the money thing all worked out." I looked down, end of interview.

"I go with one guy five years. One more lonely heartache. I want to love him, but I can't without some tenderness. He doesn't care. He got careless too, bad manners. He never took me out, except maybe Tastee Crust. I never went to a real restaurant with plates and forks and stuff, and where they have real plants. He used to wipe his nose stuffs on the plastic tree just to make me mad. I mean he still does, probably. But not with me. We broke up two weeks ago."

"Since fourteen?"

"That's old enough around here. Nineteen. God, I feel like an old maid." She looked up, past me, her face a study. She stood up, leaned close with her smile and swirling vortex. She touched again and said, "I like you. I want to know you."

She walked away, past another study. It was older than nineteen, more than twice as much. I found my sea legs and drifted into trouble—"Oh. Hello."

Renette, hips cocked, claws showing, asked the stupid question: "What's going on?"

"What do you mean, what's going on?"

She too walked away, without saying she liked me, wanted to know me. Cambodia seemed far away. In only a night and a day here was the fun kind of trouble. I thought I should choose, the young one or the old one. And a laugh bolted into me from above because I knew as clearly as a man can know anything that I didn't have to choose anything and it didn't make a pinch of shit worth of difference. I laughed and chose the cooler. You're safer with a buzz. I popped a champagne, drank it quick like a Socco Soda, letting it foam down my chest, just as my partner had taught me.

Out the kitchen door, Jack said, "Gimme that shit," and drank the last half in one pull and then went off like Old Faithful.

"You're a swine," I said.

"So? Look at you!" He wrung out my tie. We laughed till we cried and popped one more.

Herbert joined in, "Oh. Marylin. I wait years for Marylin. She fuck big ugly animal. Pig farmer. Smell bad. Gone now. Is okay."

Masao drove his rusty pickem up truck across the lawn, got out coughing "blow job!" Herbert said it was subtle and cultural for Masao, the trick of coughing up his life ambition. Marylin lingered in the kitchen. I went in.

"Oh, there you are," she said, like she'd looked everywhere, like we had a date.

"Here I am."

"It's about to start," she whispered, close, touching with two hands. "Can I sit by you?"

"No. I'm best man. I have to stand by Jack."

"That's neat," she said, scrunching shoulders, watching my eyes slide down. She gave up enough slack to pull me deep.

"You have a lovely bosom."

"I'm glad you think so," she said, leading from the kitchen to the patio. Nodding hello, hello, hello past many new friends, my skin got tight—"If you want to come to my house when this is over, you can look at it and feel it and do whatever you want."

"What?"

Renette waited down the hall. Marylin blew in my ear. I breathed short and blessed the moment, knowing that I must be the kind of rotten fucker women complain about, because I loved the pressure, didn't care what happened. But I turned and said, "I have a girlfriend, you know. I won't... flaunt this. And I don't own *Whirlaway*. I work on it."

She blinked, slithered. "Is there anything else?"

"No. No, that's all."

"Good." She led on, straight down the double barrels. She offered her hand. "Hi. I'm Marylin. Harry tells me you're some woman."

Renette growled—"Hello Marylin." Then Marylin didn't exist. "You're fucking up, Martin. It's about to start. You don't have your boutonniere, and you don't know what to do." Renette was ice, crushed.

"Do? What do I do? I stand there."

"That should be a neat trick." Marylin left. "What's it gonna be, Martin?"

"A good time had by all?"

"Anytime, Mister. Anytime." She left too. I liked it. It called for more champagne. Then I would invite Marylin to the bathroom, for five minutes, look see, maybe touch softly with tongue. Maybe ten minutes. I wasn't so cold and insensitive after all.

Sweet, sad guitar said all gather now, so these two may join forever. Louise looked like a declaration of glory, or victory, or virtue, or some bullshit sentiment people like to express when they change their lives forever, because the old life was shit, and with enough ballyhoo, maybe the new one will be better. She wore white in white on white, sequin sparkle on her veil, baby gardenias round her head, scent flowing down her gown, split one side for good thigh. And Jack, in a hundred dollars of shirt and tie—Louise took a loan—coked, stoned and drunk, rolled like flotsam on a gentle sea. On one side Louise shone bright with expectation. I stood on the other side of Jack and pushed him back up.

The priest was Buddhist, spoke of transcendence: We arrive, grow restless, grow beyond. I grew weak—too much transcending, too much drink and snoot. The Buddhist spoke of dissatisfaction and change, the synthesis of life. He spoke of sweet going sour, sour turning sweet. I looked left at Marylin, shameless beauty. I looked right at Renette, love with no faith. I looked down. Visions of Cambodia snaked through the grass, long odds on life tallied down there too, with ache, tears welling behind the dam.

The Buddhist spoke of nothing, the strength and peace of it, and the truth. We are nothing, then we can see. I sought nothing. Jack whispered, "Don't mean shit." I laughed, and the dam broke, and then these goddamn tears were rolling down my face.

The guitarist played. Jack looked stupid, Louise amazed. And transcending, I stepped past Jack, kissed Louise, said she was the most beautiful. She blushed in belief. I wove a quick exit to the bathroom.

Cold water cooled my eyes but wouldn't shrink the knot in my chest. The mirror showed a close-up of pain. I squinted down to the pores of it. A knock made it worse—"Who is it?"—because I knew who it was, knew that the loveliest bosom in the world waited outside to come in, for the gift of life.

But opening the door on Renette changed the gift. She smiled sadly, put a finger on my face. "I cry too at weddings." She hugged me, because she loved nothing more than rank, base emotion. And maybe I gave in to it—the pain went away. I knew nothing. With help, I arrived there.

Yet amazed at the science of a hug, comforted in love, I watched

Marylin looming, circling, watching from the French doors. She was like me, I thought, but suddenly the game ended, no more fun. "I need a drink."

"Me too."

We walked solemnly to the bar, where Renette ordered the sweet bubbly, the Italian one, yes, it was her very most favorite one of all, and sure enough she giggled and daintily snukked when the teensy tiny bubbles stuck up in her nose hairs. I poured my own from a bottle on the bar, it was so handy, and not all that bad.

A big dumb guy behind the bar pulled Renette around to the back side and said, "Help me here, little Darlin'," and let her wear his cowboy hat.

She loved cowboy hats, and with a sincere smile on her face told the cowguy, "It was so pretty."

I drifted out feeling Marylin's hidden gaze. I sensed it and drank more champagne to sharpen my intuition. I lay on a hammock in the shade by the beach, where she could find me. She swung with it, floated down alongside so my arm was around her. I turned her way, let a finger light on her chest—tiny fuzzes stood up over goose bumps. I whispered, "I'm skiing," lifted a seam, slid easy down the snow-white slope.

"Believe me," she said. "You'll be sorry you started here." Indifference and a non-smile made her look wise, like perfect intuition was on her side now. Her eyes spoke and her body moved. I came off the slopes. "My boyfriend wasn't like you."

"No?"

"He was weak in character. He lied. I hope you don't lie. He didn't lie to cheat me. He lied. Simple lies, everyday lies, bullshit lies."

Pigshit lies? "I lie. I lie as we lie here. We lie."

"And he smoked. He promised to quit years ago, and he did quit, until now. He knows I won't go out with anyone who smokes, and I sure won't live with anyone who smokes. Yuck. He even lied about smoking. He reeked of it."

"He smelled pretty good otherwise?"

She looked mean and said, "Yes," slid forward and pushed off. "I have to go now. Are you coming with me or not?"

"You remember the dog who had a bone, dropped it in the river for the bigger one down there?"

"We could leave for awhile." She leaned back, stroked my neck. "Let me tell you something. I'm really horny, and I like you. I look better naked. I promise you, you're going to call me, and it won't ever be this easy again."

Heart thumping, the pain came again and went to my head. "We could...smoke a joint in the bathroom. Or something."

"Good. You go in the bathroom and wait for me."

"How could he?"

"How could who?"

"Your boyfriend. Want to smoke again?"

"He's not my boyfriend. I really loved him. I don't want to talk about it again." She took my hands, stood up, stretched past touch, floated away with one look back, gone.

"Phone?" I did want to fuck her, honestly I did, and would regret for years not tailing along that day, wondering why in the world I did not.

She sighed, "Eight six nine. Oh nine, oh nine." And she drifted through the crowd, leaving me pinned to the hammock, flags up. I thought: car wrecks, dead puppies, Cambodia. That was easy. I craved a smoke or two, watching the bay, watching Herbert and Masao in the shade with pixie dust, laughing at the rubber legs that carried me over and with another blast I understood nothing, at the summit once again.

We drank, until the fat woman caretaker waddled out. "What you do here my house?" She grabbed the snoot bottle. "You want police? What you tink, dis place? I calling police."

"What this is?" Jack was behind her. He took the snoot bottle. "What this is? Drugs? At my wedding? I'll deal with this scum. Go inside."

She waddled off mumbling, "Good ting too, some kind scum." Jack sat, finished the snoot, drank and talked with Herbert and Masao about football and pussy. I watched, slept the drunken sleep, dreamed the twitching dream, felt sundown on my skin, dreamed that Masao confessed, that only half his women took the snoot bait, the other half he paid direct. Now he was broke and couldn't get laid.

I dreamed of Jack scorning the charter trade, then I dreamed of talk of gale warnings in all channels. But the gale only whispered in the lee of the volcano, and I dreamed of Jack and Herbert trying to remember the last time a freighter took shelter on the bay. Herbert said, "Not in this life." Jack said he hoped it would blow forever. Masao bet he get one piece Renette, if no one wake up Martin.

I woke in the dark to a warm hand on my face and the moment in between, before time and place, before fear, before pain—one moment, bliss. Then it ended. Wind chimes tinkled somewhere off. A baby cried in and out of hearing. She pulled me up. She wore a cowboy hat and said, "It's time to go home." She hugged the pain away again and led the way, took me home to ribs and sausage casserole and early bedtime and the TV drone, *Three's Enough* or *Eight's Company*, the one with too many Negro children. I lay still, very still, and got frisked for love, a hot mouth everywhere and finally at my ear blasting, "I love you so much!" I lay there, adequately stiff for three whimpers. She rolled off. I considered guilt, but she said, "God, that was nice." Sleep came on like a mugging.

Morning came too soon. A month's mail waited, junk, including the red notice from the U.S. Coast Guard for Captain Jack Witte, certified, return receipt requested—show up in five days with a written accident report, or lose your license. That was last month. Now on the phone the car rental place in Honolulu wanted Mr. Witte. The car was two weeks overdue, had been reported stolen. I said don't worry, Mr. Witte will be in touch directly.

At the airport I hugged my girlfriend, my nurse, thanked her for hospitality and understanding. She said you're welcome. We lingered. I wondered if it was communion, or convenience. She pushed me off.

"Go." I went, like a child to harsh punishment. She too looked sad with no mystique, another child with whom I wanted to run and hide under the covers forever, because convenience is better than hell.

Instead I flew to Cambodia and forty minutes later sat in the hot dusty shade under *Whirlaway*, unable to think or move. Yesterday was gone. Clouds blew in thick on a hard wind. I would drive to the rental car place for extension, but the car wouldn't shift. So I sat idling with golden oldies in the bleak and graying afternoon, remembering what the action was when I first hummed those tunes.

A prisoner of war left to himself can substitute the past for now; remember sanity as it was in other times, and in this way survive.

I worked. I worked, and I laughed. I'm no fucking worker. Look what happened to me. I worked. Happy work, mostly, it drew hands to tools, turning screws, twisting nuts, clamping clamps, wedging pieces, soldering, puttying, sanding, caulking. I fared. Arriving early with a "Hey niggerboard, how do you do," I pressed it to the bosom of *Whirlaway*. I pushed. I pulled, pushed and pulled, until the strokes shortened because shoulder muscles shortened then balled into knots. Pain felt good, down to the bone. Resin dusty at dusk, I slid a palm across her skin. A smoothness so profound and silky soft drew a moan, "Marylin."

Jack came back three days later. I sat in the new rental car listening to newstalk radio, AC on, racing the windows, over the edge. Jack eyeballed *Whirlaway*. "What the fuck did you do?" like his work was important and skilled, and mine counted for shit—oh, I read him alright. But Jack wised up quick. "It looks good. I see what you did."

I gave him his wedding present, a letter from the Coast Guard with a ribbon around it. "Have a nice day."

All the parts, exotic woods, big welds, little welds and splices were in and done, except for the new spreader, but the rebuild dragged on. Refitting imperfect shows up in bad weather, so Jack lectured on craft, care, precision and peace of mind in heavy seas. I said, "Foo foo...foo...foofoofoo." Jack trashed four knuckles on a through hull fitting that day. I hooked a thousand tiny holders to a thousand yards of wire and screwed the holders to the seams between hull and deck. Jack said any fucking idiot could do that. I heard myself breath by then, felt the dust ball in my lungs. "I'm not just any fucking idiot," I wheezed.

Carry painted the bottom. Jack cursed the motherfucker who shipped the new spreader—no show. He aligned the shaft with a micrometer, cursed heavy trades, because early spring was worse than lingering winter, sometimes with tradewind storms lasting weeks. And high season wouldn't last forever.

I said, "High season. Season high." I varnished new woodwork. Death fumes coated my lungs with soothing buzz.

Then one day it was done. In came the paint preppers for three days of measure, mask, paper, tape, measure again, wait two days for the motherfucking wind to die down, then spray the bitch, because the work doesn't stop, even when it's done. Sheer will finished it. The hands were nothing—appendages on dead men. Only spirit remained. My hands swung free on dead arms, shuffling off to Fatty's.

I was early, or late. I found a body slot, slipped in and froze, except for breathing. Sticky skin gets tight in goosebumps when clouds blow under the sun. Fatty Renken showed up after awhile with a big plastic laundry basket of reef fish—little angels, wrasses, yellow tangs— all the nippers who trusted me, ate from my hand—"How they died?"

Fatty laughed, "Goddamn quick."

"Dynamite," the Mexican said.

"They eat quick too," Fatty said. "Sweet as sugar." Fatty was the troll under the bridge. "Takes more ofum is all."

Inside the basket was a vision of death, a mound of corpses, faces in the rug. I drifted out and sadly, in my heart, sent these acquaintances too to hell.

The stick would have to go up with the old spreader because Jack got red in the face pissed off at no new spreader and beat the old one straight with a hammer till it lined up with the holes in the new tang.

He said the only motherfucker on the face of the earth who says you can't refit an old spreader is the cocksucker selling new spreaders. After hundreds of calls for parts, contractors, jobbers, welders, painters and money, I made one more.

"Sam. We leave."

"I'm coming down."

The yard bill came to seventy-eight grand—forty-three paid, thirty-five owed. Carry's bill came to seven grand, but Buster Frank said no one ever mentioned it to him, working Carry against the deductible, and he'd seen it tried many times. "Oh, it's great for you guys. Not so great for me when the insurance company comes for the audit. Fuck no I won't buy that."

Jack clenched his fists, stepped up—"You got to be some kind of cocksucker charging thirty-five an hour for a motherfucking boat nigger, and what the fuck kind of deal is that?" Buster Frank walked away.

Carry piped up, "Cocksucker." Sam said don't worry.

Seven-fifty an hour times Jack and me came to six grand, minus the cash given, which left enough for the deductible. I said, "No. Nonono, nonononononono... Go home broke. Start up again with no dough?"

Sam looked down. "What else can I do? They won't release the boat unless they're paid."

I walked away. Jack followed, then Carry.

Whirlaway hung in the lift, swaying in the breeze on her way to the water, looking shiny, brand-new and ready again for the sea. Ragtag, broke and broken, eyes stuck on a burned out squint, I remembered the legends. Some boats are lucky, some are not. She fell off a dolly in a storm in a California yard and got rebuilt. She got raced hard once by weekenders who treated her like a rental and pushed her too hard, too much sail, taking a knock down that held her down in a heavy sea, spreaders dipped long enough for long odds on her rising. She'd risen. A mad drunk on a sportfisherman rammed twelve boats in the harbor to either side of her, missed her by inches. She'd broke her mooring, drifted past a reef with two feet to spare, then past big rocks on the other side that should have holed her and sunk her, but didn't. She drifted in, laying herself gently on the sand.

She soaked up Jack and me, filled our lungs with dust, sucking eighty grand from the stratosphere to bring herself back up. Now she drew Carry aboard for the hard sail home. Herbert was due that afternoon. The barometer fell a millibar in two hours. Jack said the fucking barometer didn't work right in all this humidity.

Preened, prim, blushed and trussed up, she lowered slowly in the straps till her keel dipped in, then down to her waterline, she looked ready to run, a gleam in her eye, fearless, to the day she would dive under the combers and soak up the souls of the last poor stiffs aboard her.

The stick went up that afternoon. Carry worked free, with a vengeance, prepping the deck step, cleaning the I-beam step the mast stands on. He found a silver dollar in the dust, which was a dollar more than anyone else made today, which looked like someone put it there under the mast the first time the mast went into place. Looking up to envious eyes, he gripped it tight, polished it shiny and set it back for luck, under the rig, because he was afraid not to, and no one complained.

New stays and shrouds were made fast, new sails bent on. New roller furling gear replaced the worn out junk from before the crash. Jack took strength in every margin regained. I watched boats come and go.

Herbert showed up quiet, distracted, as if Cambodian reality shut him up. He hugged his friends with affection and pride because we had saved a boat.

Carry assembled clevis pins and turnbuckles. I caulked the step boot. Jack tuned the rigging and said "Aw fuck. We forgot the radio antenna." Herbert took it, sixty feet up.

I went for one more call, to Weems. Weems took it and said hey when I said hey. I said it was okay, *Whirlaway* gained value every day, and with no delays, problems, bad weather, poor health, late shipments, no-shows and/or miscellaneous, she'd be back in the water in a month, two on the outside, maybe three, running charters, making payments.

Weems said, "Don't move that boat."

"What?"

"Don't move that boat. It's been decided that the bank can sustain no further losses. Your boat...uh, the doctor's boat will be foreclosed and seized. You're not to move it."

"Foreclose and seize what? She's a pile of bones. She's worth thirty grand in parts. That's thirty, down from two ten. What's the sense in that?"

"It's not my decision."

"How can you seize a vessel halfway through a rebuild?"

"We would hope you would continue."

"Continue! For what?"

"You said you loved that boat. That's for what. Or was that just another story. Besides, we're willing to consider crediting your deficiency judgment with a reasonable hourly wage if you continue working."

"I called you the day we pulled her off. We risked our lives on that bitch."

"You certainly did."

"I told you then we wouldn't work drydock if you foreclosed. You said go ahead, get off the rocks. You said go ahead, make it right, get back. You said, 'You fellows get the job done and get your livelihoods back.'"

"I don't think..." He paused a long time and said, "This isn't my decision. It was made by the board."

"It's called a verbal contract in Hawaii," I said, wondering if it was. "You broke it."

"Don't move that..." I hung up, called Sam.

Sam said, "No contest. You're bound as debtors. Surrender the property."

"Bullshit. A guarantor on a note does not a borrower make. Nuel's the debtor. We only leased the bitch from Nuel."

"In that case you could argue against piracy."

"Piracy?"

"That's the charge. I'm fairly certain you'd clear it."

"Christ."

"What do you want to do?"

"I want to go home. We're heading out tomorrow."

Sam doubted a seizure. Legal fees run around thirty grand on a documented vessel. Another five and airfare for the Federal Marshal, and Sam's fees as custodian would run another ten.

"How do you know they'll use you?"

"I'm the only adjuster in the state with custodian insurance."

"Then you can tell us when you're coming."

"Go."

"Thanks, Sammy." But Sam had hung up. I didn't care. Out the door, heart thompin' one mo time, back from the living dead, racing down the stairs and across the yard to another hot horizon going gray and milky amber. The unsettled ocean frothed foreboding, and a windy shadow blew in from the east. I inhaled it. Whoever would have thought so many people in the world would knock you down, then kick you? Then kick you again? Was this the alternative to nine to five? Ah fuck it—with someone big as a bank, somebodies big as bankers to beat, life was as much shit as it had been, but victory was a sporting proposition again.

~~~~~~~~~~~~

# Death

Slamming into reverse at sixty was what the Weems call felt like. Stealing money from a bank on paper is one thing. Everyone does it. It's red, white and blue. You let them put you in a corner in exchange for what you want—then they try and steal it back—making you steal your own goddamn boat. There ought to be a law.

Jack, Carry and Herbert worked last minute nuts and bolts. Jack saw it coming, not the tremble or the sweat, but the twisted smile. He came up dockside.

"I tried for two free months. I think I got more." Jack smoked on it. "We're in foreclosure."

Jack flicked his butt, breathed short and turned red. "They said they wouldn't..."

"They did. Sam says we're cool on a piracy rap. They can't hold us back. They have to tell Nuel, and he has to tell us."

"Not to move it?"

"That's what they said. I told Weems we were two months from back in the water and she was still a pile of bones."

"What'd he say?"

"He said they'd pay us a fair wage, credit against our judgment, maybe, if we finished her."

Jack laughed, lit another smoke. "What now, Harry?"

"Now we run. Home and charters. Now we make no payments. Now we push the bitch. Hard. Now we make some jack, Jack, for when they take her away and we skip out quick. Now we focus on the difference between holing up broke in ninety days or heading out with a couple grand in our pockets."

"Yeah?"

"Yeah."

"Just sail home and run charters?"

"Weems doesn't even know where she lives. Sam'll tip us off, I think." I turned back toward the office. Jack followed. "We get two days jump on them figuring out we're gone. Maybe a week more for them to reach Nuel, and maybe another week for Nuel to reach us. I think I can tweak all the breaks for another week or two."

"How?"

"I think our lawyer will inform them that their lawyer will have to reach Nuel's lawyer, and that all future dialogue must interface obtusely to the defendant and obliquely to the lessees."

"Martin."

"Yes, Jack."

"I'm sorry I called you a no-skill, worthless cocksucker."

"I expect it from you, Jack."

"Martin."

"Yes, Jack."

"Who's our lawyer?"

"You must be tired, Jack."

Upstairs at the typewriter I sent a letter to Weems—Whirlaway Charters would sue for breach of contract, loss of income, drydock fees, loss of livelihood and slander, a million easy. Jack watched me type. He smoked hard. "We'll teach them to fuck around with the odd couple," he said. I signed off. Jack said, "We'll have another five days until that gets there."

"No. It goes overnight mail. I want to convene the directors post haste. They'll take two weeks on invites." I dialed Weems again and got his mailing address from his secretary, then asked for Weems, read him the letter and said, "You'll get it tomorrow, but I want to let you know it's coming so you don't do something butt-fuck stupid in the meantime."

"I see."

"That's good."

"Is this a threat?"

"Yes, Weems. This is a threat." I hung up again, typed the envelope and got pissed at the shakes.

"You shoulda been a lawyer, Harry."

"Too dull."

We drove to the P.O. for the ten dollar special. God Bless America, the Post Office took a check. We drove back quiet, just like that morning a long time ago, focused on money and yachting. Except that today a horizontal rain beat like small rocks on the windows. Jack steered with both hands against the buffeting wind. He said, "Heavy trades can last six weeks in spring time. We got no choice. Gale warnings lifted this morning. It's rough, but not like it was."

Way past pride, scared shitless, reminding myself that fear is part of courage, I wanted out, out at any cost, out. We pushed on. Jack would run her to the fuel dock and fill the tank quietly while I would go for groceries and the bill, with finesse, because Bastalani was on in the store. Jack stared at the storm as if into the Valley of the Shadow of Death.

Word gets around a boat yard when a yacht gets marked for the chains. The man who ran the yard threatened his own seizure ahead of the bank's. Fuck as fuck can again—Bastalani said, "The way it is. You no win. You lose boat." So she wrote the chit for four bills in beer and groceries and another hundred-forty in fuel. She say no worry, it late, man go home. I signed it. She wagged a fleshy finger in my face. "You go home now. You have good luck. Aloha." She made me want to stay. She made me understand love.

The phone rang, Buster Frank for me. I shook my head. She said, "He no here now." She listened and said, "I tell him no leave?...Tell who? Tell him keep boat here?...Wait I see." She cupped the phone, smiled sad and into it said, "He gone. Boat no here no more...Yes...I know."

I kissed her gently. She accepted it. "You have shown me love," I said, wiping the tear forming in my eye for such a rare and golden beauty as that which she gave, from the heart, in the trenches.

Jack was happy—another four bills in groceries, a hundred-sixty and squeezing on the fuel. Wind and rain wrapped around the big steel sheds, swirled its way through Kewalo Basin in erratic strength, rough gusts, nasty whispers.

Rain slanted, stinging faces. I yelled over it, "We're gone Jack! Buster's on his way with chains!" Jack yelled back—he and Herbert would take the boat down the beach two miles to Ala Wai Marina, wait there, cross tonight, close to the lovely dawn. I could return the rental, ride the shuttle down.

Herbert and Carry were ready, though Carry wanted his deep water debut clear and sunny, just like in the magazines. Carry Lowe had never been out of sight of land, but he'd seen plenty rough weather on TV—so rough he was even rocked by it, felt the pitch and yaw of it right there on the couch. He looked happier than Jack or Herbert, because a first timer still knows in his heart the glory of adventure. I cast them off, watched a header push *Whirlaway* sideways out of control, into the channel where she'd have hit a passing boat but by chance slid into no traffic. She heeled under bare poles, made way when the prop stopped chucking bubbles, gripped water, motored out. I split too, don't look back, passed Buster Frank going the other way in a huff because he just got fucked for five more bills. He'd turned sixty-eight grand with no risk at twenty percent over cost. He'd wring another seven grand from Carry's work. He broke a sweat twice, yelling at Sam for his money, and again, driving back in the wind and rain.

An hour later I caught the bow line near the fuel dock at the Ala Wai, tied her off and saw the hard squint the preview had etched on the faces aboard. Jack yelled that the old spreader works great, called the spreader guy a cocksucker. I got nauseous walking up to the bar by the dock.

We'd been there before. The place was marked, good for plastic, so we could charge a hot meal, so we could tie our guts in knots on credit and never ever pay the bill. It was one of those bad times, when a con man understands the meaning of too smart for his own britches.

At a table away from the windows Jack ordered brandy all around. And we waited like mourners for liquor at our own wake. I felt a big shit coming, best deal all day.

The can was a mosquito swarm. Some stiff in the next stall blew more air than a humpback whale, made a tiny plop and said, "Oh boy," beat his thighs like bongo drums, grunted hard, sighed and said, "Great. This is really great."

Not I. I slipped a two footer easy as greased eel, wished I could measure it to see if it was a record and left the stuck stiff in the next stall grunting. But arrogance got me, hit me at the sink with another shutdown, first time in months—stuck. Froze solid, on a motion, the short dry wheeze of the paper towel dispenser, like the little metal box had hung on the wall all this time, maybe since eternity started, just for this moment, when it could give a towel to me and size up my entire ridiculous existence with a wsht, wsht, wsht, wsht, wsht—no matter how many paper towels came out, another one primed and waited with the same verdict. My arm got tired, and I realized all at once, as if in epiphany, man, it's...paper towels. All I needed was a little ache, a little pain. Relief equivocated back in the gray light of the pub, back in the fold of quiet despair, where cheap carpet and plastic tables took over, and a sorry ceiling fan with bad bearings made the same snide comments the towel box had made. Carry slurped his brandy. "What's everybody look so sad for?"

Herbert looked at Jack. "They no find us here. Two, three days. I got money." He patted his fag bag.

Jack wouldn't wait. "You don't wait on a tradewind storm. It's dropped off some now." Herbert nodded, looking down, knowing Jack was right. "I wish I could tell you to go home." Herbert shook his head. "I wish I could go home." Herbert was still. Jack looked at me, then at Carry. "Carry. You can go home."

Carry shook his head. "No man. I'm going."

Jack hooked his brandy. I slid mine over, ripped off a fart. Jack spoke to his new brandy. "Johnny one note. A guy who's never been. And a cocaine addict."

Herbert smiled. "We have one honk?"

Jack got up. "You go ahead. I need a nap." He moved to a booth on a dark wall and curled into it.

Herbert opened his fag bag and dug around until he came up with some yellow pills. "Jackson. You like sleep? I got six hours. Right here." Jack was silent.

"We leave in three," I said.

Herbert said, "No. Two a.m."

"No. The pacing starts at eight. We'll go around ten."

Herbert popped the pill, downed it with brandy, dug through his fag bag for some white pills. "I sleep now. Then I wake up."

I doubled up with the grimace that looked like painful glory, like maybe another record was on the way. "Excuse me." I went again.

Behind me Herbert said, "You hungry? Like one Captain Platter?" Carry said that would be fine.

The can was empty. I got halfway down to seated when my guts cut loose, lost control. It was a relief, but I got stuck again, stuck bad—mosquitoes lit for hot buffet, bit hard, for pain and then blood, but I stayed stuck on the worse stuck a man in a bind can get stuck on, which is God—God right goddamn there in a scuzzed out dark shitty crapper trying to separate myself from the dirt inside me. God settled in, solid like concrete—no motion, no sound, past pain with perfect sense, like a vision, until the dirt poured out whenever it wanted to, but there was no separation at all. God was present, tangible and inseparable from the sides or the top or the bottom, was the source of all order turned to shit.

God had no arms or legs or head or hair or knotted guts or stretched asshole that cut loose for a stream of hot shit that spewed so long and hard it must have took the molten soul itself with it. Mosquitos didn't light on God and suck the blood—no, those things were just another part of me, and I basked in the Presence, in the Light, of a new order, which was way over the rainbow, way past logic, chance or free will.

A long time later between a shit and a sweat I cleaned myself, went back. Jack and Herbert snored. Carry belched oysters, scallops, fish and shrimp, deep fried, with fries. "Man, that was fine."

Fetal in the dark in the booth by Jack, guts easing up, I stretched out too, drifting away.

The wind at the door huffed and puffed and blew the little pub back, froth and spittle splattered the windows. The door blew open, and the wolf howled in. The door slammed shut and the little pub shuddered. Herbert sat up, rubbing his eyes, grubbing for his wake up pill, downing it quick. Jack sat up, trying to breathe. I watched a naked bulb, focused on the weekend, as if the channel was only time and I could meditate through it. Carry lay back, meditating gut bombs.

Low, hefty laughter and drunken voices drifted from the bar. Two more bodies in from the weather turned when Jack asked the time. "Six," Herbert said.

"Herbert!" A scrawny drunk swaggered from the bar, sloshing his drink. Saltwater dirty with weather brown skin, a greasy ponytail, three earrings and a green splotch tattooed over both shoulders, he ambled over. "Herbert!"

Herbert looked away. "Bobby Cobb. What it is?"

"What is... What it's... Ah fuck..." He stumbled, splashed gin on Carry, stopped, stared at the wet spot on Carry's shirt, then at Carry. "Sorry there, Slim," he said, wiping a paw across Carry's chest. He stood up straight. "What it is?" He turned back. "Rhino! What is? Herbert wants to know."

Rhino's head, low over his drink, ticked back once over a soft grunt.

Carry wanted to fight Bobby Cobb. Herbert looked indifferent. Jack and I knew Bobby Cobb and Rhino Tasupei from the harbor time, westside. Bobby Cobb was a harbor rat, come west from Jersey to call himself local, to be Barnacle Bill. Some called Bobby a jinx, albatross, bad man aboard. Some said he saved the day, one day or another. He had the miles.

Rhino Tasupei had a big jaw, big top lip, low slung neck, dead ringer for endangered species. Some said his name rhymed with wino, others said it rhymed with cocaine. Rhino was a moke—three hundred pounds of Tongan made of pig meat, white rice, reefer, liquor, snoot, piss and vinegar. But he was half blala too, slow to anger, slow to speak, steady aboard and not a bad guy, if not a good guy too.

Bobby Cobb looked like a weasel, added up like a scumbag. He wobbled near Carry, drunk in self-defense, a plea for good cheer. Carry impressed his shipmates when he said, "Step back, dirtboy."

"Well excuuuuse me!" Bobby Cobb shouted. Then he stepped back. "Hey! You got *Whirlaway* out there!"

Jack lit a smoke, slid out and went for a leak. "Order me a coffee will you?"

"Coffee?" Bobby Cobb yelled. "Fuck that! Hey! Bring my man a... a... a drink!" He staggered in a circle back to Herbert. "Shit man. We just... We just over here. *Tootsie Roll!* Man, we come over on *Tootsie Roll.*" He drank and wobbled. "Yesterday, man. Slept on the goddamn fucking dock last night, man. Shit."

"You sail over *Tootsie Roll?*" Herbert asked.

"Yeah man."

"How it was?"

Bobby Cobb fell forward banging his glass on the table. His drink shot straight up—he ducked under—and down on his shoulder. It soaked his greasy shirt, dripped off his chin. He leaned on both hands leering. "See man. I won't wilt!" Carry stared back. "Punk fucker." Carry didn't move. "Shithole."

"How it was?" Herbert asked again.

"What?"

"*Tootsie Roll.* The channel."

"Big, man. Very big."

"How big?"

"How big's a spreader, man? Twenty feet?" His head ticked. He stood back up and wobbled. "Oh man. Hey, Rhino! We got a ride home, man! Eeeyihaa!" He swung his glass, flinging the last drops over Herbert and Carry.

Carry went off, flipped the table at Bobby Cobb. "Come on peckerhead. Come on. Come on. Come on." Bobby threw a saucer and missed. Carry crouched with a steak knife, lunged and caught Bobby on the arm. We took note; Carry Lowe was for real, wanted to kill a man with little provocation, less return, even less thought of consequence. Bobby smiled—he liked getting cut.

Herbert jumped in. "Hey! Hey! Hey!" He pulled gently on Bobby Cobb's arm, and Bobby fell down. Herbert asked please for the knife, so Carry's life would not be wasted on a worthless task. He reached out. Carry gave it up, hissed, "Ooh yeah. Rough and tough. Very tough." Bobby Cobb grinned, trying to see it all as tribute to his salty soul.

Jack came back, all clear. "Carry boy. Alright."

Bobby Cobb whined on the floor, "Jesus, man. You got no beef with me."

Rhino stood up—atoll rising. He lumbered over. "I got no beef with him," Carry said. Rhino slapped a mosquito on his ham shank neck, "You go home now?"

Herbert said, "Hey. Rhino guys want ride home."

Jack smoked and thought. "I don't know. We're crowded."

"We need," Herbert said.

"Shit, man." Carry wanted something else in yachting.

Bobby Cobb picked himself up. "I got fifty-two crossings on this motherfucking channel, man. Rhino got a hundred eighty."

Rhino said, "We like ride home."

I sipped. "He's drunk."

Rhino stepped close. "I no drunk."

"He's drunk."

"He no drunk too. He play drunk. Bobby! Stand up." Rhino grunted, bent over, picked up Bobby by the scruff.

"I no drunk, man."

"He no drunk. We like ride home."

Jack said, "We might not leave till tomorrow. I'm watchin' the weather." He drank his coffee.

Rhino said, "Fuck you," walked back to his drink.

"Yeah. Fuck you, man," Bobby Cobb followed.

Carry said he wouldn't go nowhere with no trash.

I asked Herbert, "Can steer?"

"Can steer. Both. Cobb not so good, not good on boat. I no like. Bad news. Rhino good."

"Fine. We'll take Rhino. Leave the little fuck here."

"No. No can do."

"Why not?"

"Long story. Rhino owe money Bobby Cobb. Five, maybe seven grand. They deliver one time da kine for big man, but Rhino fuck up and lose load and Bobby Cobb save him with money. Now Bobby Cobb got big dog, Rhino. He say Rhino pay off debt when Rhino save his ass too. Maybe. I no think Rhino go if Bobby no go too."

Jack stubbed his smoke. "Fuck it. Let's go." He stood up and strode for the door. "Hey!" he called. The two at the bar turned. "Come on!" Jack was out the door. The wolf blew in. I tasted burned coffee, felt its fetid warmth become one with the empty pub; moldy and overcooked was what shelter had come to. The wolf howled in, and God arrived again too, or maybe God was The Wolf, and though nature appeared at times heartless in its indifference, it was balanced and perfectly ordered, and no matter how hard the fist jams down your throat, small blessings abound, if you only know where to look. Take the time between waking and walking into the horror. Blessedly compact, it left no time for fear. Thank you, God. This last hot, overcooked slug is in tribute, to You, yay though I walk into the teeth of it.

Whirlaway rode easy at the dock. The trades blew her off so the surge didn't hurt. Immersed in fluids, pressures, contacts, voltage and ignition, Jack covered fear with busy. Herbert covered with foul weather gear. Carry watched. Bobby Cobb and Rhino on deck released all the spring lines, and Jack yelled tie the springs back on and don't touch another goddamn motherfucking thing until told to do so. I cut half-inch nylon braid to twelve foot lengths and rigged safety harnesses, bowlines to hog clips outboard, shoulder wraps inboard.

I wrapped Herbert. Carry wanted it wrapped around his waist. Herbert said, "No. Big wave take you off, line pull hard here,"—he chopped a palm on Carry's spine. "Go pop. Wear high, on shoulder." Herbert tied me in. I called to the new boys, "Line and hog clips below for safety harness, if you want one."

Bobby Cobb yelled, "Safety harness? Fuuuuuck!"

I wanted Bobby Cobb overboard, but then again he and Rhino were two more weathered hands in the face of extreme conditions. And for a couple of macho idiots, they were tried and true. Airfare home was forty bucks, twenty minutes, and the airline guys took checks. But then you really got no choice but to take the long and bumpy road, if you're serious about being a macho idiot.

I watched the seething night and remembered a guy I went to high school with, who moved to Denver and sold real estate, in a suit and tie, in an office on the eighty-fifth floor with climate control—vents misting scented climate into the room. Now what kind of a life is that? I cast off.

The harbor fell away quick, trades astern. Jack hung a left and the first wave came over the bow, in our faces, no flinches, because the adrenaline was pumped up bigger than the weather was on the safe side of Diamond Head. Three more waves broke over the bow, bigger. Five miles to Diamond Head and the Molokai Channel. Jack gave Herbert the helm and pulled me along. Below he said in low tones of fear, "Where's my safety harness?"

"This mean you no like die?"

"No. It only means I want to overdose, not drown."

Bobby Cobb showed how much macho bullshit he was good for, in case anyone had forgotten—he walked unharnessed to the bucking, surging bow, stepped up on the pulpit and yahooed the storm. He came back after taking a few waves, laughing, "I no drunk now!"

The weather wrapped around Diamond Head hurling ten-foot seas and thirty-five knots. The rock came broadside in another ten min-

utes, and the show was on, first waves breaking near the lower spreaders, fifteen feet. The wind slammed forty-five for a knockdown so fast
that forward speed held, the trough fell before she did, and the hollow beneath her made for free flight before she crashed hard enough
to break her back.

Like mountain climbers on a sheer face, all hands clung to the ver-
tical wall, the deck. Another comber pinned her down, and a break
between sets gave her time to rise. As she rose, Jack crawled below to
check the hull. It held, no leaks or seeps, but when she crashed again
in the next trough, he knew she wouldn't hold another hour, much
less all night. He climbed back up and yelled, "Not so close! Fall off
thirty degrees! Bearing backside Lanai! More at a slice now than head
on, toe to toe, she crashed without the crunch. The compromise was
slippage south—missing Lanai meant continuing farther south for the
Big Island—across Alanuihaha if she could. If she couldn't, it meant
sliding sideways, next stop Tahiti.

What ensued was not the kind of sea adventure in which sailors
trim this sail or pull that line and survive this set to the next, when
new heroics would save their asses yet again. What ensued was a
mauling. The evening became unreal, insanity unfolding, a nightmare
solidified on the boiling cauldron of the sea.

Bobby Cobb yelled for sail. "Raise sail! Raise sail! Raise sail!" and
so on, until every man aboard wished for a gun. He was uncanny staying aboard with no safety harness. Hope was a consensus, the sea
should take him. Jack motored into it, or as close to it as he could,
falling off as much as he dared.

That meant a narrow slot of ten or fifteen degrees—to port of it
she got clobbered, to starboard lost. It was a narrow path to home,
but even in the slot she lost way every fourth or fifth wave that
knocked her down. Engine failure meant probable death. It red lined,
screaming, when her bottom came out of the water. Then the vision
was prop blades flying free, through the hull. I relived the minutes
of replacing the blades after cleaning, wondering how much sanity
was left when the cotter pins went on that now separated us from the

cold black boil. The engine gauges read good levels—1500 rpm, 190 degrees, shooting to 3500 and 210 when she cavitated twice in a row—lost her grip on the water and whined *Screaming Jesus, this is thin air.* I went below to check it over, new injector mounts, belts, heat exchanger and saltwater cooling muffler. I came back up quick. "Fuck it—spin cycle down there. I hope it works."

Carry Lowe lashed to the taffrail was separated from infinity by twenty-four small screws holding the taffrail to the deck. He was separated from his Captain's Platter ten miles into the channel, first stretching his neck to puke over the rail, then puking with no stretch, over his chest, into his lap, holding his breath for the next sea aboard. He came up clean, huddled there white knuckled.

Bobby Cobb showed his stuff, fore and aft, fore and aft, yelling, "Sail! God wanted boats to motor... He wouldn't invent sail!..."

Herbert was next, sprawled sick on the cabin near the mast, grabbing a grab rail on the high side, worthless.

Rhino sat on deck also high side, wedged between the cabin and a stanchion that wouldn't have kept one of his thighs on board much less the rest of him. He kept his center of gravity close to the deck, gripped the grab rail and watched the helm like a moke from the wax museum.

On the cockpit floor, tied to the binnacle and hugging it when the ocean came aboard, I watched the helm too.

Jack couldn't head farther up, he couldn't fall farther off. He yelled into it, "What the fuck!"

Rhino slid aft six inches, looked hard at Jack and held up thumb and forefinger. "Sail. Little bit." Jack nodded, released the jib sheet on the high side, readied the sheet on the lee side. Rhino sat by the roller furling line but wasn't ready for the brand new drum we fucked the insurance company out of. Slick as snot, it wanted sail right now with the wind. The jib slammed open, wedging Rhino's hand between the line and cabin roof, cutting deep. He reached back for a handle, freed his bloody paw and ground on home.

Far forward Bobby Cobb shrieked with delight—sail. Rhino made the jib line fast and held on for the next sea aboard. She punched through, and though she could point no higher, she gained to four and a half knots, to a two-to-one shot. Then we rode, adapting as some animals do to violence, measuring the night in heartbeats, learning how long a night can be. Jack steered two hours. I watched the engine gauges from the cockpit floor, wishing for a Captain's Platter in my gut so the heaves would have something to latch onto. A new vibration came through the binnacle post—Jack shaking.

I yelled up that I would take it. Jack didn't hear. Bobby Cobb, on one more round, yelled that a man who gets seasick is the worst kind of pussy in the world, and that it'd be a cold motherfucker in hell before he shipped again with this kind of shit. He said it wasn't right, some assholes calling themselves sailors, but not him and Rhino.

Then Bobby went below. "Martin! Take it." Jack followed below. Standing up and fighting up the narrow slot led in one step to horror—and the calm before death. The scene through the companionway, in the cabin was one of few words. Jack braced on the nav table and watched Bobby Cobb, who rummaged for a beer. Bobby found one and drank it, grinning at Jack, scoring those painful points he could dredge up later with gusto, and with love for those rare moments a real man lives for.

A black wall of water on the black wall of night brought me back to the helm—too late. It crashed with the worst beating of the night. The bodies in the cabin tossed like liar's dice. Those on deck buried their heads. I ducked too for the next wave aboard that pinned her down as if it would hold her there. I squeezed blood from the helm and spoke low, coaxed her up. "Come on boat. Come on boat. Stand up. Stand up." She stood, and I kept a closer watch.

In another hour the chaos got worse. Jack had stripped naked in the cabin and crawled into a berth to beat the chill. Bobby Cobb was back topside yelling that the skipper was the goddamn biggest pussy of all. Rhino told him, "Close hatch."

Jack went next, giving up his coffee and brandy, crawling naked from his berth to the head, to hug the toilet, drive his guts into it.

The wind hit fifty, then fifty-five, seas to the upper spreaders, thirty feet, less than halfway home. I stayed in the slot, but that was all. She wallowed, rose slower, took a pounding with every wave. Then my legs quit, gave out, sat me down, no more, because a man who keeps on fighting to stay alive sometimes dies one piece at a time, and sometimes doesn't even know it. I stood up. They melted. I breathed deep, stopped the shakes and queued up for the white bus, then they came again, the shakes, like a private little storm. Herbert looked dead on the cabin top, his bloodless grip the only sign that he wasn't. I called him. He didn't move. Carry, in back, watched from inside his nest of steel and lashings. Rhino moved.

He came back slow and took the helm, one foot braced to starboard, the other far to port. I slid back down to the cockpit floor and looked up like a newborn baby, ready to die of exposure if I didn't go below, certain to die of gut wrenching if I did. I wondered if death too becomes dreamlike on its approach, and I struggled below on instinct, for better odds.

It was then that Bobby Cobb fell into the snake pit between his ears. "Awwwwright, Rhino!" he yelled. "We'll sail these pussies home!" In a wink he freed the roller furler, let the wind slam the jib wide open—slamming the mast too. All eyes bulged up to the explosion, the sudden burst of horsepower on all points of the rig, arcing all of it like a big bow ready to fire itself into oblivion, straight through the hull to the bottom.

The mast didn't break, and in another stroke of luck, a rogue wave caved in from the blind side and knocked her down. Stick in the water, the big jib worked against her, holding her down like a purse seine. She couldn't lift the tons of water in her jib. And from somewhere underwater, Rhino had the wits to throttle down, quell the screaming engine.

Whirlaway had no helm, rudder flat on the surface. Rhino spun the wheel hard starboard, digging the rudder in. The boat groaned in a slow pivot downwind. Painfully she rose.

Painfully I rose, breathed once deep between vicious gusts and looked up to see the skinny rat who tried to kill us. He stood grinning beside Rhino, in a blur, stupid but still ready. I buried a fist in Bobby

Cobb's gut. The intention was understood, the punch weak, and Bobby laughed, but he puked too. I told him he was a pussy and grabbed a winch handle to kill him, because it was necessary. Rhino spun her straight into the wind. The jib flapped madly, too berserk to come home to the roller furler. Jack was back up. Bobby Cobb called weakly, "Fucking pussies!"

Jack heaved on the furling line. I cranked the winch, gained an inch, then two, then the wind took it back.

Rhino called to Bobby Cobb, "Get sail!" Bobby Cobb grinned, grabbed the sheet at the cockpit and pulled what he could to him, then hand over handed to the foredeck. Stepping into the melee, forward of the mast, he caught the clew ring square in the jaw. Bobby Cobb's jaw caved in, turned to mush. He ran forward with the clew, and I gained at the winch. The jib came in.

Bobby Cobb came back with half his grin stuck in place, the other half gone, wobbling again as he had earlier that night. He made mush noises—his mouth no longer formed words. Sinking into shock, he looked for something to hold onto. Herbert called from the cabin top, holding out the boat hook. Bobby Cobb reached for it, but the boat hook got shorter.

Carry yelled up, "Hey, Bobby!" and tossed him a line, untied at the bitter end.

Bobby wobbled and made more noise. Jack watched the boat, moved to the helm and took it from Rhino, who moved toward his former position. Bobby fell then, aiming for Rhino, falling on me. I shoved him over to Rhino. "Take care of your friend!" I howled at the howling night.

Rhino held Bobby by both arms, looked into his pulverized face, into his eyes as he went unconscious. Then Rhino looked abeam at the water mountain rolling over. And the evening was made perfect when Rhino let go of Bobby Cobb and hung on for himself.

Jack spun the wheel away from it, then back into it. From under the deluge she rose, one man gone. Rhino sputtered. "Bobby fuck up," was Bobby Cobb's eulogy; "fall overboard," his epitaph.

The five little Indians left aboard felt uncertain gratitude that Death had taken the worst among us first. Herbert went back to his cabin sprawl. Carry tucked his head between his knees. I melted again to the cabin to stop the shakes. And dressed only in pants, Jack called Rhino, take it again. Then he followed me below. I trembled by the cooler, "Care for a beer?"

Jack nodded. But wind and seas made the cabin unbearable, drinking difficult. So two down and outers bracing for a couple warm ones in whatever spirit remained, down to the breathing and the pulse of it, lost all the words and wit between us, all the life pounded to pulp.

On deck again, I sat on the cockpit floor. Jack took Rhino's spot, high side by the cabin. Rhino steered eight hours, to first light, when the island of Lanai showed its lee side and sheltered water dead ahead five miles.

Rhino took her in. Once in the lee the trades wrapped, reaching around but down to thirty. The sea swelled there to four feet. Herbert moved first, testing his arms and legs, rising to a stoop, making his way back and sliding in beside Rhino. "I take." Rhino gave it up, sliding around to a cockpit seat. He sat. Carry unlashed himself, stood up and watched the wake. Jack moved into the cockpit, and I went for six.

We drank it quick and quiet. Carry went for another. Herbert broke the silence. Looking hard around the little circle, he say, "Bobby Cobb go south." No one spoke. Herbert looked at Rhino. "Bobby Cobb go on yacht, drunk, no can stand up so good. Yacht look like guys in hurry, offer money. He go." Herbert nodded, responding to his own coaching. "Right, Brah. Bobby go. He promise send postcard, say he always want go."

Rhino drained his beer, crushed the can, flipped it overboard, sat back and slept.

The next five hours to home were gray, wet and bumpy. *Whirlaway* couldn't point, but she leaned a shoulder into it, berserk with a will of her own.

Homecoming was grim. In the wake of beatings and broken spirits, death and the kind of violence most souls never imagine, much less see, she made her mooring. A surf shop boy ran the dinghy out and came alongside with aloha. He shut up quick, seeing the faces aboard.

We rode in quiet, hardly looking back at *Whirlaway*, who looked bedraggled, resolute, too dumb to die, covered with the black, greasy film saltwater turns to on a boat. Fixed and fresh painted but forlorn in the grim veil, sheets, halyards, reef lines, leech lines and harnesses dangling loose or scattered about, she looked gangfucked on her way to the ball and left for dead. Yet she rode easy on the mooring, as if ready to go again, as if she really had more pride than sense.

"*Whirlaway*," Herbert said. "Thank you." Rhino grunted.

Louise and Renette waited on the beach, knowing we had died at sea. Soon after the second hug came the news: a man named Sam had called and left an urgent message to call him back. Jack smiled and lit a smoke, shuffling up the beach. "Take the whore," he said.

"Nice," Louise said. "Real nice."

Renette led me by the hand, smiling and calling me sweetie, saying she had some plans for me.

 # The Beautiful Dream

It wasn't easy, walking out after fucking Renette one time, but it wasn't hard either. She got passionate, got down, wanted it nonstop, like the high hard one was proof of survival, of love. I begged off— out from under deep knee bends. She rolled off, sighed big and said she'd been thinking, "about us," and if I wanted to stay around, a few things needed changing. "First of all..."

No thought, no purpose encumbered one foot then the other for five miles up the beach, around the bay, until sand under foot was all there was, until a man was nothing but tired flesh on aching bones— stop, feel the slow, wet, cold rise between the toes. I lay it down behind a dune, curled my feet under my butt, cupped my hands for a pillow, slept.

Waking in darkness, I bolted up—pounding heart and electric second over the hollow, bittersweet, between nether and now...

But only the world waited below, with a gentler pulse timed by lapping waves so tame that tourists wallowed daytime in the shallows. Violence was only a memory, best forgotten, if not now then soon. "Boom." And life went on, there, soft, dark and sandy.

And there in the dark and lizard tick, a man felt the balmy breeze seep into his skin, felt sand fall off, grain by grain by grain...heard himself make long gutturals like rocket boosters piercing darkness to orbit then sh...exist no more. Retreating to the high plateau for sage brush, coyote song, he reached nowhere, good. Buzzards swooped through the stars for whatever was left but in vain, only Spirit remaining.

Up again, then standing, then one foot then the other, a man just like a man I saw once walking down the road, wrinkled from a sleep in the sand walked through the valleys between the dunes, through the canyon between the condos to the street. Walking with traffic down the street, I came to place, a bar.

Fuzzy noise with a downbeat and smoke swirled thick with social need, people looking for people to take home, for the feeling— thicker still with people glaring hard at the spirit drifting in, people amazed, afraid maybe. A meteor in the distance trailed a smile, approaching, staring, waiting, then gripping the spirit arm, leading it to a stool at the bar. "You look run hard, Harry, put away wet." Jack called into space for one more tequila grapefruit in a bucket, make it a double. He handed over a light jacket. "You got to wear a shirt in here, Harry. Don't look down. You can fake barefoot. Here. Comb your fucking hair."

"Why a bucket? Why not a glass like everybody else?"

"Because you get more juice, so you won't get drunk so fast. You want to be a goddamn alcoholic all your life?"

"No." I'm no juice head, I want back, feel good, young again. "Thank you."

"Don't mention it."

Double tequila grapefruit in a bucket, a cigarette, a light jacket and combed hair led to a smile, like everyone else. "You got sand in your ear, Martin. What'd you do, break loose of the fuck farm and rack out on the beach?" Yes. "I figured. She said you split for no reason and headed up this way. She's pissed." Yes. Jack smiled. "What'd Sam say?"

I don't know.

Jack spoke to his drink. "They can come get the bitch. I don't care. I'll run the whole bunch of them out in the dinghy. I don't ever want to go aboard again." He pulled ten bills from his pocket. "Here. We got paid for the private charter before the crash. Seven grand. I put

five in the account to cover bad checks at the yard." He shrugged—
"They put you in jail for that shit. Here. We get a grand each."

"No pockets."

"You're worthless."

"Yes."

Like a moon from behind Uranus, Carry Lowe orbited into view.
"Nuel called."

"How Nuel is?"

"He's fine."

"Well. Good." Jack watched his drink. Like life, it went empty.
"Three double tequila grapefruits in buckets," he called.

"What you tell Nuel?"

"Jack wouldn't talk to him. He made me talk to him."

"What you tell him, Carry?"

"Told him it was fucked."

"What'd he say?"

"Nothing much. Said you'n Jackie's fools for not sinking her when
you had the chance. Said you don't get a chance to sink a boat like
Whirlaway every day." Carry drank his new drink.

"What'd you say?"

"Told him he's fucked. Told him if he'd been around last night he
might have got his ass throwed overboard too."

I gagged, like good old times at The Q-P DO. Jack laughed. I
looked fore and aft.

"Carry didn't say 'too.'"

Carry grinned, "Man that was something, wasn't it? Old Rhino. I
liked that fine. I don't believe I ever will forget the look on..."

"What'd Nuel want?"

"Wanted to know what you'n Jackie fixing to do."

"What'd you tell him?"

"Told him how the hell do I know? What'd you want me to tell
him?"

"Tell him Jackie'n me are gone. Tell him come on, sail his yacht to
Florida. Only five thousand miles upwind."

"Seven."

"He said he's looking into that." Jack choked on another laugh. "Said he talked to a few boys around his place, and he says he's getting tired of the whole deal too. Said he thought it was good to have a decent boat over here, and he really didn't mind giving a couple fellows something to do, but he might just go ahead and sell the whole show. Said he had a guy in Michigan might pick it up. Just write a check."

"Made out to who?" Jack said.

"Whom. Forget it. Nuel can't sell. His boys who do the work won't pass the interview."

"Said he didn't really need to talk to you boys, but it'd maybe be best if he did. Said to remind you, 'We all in iss tuh getha, Bubbas.' Said you boys'd hear from his lawyer one way or another, and it's always good to work these things out on a amicable basis if possible. Said he was out 'fit-ty thouzndollahs' and now the bank wants another twelve for the last two months and this month too."

"Tell him come get it."

"I can call him. I got his number right here. We buddies now—he told me call him, anything came up. Said it wouldn't be forgot, me keeping him posted on the situation. Said if he didn't answer just keep on trying, he'd be back pretty soon from flying his new airplane and a fellow was in town for some office buildings he's fixing to buy. Said it was his private line. Not everybody has this number."

The down and outers laughed, drank. Jack chewed ice. Carry called for three more. Jack said Herbert flew out that afternoon to Hilo, had to check on a load of seafood."

"Rhino get back to the westside?"

Carry said, "Yeah. He walked."

Jack hung his head, "We wouldn't have made it without Rhino. We'd be dead."

We drank on it. Jack ordered three more. I turned slow on my bar stool, leaned back on the bar. "So Nuel wants you to spy on us."

"He said he already knows exactly where you are and what you got."

"Did the bank call him?"

"Yup. Said he already hired a couple three lawyers."

Smoke swirled with thoughts: marshals on the way for a seizure, bank foreclosing, down and outers deeper and farther. Two bimbos stepped up, ordered up, hung around. Carry told one she had nice thighs. She said thanks, so Jack told the other she had great ankles. The women giggled.

I picked a quarter off the bar, motored slow through the haze. Outside was clear, starlit, still, a deep breath cool and fresh. Soft clanging followed the quarter through its tumble. A monotone signaled the far end, ready and waiting. Different was better. Eight six nine, oh nine oh nine.

Chemistry, timing and few words measured want. Hot breath fogged the glass.

"Hello."

"It's me."

"You're back."

"Yes."

"Good."

"Yes."

"You sound tired."

"Yes."

I was gone. Silence explained. "You need a place?"

"Yes."

"You have to be quiet. My parents are sleeping."

"Sh."

The half mile took as long as two on a slow drift. She wore a see-through nightie for a presentation reflecting another kind of insecurity, because she was perfect, needed no presentation. Her eyes reflected too, a sadness that her body ripened, her spirit aged. She stood in the doorway backlit, perfect and in need.

"You probably had some raggy old flannel on when I called."

"Yes," she relaxed, "Come in." In a step I was in her embrace, in her whisper, "You look so old."

"Mmmmmmmmm." She pulled me in, led down the long hall to the studio over the parents' house. The little room had a single bed, a table, a bottle and two glasses. She opened and poured. "Where do I sleep?"

She served wine. "Wherever you want." I drank like it was water, stood stupid, lost again, A to B. "You look like... You look awful."

"Some. Yes."

"Some what?"

"Quite a bit. Nothing. Really. Please."

She sat on the bed. "It was bad?" I shrugged. "I thought about you. I think I missed you."

"What did you miss?"

"I'm not sure. Maybe I didn't miss you. I think it was the dilemma you were in that I missed."

"They teach words like dilemma in junior high now?"

"I learned it in sixth grade." She slid free of her nighty. "I have men wanting me all the time."

"I know."

"You too, but you were different."

I sat beside her. "Stuck." I drank. "Maybe still stuck." Her young and perfect body there before me was inanimate, breasts and thighs as arbitrary to the scheme of things as lawn furniture, and I feared the moment, knowing what was lost on the nightmare seas. She crawled under the covers, signaled me in, so I stripped and got beside her, lay my head down, closed my eyes.

She doused the light, lit a candle. "Good night."

I wondered if a beautiful young woman in flickering shadow was another dream, another convenience. Darkness, no violence, no fear, oozed over with warmth and a touch. "Why is tonight different?" I turned to her, and God stuck me again, filled the space between us with solid time, with the distance between two nights, between a touch, stuck me in the relative span of chasms. She held still while I closed the distance more slowly than the distance closed. She rose to it when my hand trembled and the moment of contact stretched from solitary one to plentiful minion. I shuddered, violence recalled. She wrapped herself around me as a mother wraps a child, as I choked on the foolish notion that this had never happened to me before.

 Nuel Revisited

It was over then, but then it wasn't. I woke alone, dead reckoned a two-knot current, heavy swell, Bobby maybe fifty miles southeast by now, unless the sharks got him. Sharks like a dead man best of all, and Bobby stunk bad enough going in. I felt better about Bobby Cobb than I felt about myself. Bobby be done.

Drifting on gentler seas, I slept again till noon, until the sharks circled close, woke me up in a sweat, sat me up with a gasp.

Jack didn't answer. Sam was in—said he was impressed how quick the Federal Marshal was on line, headed for the beach, until they got the letter. The bank now had lawyers in Honolulu.

Small victory is life to a beaten man. A man who thinks nothing will survive him likes to make a few waves going under. "How long will that take?"

"How long do lawyers take? They'll reach your lawyer, maybe work out a deal. A month anyway, maybe two. They don't know foreclosure costs. Don't forget, if you lose, you pay what they spend."

"What's it cost?"

"I'd say ten grand legal, five for me, a few for the Marshal and then miscellaneous. Then the boat comes over here and gets tied to a dock and goes to hell for six months or so. That boat should bring eighty, ninety grand at auction. Distressed. Uncertified. That puts you down what, another hundred or so?"

"Did you explain that to them?"

"They didn't ask. I'm telling you. You tell your lawyer. He'll tell their lawyers."

"We don't have a lawyer."

He gave a name and number. "He's alright, sometimes."

"We got no money."

"You rebuilt her. You're back in the trade now. Run charters. Make money. Make a business again. You'll know what to do." The Squire was a sentimental fool after all.

"Yes, sir."

"You owe Buster Frank for fuel and groceries. I told him I wouldn't cover that."

"No. I wouldn't cover it either. Tell him we won't forget his help in hard times."

Sam laughed short. "Maybe you got a lawyer."

"Thanks, Sam." But he'd hung up again, and I laughed short too. "Stealing from the rich, giving to the crazy," I told the empty room.

Jack answered from a hard sleep. "Hey."

"What?"

"New plan."

"What?"

"Back to old plan."

"What?"

"Run charters. Make money."

The pack crumpled, the match struck, the long first drag. "When?"

"Tomorrow? Think about the business with no payments."

"Yeah?"

"Two good months is ten grand walking money."

"They'd just let us keep it?"

"Attitude, Jack. Attitude."

"I could use a few grand."

"You guys out late?"

"Yeah. Strange. It got wet. She said, 'It's like a damn burst, isn't it?' Man. Strange, like sticking your dick in a bucket of paint, you know what I mean?"

"Carry fall in love?"

"He got a blow job. Then I had to listen to his life from day one. Fucker cracks up. Bad drunk."

"What's he doing now?"

"Sleeping. He's going home today."

"I'm coming over."

By the time I made Jack's place the bank's lawyers had called, but Jack wouldn't talk. Nuel's lawyer called too—Carry talked—got asked for everything he knew. Carry said he knew Nuel was no damn good, going around like he did, sticking rebar up little boys' backs, cutting people's heads open for the money. Carry said Nuel cut open a head on a old woman knowing she'd die but that didn't matter on account of the Medicaid, which he needed for a payment on his empty office buildings in Utah.

Carry got going on the old woman and did good, till he cried on the phone that the old woman was his grandmama. Nuel's lawyer got short. Carry said, "Prejudicial. Leading the witness!"

Sam's lawyer should have been cheap, asking the same questions over and over into pure confusion. He wanted a hundred thirty an hour. "We like a thousand dollars retainer and then we like to keep the account balance at a thousand dollar minimum. We can work off it from there. You can bring it up to the minimum once a month, and we like you to pick up any overage within ten days."

"Overage. I like that. I'd like some overage." The lawyer said nothing. "Is the meter running now, or you taking a break?" The lawyer said nothing. "What's the rate for a couple convicts in a bind, on a personal send up from Squire Sam?"

"Hold on." He took a breath. "Okay. Eighty bucks an hour. Get me three hundred today and we're a team."

Fuck me in the ass, a little voice said—it's a drop on a hard close. I sighed.

"You want to call me back with an answer?"

"No. We're on. Call the bank's lawyers and send them a few memos and some injunctions and restraining orders and a habeas posthumous."

"I'll call Shel this afternoon." Sheldon Hyde was a bank lawyer. Shel and this guy would have drinks, maybe dinner. They'd come to a just and equitable interpretation of The Law.

Driving Carry to the airport on a full tank, a cold pack and a bag of hotdogs was good. Cruising between the volcano and the ocean in strong winds was a comfort, anarchy at hand. Jack popped a cold one, unwrapped another red hot, "Boy. It doesn't get better than this."

Carry wadded the empty bag, wished that he could stay, spoke in fragments: "I can...work...a boat."

"Wish we could afford you, Carry."

He looked out the window. "I don't need much."

"Neither do we. We don't get it."

"I want to learn. I want to know how you do it."

"We don't do it."

"Yeah you do. You eat shit just like me. But you guys got a yacht and a condo on the beach and some fine women."

"This ain't Russia for chrissakes." Jack popped a beer.

"Yeah. I got Wakiwaki Waikiki." The bay blew frothy. "We could take her." Tradewinds swooped down the littorals, bullied the little truck. "Tahiti, New Zealand, Micronesia. It's all downwind."

Jack turned at the airport, pulled up to the terminal. "Carry. I swear if we steal the bitch we'll call you first. You're on." Carry was consoled, certain it would come to pass. He lit a smile at the promise, grabbed his pillowcase, squeezed off a couple handshakes for a couple twenties, and he split, ambled down the concourse on bowed, skinny legs.

"He's right there," Jack said. "Gets too emotional though."

"Not like you, huh Jack?" Jack thought it over. "That screw headed fucker goes to our school," I said.

Jack thought that over too. "You got a bad attitude."

We cruised a few booking desks, got good wishes all around from those who bet against *Whirlaway's* return. The woman at the Jesus Christ Activity Center gushed thanks to Jesus, said she'd been ten hours a day, six days a week for seven years in that wooden booth, five-by-five-by-five—just her and Jesus. Two couples came up talking snorkel. She hallelujahed and sold them *Whirlaway*. These guys are heroes, praise The Lord.

Two more came later on the phone, and though eight normals broke even in a former life, six with no mortgage meant a bill and a half each. Life got fat on two spins of the axis.

I stayed up late with thirty bucks worth of groceries slicing up for ham sandwiches and garnish, because the lunch guys were owed two grand. The lunch guys charged six bucks less and did all the slicing so it was a pint less bleeding too. At least the work helped postpone the cruel choice of beds. Renette called at seven, asked if I'd be staying again with Marylin. It was a lucky guess, that was all. She didn't know. And I didn't care. I flashed on the difference between greasy food, country sentiment and horsefucking on the one hand, and youth, soft touch and sensuality on the other. Fuck Renette. I said no.

"Are you coming over then?"

No. That was easy. She hung up. I called Marylin and got no answer, so the rest was easy too—two more beers and the couch, calm seas to three a.m., junk movies and sleep. Louise turned it off at three, and the deepest sleep in months took me to six, time for a money-maker.

Coming aboard at first light was harsh—ransacked and looted, raped and robbed, strung up and left to die, salty, slippery, bloody, reeking of puke and shit, *Whirlaway* was not ready for the prom. Buckets and brushes and soap got us in a sweat by sunrise. Jack took a break to board the six normals.

They showed up on the beach, puffy, plump, pale white, prosperous and dull. Jack told them don't leave the cockpit. He put one at the helm, pointed a landmark, the snorkel adventure grounds, and said don't fuck up. We worked. Jack said it was good, the sweat was mostly liquor, and anyone who paid a Christer good money for a boat ride could find happiness in the cockpit. He moved them to the cabin top then and cleaned the cockpit. The blood came up with bleach and cleanser, and the light spots looked better than blood.

At the adventure grounds the normals held their noses, jumped in.

Jack told them, "Stay out of trouble." An hour later he said, "Get out. Help yourselves to sandwiches, go ahead and have a beer." We motored home quiet, flushing the bilge, cleaning the cabin. We took a break to tie up at the mooring. I drank a few beers while Jack took them in, and everything seemed back the way it was again, hard work, chronic fatigue, too much drinking.

But four more normal normals and another eight Christer normals from Praise The Lord Bookings were on for tomorrow. No calls from Honolulu.

I called Marylin. She said, "Oh, hi!" She was busy. I let Renette go.

A normal next day came aboard pasty, plump and dull—and aggressive; gold and diamond bracelets, chains, a watch, an idiotic ring with big diamonds, three rows, eight to the row. Jack said, "I might get a big gold diamond fucker like that."

The golden normal wasn't put off, but instead got encouraged, became host, loudmouthed over extremely famous and expensive boats he'd actually been aboard. He pierced the dawn tranquility. A Christer said, "Those with all shall have nought. Those with nought shall have all. See His glory—on the water." The other Christers chuckled. They knew.

The golden normal said, "I own twenty-seven buildings in New York."

"You must be a doctor," Jack said.

"No no. I earned my money."

I said, "If Jack here owned twenty-seven buildings in New York, he'd be dead in a week. They'd put on his gravestone: Old Jack. R. I. P. Pussy and Drugs."

Jack said he wasn't that old. The golden normal shut up. The Christers looked stunned, then dropped into Bible speak—He, Him and His, blissful glances up. After an hour of it, the boat felt like a loony bin. Jack boomed, "What's all this 'He' bullshit? Is there any chance He might be a woman? Or a whale? Is He a vegetarian? Or does He like to take it in the ass? I mean what the fuck?"

I went forward for the anchor, feeling more stable in a way, back to abnormal with all the normals hushed, making money, dishing insults. I called back, "Yeah. What the fuck?" Then we laughed, out of control, coping again.

The next four days made two more grand in receivables, no calls from Honolulu. A month of high season remained. I called Nuel's lawyer for a reading on the situation. Jeremy Oulette was "looking for data," considering slander as grounds for an "action."

"Let me make it easy: Nuel's used up four states. He nearly killed a boy. He's the rottenest, lyingest, immoralest, scummiest no-count piece o' shit God ever put life into. I'll testify. How's that?"

Oulette said, "One moment." He wanted it all, mumbled, "immor... scum... piece... shit..."

"Jeremy. Did he give you any money yet?"

"I uh..."

"You know he's done in Florida. Cut an old lady's head for the Medicaid. Ask him. You better get some cash up front so you have something to draw on, a working account with some overage."

"Maybe."

"Anyway, we want Nuel to have a firsthand report on the operation, condition of the boat and so on. Airfare's cheap and you'd only need two nights. We'll go out sailing and show you the boat, maybe have some fun."

"I don't need to call it fun."

"Nah! Fuck the fun. We only want what Nuel wants, settle this thing amicably. We're making substantial money now, so we can show you the numbers."

"I think an inspection might be good. I appreciate your cooperation. I'll speak with the doctor and get back to you."

"Ten four, buddy. Check you later."

Tad Givens called the same day for his check. Jack answered. "Who the hell is Tad Givens?"

"He's our lawyer." I wrote the check. Givens said he had a call in to Shel, and he'd advise when he knew.

It was only three o'clock so I called Shel and left a call back for Oulette. I called Oulette and left a call back for Givens and capped off with a call to Givens, call back Oulette. "That should get us another month. I'll follow up tomorrow with calls from new clients."

I called Marylin. She said, "Oh hi!" She was courteous and pleasant. "How are you? How've you been? How are things going?" She was so excited because she'd gotten back together with her boyfriend, but it was so different now, since she discovered...she didn't know what, he was such a nice person when he wanted to be. She guessed she loved him.

"Love is a wonderful thing." She made perfect sense, like a dream—but it was all green cheese, no sense at all, another zero on a fractured sofa on a hot and windy afternoon. No, you can't bring it back from a dream.

Jack came in pissed—no charter tomorrow, no money, only a solid day of baseball and The Beaver. "How's it looking, counselor?"

"Peachy."

"Fucking-a." He downed a beer in one slug.

I hit the shower in a funk. Marylin was a coincidence, not cosmic. The funk got thick at Renette's—she opened the door, stepped out with a hug and a promise: I was the love of her life. I'd never felt so bad on dry land.

She took me in, warmed the other half of the dinner she'd made for two—fried egg and salami sandwiches with chocolate milk, ice cold the way she liked it—while Margarita, the parakeet, sat perched over the table on the fake chandelier, dropping tiny anchovies on to the plastic fern. Then she took me to bed for a back rub and easy sex with no demands. In the morning she made coffee even though she didn't drink it and sent me on my way.

A week passed into routine, approached normal. Up at six, work a snorkel adventure with an occasional sunset. A guy could work the beach too, between charters, pointing out the boat, closing quick on normals with no plans for tomorrow. Homecoming was meat and potatoes, TV and reefer, bed and the love chase, orgasm and sleep.

Givens called. Shel liked the slow pace—still no word from him, except for filing foreclosure, assuring Givens on a seizure, directly.

Givens, ready for action, needed more money right away. I said, "I'll handle the action. We got no money."

"I thought you were running charters."

"Right. We made two grand last week."

"So?"

"We spent it on sandwiches."

"What?"

"We owed the lunch guys two grand."

"Look. I don't need to know your business."

"That's what I said."

"It's not up to me. The boss says another six hundred this week or we're off the case."

"Off the case. I see. I'll talk to my boss. We'll see what we can do."

The next ten days grossed six grand. The lunch guys got five hundred and agreed to easy payments. The down and outers got twenty-seven bills and half a honk each. Fat and sassy set in with easy groceries, rent on time. Guilt over Renette's love was replaced first by acceptance, then comfort. Discretionary income put a new slant on life—I could now see the need for nuclear weapons in the world and a solvent Pentagon. Rising early, working hard, getting paid, and then coming home to some decent meat, potatoes and TV was good, sunburned and bone tired. Some better-than-average sex made it all tolerable, a suburban route to the end.

Hungry wits stay sharp. With no hunger, a man can count his years left, plan for the future, retirement and old age. But hunger lingered, crouched on a rafter watching the infant prosperity. We knew good times were like hard times, only a phase, so we took the girls to dinner with champagne, dancing and drugs, like no tomorrow.

One night Renette asked, "Do you love me?"

"Sure." She cried. "No shit, I love you so much I want to die." She sobbed. We fucked twice, forty minutes of in-out. I wondered if women wonder who a man fantasizes.

"I love you more than life itself," she said.

That's not healthy, I didn't say.

Another week passed and another. An invoice for twenty six-hundred came from Givens. I got back to him: "You're fired."

"We'll litigate."

"I recommend Oulette." I hung up, called Oulette. "Givens is fired. We need a mouthpiece."

"Mmm. Can't. Conflict of interest."

"What do you mean? Nuel's our partner."

"You know what I mean."

"You mean Nuel's working against the partnership?"

"He wants me to research action on a breach of partnership."

"Did he pay you?"

"Yes."

"You talked to Shel yet?"

"I have a call in to him."

"You still going sailing?"

"I can't talk to you again until you retain an attorney. Then I can speak to him. We have certain ethics, you know."

"Very certain."

"Goodbye." He hung up. The infant choked. Hunger fluttered, descending softly. At least prosperity died with a whimper not a bang, with a lawyer on the phone, not a marshal on the beach—not yet.

Real insight came with feeling good—the shakeup, move out, hit the trenches was back. Real life was on again.

I felt old, getting older, nothing to show, trapped in workaday with an older woman. I wanted out, which was all I'd ever wanted.

The early movie came on, a lovable, laughable comedy, so I eased up for it, because Jack said I never did, and I'd be dead a long time. But just as daytime TV in the suburbs got me numbed, got my stomach thinking of supper, my dick thinking of the home girl, eyes heavy for a nap, the phone rang.

"Hey, Bubba."

"Hey, Nuel."

"I thank I got it all figgad out."

"Tell me."

"I will. A bank wants—em-me see—nineteen thousand sebm

hunnit 'n sebmy two dollars'n fit-ty shree cent."

"Fuck it, Nuel. Let's call it twenty grand."

"Course now I want my fit-ty thousand dollars too. What I'm willin' a do izziss: I'm willin'a add it all up'nen each one de partners pays one thud. Jist like we said in a beginning—one thud, one thud, one thud. At means each a you boys pay right around twenty fo thousand. You can jist pay me if you want to, 'n I'll pay a bank."

Nuel hit home, had lied about the loan, went cahoots with Bascum, sabotaged the business, taken his partners down to dirt poor for a point, his superiority. He sliced up a boy and left him for dead. It was attempted robbery, fraud, murder and graft. And here he was again, another go at control. The Doctor was in.

"Gee, Nuel, that sounds like a swell idea. And what a deal for me 'n Jackie."

"Well. I hep you boys if you let me."

"I'm kind of dumb at this stuff Nuel, well, and me 'n Jackie can just...write you a damn check?"

"At's right. Right away now, 'n I'll take care of it."

"I'll go ahead and say yeah for me, 'n Jackie, I think he'll see it's a good deal, shit, just clear up the whole damn thing. You go ahead and pay a bank, and we'll send you what we owe you from charter money."

"Hell I can't afford a pay for you'n Jackie. Jist send me yo forty-eight thousand 'n I'll pay a bank."

"Nuel. You won't believe this—I'm embarrassed to tell you. We spent our last forty-eight grand."

"Shit. You boys. You don't listen. If you do like I tell you to do, you set aside twenty, forty thousand dollars. Jist set it aside. Don't spind it, don't even touch it. No way. At way when you need it, you have it. But you jist don't listen!"

Nuel was merciful and patient, but sometimes his flock crossed him. "We're sorry, Nuel."

"Well, Bubba. I gotta do what I gotta do. I want you'n Jackie a know it ain't personal, no sir. Iss bidness. Ass all. Don't have a damn thang to do with how much I like you boys."

"Well. What you gonna do, Nuel?"

"You jist be careful, Bubba. You be real careful."

"You mean like listen for fat guys in the shrubbery with machine guns?"

"You never make another dime, Bubba. I git it. You'n Jackie just won't learn, 'n now I beat you at your own game."

"I got a idea, Nuel. Let's play a game where we see who gone cost who more money, rat now."

"You fuckin' with a wrong guy, Bubba."

"I might just cancel on a inshurnce tomaw mawnin', head on out 'n c...c...cu...cu...cut her loose." That shut him up; he knew I'd do it, and he hated it when I mocked his gritgeek speech defect. "Hey Nuel, you looking for a new state to cut heads in?"

"My lawyer'll know howda get me."

"Yeah, he's coming out sailing with me 'n Jackie."

"Yeah. He told me you been talkin' in his ear."

"Yeah. Told him you a killer. Told him you didn't have much money, what with deductibles and all."

"You got a new girlfriend, Bubba. She's a little...elderly for you, isn't she?" Score one for Nuel. "How you feel, getting old, ain't got shit, no way to get shit?"

"This might be the last time we ever talk, Nuel. We come a long way, you and me. You gonna hang up in a minute, and when you do, you try and figure just how much money a guy like me, in a position like I'm in, can cost you. Worst case scenario, Nuel."

"You keep an eye out, Bubba."

I hung up. I would have traded another shot at Marylin's tits to see him then, would have traded for Bobby Cobb going over.

 # Herbert

I spent an hour looking for Nuel's old hospital or new insurance company so I could report on Nuel's cocaine habit. I looked for the third wife too, the one Nuel offered fifty grand for a hit on, in front of four witnesses I could subpoena in a skinny minute. I got hot by four, tired by sundown, drunk by dark.

Jack said Nuel would fall soon enough. "Why make waves now, when we got a free boat?" So normal life went on, with a watch out the window. No day's money got counted until leaving the mooring, because a cancellation meant refunds, until we got the normals into the water. Three grand each squirreled away safe was enough for airfare anywhere, rent and deposit and some groceries too, enough for another year of living, after a fashion.

Nuel had overhead, on the run, but he kept contact with Oulette. He went north to Pennsylvania to cut a few Quakers after ruining a perfectly good melon in Florida. He still had over forty states left but he couldn't handle a judgment now, not with another malpractice, and maybe another wife.

I felt good about Nuel, because the chase would soon end. I felt bad not knowing when, called a lawyer of my own to prep for personal bankruptcy, to keep it clean for a new start, somewhere, new strength, somehow.

One day drunk, stoned and wondering when, Jack said, "Hell, we ought to run an ad in the local paper, sell the bitch, mooring, dinghy, brochures, T-shirts and all."

I took a hit, drank my beer. "Selling a yacht we don't own and a business covered in shit and lawyers doesn't bother me. It's the timing. We need two months to sell."

"Call it in anyway. What if we called two months ago? Besides, I think you'll get us another two months."

"I'd be surprised if we got another two days." I called in the ad. The phone rang as I set it down. I gave it to Jack. "Your turn."

It was the tour operator from Honolulu who sent the private charter before the crash. She had another—a Fortune 500 corporation— seven days starting tomorrow. She'd pay a thousand dollars a day but no more.

Jack sat up straight. "I don't know. Let me check our schedule." She said don't bother. "Well. I guess we're on then." She said good, westside, seventeen miles around.

Poof—the down and outers, catbirds at last, planned a grocery and beer run. Departure tonight for the westside for a week on the hook meant refuge, no marshalls, no surprises, peaceful slumber, cash money.

"I never had six grand at one time before," Jack said.

"Yeah, you and Dave Rockefeller practically asshole buddies now."

"I like the charter business now. I think we should keep it."

"Jack. We're stiffing the mortgage."

"Oh yeah. I forgot. Oh...we need some snoot."

"What? We doing too good?"

"I want some. That's all."

And as if some days were made for beating the bear, a familiar knock on the door announced the arrival of the snoot.

No one saw Herbert in the month after coming home, not to worry; a busy man in import/export will surface when he's ready.

Herbert showed up fifteen pounds thinner with thinning hair, normal pallor. His nose stuck out from the weight loss, hungry for more snoot. He carried a six-pack and a soiled paper bag, a smile fixed and shallow. "Ey, Brah." He sloshed down a pill then plopped on the sofa.

Jack said, "Hey. We got a big charter, right now. We need a deck-hand." Herbert sighed.

"Hide out with us for a week," I said. "Just stay aboard and shag beer and help clean up." Herbert smiled. "You look bad."

"What you go now for? It dark."

Jack shagged a beer. "*Whirlaway's* going back to the bank any time. We want to get out of here, run one more charter."

"Nah! They no come night. Sit." Perfunctory and domineering, he shuffled to the table, wide-eyed and unkempt as a snoot bum. "I want show you. Turn out light."

Jack doused the light. Herbert set his bag on the table, careful, like it was a baby. It opened to another bag inside, less worn, and a plastic freezer bag inside that. Inside that an uncut kilo brick glowed like moonscape. Herbert opened the plastic. "Oh, God," Jack moaned. Herbert's fixed smile twitched. The brick shone, buzzed vibration.

Herbert said, "Sixty thousand cash."

"That's half this condo, and this place never was much fun."

Herbert pulled a mirror in a velvet sheath from one pocket, a fresh blade from another. He feathered the brick, dusted the mirror, fluffed and sculpted two lines—a night on the town, turbo.

Herbert smoked his, said his nose was gone and noses are passe anyway—"Smoke more better. Healthy. My doctor say."

Jack took the snooter. "I'm passe." He snukked it up and braced for the slingshot. The tremor did not come. Instead he sat down grace-ful as a dancer, nodding.

I next leaned and snukked and floated free, ignition, lift-off, orbit, smooth as sipping whiskey, no heat, no jolt.

"Uncut. Ninety eight percent."

"Could be habit forming."

Herbert's smile got warm and honest. "It is." He laughed. "But only psychological."

The drug talked for an hour then—Herbert said Rhino got a post-card from Bobby Cobb. Jack laughed and dusted the mirror. Herbert laughed too. "Rhino no dummy you know. Rhino like save ass, same like any guy."

Jack recounted all the lawyers. Herbert said, "Maybe I know one man like buy."

"You find one man buy, you get five grand."

Herbert laughed. "Why you pay? You keep money."

"Send the man."

He scraped the brick. On the way to Jupiter, Herbert said he was doing good.

"We like buy some?"

"Why you like buy? Take."

"We like buy some for later."

Herbert cut a chunk off the moon, an inch square, a half-inch thick, maybe a grand wholesale. He called for a saucer. Jack jumped. Herbert laid it on, and Jack said, "We can't take that much from you."

"That's a first," I said.

"You share."

"I don't get it."

"You got."

"You in a situation?"

Herbert's smile went shallow and anxious again. He looked between us, "Herbert say he doing good."

"You in a bind?"

"I like... I like sleep here one night."

"How you going sleep on this stuff?"

"I got pill for sleep."

Jack said, "You can stay here all week if you want to. Louise won't care."

Herbert shook his head. "One night. I leave tomorrow."

"Sure."

"I like borrow two hundred dollars."

"You got sixty grand in snoot here, and you need two bills?"

"What? You never hear nigger rich?" We laughed. I asked why two hundred. "Need airfare."

I shagged beer. "Who knows you're here?"

"Nobody. It's cool."

"You in big trouble?"

He shook his head, no emotion. So we drank beer, talked two hours more, until Louise came home—Herbert hid his moon rock quick and shook his head. But she was hip to tootseroony and wanted hers. Herbert fessed up grinning, prepped new lines. I passed. Jack smiled. Louise said she never felt honk vibes so strong before. Jack smiled bigger, snooted again and lay back on a seven year journey to the next galaxy.

The new blast made more talk for another hour. Herbert spoke melancholy and life. He sought reason. He said his aversion to violence in the late 60's ruined his football prospects. He would have made it in football if not for that. He made it instead with a spiritual career.

"What's that?" I asked.

Herbert said he was a priest in the Church of Cocaine Now. Nobody laughed. He said he made a moral contribution, gave his congregation a lift. His flock agreed, see the tithings they paid. He rambled on, dead serious, laughing time to time at his own nonsense or at this guy or that guy. I drifted. Jack zoned. Finally the tunes took over. We smoked a joint. Near two I slept.

I was up at five. Jack looked like a dead man, eyes open, in the recliner. Herbert on the lanai looked south at the night, paced for dawn. I put coffee on, packed my ditties. Jack wrapped his chunk in plastic, grabbed some T-shirts.

Herbert came in and set out saucers and cups and served the coffee proper with the creamer and sugar bowl—for a formal sit before sunrise, together. The ritual was proper and silent—until laughter over a small eye-opener. Hot coffee warmed our buzzed-out bodies. One mosquito up early, looking for an ear to buzz into, lit on Herbert's arm. He watched it pierce his skin, sink its needle to the nub as the hind end swelled and turned red. Herbert slid a thumb and forefinger to either side of it. Then he squeezed the skin white, slow, bloodless, tight. The mosquito sucked hard. "He want one free blast," Herbert said, letting go.

The mosquito bulged and burst. "I get one big guy mosquito bite." He smiled. "I like see him go off like that." Herbert smiled. "I go now. Best for girl." He glanced at the bedroom. Louise snored lightly.

I walked to the window, walked back. "Herbert. You been fluky since you got here. What it is?" Herbert shook his head.

"You need the truck?"

"Yes." Jack gave him the keys, told him which beach we'd anchor near, and if he didn't tell anybody where we were, we wouldn't tell anybody where he was. He puffed up with emotion, put his arms around us. "Some times come," he said, "when you know who your friends are."

"Fuck this, Herbert," I said and split, out the door. Jack and Herbert followed down the walk, past the ten-by-ten pool that was mostly dead leaves and kid piss, across the deck to the sand, down the beach thirty yards to the high bushes. We lugged the goddamn dinghy one more time down to the lapping waves. Unseen in the darkest of night, the break rolled gently, stood up quick and tall and whomped down all at once. Herbert held up one hand and waited, counting.

He counted a set and a half and waved us on—now. He pushed the dinghy knee-deep, waist-deep in the break. He pushed hard once, and we were beyond it. The next wave rolled under and whomped just as the little outboard sputtered to life. We rode out looking back, watching black go silver. Dawn made the sea big, the sky immense. Quivering light framed Herbert's silhouette, his arms raised like the ancient god, Maui, who pulled molten rocks from the sea with his fish hook made of bone.

Cocaine all nighters don't lead to good impressions next day. Neither sunrise, nor the rising heat of morning, nor the three-hour cruise to the westside, nor a half dozen aspirin could smooth the wrinkles of the night before. Jack had an inspiration near brunch time: another blast, which led to just one more little lift at noon, to get through the three-hour sail, to earn our daily grand. Two cold beers quick helped for awhile. With the old stability faked, clean T-shirts, fixed smiles and bloodshot baggy eyes we stooped to the task.

Sixteen normals stood on the beach looking like Tweedledee and Tweedledum, Dee, Dum, Dee, Dum, Dee and so on down the line. They wore baggy shorts and Hawaiian shirts and carried little cardboard barns. Loyal long-termers—middle management averaging a hundred-fifty grand a year, they approached in single file, eyes ahead, and did exactly as they were told.

Each little barn held a salami and cheese sandwich, an apple, a brownie, a pickle slice and one piece greasy fried chicken. Jack said, "Time for a grocery run." He headed out Pailolo Channel, where the swell rolled but didn't break, eight to ten feet. *Whirlaway* surfed down the backsides, through the trough and nearly up the fronts, hung up halfway, punched through and shot the curl again. In three hours Jack scored fourteen perfect lunches still in their little barns. One was soup on the stern deck. One stayed down.

I accepted the gratitude of the man who kept it down. Jack dinghied the rest in. I dove for a look at the bow anchor, secure in twenty feet of water. And for more security, what with the good life and no mortgage, I set a stern anchor way out back. On board I threw the sandwiches over and grooved on the salami oil slick. Jack got back and asked if I was cracking up again.

"That shit'll shorten your life," I explained.

We ate apples and chicken in the cockpit with a six-pack and talked—the Feds could be on our beach right now, or in a week or two or whenever, and it would be ugly. Yet in the balmy trades, the pinking tropical sky and an easy anchorage, there aboard a yacht so fine as *Whirlaway*, a quarter mile from the beach and four thousand hotel rooms booked solid at something like a million bucks a night, it wasn't ugly. Magical—as in the long odds pay-out on a horse sure to lose—seemed more the memory in store. Magical and sad, since *Whirlaway* swam fast and sea-kindly as a boat could, saving her boys from certain harm too often. *Whirlaway* in that milky amber light, and how she always got her way, filled the evening with a swarm of goosebumps.

Jack said, "You know it's something. You take two geeks side by side and one of them is a waste of oxygen, and the other one knows how to have a good time. It's amazing. They don't look that different." Jack liked the guy who didn't puke.

Reverie ended when a faint voice carried from the beach. Louise waved her arms. We went in, since *Whirlaway* rode well enough at anchor, and a sit-down cocktail with table service sounded good.

Louise hung her head, arms folded. When the dinghy was high and dry, she said, "Herbert's dead."

Jack sat on the dinghy. I sat in the sand. Louise said no one knew what happened. Herbert was on his way to Hilo again this morning. He hung around a few hours till the commuter flights started, drank a pot of coffee and lined up a few more eye-openers. She offered him a drive to the airport but he said no, more better if he took the truck.

"I don't know from there. The girl said he called her from the airport and sounded...crazy. She said he ate so many pills, especially when he got nervous. He couldn't talk right. He said he didn't know if they saw him, but they looked like they were waiting for him. He didn't know where to go, but he was on his way and she shouldn't hang around the place."

Louise shrugged. "Then he got the truck and headed up toward the crater, and about ten miles up he flipped the truck doing...they say eighty." She sobbed. "It burned up."

"Burned up?" I asked. "Trucks don't burn up when they crash, except in movies." Jack lit a smoke. Louise cried. Night filled in. And there we sat, questions giving way to the fact. Small talk set in. We pushed the dinghy back out between breaks for a long, fitful night. Louise slept aboard with Jack. I sat in the cockpit watching for shooting stars.

The night lasted as long as the charter business had, Herbert recalled in every phase. Yet dawn came too soon with nothing but memory, numbness, tingling and sixteen middle managers from one of America's largest corporations. The normals sat and rode. Jack steered. I stood back at the taffrail. All eyes looked across the water, as if for meaning, and every so often one aboard who lived securely would make his way aft to puke.

So the week went. Louise came back down the next afternoon to report no one on the beach, no phone calls. Herbert's cousin had come by, asked for *Whirlaway* next Sunday, for a memorial service, spread ashes.

Jack said "Yes, but cousins bring own liquor. And tell them limit to fifteen people."

"Where did they get the ashes?"

"God, Martin. You're so morbid."

"Didn't Herbert burn up with the truck? What'd they do, get out there with a whisk broom and dustpan for the do?"

Louise didn't know, but she said in a huff that she'd be sure to ask around. She walked away to where it was hard to hear, except at the very end, when she looked back and said, "Wake up, Martin."

The next four days were carbon copies. So were the next forty-eight normals. Down to drudgery and mourning, work and beer, the quiet settling thicker than bad times in drydock. The three hour cruise home would have been a time for cutting loose, a time for victory and thanks to lucky stars for life outside the Fortune 500. It would have been a time for letting the bitch run free, no dead meat on board, sails trimmed for speed, a rare time in the trade, most likely with Herbert aboard. We motored at a reasonable speed, drank beer and breathed deep.

Near the point at the Pali, Jack said, "I want out."

"So? What else is new?" I kicked the throttle up a few hundred. "I want out worse than you. I'll tie a red goddamn ribbon around mine and give it to you for your birthday, early."

"I'm getting out." Jack stared down, resolute.

"Yeah? You going to walk away?" He nodded. "Suits me. I'll call Nuel's lawyer, let him work it out... Nah. I'll call Shel. Tell him, Jack says fuck it." He shagged two more beers. "I don't know about Herbert."

"He burned out. What's to know?"

"Did he burn up?"

"What are you trying to say?"

"I want proof. Body ashes have a certain feel. I want to see."

"You don't think he's dead?"

"No."

Jack thought it over. "You think he crashed the truck to shake the bad guys?"

"I don't know."

"That's what people think when a friend crashes and burns."

I sat back and drank. Another family had asked for a memorial cruise a few months back, to spread uncle ashes near the fishing grounds he worked for years. Jack remembered. "You remember Herbert wouldn't go?" Jack nodded. "You remember what he said?" Jack shook his head. "He said he'd only go once on an ash cruise, his own. I asked him if he'd pull some shit. He said he'd try, swells out of nowhere, maybe some waterspouts, little ones, and maybe some storm clouds quick."

"So if he doesn't show, that proves he's alive?"

"I guess it might not prove anything."

Jack stared off. "You remember what you told Louise the second time I quit her?"

"No."

"She sat down there and cried about four days straight. You told her, 'Let it go.' She was okay then. Thanks, Martin."

I headed forward, tired of it. "You came back, Jack."

Departure and return sank in like the sun sank into the sea. Back on the beach after the best week ever in the charter trade, I said, "I guess it's party time tomorrow. Here. One thirty." The Herbert memorial cruise was at two.

Jack said, "I guess so," and walked up the beach.

I wanted quiet. Renette let it be, early to bed, no chase, sleep.

Sitting in the sand midday talking bullshit with Masao was what life came to, was Herbert's memorial, was a bullshit eulogy to a wasted life. Masao brought an uncold six-pack and said his new phone was unlisted, so the bitches wouldn't be calling him up all the time. Renette said he could paint his number on a billboard and be safe.

Masao said that kind of talk was unnecessary. She said maybe she was wrong.

The family came at two. Marylin brought Tiny Little, whose bib overalls stayed up with fat compression. I stared, couldn't help it— Tiny needed a periscope to see his dick, and plane geometry said he couldn't reach it.

Marylin looked like Daisy Mae, her cartoon tits out there proud in flowered rayon, open three snaps down. Mud splotched her legs like pig farm beauty marks. She clung to Tiny Little. He had bushy, bristly hair, also flecked with mud, and mean eyes that told the world he knew he was ugly. He was pissed too, ready for a stomp, but the ocean scared him, so he listened near water.

Jack didn't know his name was Maka but thought it was Tiny Little—"I guess we'll run Tiny Little out first." The fat man stepped up, looked down and then at the dinghy.

"I no go," he said, and lumbered back up the beach. Marylin ran after, pleading uselessly until she looked back and waved. Her blouse flapped in the breeze, baring her swollen belly. Poof, gone.

Renette whispered, "If it comes out with green eyes and a shitty outlook, Tiny Little might kill you."

"Go on, get aboard." Cousins, uncles and aunts waited while Herbert's mother hobbled from the parking lot. Cousin Takao carried the bronze urn.

They crowded the cockpit, quiet and still, opened their coolers, drank and ate. The afternoon was flat calm, no breeze, like dead man's breath on the bay. Jack announced motor, no wind. The family looked up like he was nuts. He cranked it up and eased it into gear.

McGreggor Point was good for deep water and road view—loved ones could remember, driving by. Herbert's mother nursed a beer and sobbed, wished for a breeze, for Herbert. Far aft Masao wished for some snoot and pussy. "I know Herbert too. Snoot and pussy everlasting is what Herbert wants right now." Renette came back and scolded. How could you be so awful, making jokes on Herbert's memorial cruise?

"You right. I slit wrists now." He went below for a beer.

Near the point I asked Takao what to do. "Sing song. Pour ashes. Go home. I got work tonight."

So we cut the engine and drifted, quiet. I watched northeast and then south, scanned the water. Jack watched me. Herbert's mother sobbed, and the other women joined. Takao sang a sad song. The others sang along.

Takao opened the urn and poured. I reached for a handful—chalky rounded pebbles. I felt them, squeezed them, let them fall. They sank slow. Takao sang another song, less sad. Jack cranked it up and steered home.

Evenings after funerals are a drag. Renette cooked dinner, because friends should be together then. Her nurturing was better than her cooking. She made hot dogs wrapped in bacon for appetizers. She said she loved hot dogs, she didn't know why, they just made her feel good. Jack said it was the shape.

Louise read my stars, fussed over my exact time of birth and navigational coordinates of the birthplace. "Your chart is amazing."

"Why is one star chart amazing and another one dull?"

"Well... They're all amazing."

"I thought so."

"But yours really is more amazing than most because of all the things going on, like karmic residuals."

"What a karmic residual is?"

"That's a problem unresolved in another life, or else in this life from a long time ago. Life changes every seven years, and then of course it really changes when you die."

"Will I be rich when I die?"

"That's up to you. You've spent this life trying to work things out and you've reached a resolution in your head but you can't free yourself in your heart, which is of course fatal for a Leo, since Leo rules the heart, and a monarch with no kingdom lives...well..."

"In abdication."

"Your father shows up here, Aries transcendent..." She gained momentum, moving from affection to conviction, sad moons rising, Mercury in retrograde, Mars in submission and Jupiter sliding sideways. "He may be part of the problem. Is he dominant?"

"He dead."

"Oh." She made a squiggly notation on the chart and studied it. "How old were you?"

"Young."

"So it was a hard adjustment?"

"Probably average."

"Were you close?"

"I don't know."

"Maybe that was it. You show massive unresolve there, and it's apparent in every phase, even the future ones."

"What can we predict here?"

"I wouldn't. Some do."

"Can you see money?"

"It's all opportunity. Free will happens all the time. That's why I don't predict. I don't think anyone should. I could predict on the basis of what's here and how I know you, but it would only be my opinion."

"What your opinion is?"

She thought. "How did your father die?"

"Liquor, tobacco, women."

"You took over the family business." She pointed out some squiggles. "All the moving around and turmoil is here. No kidding. See..." She talked through orbits and transcendences, asked for dreams that came more than once.

Jack leaned on the counter, crunching a carrot. "He dreams of no stiff in the box. He told me."

Louise set her pencil down and held her temples. "Oh, jeez."

"I think Herbert's not dead."

She shrugged. "I told you, it would be an opinion."

"What your opinion is?"

"Well. You might be psychic. Is there anything you know, really know, in your heart?"

It was only a silly moment, a game, but a tough one. I smiled, dead serious. "Louise. I want one more star chart." She looked down. "I want Herbert's chart." She nodded.

Renette said it was soup, but it wasn't. It was pork ribs, rice, bread, potatoes and corn. I dodged the load, got up—"I'll be right back."

"What? It's not good cold."

"Ten minutes. Can I use your car?" And out in the night, moving, a troubled mind threw the clutter out the window, took the day down to dark and fast. Speeding toward the bar of the heavy snoot drunk when Takao was first met, I cooled off, took twenty minutes to clear the air of he-said she-said, left all the crap in my wake.

I went in for a beer, then left and headed back, taking the cane road shortcut I couldn't find coming the other way.

I pressed it to eighty, then ninety, and the flashing light came on. I'd found Takao. A light blinded, then got lowered. "You speeding what, ninety? One hundred?"

"You know me."

"Yes. I know you. You speeding ninety."

"I speeding to find you. Now I find you."

Takao looked up the road and down. "What you want find?"

"Herbert's mama. Herbert got trouble."

Takao looked stupid. "Herbert got no trouble. He dead."

"Where she stay?"

"You know end of cane road?"

"Yes."

"Go past. Past Dairy, up and to left. No, right. You find. Only four houses. All Herbert folks in same house tonight."

"Thank you."

"Go slow." I pulled out slow, spent the next hour on dark cane roads past Dairy Road, to left, no, right.

Finally a gravel road looking like the route to the end of the world led to four houses, one lit up, door open. Inside, after aloha and a beer, I took a step toward Herbert's mother. She didn't move, look up or down or to either side. "When was Herbert born?"

"March five. Nineteen fifty-two."

"What time?"

She looked up. "Morning. Early." She pointed next door, sobbed again.

"I'm sorry." They walked me out, saying shush, no sorry, good that memory begin with Herbert's birth, and begin now, with family for comfort.

"You come back. Anytime."

I drove home slow, dead tired. Herbert wouldn't put his family through that—yet a man might do what he wouldn't do, if he must. Jack slept on the couch. Louise lay against him, barely awake. Renette smoked a cigarette at the uncleared table. Thick white grease covered the ribs, the hot dogs, the bacon. I moved softly over one scoop rice, one beer.

Louise woke Jack. I wrote on a scratch pad: March 5, 1952. Dawn. I wrote the navigational coordinates beneath, tore off the page and gave it to Louise.

The Wittes went home. Renette went to bed. I drank alone, then drank some more. I watched a late movie, then walked down to the beach, where a clean, crisp break glowed in its foam, its fluorescence alive in the moonless dark.

Louise called early. "Martin."

"Yes."

"Hard to tell."

Neo
Funda
Mentalism

Jack woke me up—normals on the beach and no lunch.

"But we quit."

"Eight people, Harry. That's a couple hundred bucks each."

"For how long?"

"Six, seven hours. Come on."

"No. How long can you live on six-hour runs. How much longer?"

"You go to sleep. I got a charter. You'll wish you had one when crying time comes around."

I followed, went for retail deli, and the day stayed numb. Questions of depth, cost and daily fun got a squint and a groan. The normals caught on quick.

One pasty young normal and his matching wife talked loud—they just picked up a fabulous condo. Now they were native, and it had tennis courts, a sauna and super beach access. They were from Pennsylvania. I wished them matching headaches and a visit to Nuel for the cure. I wished them gone, into thin air.

Another normal asked about the local fellow with the tiger tattoo—the one who chummed fish off the stern with one hand and caught them with the other.

"You mean the guy who knew the fish names, Latin and local, and which was good to eat and how to cook?"

"Yes," the normal said. "Him."

"He left town."

Seven hours and two six-packs later it was done. Jack talked practical—you got to get while the gettin's good. "That's eight bags of groceries. Good groceries. That's a honk and a half with champagne. Shit, that's half a month's rent."

I left him in the sun. Inside was worse, pressure cooker hot, like it would go off, splattering the neighborhood with boxes, T-shirts, invoices, bills, stationery, poison-pen letters, dirty dishes, old air thick and reeking of burned coffee and butthole. The table was a heap—newspapers, a radio, odd shit. Tomorrow's manifest on top showed ten normals. I cleared the sofa with a one-arm sweep, put the fan on low moan and lay sorry bones down. I hit the answer box: *Call Sheldon Hyde, Honolulu.* I rolled out.

Jack leaned on a wall in the shade, hanging his head with a smoke hung from it, like he knew it was over because it was over and couldn't go on. I told him anyway. "I don't care," he said. "Tell them come on." He crushed his butt on the cement.

"We got ten tomorrow."

"Tell them come Wednesday. I don't care."

We went in. I called. Shel was on another line, had a client waiting, was overdue in court too. "What about lunch?"

"I beg your pardon."

"This is Martin Lusk."

"One minute please."

I covered the phone. "He's dropping everything. I think we're important."

"Cocksucker."

"Hello! Mr. Lusk?"

"Mr. Hyde."

"Yes! How goes it?"

"How it goes."

"Yes! Ah...look. We've reviewed this situation for our clients as regards you and Mr. Witte, and Mr. uh..."

"Nuel. The doctor. The debtor in this situation."

"Yes! Actually we're dealing with him separately. The fact is you and Mr. Witte are now in possession of the documented vessel *Whirlaway*. Is that correct?"

"Are you writing this down?"

"No, of course not. You can speak freely."

"I'll speak freely. But I think you should write this down. That way you'll get it straight the next time you speak freely. Okay, Jack and I caretake the documented vessel *Whirlaway*—have did so ever since we rebuilt the documented vessel *Whirlaway* in drydock. We put in the time and the work, Mr. Hyde, good faith. We wrote it down. We're ready. You come get the boat. Wednesday is good for us."

"Look, Mr. Lusk, we've advised our client that a seizure and sale at auction would possibly not be in their best interest..."

"Possibly?"

"And you must know it wouldn't be in yours. This judgment will stand against anything you earn, a hundred-fifty thousand, Mr. Lusk, plus the twenty-five thousand or so in late payments, give or take. The vessel is appraised at what? Two ten? Two twenty?"

"Give or take."

"We're in an unusual position with the doctor, but we feel we can persuade him to concede his interest in the whole affair. That means you fellows would pick up the equity and simply take over payments. It's what we think is a rare opportunity for you and Mr. Witte. You wouldn't qualify for this kind of loan otherwise you know."

"You'd be surprised."

"Yes, I'm sure I would be. We'd like you to come over and sign some papers and work out some details. When is convenient? You say Wednesday is good for you?"

"Hold on."

I covered the phone and grinned, cupped the talk end just like when it had seven grand cash in it and I didn't want to spill any. Jack smoked hard. "They say Nuel's out with an easy squeeze. We take over payments and it's ours." Jack smiled. Then he nodded. I smiled too, shaking my head, sliding my palm off the bung. "I'm getting out, Jack."

"Yeah?"

"Yeah. I got a life to live."

He nodded again. "Me too. Tell him come get the bitch."

"Mr. Sheldon."

"Mr. Hyde."

"I meant Mr. Hyde."

"Yes."

"We don't want it." He waited. "We're a couple poor, dumb stiffs got worked over bad by your client's client. It's a no-win deal, Mr. Hyde. We understand the premise, which is proven commodity, which is two sunburned grunts who know the ropes, who might look iffy in the risk column but who, for chrissakes, got the bitch back in service. So now we have a chance to bust our balls for about fifty bucks a week if we make payments. We don't want it. You see, Mr. Hyde, we used to be con men before we got into the boat business, and frankly, we're thinking of going back to that, you know, suits and ties and offices and all like that?"

"Yes. Well. I honestly wish you and Mr. Witte didn't have to take the vessel, feeling like you do. But I'm afraid it's kind of like Old Maid, isn't it?"

"Mr. Hyde. I'm not a lawyer, so what do I know? But I've been to jail. I know that short of court, the law is like a football game—the team most psyched most often wins."

"You're not entirely wrong, Mr. Lusk, in theory. Unfortunately for your side, this is not theory."

"Yes, Mr. Hyde. You have clients waiting, so we'll say goodbye now. I'll call my lawyer. Mr. Jack will call his lawyer. We'll file personal bankruptcy faster than you can say liquidated damages. Then we'll get our team coming at your team with everything we got in the way of breach, malfeasance, moral turpitude, fraud, loss of income—Mr. Hyde, your team is a much bigger target, you see, than our team."

"Mr. Lusk..." He trailed off, a crack in his voice. "Do you have any ideas?"

Victory. "Yes. I have an idea."

"Go ahead."

"Give us a hundred-twenty days to run an ad and sell. We can sell her. She looks too good not to sell. And she'll sell quicker as a Bristol clean charter boat in operation than she will as a dirty bucket on desolation row."

"Why a hundred-twenty days?"

"I don't know, Shel. Give us a hundred-eighty. Give us two weeks. I don't care. Come get the bitch Wednesday."

"Hold on. Hold on." Shel held the phone and mumbled, came back in a minute, "Mr. Lusk. We think we can give you a hundred-twenty days to sell it, but I'll have to get back to you to confirm. Okay?"

"Ten four, Mr. Hyde. We can give you until tomorrow at this time. And we will need your confirmation in a letter, please."

"Thank you. And you have a nice day."

"Likewise, Mr. Hyde." We rang off.

The big back door groaned open at last. I breathed deep, laughed, shook my head. Jack didn't speak, went for a beer. "You're so fucking smart."

"Smart enough to save your ass."

"He wanted to give it to us. You said no."

"We can still get it, if we want it. But maybe you don't understand plain English." I sat up, raised my left hand, right hand on heart. "God should strike me dead if I have any intention whatsoever of staying in the charter business." Jack stared, puzzled, pained, unbelieving. Wasn't it what we did, wasn't it the dream, after all? Had it not taken its pound of flesh, but saved us from middle management, the secure life and terminal d-u-l-l? Was it not the difference between us and the normals? And was it not ours, now, on a platter?

I clutched my heart with both hands and choked. "I think it's the big one!" Jack laughed. Then he stopped. Then he walked out, leaving me alone in the clutch, in the ruins, bleary and weary but wide-eyed and face-to-face with middle age, poverty and other prospects for a man with nothing left to give. The funk buzzed. Burned coffee and butthole mixed with relief and anxiety.

Sick as shit of this place is what I felt. The crummy little condo closed in with its fake tropical decor and real tropical depression, furnished like a grade B movie from the fifties. I lay back and groaned with the short-shaft fan, wobbling on bad bearings at low speed. The place looked tired and sounded tired, until distinction dissolved between me and the baggage—cheap shit acrylic, moldy coffee cups, papers, files, dirty towels, fuel cans, patch kits, pumps, life jackets. No fleas—I wondered why. I wished for a plug to pull, so I could sink the dump.

I sat up. But it wasn't so bad with four more months, good dough, no payments. Good season was ending, but the summer crowd would turn a few grand, so fuck all. Money was the thing, summer coming on. I missed Herbert—Herbert and the summer girls, Herbert and the cornball animal bullshit that so tightly conscriped what the poor boy knew of society and women that he kept himself down—Herbert and the spirit of Aloha, which was the all of covering his friends, giving everything he had.

I turned to a blip in the monotony, a high note in the low, dull fugue. A Japanese man in the door, in a blue serge suit, didn't look local but spoke the idiom. "I like buy boat."

And standing up in a rush of recognition of small signs, of connections or messages or whatever you want to call it, enveloping myself in joviality, like a used car salesman caught napping, I greeted what I knew was opportunity. "Hey, what it is, come in." A new Lincoln down the walkway had rental tags—out of town money, or paper bag money. Either way was money. I shut the door. "So. You saw the ad?"

"Yes. I see ad." I offered beer—"No please."—and flashed quick— no address in the ad. I bulldozed boxes, cleared a path around the couch and laughed, cleaning day today.

"*Whirlaway* is a fifty-foot racing sloop."

The man bowed. "I know boat. You have books?"

"Yes, of course we have books." I looked left, then right. "I just don't have them ready now."

He bowed again. "I come back. Tomorrow. Same time." He turned to go, then he turned back. "You like stay with boat?"

"No. I like go away from boat. My partner, Jack, drives boat. He may like stay."

"Good."

Jack was in the door. "No," he said. "It's all for sale." The man nodded. "We'll have the books ready by tomorrow afternoon. I'm Jack, by the way."

The man bowed. "Moki." He went to the door.

"You knew Herbert."

"Yes. Tomorrow, yes?"

"Yes," Jack said. Moki left. I dropped again to the sofa. Jack came in—"Strange."

"Smart."

"Yeah?"

"Yeah. He got the drop on us. He knows the real picture."

Jack kicked a pile of papers. "I hate this." The papers floated down, slid into corners. The room looked the same. He popped a beer. "So tell him we're alcoholic drug addicts. That's why we fucked up so bad."

"I won't have to tell him anything. He's good. But don't worry, we only have to sell a boat we don't own and cut a secret deal on the side."

"You think he will?"

"Piece of cake," I told him. Jack said fuck and split. I slept three hours with no dreams.

Moki came back to a different picture, cleaned and vacuumed, nearly too different from the day before. "What? No charter today?"

"Sure. All done by one, chop-chop." Jack lied. Then he covered— "But you don't get a charter every day. Sometimes the wind blows hard for two weeks. Then what? No money. Tough business. You get tax breaks though, and big money when the weather is good."

Moki nodded. "I like."

We reviewed the books, the saga of Nuel, the significant cash flow. In the end it showed potential and a very good week before the crash, two good months after. Jack called it a million dollar idea. Moki took the books for his computer. "No such guy, million dollar idea," he said. "Only million dollar implementation." He left.

Jack called after him, "Don't forget the depreciation!" It took two six-packs to figure how heavy he was, how hard to choke the goose. Jack worried—he might have to stay on to run the boat.

"You wanted to stay on and run the boat. With Moki on the loans, you can walk anytime, which you can't do now, not without a bank on your tail."

"Yeah, now I'll have the Hawaiian Mafia after me."

Hard work soaked up anxieties and mournful recollections for two more days—wind, sun and spray beat the worry, left the leather tough. Money made sense after a life of hunger.

Moki came back the third day to talk purchase. I said, "No, first we sail."

Moki begged off—he got seasick. So a cash laundry was the obvious objective, the understanding in a glance between the down and outers.

Jack asked if Moki need one captain to make deal. "If you like, yes. If you no like, no. I send one man tomorrow for sail with you. He tell me if boat good." He'd killed enough time—"Tomorrow maybe. We talk." He left. Jack moaned and groaned: He hated the charter business. But what else could he do? I left too, for a dark bar and several cold beers.

Moki sent a registered marine surveyor who eyeballed stem to stern. But an old Coast Guard inspection trick led him by the nose—Louise and Renette all greased up, bikinis wedged up in there, polishing brass. Jack played personal valet, deferred to his superior, shagged cold beer and said go ahead, look up her asshole if you want to. The guy only glanced at the bilge, survey passed.

Yachting time was late, twenty-five knots through the slot, so we motored around the corner for the easy ride home, all downwind. She was hard to live with, to weather, could hardly gain an inch upwind and beat you to death trying. But give her headsail and plenty main, she ran downwind like downhill. Jack played the swell, surfed off the ten-foot crests to eighteen, twenty, twenty-two knots, twice the speed of surveyors.

The run was a thrill, fuck the reach, home by dusk, back on the beach by dark. She held up to last year's value.

Moki came back with the written survey and appraisal. He said boat good, business one mess, maybe better with right management. "Yes," we confessed. "Decent management is all it ever needed. We don't know how. You like buy?"

"Yes, today, cash." Jack shagged beer.

Too fast, slow down—"Boat not ours to sell, but...if you follow, you can take over Nuel's loans—boom! Sixty grand equity right now."

"I like." Jack smoked like a fiend.

"Okay. We got the mooring, dinghy, outboard, brochures, T-shirts, and goodwill."

Jack said, "And two years of our lives. Call it a hundred-fifty on the boat, another hundred on the business."

Moki said, "What, you nuts?" He stood up, walked to the door, paced back. "You no see value of me? I bail you out."

It was jugular time. "You no see value of sixty grand equity?" I asked. "You no like nice place for bury big kind cash? You take four tourists, call them twenty tourist, make...thirty grand a month, sparkle clean."

"What and pay tax? I got plenty holes for bury cash."

"Not with expenses like this baby. You can run fifty grand a month through her and show no profit. This is a yacht!" Moki stayed mum.

Jack came in—"Fine. No deal. Goodbye, Mr. Moki."

Moki bowed and left. Jack looked nervous. "We got a hundred-ten more days free. That's worth something."

"We got a judgment coming on."

"Maybe he'll call back."

"Maybe."

Three more guys called that week. All three read the books, kicked the tires. No question—it needed renegades or refugees to make it worth a damn.

Moki called Saturday. "How you feel now?"

"Come. We talk."

Moki came in saying he liked *Whirlaway*, had decided to buy the boat, we keep all the garbage.

I shook his hand. "We decided the same thing—the bank's ready to close in ninety days. We got three other people looking, but we like your approach to the operation. It's more realistic. Earnest money deposit will bind the deal. Ten grand, made to Whirlaway Charters."

"Good. I like." He wrote the check to *Whirlaway* and the bank. "This way more better."

I took it neat. "How you know Herbert?"

"Herbert good boy. He get crazy, too much drug. He lose big opportunity." We wanted more, but that was the end of the story. "What you do now?"

Jack said, "I'd like to drive the boat for you." I laughed.

"And you. What you do?"

"Take it easy for awhile. Maybe try and sell a mooring and a dinghy. Maybe lay in the shade for a year or two."

"Not good. You young man, need opportunity."

"I'll let you know, Moki. Okay?"

"Okay.

"Meanwhile I'll write an agreement of sale, tell the bank we got a buyer. We talk tomorrow, maybe next day."

"You no wait too long."

"No no. We no wait," Jack said.

"Maybe I talk bank."

"What for?"

"Maybe get cheaper."

"Maybe get nothing. We'll call you when we need you." Moki left. Jack relaxed. "Well Jackie, we just made ten grand if we're willing to try for the forgery merit badge." Then I called Shel. "Mr. Hyde. I think we have a buyer."

"Mr. Lusk, it's not your place to think on this. Send prospects over. We will qualify."

"Mr. Hyde. Why be a peckerhead now, at this difficult time? Why this...hostility?"

"Are you quite through?"

"Quite. Qualify my ass." I hung up, called Weems, collect, in the trenches again. Jack liked a good show, swilled beer until it foamed down his chest, just like old times. "Weems. Long time. I know we can't talk direct without the committee and some memos to Shel so he can call Oulette and Oulette can call Givens and Givens can call us and you can do that if you want to, but take a minute and we'll save months."

"Go ahead."

"We got a cash buyer but I can't take it anymore with these goddamn lawyers! They're tearing apart what I'm trying..."

"Hold on. You say cash. That's on the mortgage balance and the deficiency?"

"Neither one. He offered one-forty cash to you. The deficiency is what? Twenty grand?"

"Twenty-four now. Plus expenses."

"I'd cut expenses if I was you. And you can call the deficiency thirty-six grand in ninety days, because that's when the guy says he'll close. And call the deficiency Nuel's."

"Don't you think you and Mr. Witte could come up with a little something?"

"Hold on. Jack, a beer, please." Jack shagged. "Weems wants to know if we can come up with a little something." It was a tender moment again, life and cold beer on Weems' dime.

"Mmmmmmmm... Nah," Jack declined.

"No...well, Mr. Weems, my partner, Mr. Witte, says we can send you some food stamps, if you think that would help."

"I see. Very good. I'll contact the doctor. And don't worry about Mr. Hyde. I'll speak with him too."

"It's him or me, Weems. This deal's not big enough for both of us. And Weems, you might let Nuel off the hook for ninety days because, well, he can't help it if the new guy won't close sooner, and if he comes up with twenty-four grand, well, you guys still do pretty good. We just saved ninety days anyway talking direct like this. And if you want my opinion, I think we ought to go ahead and wrap it up like this, direct."

"Thank you. I'll consider that." We rang off.

Jack shagged another round. "Call Oulette and fire him too."

"Nah. He's expensive and not a bad guy, and Nuel's paying."

The good mood got dusted in the last of Herbert's moon rock, trial celebration.

Jack snooted and paced. "We got three each now and another five each from Moki. We ought to make another, say, six each in the next ninety days. Fourteen grand. That's enough."

"We got three each. That's all we got. We're a long way from it."

"Yeah?"

"Many moving parts. Many megalomaniacs. How many phone calls you think will be made in ninety days?"

"I got confidence in you."

"Thank you. I suppose that helps."

"I'm sorry if it doesn't." It was truce, relaxation like never before, compass heading on liberation. We talked forgery, reviewed the fine points and finesse of it, wondered whether we'd best sign the endorsement on Moki's check or cop a bank stamp? Jack said, "Fuck it," and signed Moki's check on the back: Weems.

Another snoot made the mood better than the day the loan cleared. I eased up on the future. "What now, Jack?"

Jack turned on the TV to the top of the sunset series—The Billies, The Beaver, The World Tonight. "Our luck is holding."

Summer was one day—up early, hump charter, many calls, much beer, cold cash. Nuel told Weems no, go ahead, foreclose, no sale, stretch it to the next century. I felt weak, top-heavy with bluffing, which is how you feel just before the other guy blows it, and so you got to keep telling yourself you're doing good, knowing it's also how you feel right before you fall on your face. Nuel called, said he told his lawyer to go ahead and get him a chapter 13 bankruptcy, "since they wadn't a way in hell I come up with twenty fo thousand dollars

by my sef on top a at fit-ty thousand dollars I awready pissed down
a rat ho."

So the bank already forgave twelve grand. Nuel got the tax credit
and two years' depreciation—fifty-three grand—and never broke a
sweat. I said, "I'm thinking Australia myself. Mighty big haystack for
a little needle like me."

"Shi... You boys. You put a big oh fuckin rat up my ass ho. Why,
at investment tax credit don't mean shit when you make much
money's I do. I need a make twiced what you'n Jackie make cause on
account of I lose fit-ty percent of it right off de goddamn top of it.
Don't you unnerstan! What's a fella's name. At boy wid de cash?"

"Fuck you Nuel. His name's fuck you, which is a coincidence
because fuck you is his first name, and you won't believe this but Nuel
is his last name. Fuck you Nuel. You want his number?"

"You boys be hearing from my lawyer."

"Okay! I'll tell you, but I got this sneaky feeling that you fixing to
call a bubba up and fuck it up—I mean fuck it all up, fuck me 'n Jackie
'n fuck yourself too, on account of you're so fucking stupid."

"I don't know what makes you so mean. I never did know, except
maybe it was because you was such a failure in life'n always knew it
and just didn't do nothing for it 'cept hang out over there 'cause a de
weather 'n fuck de dog wid Jackie."

"I already heard from your lawyer, Nuel. He's not as dumb as you,
but he's dumb. You have him call whoever you want to. Won't matter. You and he know who's winning this one. It's me. You're about
to get fucked for twenty-four grand and I'm the fucker, and ordinar-
ily I'd be glad to fuck you and know you know I fucked you, but
you're a special kind of guy, Nuel. I enjoy telling you like this."

"You wrong, Bubba."

"I'm right, Bubba. When we get off the phone here you can sit back
with your eightball and your wine and think of me walking out of
here. I will be invisible, Nuel. You are documented owner of a boat
on a mooring right here in front of me. You are somebody. I could
move next door and they wouldn't find me. You want to sell the bitch?

Try it. See where you get. You are a target Nuel, and you may be better at that than anything you ever did. Come on, Bubba. Let's see
what you got. Bye now."

I hung up, hoping Nuel bought the act—insane, nothing to lose—
hoping Nuel would pay the twenty-four grand. I meditated the act of
acting, insanity, nothing to lose, or maybe I only wallowed in the
idea.

Weems called the next week—Givens filed a lien on the vessel for
his unpaid bill. I said, "Fuck that guy—or take care of it, whatever you
want." Oulette called the next week. Could he still come sailing, he
and his wife, because, well, they were back together again and were
maybe coming over and, well, a sunset sail never hurt a romance.
"Jeremy Oulette, hardly anything warms my heart like a marriage
saved, hell yes." Lawyers; two boat rides cost a hundred bucks, ethics
out the window.

The bank turned down Nuel's offer of eight grand, holding firm at
twenty-four or foreclosure. Weems called and delivered the news
with a newfound fighting spirit: No deal. I did my best—"Will you
relax, Weems? At this phase of a multifaceted negotiation, everyone
gets excited. Strongest player is him with least to lose. It's the physics
of downside negotiation. Relax, Weemsy. It's a done deal."

I felt heady, like a successful invader from the third world, felt good
about it, until the Girl Scout lecture on karma. "After all," Louise
pleaded. "Nuel's your partner." Imagine the mayfly telling the arach-
nid about cosmic sheen, lecturing me in mottos for the new and
lovely age. "Don't forget," she said. "What goes around comes
around."

"Did you ever give your little brain a chance to consider that it's
been around and now it's coming back? Did you ever stop to think
that this whole event pains me, that I'm only the messenger, bringing
the news back around to Nuel?"

That shut her up. I was on a roll.

Oulette came over with his wife for a champagne sunset sail, some
groovy jazz and good cheer. He bought dinner. Nuel had moved to

Michigan, where he complained of cold weather in July. I raised a toast, "To Nuel. Our partner."

Snug in stalemate was good for charters two more months, holding Moki at bay. Jack wanted to stroke it another month, against crying time. But a new lawyer called, Moki's, insisting that either he talk to the bank or the deal was off. I said I couldn't talk with lawyers. The *Whirlaway* code of ethics required that principals talk direct, no lawyers allowed. "It's a tough situation for you guys, to the best of my knowledge, at this point in time, but it's an unwritten rule around here and I'm not the kind of guy who goes around upsetting the apple cart, if you know what I mean." I hung up on him too, feeling a strange momentum, like the cocaine delusion effectively applied. I feared overheating.

I considered a future of conquering men in suits and ties on the phone. But life is not practical—look at the men on the phone. They know what they have, where they can go with it, what they can get— know it daily, pulling themselves from dreams of something better, something faster, something to make their hearts giddy up. They are normal, chasing the dream. Herbert said it best, "Just when you got it all good, for life, you die."

Moki called. "You one crazy fellow. You like opportunity?"

"Get your money ready. We close in ten days."

"Yeah yeah yeah yeah yeah."

"I got to go." I hung up on him too, it worked so good so far. The world turned when I said turn. I sat still. Dusk got dark. Maybe drug smuggling, or maybe the retail end—plenty women, no worries because death is quick, which is good, and anyone thinking different is a fool, and between the living and the dying is the rush and the money, unless you go to jail.

I hate jail. I hate too much, but I've been around. Nuel said *such a failure in life*—score one for Nuel. Maybe you don't get into the melon cutter union if you can't fake some kind of skill. Nuel fooled someone. He'd thrust himself to the income stratosphere, brought down a half million annual by telling people they needed their heads cut open, their brains sliced up for better living in the suburbs. Nuel didn't have time to spend it all. But he could blow thousands at a whack, desalinators, windmills, oil wells, thoroughbreds, empty offices in Utah, yachts. Nuel didn't care—plenty more melons where those came from. Nuel was anti-abortion, needed inventory.

Such a failure in life. He knows I won. I know it too, and he knows I know it. Then he kicks me in the nuts calling me a failure, and we both know that, too.

The tropics was what I'd come to, where balmy weather and the deep blue sea make waking dreaming. *You one crazy fellow.* Moki saw the distance between me and the world, knew that a man so removed values life now, death quick, with the rush and the money in between.

A feeling is what I'd learned from the dream, only a feeling, warm, clear blue, seductive in its isolation, beautiful in its whisper. It feels like home, and the skin draws tight in tingles in its blessed presence.

The phone rang late. "Why you call so late?"

"I change mind. I no want boat for one-fifty. I want for one-forty. You give back ten grand. I talk bank myself." He sounded far away, wide awake.

"Do you think I'm crazy?"

"No. That why I want boat for cheaper. I bail you out."

"Do you think I'm crazy?"

"You call bank and tell them. I call and tell them—you steal ten thousand on deal."

"Do you think I'm crazy?"

"Maybe you crazy. But you no get my ten thousand. You watch. I walk away. You owe."

He sounded pissed, hot for the deal. "Okay. No deal."

"Yes, I think you crazy. I think you be very poor too. I walk away from *Whirlaway.* You see me walk away, you say I fuck up too bad, should not let him go. You pay back."

I laughed, "Moki?"

"Yes. You crazy!" He hung up. I hung up too, slowly, wondering by the time the receiver settled down why I dreamed of Moki. I felt good, knowing how to handle such a call if it really came.

"Where are you?" said a voice in a dream. I was gone, in a cool place with no smell, no crowd closing in, where a man could sleep soundly, dream of a country woman finding him far away, working him like a miner on a vein, searching.

~~~~~~~~~~~~~

 Whirlaway

For my fourteenth birthday my mother said *whatever you want*. She split up with the old man that year and then he croaked, hard time for a kid, must have got to her on my birthday. I went easy on her, what the hell, no cakewalk for her either. I chose spaghetti, just spaghetti, no salad, no squash. She said, "You don't want the squash?" I said spaghetti, and a few cherry sodas. And a movie, a double feature at the drive-in, first *Mothra*, about a papier-mache moth bigger than the Rexall Drug Store, who attacks toy trains in Japan. Second was *ZOT!*—this guy discovers this ancient medallion and figures out the secret code on it. As long as he has the medallion, he can point one finger and cause sharp pain—people, machines, anything—so he practices in his office on a fly. If the guy yells *Zot!*, everything goes slow motion. It was neat seeing the fly buzz around like he was drunk. Later on the guy got pushed out a window on the fortieth floor. He yelled *Zot!* No problem. He fell slo-mo.

And if he pointed at something and yelled *Zot!* at the same time, instant annihilation—wasted the fly.

Sometimes I walked the beach pointing at normals, condos, tropical shopping malls. "*Zot! Zot! Zot!*" Jack called it my workout, staying in shape.

In high school my report cards frequently said I could do better, and then came attitude. I was doing better now, could not have given less of a shit about not being appointed hall monitor or patrol boy, stayed cool in the hall, looked before crossing. I still got pissed at people in authority—thought they caused all the shit I wanted to *Zot!* I used to get pissed off at September too—who ever heard of getting pissed off at September? But my attitude was getting better, getting focused, with results. Even Jack said so, and he'd complained more than any of my teachers ever had.

Then one day it was over. It was over just like it was over when she crashed on the beach and when the masking tape came off in dry-dock. Except that now it was over, no more, over, nothing left but life out front, a few grand in hand.

It was over—falling away in layers over, pared to the bone over. I woke up mornings with a shout: "It's over!" and a whimper.

Closing took time, like Jello. Nuel told Weems he was headed to Wisconsin, from Florida—he hated Florida, so many old people, so much sun, and these goddamn waves. They settled at twenty grand. I had hoped for more.

All the lawyers went away, and Moki signed the dotted line ninety days after writing his check. Shel told Weems he suspected another fucking. Weems said he would ask the committee for funding, so Shel could track it down. Moki didn't press it—got the mooring, the dinghy, the brochures and a *Whirlaway* T-shirt for himself, size small. He like.

Renette put it on the table—her love was one way, no return. She knew I was a leaving kind of guy, exits were in my planets. She wanted me to know: I'd only leave her once. I breathed deep once, saw a woman pushing fifty, leaning hard. She split in a huff.

She came back in thirty minutes for an okay, maybe it could work. I said I had to go, but I'd be back, most likely.

"What does that mean?"

"What does it sound like it means?" She did another huff.

But I did have to go, get off the battlefield so the war could end, had to go because I was a going kind of guy—because going proved

I could, and once proved, I could come back. I had to check in on the world, that's all.

"What are your intentions?"

"Intentions? I never had any intentions! In my whole fucking life I had no intentions!" She split again, two days this time. I felt freedom. I felt nowhere to go. If she was around she'd be rolling a joint, studying the TV guide, watching TV—with nothing in common we'd shared the same hideout two years running, between her legs. It ended the next day. She had a date with a guy who'd just got divorced and released from a nuthouse. She stayed with him a week. At least she was consistent.

Jack adjusted easier. He was married, for one, and Louise wasn't even thirty. And he had a job, driving *Whirlaway*, so his days didn't change much. Moki's nephew, Dennis, worked deckhand. I sat on the beach with the feeling.

Maalaea Bay in shimmer, sun on the water with a late summer breeze chasing the heat away. It changed when a little boat sailed into view. I knew those guys. I knew that boat—an old beach Cat with fat stems for running up on the sand when Waikiki looked like this, before it looked like Hong Kong. The boat was older than the poor stiffs who ran her, but the stiffs showed more wear, stress crazed and brittle skinned from too much load, too much sun.

Out there past the point, slipping to Lanai, they pushed hard, upwind in thirty knots, straining to reach flatter water so their outboard engines could keep their props submerged. They could go to inboard diesels and solve the problem, if they had the five grand for the conversion, which they didn't, because they spent eighty bucks a day on outboard fuel and repairs. They'd be home in three hours, or maybe two if the breeze let up.

It changed again when a young bride on the beach scanned the bay slow, her four-carat rock dazzling in sunlight beside her clearly successful groom. "I really love the ocean," she said.

I lay back and read the clouds.

If you look hard enough you realize: they make no form. I went inside.

Jack sat on the sofa, still, smoking, waiting. Nothing moved but eyes in sockets. I sat, dialed the airline, got a flight for later. Jack said, "You can be poor here, or you can go to America and be poor and cold."

"I have to go."

Jack nodded, crushed his smoke, went out for beer. Louise was easy, said it was good, departure today, the twenty-third. "The twenty-third is an eight day, because you count the year digits too on a major life event." I was an eight. Everything made sense, at last.

She didn't know where Jack ran off to, so he was easiest of all, a note: Thanks for the swell weekend. Your pal, Martin.

Then I was gone, really gone.

Paradise never had a chance—that was first thought, engines droning in bullying trades late in the day. The shallow, green sea below turned quick, deep blue, and fell away warm and crystal clear. I dove twenty feet and sighed big, got down in the groaning peace of it. Fish understand—angelfish, odd wrasses and tangs darting red and electric blue through wobbly sunbeams, coming to crushed bread like hungry children, fearless of me and sharks cruising below.

I sometimes ditched my snorkel, mask and fins and dove back in for a long free swim, looked down in the blur and wondered who looked back. Back on deck I waved one hand in the air while straining my eyes to see the bottom, signalling when Jack got the bow over the hook. Then I straddled the roller, gripped the line, put my back into it and heaved, and cursed my lot in life.

Over the Molokai Channel at seven thousand feet in last light, a familiar voice one row back asked, "What are those things, those things down there? Those white things. What are those white things down there? Waves? Are those things waves?"

Her new husband said, "Yes. They are waves."

She breathed deep and approved of waves. "I like the ocean."

I slept, dreamed of wind and horizontal spray, not so bad once it broke you down. It led to nothing, which was restful, with nothing to rest up for. I woke to a voice announcing final approach. I stepped into autumn.

It poured down my collar, froze my feet. I needed clothing, had forgot about autumn. The new wife stopped on the tarmac, hugged her new husband. "God, it's good to be home." I'd forgot the people, the cars, the rush. The new wife touched me. "Going into town?" What the fuck. "Want to share?"

Did I ever. So the tables turned; I became helpless, strange and ignorant as a tourist ever was. She effervesced. I envied the new husband and considered life on the eightieth floor in a suit and tie with a beautiful wife and plenty money. She chattered over her week's plans, a restaurant here, a bistro there, a party on the weekend, an outing to the country.

They got out in town and said goodbye. Then they were gone. So were reefs, prevailing winds, storm fronts and honky-tonks, thousands of miles away, in the middle of the ocean.

I got a six-pack outside a hotel and checked in, took a hot shower, chilled again in five minutes, drank the last three slow and felt good— or at least sleepy kept pace with cold.

Liberation came in the morning, sank in at breakfast, no pineapple but a real morning paper with headlines and news, in the world again. Outside it was metal and flesh, flowing fast, swept like scuz in a current round a point. People jogged, looking pained by choice. Money was everywhere.

Into the flow was going somewhere, for shoes and socks, a jacket and long pants, and a bookstore.

A ten-paperback rack blocked the door under a banner: BEST-SELLERS. One was a book about a car that came to life and scared people. Another was about true love in Texas. One teased: one more dark and dangerous depth of an as-yet unforeboding ocean, waiting out there to get you.

Two more covered true love in New York, and two family sagas were based on wealth and true love in New York and Texas.

One was about city crime, and the last two by the same woman, her name bigger than the titles, were about the true meaning of being a woman and the thankless task of living a woman's life. Both covers told in bold letters of ANOTHER BLOCKBUSTER BETTER THAN THE LAST ONE! They delved into fame, the media and foreplay.

Browsing was dull, like the same author, or authoress, had rendered all of life down to suburban narrative, he said, she said, did, did, did.

I went back the way I came. An armored money truck honked me up the curb as I fashioned a narrative, about this guy who gets way-laid in the tropics—and comes back to knock off an armored money truck. They were everywhere.

A wino outside the hotel puked on himself, blubbered for spare change and got a dollar from me when I headed up for a few hours with the windows closed, shades drawn, no wind, no spray, no sun, no winos.

I woke up choking, stuck my head out the window, breathed deep, and slow, past the fumes. No more oxygen in the room, like lungs had become lint traps. Do people get used to that? On the bed another hour I sought the feeling, found it in the tall channel, wondered if the channel was tall today. The clock ticked.

Thirty minutes to checkout, three percent of net worth gone in one day. Nice, but life would probably last more than a month. So I called Lyles, who drove *Whirlaway* in the trade, in San Francisco. Bonnie answered.

"Hey," I said.

"Martin! Where it is?"

"I don't know. You could call it the Cheap'n Sleazy Motor Lodge. I got friends out front already counting on me."

"Fuck that! Come on, it's my day off. Lyles'll be home soon." Lyles drove a ferryboat now. I felt closer to home too.

I got wine, because Lyles and Bonnie loved wine. Bonnie was generous with hello—the hug, the wiggle, the kiss. She wanted stories.

I wanted to wait, especially on the storm at sea, my best good-as-dead story, because one time telling was enough. "Fuck it then, let's go to the grocery. How's your love life?"

"I fell in with a woman, oldest woman ever, past forty."

"Not so old."

"Past forty-five."

"Does she look good?"

"Yeah. She looks good and smells good too."

"You mean her pussy smells good?"

"Goddamn, Bonnie."

Bonnie giggled, "I can even make Lyles blush." Bonnie had around fifty thousand sea miles and spoke fluent bilge. "Sorry. I'll be sweet. What happened? Are you in love?"

"I don't think so."

"Is she coming over."

"No."

"Are you going back?"

"I don't know. She's already fucking around."

"Ah, fuck the bitch. She's a retread. You need a young one, Martin, with big hips, for babies."

"Yes. Babies. I forgot about that, and the clothing, indoors and no air."

"Yeah, I been there. It goes away."

A short, wiry man at the meat counter looked the same as two years ago, or three, now bald on top, long on the sides to fold over, but the fold slid off. And now he could grab a chicken, slice it ass to elbows in twelve seconds flat, bag it in two more and up the price ten cents a pound for the cutting. I watched him cut three chickens, factored four chickens a minute, say fifty minutes in your average hour, eight hours to the day, two hundred fifty days to the normal year, times three years. Was this guy cutting chickens while the ocean climbed clean out of itself and tried to kill me? Bonnie whispered: "Storms at sea are better, huh?"

She went for produce, leaving me with storms, chickens, fluorescent flicker.

Perspective got aligned an hour later when Lyles got home and the wine swill started while I told of crossing the Molokai Channel in twenty-five foot seas and fifty-knot headwinds. Lyles said, "That's chickenshit," and told about a real storm at sea. It was either off the coast of Maine in the Marblehead-to-Halifax race or on a delivery back from the Aleutian Islands, he couldn't remember which, except that the boat was big and heavy, which was good for those conditions, since you can't live five minutes in water so cold. Every man aboard got sick but Lyles—he'd never been sick in his life. He got sick too, but that was only after some green meat, he was so weak, had to eat to run the boat, even after he got sick, which he never was. "Green meat doesn't count, for chrissake."

Two more jugs led around the Cape of Bullshit, into balmy weather, strange ports and deep slur. Lyles shrunk all stories but his down to small dimensions until everybody's stories could fit into a thimble, except for his stories, until Bonnie said, "You're a big mouth and a bore and full of shit, so just shut up." Lyles came up smiling. He apologized: he and Bonnie had to go to bed. Bonnie blushed, and they were even. She yelled back from down the hall, plenty sausage for breakfast. Strong people, Lyles and Bonnie—alcoholic but strong, maybe strongest of all.

Then it was late, dark, solitary, and a phone call over the ocean to what used to was was simply action following sentiment. Renette was happy, then sad. Nothing changed in a day. I said I was cold. She said nothing. I said goodnight. I laid out two couch cushions and attempted sleep in twenty-foot seas.

Lyles and Bonnie were up in the dark drinking coffee, smoking cigarettes, talking hangover. Droopy and forlorn, their low lit mumbles outlined life that day. I lay still another hour, till charter time, then I lay still two more hours. A shower, reheated coffee and the sausage led back to the question: Now what? The flat creaked and whispered another hour, cold breezes leaking through hinted winter on the way. You forget cold and penetration—cold and quiet. Waves crashing, on

the other hand, don't go away. I wished they would, drank more coffee, got wired and saw that a man repressed too long can crack up,
ditch reason like excess baggage, stay afloat with no ballast. The
room moved. I gripped the rocker.

Two weeks later was better. A hundred miles around the block and
around town, bus rides another hundred and the ferry round the bay
odd days led to difficult thoughts at shorter intervals, like labor pains.
I gained insight on the marriage bond. It has to do with fucking, with
people having sex with each other every day, until that other flesh
becomes coupled so regularly with your own that a separation is
internal. The solution to this growing gnaw in my gut was easy. But
action got stuck at the little plastic box with all the numbered buttons
and the tone that said hurry up. I got stuck on basic movement, stuck
still, wondering what next and what for.

It was another day in the empty flat, not too hot, not too cold,
quiet, the old house creaking like a spar under load. A vacant stare
at naked walls had a life of its own, flitting corner to corner, trapped,
afraid. I called the ex-wife.

When did I return, why did I wait so long to call her? I told her the
truth. "I don't know. Just relaxing here with Lyles and Bonnie." She
liked Lyles and Bonnie alright, but they got so pushy, drunk, wanting
Fran to go to bed with them, and enough is enough. She didn't want
sex with Lyles or Bonnie. But a bottle of wine with a former life partner sounded good. Did she mean partner from a former life?

She waited outside, too tired for the insistence, the cheap wine and
sex talk. "And the worst part is they'd ask you to leave." She knew—
they'd asked Brandt to leave.

Fran talked about *my life*, who was part of *my life*, like it was a unique
piece of furniture. She pulled up to a chic trattoria in a chic neighborhood—chic and freezing. In a warm corner she unwrapped and
ordered a nice zin. She leaned close, in confidence. "I love zin, don't
you?"

"I'd die for it."

She looked cross, hoped I wouldn't start. She settled in, got comfy and wanted to know about the love interest, how we met, what we shared. I recounted the hard times, the sky falling, poor health and plentiful sex. "Interesting. That's what people do here. They nurture each other. They save each other from themselves." Fran was unhappy for a long time, but after her course in Reality Restructure for Now, she saw the why of it. "I used to do it too—with Brandt. We broke up, by the way."

She took the course and ditched Brandt. Now she felt stronger every day, dating again and hating it, of course, all these guys with their bullshit and money. All they want is sex and convenience. "I know they see more than that in me, but you know what I mean."

She'd paid a grand for five lessons.

"It isn't real, you and this woman. A neat fit for the puzzle parts. All you get is new parts to work on, maybe some company at night while you cry out for help. What else do you have with her?"

"You had a tough year too, huh baby?"

"Patience, sharing, faith, mutual independence." She leaned near again with her famous smile, benevolent sadness, perfected over the years. "Do you talk to her, about your doubts, your dreams?"

"No. It was mostly just greasy food, reefer and sex." She looked disgusted but turned to the bright side, her new beau, Erroll. She grew animate—Erroll was strong, needed nothing, no one, wanted the same and enjoyed a zest for life.

"We're giving a party tomorrow night. I'd love for you to come, and bring Lyles and Bonnie. They'll behave with Erroll around—and me."

"Was his name always Erroll?" She smiled patiently. "A party sounds good. I'll tell Lyles and Bonnie."

"Erroll sells computers. I know you'll like him."

"I'll fake it if I don't."

"Thank you."

Joining Lyles on graveyard that night was good. Running harbor pilots and drunk crew under the Golden Gate in pitch-dark on pitching swells was strong antidote to introspection on love and life. A joint on the stern deck near the diesel roar, a couple beers and big seas made the night something to grab onto.

After a nightcap at home near sunrise, a mere quart of wine, Bonnie made coffee. Lyles said, "Well, what's your plan?"

Plan? I had no plan, except a natural itinerary of seeking more pleasant forms of oblivion.

"It's time for a plan."

Bonnie served. "You can stay as long as you want."

"No he can't. Martin, you need cash?"

"No."

"Are you ready to go tomorrow?" It had finally come today. The sun rose outside.

"Sure, I'm ready." Lyles bellowed a toast to initiative and sunrise, brandy all around.

But Bonnie said, "You can't leave today. Fran's party."

"That's right," Lyles said. "One day won't matter, and besides, you might get laid. I think you need to get laid."

"I got laid so much I need a rest."

"Yeah, but those rests only take two days and you been a couple weeks without. Besides, she was too old."

"Too old for what? It's not like a bar of soap, you know."

"Nineteen is better than soap."

"You're full o'shit," Bonnie said. "All he talks is nineteen this and nineteen that. We get one, and who do you think does all the work?"

Lyles shrugged and said that one didn't count; he was drunk and played out. He cracked another bottle.

I begged off for a nap, had a life to map and would start with sleeping. Lyles called me a pussy and poured another round. I lay on the sofa. Bonnie went to dress. "You should forget boats," Lyles began. "Boats are nowhere. I'm done with boats. I'd never go out again, not unless I had to, for the money. But you, you ought to quit fooling around, especially when you're no goddamn sailor in the first place."

"I quit, Lyles."

"I sailed all over the world. Corsica, Sardinia, Melanesia. Islands where...big-titted beauties swim out when you get there and all they want to do is fuck you." He cupped his hands where his big tits would have been. Bonnie watched from the kitchen door, fixing her bra, buttoning her blouse, listening like it was truth. "But you. You need to get out of boats, Martin. It's time."

"Fuck boats," I agreed.

"All boats are always sinking," Lyles said.

"There's always somebody at sea in a storm," Bonnie said, remembering those people being thrashed at sea this very moment.

"Always somebody shipwrecked," Lyles said. Bonnie drifted out.

"Fuck boats," I said.

Lyles drank, finding his stride. "The thing of it is, Martin, you got to deal with the phases of life. You got to stop moving around. You're too old. You got to get a woman and make a home. You're gonna die Martin, with nothing to show for it."

"Mmm. That would make me sad."

"Only one thing makes a man immortal. His children. I'm having some. But you got your mind on another trip. All over the damn world..." He paused, on the world, continued with what was wrong with it, how to fix it.

I woke at noon, run over. I got up two hours later, and an hour later Bonnie came home. Lyles woke up, stumbled down the hall and pointed a finger. "You think too much. Don't drink enough!" A cork got popped, afternoon turned to evening and life eased up some, made some sense.

Fran's party didn't. One foot inside the door was scrutiny. Housewives once hippies hid their fat in baggy gowns, let it droop under pearls. Political women held goblets at their chests, talked aerobics, surveyed new guests coming in. Two women got loud, really angry about the President and women—that dickhead—and the price of feta cheese.

A young man in used clothing, dry-cleaned and retailored, talked loud about blacks attacking blacks in South Africa, and how the evil whites were behind it. "But it's our best move, really. It will force the hand of the Indians." He held one hand limp at waist level, for sensitivity, sipping what looked like a nice zin. He didn't look black.

Most of the other fellows wore bomber jackets and fly-boy scarves and argued rates and points in heavy flak, going in low for a strafing run. One peeled off formation, approached gracefully, tall and handsome with a big money haircut, right hand limp, urban. "I understand you own a fifty-foot racing yacht in the tropics." It was an offer to open, who had what.

"No no. I never owned it. I was a boat nigger."

"Ha!" laughed the tall one. The young politico bristled, raised an eyebrow and half a lip.

Fran swooped down like Loretta Young. "Martin!" She led a tall woman by the arm but swung free for a hug and a kiss for her eccentric, salty friends. "You've met Erroll?" Erroll nodded briskly once and beamed, proud profile.

Bonnie said, "Shit, Frannie. Looks like he stuck it in the pudding already."

Fran blushed. "This is Nancy. She knows all about boats." Fran took Bonnie and Lyles away, for a drink. Nancy looked bored, well built and pretty enough, her skin leathery from wind and sun. She stood stoop-shouldered, waiting.

I looked her over and said, "Stand up straight for chrissake." She did, smiled briefly and stayed mute. "You know all about boats?" She nodded. "Boring, huh?" She nodded again. "I hate boats." She nodded again. "Fuck boats." She laughed.

She opened up. She'd set off with an urban daredevil a couple years ago on a passage planned for twenty-one days. They ran out of wind and then provisions. They drifted fifty-two days. Finally spotted by a passing freighter, she got picked up or towed home or given a hot lunch or something. Her date croaked. "I was young. I didn't know anything." She got choked up. "I made it, and now I'm alive and another person isn't."

She covered her face. I drifted off, into the study where a sincere fellow praised his close friend, the son of Jacques Cousteau. He called the old man Jacques and recalled a casual lunch in which the future of the planet had been determined. The sincere fellow wanted the best for the planet, sincerely, but he wished he could make half as much money as Jacques' son did by simply begging in a suit on behalf of planetary welfare.

Drifting back through the kitchen, I slid into a snug corner, onto a convenient stool, with a nice zin. A contemporary woman named Judith said, "James might have a business card that says real estate, but really he's a writer. He hasn't written much, but he will. God, he spends enough time thinking. And he's so creative. Nod, our youngest, was conceived near a Guatemalan pyramid. That was James' idea! You know about pyramids and all." She and James both felt Nod began life with a creative edge on the other children at day-care, most likely because they were conceived with your average after-the-late-movie fuck in the suburbs, on beds most likely. "How boring. God. I hope I don't see another child named Travis."

James got drunk for the conception on "a very exotic" bottle of Guatemalan brandy. "He thinks of everything." Both she and James ditched their underpants two days before the conception too. "It's best to let your genitals breathe. James got a vasectomy after that. We just don't want any more."

"Your pussy can breathe," it was time—I couldn't help it. "But can it whistle?"

The men restrained a laugh at this insane comment, the women continued, denying existence to such a swine. I finished my zin just in time—James and Judith began on their love of the oceans.

I stood up. "I'd love to stay and chat, but I can't."

Outside the cold felt good—more oxygen, less bullshit. Long breaths in the cold with a low rumble felt like a jet engine at altitude. But the engine stalled on a laugh—thirteen grand left, and I'd drop one right now for Jack in a tag team inside, and some warm weather. Jack could talk to these fellows.

I looked for Herbert in the stars, but it was too cold—Herbert wouldn't stay this far north.

I walked, because a few more miles seemed like where I ought to be, walked all the way from urban chic down to the rail yard, under nightlights that made everything unreal as a plastic model, laid out perfect by Lionel. A McDonald's sat across from a mortuary. The little man with the lantern in his hand and a dog at his heels came out, went in, came out, went in.

Live, eat hamburgers, die, we never close.

Tracks near the water led to a bar, where three hours passed easy with the feeling, warm weather, several beers. Into the night again, until the fear seeped in with the cold and grew tall as a channel in storm trades, mounted itself into great walls of water threatening collapse at the spreaders, told me eye-to-eye that the truth was that life was no life at all. It was slow death, except for the action. Renette made no sense, except for shelter from one more storm.

So I called. She wasn't home. I wondered where I lived and walked back to Lyles' place, fatigued, wide awake. I dreamed of sitting up bewildered on Lyles' couch.

Morning rolled in like fog. Lyles sat on the sofa, had the day off, time for a talk.

"Not necessary. I'm going back. I'm a fuck-up. We need warm weather. Fuck-ups."

Lyles made coffee. "Maybe you should go back. Maybe not. I think I can get you on, down at the dock."

"Fuck boats." Renette was still out. Jack too, humping it for Moki, ten normals on a snorkel adventure.

But Louise was in. She breathed short, sounding aggravated and put out that he wasn't there, like now the full load of Jack's angst was hers to bear too. And I got stuck again, in the mud, which is what going back looked like, the heap, the crud, the shit. "Come home, Martin," Louise said. "Martin. Come home." *Come home*, she said. It was a concept I'd never once considered. "I feel trouble inside you. That's good, you know..."

"Do you hear opportunity too?"

"Hush. I'm hugging you. Can you feel it?"

"Of course. Can you tell what I'm doing to you?"

"Unrest is the first step toward growth."

"I feel ten feet tall. How is Renette?"

"It goes both ways with you and her. She has a new boyfriend. He's twenty-eight or something. He's very quiet. She moved in with him—Martin—it's a better match, her and this new guy."

So the long trip back began on confusion, nausea, a dash of the dizzy. Lyles poured.

Night lingered, warmth waited, and I longed for enough of it to sweat. Departure was for five a.m. in a window seat behind the wing. Seatbelt fastened, I felt a tremor coming on, coming up from somewhere so deep it began from far faraway—I felt the glue unsticking, parts moving freely. I watched from above, looked down on a grown man choking sobs at prospects for a trip to the tropics. A fat man sat down beside me. I turned away, sobbed against the glass.

Breathing came easier when the big jets whined, roared, thrust up and away, circled once and turned west. The fat man leaned over, "All roit now, mate?"

"Yes." The airline magazine told many wonderful things about many wonderful places. The fat man said, "Maybe I can help." He breathed short and hard like a fat man. "Sometimes saying is the first time seeing." He talked like an Aussie shrink. "Try it: My parents were sad."

"My parents were sad." True enough, but so were everybody's.

"Last year was difficult."

"Last year was difficult." Big deal. It was tough for everyone, except maybe the guys Fran hung out with.

"I love getting away." Fat bastard had me smiling and sniffling at the same time. "Rainbows," the fat man said.

Rainbows. I hadn't thought of rainbows. "What now, Doctor?"

"That's easy. Next stop Paradise. It's beautiful, you know."

Jack waited in his spaghetti sauce aloha shirt and baseball cap—ten normals waited on the beach but fuck it—"I told Moki go fuck yourself, my partner's coming in." I didn't believe it, because Jack Witte was an opportunist, like me, like the rest of the sharks. But Jack was there and said the right thing, and the sentiment counted.

"This place is crawling with you know what, but I'm amazed how good the married life is turning out to be." It was just last week he got a young one on board late, twenty-three or so, much nicer than the beauty who ditched him at sunrise. He was really looking forward to it, but it was no good. "I felt old. And bad. I remember getting down there like no tomorrow. But this one, twenty-three, and it had the same vibe down there as a major intersection, rush hour. These fucking kids today. I tell you it's a changed world, Harry." He lit a smoke, popped a couple beers for the ride. "Besides, I love Louise."

"That's convenient."

"Yeah. It is. Maybe that's what it comes down to, Harry. Maybe that's why you came back."

"You think we're just a couple old-fashioned guys who know when to turn a circle by the stove?"

"I think you can get a new girlfriend easy as pie."

"I don't think that's why I'm here, Jack." And we rode quiet a mile or two, just like old times, but different, more like new times. "Pull over, Jack."

"What the fuck for?"

Scenic Lookout sits eighty feet over the water. You can get down another twenty or so on a steep slag trail, but it's easiest if you just jump. If you wait, you won't. It's not thoughtless—you shouldn't belly flop, and feet first needs a hand over the asshole so the water won't jam up.

I chose the swan, mostly because that was the mood I was in and I saw a guy on TV who simply leaned forward, out, then he sprang, arms wide, as if flying over the sea.

Falling is fast but slow and takes all the time in the world if you don't rush it. Impact is blessed, and if you relax and ease into the reach and pull, then the two miles to the beach by Jack's place is only a process—and a feeling.

"It's an accomplishment," Jack said, every bit as great as monogamous love with Louise. He waited again on the beach for my second arrival that morning, calling out to me when I was thirty yards out, news of a roast in the oven, a coldpack in the fridge, a new TV with color and remote.

I sat in the sand under some palms, watched the water. It shimmered in calm places, frothed under gusts. It rolled easy in breathing undulation. It matched my breath, then it matched me. It was what I came to, long way around.

Whirlaway

Design and composition by Gael Stirler, Tucson, Arizona

Text composed in Weiss with page heads in Futura

Printed and bound by R. R. Donnelley & Sons Company,
Harrisonburg, Virginia